"What difference does it make to you, anyway?" she replied, feeling a little desperate now.

Her resistance was crumbling under the power of this somber, intense Noah.

As soon as she uttered those words, she wished she could take them back, because he started to walk toward her. The expression in his gorgeous but compelling brown eyes had Rylie backing away, completely forgetting the truck behind her until she bumped into sunset-warmed metal. From bra line to hips, she felt the heat; however, that was tepid compared to what his look stirred inside her.

When Noah was toe-to-toe with her, he framed her face with his hands. "Only this," he whispered against her mouth.

The Puppy Prescription

Helen R. Myers
&
USA TODAY Bestselling Author
Christyne Butler

Previously published as *Groomed for Love*
and *Puppy Love in Thunder Canyon*

H HARLEQUIN® MUST♥DOGS

Recycling programs for this product may not exist in your area.

ISBN-13: 978-1-335-04182-1

The Puppy Prescription

Copyright © 2019 by Harlequin Books S.A.

Groomed for Love
First published in 2014. This edition published in 2019.
Copyright © 2014 by Helen R. Myers

Puppy Love in Thunder Canyon
First published in 2012. This edition published in 2019.
Copyright © 2012 by Harlequin Books S.A.

Printed in U.S.A.

CONTENTS

Helen R. Myers is a collector of two- and four-legged strays, and lives deep in the Piney Woods of East Texas. She cites cello music and bonsai gardening as favorite relaxation pastimes, and still edits in her sleep—an accident, learned while writing her first book. A bestselling author of diverse themes and focus, she is a three-time RITA® Award nominee, winning for *Navarrone* in 1993.

Books by Helen R. Myers

Harlequin Special Edition

It's News to Her
Almost a Hometown Bride
The Surprise of Her Life
A Holiday to Remember
The Dashing Doc Next Door
Groomed for Love
A Man to Count On
The Last Man She'd Marry
Daddy on Demand
Hope's Child
It Started with a House...

Visit the Author Profile page
at Harlequin.com for more titles.

GROOMED FOR LOVE

Helen R. Myers

Chapter 1

"Rylie, sweetheart, you are the best thing to happen to Sweet Springs since they started putting in drive-through windows at pharmacies."

Rylie Quinn, the new groomer at Sweet Springs Animal Clinic, grinned at Pete Ogilvie, the eldest of the four war veterans who conducted a daily coffee klatch in the corner of the building's reception area. It was she who'd dubbed them the four musketeers after characters in the famous Alexandre Dumas novel, and Pete himself Athos, after the eldest of the adventurers, because the former marine was the boldest yet most complicated of the group. He also had somehow taken Jerry Platt under his wing. At sixty-six, Jerry, whom she called D'Artagnan, was the youngest and had become the fourth member of the veteran group, as D'Artagnan had become the fourth musketeer in the story.

"Why, thank you, kind sir." Holding out the hem of her maroon smock, as though it was a skirt, she offered a quick curtsy, bemused, even though the comparison was confusing. She suspected he hadn't meant to imply that she was appreciated because she was a convenience. "All because I asked Mr. Stan if he wanted sweetener in his coffee?"

"That's right! None of us can tell him that he's being an old grouch the way you can and still bring a smile to his face."

Stanley Walsh—aka Porthos, as far as Rylie was concerned—was sixty-nine, the second youngest, and an ex-navy man, as well as a retired master sheet-metal fabricator. Sometimes—like today—his hangovers caused him to grouse a little more than usual, which was saying quite a bit, since Stanley had a dry sense of humor to begin with.

"That, along with being as bright and as pretty as a black-eyed Susan, which is about the only damned flower that can survive the summer like we had with any grace. Whew, can you believe it officially became autumn yesterday?" Pete asked around the room. "If you hold that front door open for too long, I swear those bags of dog food stacked on the shelves over there are gonna pop like popcorn in a microwave."

As others grunted their agreement, Rylie said, "I'm sorry for the strain it is on animals, but I sure don't mind it being warm. I was born and raised in the desert country of California. That said, I'm getting seriously partial to your trees here, especially the pines." She had arrived in this Central East Texas community early in July, in time to attend Dr. Gage Sullivan's marriage to Brooke Bellamy last month, the niece of the lady who used to be Gage's neighbor. That neighborhood, as well as several parts of town, was enhanced by pockets of the pines and hardwood trees that had once earned the region its other name—The Piney Woods. She told the men, who had also attended the wedding, "If I had Doc and Brooke's yard, I'd sleep with the windows open every night to listen to the breeze whispering through the trees."

"Well, don't try it here, even if your fancy RV's windows are high off the ground," Roy Quinn said from inside the reception station in the center of the room.

As usual, her uncle pretended to have as gruff a personality as any of the old-timers, but Rylie knew the middle-aged bachelor saw her as the daughter he'd never had. "I wouldn't do that. Besides," she reminded her only relative in the area, "as far back as those trees are beyond the pasture, it's easier to hear the highway traffic out front." The clinic was on the service road of a state highway that ran north to south on the east side of town. The overpass that led to downtown was only a few dozen yards beyond the clinic's parking lot.

"Good. Keep those miniblinds shut at night, too. What we lack in woods, we probably make up for in Peeping Toms and lechers, and word's getting around about you and that RV being parked in back."

As he spoke, he glanced over her shoulder to fork his fingers from his eyes to Jerry, who tended to think of himself as quite the ladies' man. Recently, Jerry Platt had the bad judgment to get involved with a certain widow in town, who had really been angling to get closer to Doc. It had caused quite a stir among the old-timers, who feared losing the congenial atmosphere at the clinic, and they were keeping Jerry on notice, too.

Rylie shook her head, thinking Uncle Roy was being silly. Jerry was more than a decade older than him! Besides, he'd been nothing but a gentleman to her. Noticing Jerry's embarrassment, she leaned over the counter to whisper, "I'm twenty-five, not fifteen."

Roy grunted. "You'd have to dye your hair gray to convince anyone. I'll bet you still get carded when you go out for a beer."

"My last beer was a week ago with you guys at the VFW hall, and you know they would serve me anything because I was with you." However, he was right; she did look ridiculously young, but what could you do when you had red hair and a squeaky-clean face that made you perfect for the front of a cereal box but was never going to trigger wolf whistles as a cover girl's would? Something else she didn't have going for her was height—she hadn't grown an inch above her five foot three since the seventh grade. To redirect Roy's focus, she reached across the counter to straighten his wrinkled shirt collar lying awkwardly over his maroon clinic jacket. "If you don't like to iron, at least take your clothes out of the dryer before they dry all mangled. Better yet, let me do your ironing for you."

"Don't change the subject." Roy playfully swatted away her hand away. "Just remember that I have to answer to your parents if anything happens to you here."

She thought about her parents, who were considering becoming foster parents since she, too, had "abandoned the nest," as her parents put it. Her older, adopted brother had struck out on his own four years earlier, finding his career restoring old homes on the East

Coast. "Nothing is going to happen to me, Uncle Roy. I was born under a lucky star, remember?"

It was her longtime joke, ever since learning that she had been born one night on the side of the road after the family car had suffered a flat on the way to the hospital. When asked as a child, "Which star?" she would spread her arms wide and declare, "All of them!" The truth was that Roy had been a lifesaver in helping her get a job here, and Rylie intended to quickly make him see that she was fine on her own before he found out the full truth about why she had made the move.

"Well, Ms. Lucky," he said, nodding toward the front, "your first appointment is arriving—along with her sourpuss courier."

Noting his grimace, a confused Rylie glanced over her shoulder to see a sleek black BMW sedan pull up to the front door. She couldn't stop a little sigh as she recognized that once again Ramon Bustillo wasn't here in Mrs. Prescott's Cadillac.

"I wonder how Mrs. P talked His Highness into delivering her pooch again."

"Behave." Rylie looked from her uncle to the four musketeers, to see if they were listening, then back to the expensive car. She knew why Uncle Roy called Noah Prescott that—Noah wasn't only the son of Mrs. Audra Prescott, one of the state's most admired ladies in society, he was also District Attorney Vance Ellis Underwood's assistant and expected successor—and he acted the part. As a result, her uncle didn't care for him, calling him a "stuffed shirt," and, after two meetings with the man, Rylie had to admit Roy had some cause for his opinion. However, Noah was maddeningly sexy, too, with his intense brown eyes, serious five-o'clock shadow that tended to keep her from having a clear view of the slight cleft in his chin, and gorgeous, wavy brown hair with enviable gold highlights. The first time she met him, she'd concluded that he must shave three times a day to keep the elegant image his tailored suits and expensive shoes exuded. He undoubtedly went for a weekly manicure, too. His long-fingered, pianist's hands had made her want to shove her banged-up, laborer's hands into her jeans' back pockets.

"Ramon must have experienced some kind of problem again," she replied. Ramon Bustillo wasn't only Mrs. Prescott's driver; he was the caretaker at Haven Land, the family estate. Last time, Ramon had needed to get Mrs. Prescott to an early doctor's appointment, so Noah had brought her dog, and it was evident to anyone with eyes that Noah couldn't wait to be rid of the adorable bichon frise, registered as Baroness Baja Bacardi. It had been equally clear that the little dog couldn't wait to get into friendlier hands, as well.

"I suspect having an audience won't improve his mood any, so I'm going to take MG and Humphrey out back. C'mon, Humph," he called to Doc's basset hound. "MG, pretty girl," he added to the large, black retriever-mix dog. "Let's go out."

"Thanks, Uncle Roy." Seeing Noah struggle with closing the car door, she started toward the front door to help, only to stumble. "Oh!"

She knew immediately what had happened—instead of following her uncle's directive, MG had come to stand beside her as though waiting for permission. Luckily, Rylie had good reflexes and grabbed the edge of the counter before falling face-first to the tile floor.

"Rylie—good Lord! Are you okay?"

Seventy-year-old Warren Atwood, the "Aramis" in the group, rose from his chair. Retired from the army and a former D.A. of Cherokee County himself, his dear wife was in a local nursing home suffering from the last stages of Alzheimer's. Rylie had learned that he was so devastated by it all that he could barely stand to be there without becoming emotional.

"Not to worry," she assured him and the others, who also looked concerned. "I should have known she would come to me first. She's still getting used to Uncle Roy." Rylie covered her embarrassment by quickly hugging the sweet-natured, long-legged dog. She thought she'd been doing so well; she hadn't bumped into a wall or tripped over anything in days. "Let's go, Mommy's Girl. Go out with Uncle Roy. You know it's your job to watch over Humphrey." She walked the black, silky-haired animal to the swinging doors, where her uncle and Doc and Brooke's basset hound waited.

"I don't get it," Roy muttered. "Dogs like me."

"She likes you."

"So much that she runs to you at the sound of my voice. She's going to give me a complex." After the mock complaint, her uncle gave her a concerned look. "Are you sure you're okay? You aren't getting all flustered over Golden Boy, are you?"

"You're sounding more and more like a jealous schoolgirl." Shaking her head, she started for the front door again.

By the time she had her hand on the handle bar, Noah Prescott had championed the outer door. Barely. She couldn't help but laugh at the awkward way he was holding the little cutie. Was he afraid that the adorable white bichon frise was going to try to take a bite of his earlobe or that the young dog would ruin his very attractive silvery-gray suit?

"Thanks for the prompt assistance," Noah muttered when he finally made it inside.

"You're very welcome, A.D.A. Prescott," she replied cheerfully, purposely misunderstanding his sarcasm. "I would never have guessed a little eight-pound dog with such an amiable nature would scare a man with the entire police department at his service."

"I. Am. Not. Scared." Checking his edgy tone, Noah added stiffly, "I'm simply trying not to get dog hair on my suit. I happen to be due in court within the hour."

"Well, you're wearing the best color to hide a strand or two," Rylie assured him, all smiles and pleasantness. "Hello, Bubbles, you cutie." She relieved Noah of the tiny bundle, who had been nothing but obliging during her two previous visits. "I hope nothing has happened to Ramon," she added to Noah. "Your mother's driver?" she added, after his odd look.

"I *know* his name. I just thought it unusual that you did."

Maybe Uncle Roy was right—Noah Prescott could be the snob Roy claimed. Unable to resist, Rylie said with several more degrees of sweet demeanor, "Why wouldn't I? Because he's *only* a driver? I'm only a dog groomer. Who am I to put on airs about the hired help?"

After staring at her as though he would like to put her behind bars, or at least walk out without another word, Noah replied with painstaking civility, "Ramon is at the dealership. The car had a flat before getting out the driveway. Mother didn't want him driving way down here on the spare, then all the way back to Rusk."

"That sounds just like her. She's such a thoughtful woman." Audra Prescott was also turning into her best customer so far, thanks to her preference for having her dog groomed more often than the average person. With a few more clients like her, Rylie knew Gage and Uncle Roy would be convinced that there was definitely a market for another dog groomer in the area. "You're a good son, too," she assured Noah, with impish humor, "for helping out in a crunch."

"I can't tell you how that reassures me." Checking his watch, he added quickly, "I take it that Mother gave you instructions on what she wants done?"

"Bathing, trimming…the cut still a little shorter since the days are still quite warm, even though it's shorter than the AKC prefers—" Turning to reach for her reservations book that she'd left on the lower level of the reception counter, Rylie misjudged the distance and bumped her elbow. She hit hard enough to gasp and jerk back, and she had to do a neat little jig to keep her balance. "Oops. Sorry, Bubbles. That's the last misstep for this visit, I promise."

From behind her came Noah's droll observation. "I take it that it wasn't runway modeling that you gave up for this line of work?"

"As a matter of fact, it was," she replied, her wicked humor kicking in. "Call me crazy, since there's only so much demand for five-foot-three glamour girls. But I just love animals too much." She kept her smile bright, determined not to let her disappointment in him show. But who was he to add a jab at her height into his cutting remark? Mr. Glass-Half-Empty Prescott might reach six feet *if* someone gave him an inch of credit for his ability to look down his nose at her. While he had the face for it, no modeling agency would hound him to sign a contract, either. "As I was saying, aside from the usual care, Bubbles will get—"

Noah silenced her with a dismissive wave. "Don't bother. That Mother relayed instructions is all I care about. Good grief, primping is primping. Any of the shops between here and Rusk would do the same thing."

Sexy, but grouchy, Rylie thought with renewed disappointment. All because he had to drive a few extra miles for his mother's dog? She couldn't resist rubbing it in a bit. "Yes, I am fortunate to have her, Mrs. Collins's and Mrs. Nixon's support, as well. They've all been very kind about spreading the word. As it happens, I'm a little different from some in the business because I've been doing this kind of work since I was old enough to know the difference between the front and back end of animals. And for the record? The term *primping* is condescending. There are a good number of health issues related to good grooming for animals, just as there are for humans."

In a moment that couldn't have been better choreographed if she'd tried, Bubbles started licking Rylie's hand as though apologizing on Noah's behalf. Rylie nuzzled the little dog.

"Aw...thank you, precious." She returned her focus to Noah. "I also don't believe in sedating animals, whatever their temperament. How safe or wise would it have been for your mother, or nanny, to sedate you when giving you a manicure or trim?"

From the corner of the room the four musketeers chuckled and snickered.

Noah Prescott stared at her as though she'd just burst

into "The Sun Will Come Out Tomorrow" and took a cautious step back toward the exit. "Just call my mother when it's ready. Ramon should be home by then."

Almost before the doors drifted shut behind Noah, Stan Walsh launched the inevitable commentary. "Whatcha trying to do to the poor guy, Rylie? You had him acting like he'd OD'd on sticky buns."

As the others laughed, Rylie stroked the adorable animal in her arms and gave them her most innocent look. "Now, Stan, are you accusing me of being an instigator?"

"Never met a honeybee who wasn't."

"It's been my experience," Pete Ogilvie offered, "that the harder a guy tries to convince a gal that he doesn't approve of her, the more he's really trying to deny he's attracted."

"That sounds like forced logic to me," Jerry Platt scoffed.

"That's because you have the libido of a rabbit," Pete countered, "and the mind of one. You think that any female who happens to cross your path is a gift from the gods."

As the men burst into laughter, Rylie pretended the need to cover Bubbles's ears. "This conversation is getting way too frisky for our tender ears, baby girl. Let's go."

Damn her perkiness.

She was the most annoying female he'd met in some time, and what was driving Noah crazy was that it was for all the reasons that usually attracted him. What the heck was going on? Rylie Quinn was friendly, good-natured, a born optimist. How could he fault someone who tried to see the bright side of things? Yet for some bizarre, quirky reason, he was discovering that he had no problem where she was concerned.

She was an irritating mix of sweetness and provocation, deceptively packaged in a Peter Pan–size body that her maroon medical smock would mostly hide, except when it wasn't fastened today any more than on his other visit to the clinic. That gamin-short hair didn't help make her look fully grown, either. The short, punkish style left her looking more like a nine-year-old boy than a woman in her early or mid-twenties, an ironic observation, since he liked his women slender and sleek. But then she did little to enhance her femininity—maybe just mascara and some lip gloss, and yet every receptor in his molecular being went on full alert the instant she was within sight.

It was those gray-green eyes that got him on edge, he decided. Sure they were incredibly framed by lashes that would make a sable proud; however, their color was that unnerving shade of storm clouds before a tornado dropped from them and turned your life inside out. *That's it!* he thought, feeling as though he'd locked in on some important detail. She looked at him as though she had a secret, and she wasn't telling. Well, he wasn't big on secrets. It was one of the chief things that made his work so difficult and, often, ugly: secrets and lies.

As Noah sped north to Rusk, and the courthouse, he considered phoning his mother again to ask if she really knew what she was getting herself into trusting Rylie Quinn. Just because her equally dog-crazy friends approved of the young woman, Rylie's claim that she didn't use drugs to keep animals calm during grooming didn't mean she hadn't, or wouldn't, in a crunch. He also didn't believe for a moment her self-laudatory proclamation that she got along with any and all critters. Maybe it was working to sell herself as the female rendition of the *Dog Whisperer;* however, she'd been at the clinic for only about a month. The jury was still out, as far as he was concerned.

On the other hand, Dr. Gage Sullivan's reputation was impeccable. He just hoped the guy hadn't been suckered in by a red-haired con artist the way his mother and others may have been.

At the thought of his mother, he sighed heavily. He accepted that he was struggling to understand her and had been since the accident that put her in a wheelchair. She had always been a pragmatic, no-nonsense person, but no more. *Who registers their lap dog as Baroness Baja Bacardi?* he thought with a new wave of dismay and embarrassment. What a title for a creature that could almost fit in a restaurant take-out box. Granted, his mother had little pleasure in her life anymore—a dog, the pool therapy, her painting and the visits from a small handful of trusted and dedicated friends, as well as her minister, lawyer and accountant. Otherwise, her society was "Livie," Olivia Danner, her live-in nurse, and Aubergine Scott, the resident housekeeper-cook. Considering the whirlwind life of a socialite that she'd juggled before, his mother's life was as shockingly different as if Hillary Clinton suddenly chose to exit the political world forever and cloistered herself in a nunnery! Under those circumstances, Noah didn't have the heart to deny her this bit of frivolity even as he groused to others over being inconvenienced. Audra

Rains Prescott had earned a certain amount of indulgences, regardless of how silly this one seemed to him.

Three years ago, his parents were involved in a head-on collision with another vehicle, one whose driver passed out due to side effects of her prescription drugs. The crash had killed his father and the other driver instantly. It was a miracle that his mother hadn't died, too. She had, however, lost most of the use of the lower half of her body. Nevertheless, there was enough nerve connectivity to trigger chronic pain and insomnia, which in turn added to bouts of depression. If it wasn't for their dedicated people on the estate, he would need prescriptions, or at least a therapist himself.

For example, Ramon wasn't just dealing with a flat tire; there was a recall notice on his mother's Cadillac that he hadn't let her know about, due to her fragile perspective when it came to all things motorized these days. It had come only two days ago, so the tire issue had been fortuitous in a way. Ramon knew to keep the more serious issue between the two of them. He just hoped the repair wouldn't take all day.

"Hell," he muttered, "if you can't trust America's classy tank, what can you trust?"

It was a relief to reach Rusk and the courthouse. He'd become the assistant D.A. for Cherokee County soon after his return to East Texas to supervise things at home. Until then, he'd been the hottest "gunslinger" at one of Houston's top law firms. Had he been able to stay there, he had no doubt there would already be talk about him becoming a partner by now, even though he was only thirty.

Coming home, it had never occurred to him to just manage the family estate and enjoy a gentleman's lifestyle, which had been an option. True, he could also have opened his own private practice; however, that didn't appeal to him, either. Divorces, will probates and small lawsuits needed good counsel to be sure, but not from him. He needed something with more intellectual challenge, and so when Vance Ellis Underwood, the current D.A., discreetly asked him if being the assistant D.A.—with the understanding that he would be seen as Underwood's heir apparent when Underwood retired—would be something he would be interested in, Noah saw that as his best option.

If only he was handling his return to a more rural lifestyle as well. While there was no denying the countryside's beauty, he missed Houston and the nightlife, the buzz and being in the inner circle of what was happening in the city and state. But someone had to oversee the family's estate—the mansion, the near-thousand-acre ranch and tree farm, along with oil and gas leases. His mother had left all of that to his father, although she had a good basic knowledge of what was what. Unfortunately, she was no longer mobile enough to keep on top of things.

At the town square, Noah parked in back of the courthouse building, where their offices were on the first floor. Grabbing his briefcase, he hurried inside. While driving, he'd already answered two calls from the D.A.'s secretary, the last time assuring her that he was as good as in the building. Court commenced in minutes, and today they were choosing a jury for a case related to the largest drug bust in the county's history. The fact that the accused was the son of a prominent family in the area was garnering a lot of media attention, and it would be the worst day to be late.

Noah rushed into the office just as Judy Millsap exited the D.A.'s office, a bulging file and her steno pad in her arms.

"Oh, thank goodness." The silver-haired, usually calm woman exhaled with relief as she set her load on her desk. "This is all for you. He's coming down with a full-fledged case of some bug or other. He thought he could get things started and then let you do the most of the jury interviewing, but he just admitted that even sitting in court might be more than he can manage."

At sixty-six, Vance Underwood had suffered a few health problems in the past year and had confided that he wanted to retire as soon as his term was over in two years. Catching something as common as a virus could turn things serious quickly.

"Do you think you should get him an ambulance?" Noah asked in concern.

"I asked. He vetoed the idea, but I insisted he let a deputy drive him home. I'll take his car and hitch a ride back with the officer."

"It sounds as though his heart doctor should be notified, as well."

The plump woman with the wedge hairdo nodded her agreement. "So do I, but it's not up to me. I will call his wife and warn her we're coming while I wait for the deputy. Perhaps I can convince her that she needs to make that call."

"Good luck with that." As much as Noah didn't want to seem too eager to take control, he was also discreet about making any comments about Mrs. Underwood. It was well-known in the office and elsewhere around town that Elise had never been given a prescription drug she didn't develop a loving relationship with.

Chances were that she wasn't even out of bed yet, let alone coherent enough to be of any assistance to her husband.

Reaching for the stack, Noah said, "Let me know if there's anything else you need."

"Pick an excellent jury."

Three hours later, Noah was back at his desk. As luck would have it, the judge had come down with the same virus that the D.A. seemed to be suffering from and the entire day's docket was rescheduled. Minutes ago, Noah had encouraged Judy to take an early lunch, assuring her that he would stay and watch things at the office. She was grateful, having missed breakfast due to the morning's hectic situation.

Alone in the office—since their clerk, Ann, was finishing a task and directly heading off to lunch, too— Noah called home to check on his mother. "Has Ramon made it back from the dealership?" he asked.

"I'm glad you called. No, he hasn't. They just started on my car and told him it would be about two hours. How can a simple matter like a flat take so long?"

Noah wasn't about to tell her, and replied instead, "They could be shorthanded. We have a lot of illness going around here, too. Or else they saw that the car's mileage was close to the next scheduled oil change and servicing and convinced Ramon to go ahead and do that."

"Oh. Well, then, will you be a dear and pick up Bubbles during your lunch hour? Rylie called and Bubbles is not liking being locked in a kennel at all."

Noah closed his eyes and pinched the bridge of his nose. "Why can't she bring her to you?" She must take a lunch break herself, and since she was eager to build up a clientele base, this would be a great way to make points with a valued customer.

"Shame on you!" his mother replied. "That's not her responsibility." After a slight pause, she said more calmly, "If you have other commitments, darling, just say so. I only feel badly for everyone having to listen to my baby acting up. I'm sure she's upsetting the other animals, too."

It was on the tip of his tongue to claim that he was due back in court too soon to do that for her, but his conscience wouldn't let him. The whole purpose of returning here was to make his mother's life as stress-free as possible.

"Judy's taking her lunch at the moment," he said. "But she'll be back in about thirty minutes. I can go then."

"Bless you, darling. You're the best child a mother could hope for."

"Give me a compliment that bears repeating," he replied drolly. "Everyone here knows I'm an only child and that you have nothing to compare me with."

At least when he hung up, she was laughing.

When Noah pulled up to the clinic, it wasn't yet one o'clock and the closed-for-lunch sign was still on the door, although Noah could see the old-timers sitting around their table. He wondered if they ever went home. Or was there anyone at home to go to? He had noticed pockets of seniors around Rusk, too, who collected wherever they weren't in the way yet could get out of the heat or cold, depending on the season. Loneliness and old age weren't necessarily synonymous—

he knew plenty of senior citizens living full, active lives—but apparently something was going on. It was good of Gage Sullivan to allow the guys to hang out here.

One of the seniors spotted him and pointed around the building toward the back.

Hoping he understood correctly, Noah drove that way, only to utter a soft, "Whoa."

He'd heard that Rylie Quinn was living in a camper in the back of the clinic, but what was parked ahead of him wasn't just an RV. It was one of those monster coach things that well-to-do traveling retirees and touring rock stars used. Didn't those things come with a hefty price tag? It seemed a lot of vehicle for a woman only in her mid-twenties. Grooming dogs was apparently more lucrative than he'd first thought.

As he exited his BMW, he gave the two-tone bronze machine a once-over from behind his sunglasses. This was a model where both sides could extend out from the main structure for extra sleeping and dining space, converting it into a virtual house on wheels. The size of the thing also had him wondering who else might be in there. A boyfriend? Husband? Rylie didn't wear a ring. Come to think of it, she didn't seem to wear any jewelry at all. Interesting bit of trivia for such a lively, even flamboyant, person.

Before he could knock, the door opened, and he looked up into Rylie's smiling face. A determined smile, he noted.

"Hey there. Twice in one day—my cup runneth over. I guess your mom managed to twist your arm? When I called her and learned that Ramon was being held hostage at the dealership, I offered to bring Bub-

bles to her, but she said you would be happy to do it."
Upon seeing Noah narrow his eyes, she threw back
her head and laughed with delight. "Oh, how funny!
She conned you."

"So it would seem," he muttered. The *why* bothered
him, too. His mother hadn't met Rylie, so she had better not be getting any ideas about matchmaking.

"Come on in, you poor oppressed soul. I was having lunch here to let Bubbles have more space, and so
the old-timers could hear each other talk. For a little
thing, she does have powerful lungs."

After a slight hesitation, Noah did step up into the
vehicle. He couldn't deny that he was curious as to
what things looked like inside. "That's what Mother
claims to have been worried about. At home Bubbles
has about ten thousand square feet to roam around,
all in a safe environment." As soon as he said that,
Noah inwardly kicked himself. Not only did it sound
as though he was bragging, but he knew better than to
offer details to strangers, particularly about the family's
wealth. Granted, one had only to drive by the property
to know they were well-off, but to him this was just
another sign of how easily Rylie Quinn could under-
mine his discipline.

"Lucky girl. At least we don't have to worry about
her getting enough exercise, regardless of the weather."
Rylie stepped back to make room for him. "I wondered how Mrs. Prescott could be feeding her all of
those treats she admits to, yet this munchkin stays at
a healthy weight." She leaned over to pick up the little
dog that—upon Noah's entry—had gone straight to her
and planted one tiny foot on Rylie's sneaker.

Noah didn't miss the move, which struck him as

possessive. That left Noah with the uncomfortable feeling that the dog could sense his conflicted feelings about Rylie. Or was the animal sticking close to her because she hated the idea of having to ride home with him? At this rate the spoiled fur ball was going to have Rylie thinking he was abusive.

"She also likes to chase around the pool," he continued, "while my mother has her therapy."

With a sympathetic sound, Rylie said, "I heard about what happened to Mrs. Prescott—and the terrible loss you both suffered. I'm so sorry."

Although he nodded his thanks, he had to look away after feeling an unexpected pulling in his midsection, as though someone was tethering them together via invisible strings connected to each of their ribs. In self-defense, he changed the subject. "This is quite a setup you have here. When I heard you had been working out of an RV, I pictured something less…comfortable."

Rylie glanced around, her expression reflecting her own sense of good fortune. "A business contact of my parents helped me get a great price and terms. It's a repo," she told him. "I didn't really need anything so big, let alone lavish, but the extra space would have come in handy if Doc hadn't been so generous in letting me use the clinic's facilities. But you never know. The clinic business keeps growing, and if things get too crowded for him—especially if he adds staff—then I'll have to work in here again."

Taking that in to mull over later, Noah's gaze zeroed in on the master bedroom at the far end of the RV. He saw the king-size bed with the blue-and-purple bedspread and small berg of matching pillows piled against the sapphire-blue, cushioned headboard. It was too easy to imagine Rylie lying there, and when his wayward thoughts started to edit what she might—or might not—wear to bed, his body stirred with hunger.

"Do you have our bill ready?" he asked, abruptly.

"Oh…of course," Rylie said, immediately contrite. "Sorry for wandering on. I know you have to get back. Actually, I have another appointment in a few minutes myself." She went to the dinette table and picked up the invoice lying there beside a half-eaten salad. "I gave your mother a discount because this is Bubbles's third visit in just over a month, meaning there's less matting than I usually have to deal with. Also please let her know that Bubbles's nails didn't need trimming this time. You're such a good girl," Rylie cooed to the dog.

After eyeing the fresh coat of purple nail polish on the dog's toes, Noah saw Bubbles lick Rylie's chin, then give him a look as though telepathically saying, *See? This is how I like to be treated.*

Accepting the bill, Noah reached for his billfold. As he handed Rylie the correct amount, he asked, "Would you mind bringing her to my car? I can really do without the ladies in the courthouse snickering at me when I return smelling like I've been hanging around a perfume counter."

Choking, Rylie insisted, "You're exaggerating. I can't handle excessive scents myself, nor can Bubbles. I use a very light touch on my animals."

Some inexplicable something egged him on, and Noah intentionally rubbed the tip of his nose. "If that's restrained to you, we'll have to agree to disagree."

"Don't listen, cutie." Rylie cuddled Bubbles again. "He's determined to try to make us think the problem is with us. I think you smell as delicious as your name, and your mommy will, too." As the dog reached up and touched a paw to her cheek, Rylie laughed in pleasure. "You are a heart stealer, yes, you are. Let me just stamp your bill as paid," she told Noah, "and—"

"That's not necessary."

"But I always make sure your mother has a detailed—"

"I'm handling this for her."

Rylie's face lit with pleasure. "How nice of you." Leading the way, she opened the door and took care going down the steps. "Gotta be careful with our precious cargo, huh, sweetie?" she crooned to the little dog. "Isn't it a beautiful day?" she added to Noah.

"It's hot for autumn."

"But the evenings are so nice. Doc has a couple of kenneled dogs this week and he's letting me walk them. Then they get to spend the night with us. As you saw, there's plenty of room, and they enjoy it so much more than being locked up in pens."

Noah lost the battle with his curiosity. "Us?"

"MG and me. My dog."

"And MG stands for...?"

"Mommy's Girl. They told me when I got her from the shelter that they'd named her Marnie, but it was soon apparent that we were going to be very close, and she's seriously maternal. She instinctively steps in to help whenever she decides I need her assistance with an animal."

Noah was sorry he'd asked. Sure, he believed there were special relationships between some pets and their owners, but *Mommy's Girl?* That was laying it on a bit thick.

Unlocking the BMW with his remote, he opened

the passenger door for Rylie. Looking over the hood of the car, he considered the grassy area and the woods beyond it where she said she walked. It was more a wild pasture than a park. "Aren't you concerned about snakes, or getting eaten up by chiggers and mosquitoes?" Texas also had more than its share of wild hogs, coyotes and an increasing number of abandoned dogs, too, he thought.

"We haven't been bothered yet," she said, shrugging. "Maybe there's safety in numbers. In any case, I tend to take a live-and-let-live approach. It's more important that the dogs get some attention and exercise. They're missing their homes, and some are overweight, so being constricted in pens for days is just unhealthy." She began to put the dog on the BMW's black leather seat only to rear back. "Oh! Please put on the air conditioner and give us a moment for things to cool down. She'll get burned."

"Try putting her on the floorboard." When he saw her stubbornly resist, Noah did get into the car and start the engine. Sure, it had gotten warmer in the short time that he'd been in her RV, but it was nowhere near as bad as it had been in July or August. As the vents quickly blew cold air through the inside of the vehicle, he reiterated, "The floorboard, please. I don't want claw runs in the leather."

"But she won't be able to see, and it's a rougher ride down there."

The Mother Teresa of furry creatures really was beginning to push his buttons. "For crying out loud, this car's shock absorbers are the embodiment of foreign skill in cushion and spring. She has no idea what *rough* is."

With a sigh of exasperation, Rylie said to the dog, "Your big brother is determined to be disagreeable, isn't he, precious?"

Big brother? "Okay, that's enough," Noah said, having had his fill of this nonsense. "Put the damned dog in now. Please." He had to get out of there before she fried what brain cells he had left.

With a mournful glance, Rylie did as ordered. Carefully shutting the door, she backed away.

As Noah cut a sharp U-turn, he decided he was going to tell his mother that her pet's groomer—cute as she was—was a nut job who needed a reality check. There were kids, even in this area, who needed help with essentials—food, clothing—not to mention finding a safe family environment. Spending any more time on inanity like this was ridiculous. How could a woman be so adorable, yet irritating at the same time?

As he circled around the clinic and cut a sharp turn onto the service road, Bubbles barked at him as the force of the turn tipped her over.

"Oh, put a lid on it," he muttered.

Chapter 2

As Noah expected, his mother was parked in her wheelchair within sight of the front door and applauded with excitement as he entered Haven Land with Bubbles. Adding to his soured mood, she immediately started complimenting Rylie's work the instant her precious four-legged princess leaped into her arms. Even if he wanted to pass on Rylie's comments and messages, he couldn't get a word in due to her effusiveness.

"Isn't that shade of purple ribbon adorable, Aubergine?" she said to her housekeeper, who was standing with the glass of tea and the small cup of medications Audra needed to take. "Livie—look at her nails! A perfect match. And she's so happy to be home."

Aubergine Scott had been with the family since before Noah had graduated from high school. She was

a single mother of two children, now grown, grate-
fully educated by his parents. Daughter Rachel was a
lawyer in Washington, D.C., and son Randolph was a
teacher in Houston. Each had tried to make the sixty-
year-old retire, to pay her back for all she'd done for
them, but Aubergine liked her independence and was
devoted to his mother.

Olivia "Livie" Danner quit her RN job when Noah's
mother had been discharged from the hospital in Dallas, and joined their makeshift family. Quiet, bookish
and athletic, at fifty-seven, she was as reserved as Aubergine was outspoken, but both possessed a dry sense
of humor that Noah appreciated, even though quite a
bit of it was directed at him. What he cared about most,
though, was that his mother liked and trusted her.

"She's as pretty as a valentine," plump and short
Aubergine declared.

"Charming," tall and toned Livie added, with a tolerant nod. "Please take your medication, Audra."

"In a minute. Oh, she smells good enough to eat,"
Audra gushed, all but burying her face in the dog's fur.
"Did you properly thank Rylie for me, dear?"

Ignoring Aubergine's barely repressed grin, he
shoved his hands into his pants pockets to keep everyone from seeing him curl his fingers into fists.
"Mother, trust me, she knows how supportive you are
of her. She all but rubs it in my face. If anyone should
be appreciative, it's her for having your business."

His mother gave him a distressed look. "I swear, you
are sounding more like an old grouch every day. And
you were raised to have better manners. Do I have to
call her and apologize on your behalf?"

"No, ma'am, you do not," he said, with only a modi-

cum of guilt. Also not happy to be scolded in front of
the other two women, he continued, "Do you mind if
I get back to work now? Vance went home sick, so I'm
holding the fort today."

"What? Then why are you standing there breathing on your mother?" Livie immediately started pulling the chair toward the living room.

"I'll get the disinfectant spray," Aubergine assured
her partner-in-protection. To Noah she said, "You heard
her, get going. You know her lungs don't need any more
work than they already get."

Noah held up his hands in surrender and quickly
backed out of their presence. He knew he'd blundered,
and the sooner he made his exit the better.

"Oh, Noah, they're only being protective," his
mother called after him.

"And they're very good at it," he said with a courtly
bow. "Don't worry about dinner. I'll eat out. Have to
work late." He didn't really, but it wouldn't be a bad
idea to work ahead.

Judy was on the phone when Noah returned to the
office and Ann, the junior clerk, was either still on
her lunch break or in some storage room hunting files.
Ann was more Judy's assistant than any help to Vance
or himself, and Noah often forgot she was even em-
ployed there. From the looks of the poor woman, whom
someone had nicknamed "the beige person" for the
way she dressed and behaved, she might have easily
just emerged from the bland walls one morning and
retreated into them at night. She rarely spoke that he
could hear.

Back in his corner, where he was framed by a win-

dow, a wall and on the third side file cabinets—the
closest thing he could develop into an office—Noah
took the extra time to check his email account and then
on a whim typed Rylie's name into the search engine
box. He wasn't proud of it, but he had just enough annoyance left in him to want to see what would happen.

As expected, there were no clear results. There was
a link to *Riley's* Car Wash, another *Riley* who could
read your psychic vibes for twenty bucks and a mas-
seuse. For a second he wondered if Rylie changed the
spelling of her name to moonlight in an even more lucrative field. Hindsight being what it was, he regretted
not having written down the RV's license plate number. That would be easy enough to check, even if they
were still California plates.

About to start a different search, he saw Judy put
her call on hold. "Noah—it's the sheriff," she called
back to him. "With the D.A. out, he was wondering
if you two could meet regarding upcoming cases he
thinks are ready for us."

"Of course." With reluctance, Noah shut down his
web browser. "Where does he want to meet, here or
at his office?"

"Well, if you come now, we'll see you right away,"
Roy put his hand over the phone's mouthpiece and
gestured for Rylie not to leave as she'd been preparing to. Curious more than disappointed at not getting
to call it a day yet, she backtracked to wait beside him.

Putting his hand over the mouthpiece, he said,
"Noah Prescott. Emergency." After that he said into
the phone, "Come to the side door. If people see vehi-

cles in front, they'll think we're open for regular business. We'll be watching for you."

As soon as he hung up, Rylie commiserated on her uncle's bad luck, while worrying about Bubbles. Uncle Roy had planned to meet the old-timers at the VFW hall to watch a Texas Rangers baseball game this evening. What could possibly have happened to the little dog? "Bubbles is hurt?"

"Audra Prescott dropped a glass. You can picture the rest. Noah is running the pup over here."

"Poor little thing. How badly is she cut?"

"Bad enough that neither he nor Ramon could get the piece out. The dog snaps at them when they try to get a good look."

Rylie wasn't surprised about her reaction to at least one of the men. "That's a surprise about her snapping at Ramon." The caretaker, who was closer to her uncle's age than Noah's, appeared to get as much of a kick out of the little dog as his employer did.

"If you ask me, Bubbles is just partial to women," Roy said. He nodded to MG. "Like someone else I know."

Nudging him affectionately due to his lingering fretting over why MG wasn't warming to him as much as he expected, Rylie said, "Either way, I know Mrs. Prescott is stressed. You go on, Uncle Roy. I'll manage this."

Although he looked tempted, he hung back. "You haven't even started your certification as a technician yet. What happens if the dog needs stitches or something else that requires she be put under sedation?"

"Then I'll notify Doc and I'll keep Bubbles as calm as possible until he's back from his emergency call.

Go enjoy your game with the guys, and if something changes that I can't handle, I'll holler." The VFW was only a half mile down the service road.

Roy seemed tempted, but the pull on his conscience was clearly stronger. "You don't have a key to lock up in case Gage isn't needed."

"So lock that side door and leave the back one open. I'll keep an eye on things until you can make it back here to close up."

Roy rubbed at his whiskered jaw. Like Rylie's father, he took after the Black Irish side of the family, while Rylie favored her red-haired mother, whose ancestors were from England as much as Ireland. "I would give you my key and you could give it back in the morning," he ventured.

Rylie loved him for the gesture but shook her head adamantly. "Hey, I will get a key when Doc is ready to give me one."

"Which will be soon," Roy assured her. He gave her a quick hug. "Have I told you lately what a great job you're doing? I'm really proud of you."

Afraid that he was going to ask questions again about why she'd quit veterinary school when she'd been in her last year, she assured him, "That means more to me than I can tell you. Now, go. Enjoy! And I'd like to hear that you actually talked to a woman while you were over there." She didn't understand why he was still single after all these years. He didn't even have someone special he was seeing. On first glance he did appear severe with his stark coloring and serious manner, but he was attractive and fairly fit, although probably a bit too shy with the opposite sex for his own good.

Relenting, Roy dug his keys out of his jeans pocket.

"I'll see you right after the game is over—unless it's a total blowout from the beginning. Then I'll head over here sooner. We can play a couple hands of poker over a beer. It's time we find out if you can finally keep up with your old uncle."

"Be careful for what you wish for," Rylie countered with a cheeky grin.

Waving goodbye, she rounded the building to wait on Noah. She knew if she didn't, he would be confused, then annoyed that things weren't the way Roy had said he would find them. Also, knowing Bubbles would be stressed, she wanted to make things go as quickly and easily as possible for her, too.

She couldn't deny that she was feeling an odd mixture of apprehension and excitement at the idea of seeing Noah again. Maybe she was being a glutton for punishment, but she wanted to make him see what others had no problem noticing—that she was good at what she did and fun to be around.

She didn't have to wait long for him. Noah must have really kept his foot on the accelerator to arrive only a minute or two later.

"What's going on?" he asked her, upon parking in back and emerging from the black BMW.

He looked much more approachable dressed in a pale blue denim shirt and designer jeans, but his lack of a tan and his Italian loafers made it obvious that he was no outdoorsman, let alone a cowboy. Nevertheless, Rylie's heartbeat kicked up a notch and she almost forgave him for his curtness earlier.

"Doc had an emergency and Roy had a previous commitment. He'll be back later. We agreed that he would just keep this door unlocked instead."

"They don't trust you with a key?" he asked, rounding to the passenger side of the vehicle.

So much for wishing that he'd come with a better attitude, Rylie thought. "I've only been here for a short while. Uncle Roy didn't get a key when he first started, either." She couldn't, however, resist adding, "Have you always acted so condescending and superior with people, or is this a side that only I bring out in you?"

Noah looked taken aback. "Me? Condescending? Serious maybe. Mine is that kind of profession. The price for putting criminals where they belong means having to fixate on the unpleasant, often brutal side of life. Not everyone has the luxury of seeing the world as glass half-full every waking moment as you do."

Oddly enough, Rylie was almost consoled by his answer. If that's how he saw her, she thought, opening the door herself, then she was a better actress than she'd hoped. "Well, all of that fixating is doing bad things for whatever charm you inherited from your wonderful mother. Maybe you should consider a job change before it starts to affect your health." Before Noah could reply, she reached for Bubbles and cooed, "Poor darling. Easy does it. We're going to get you feeling better. I promise."

The pink towel the young dog was lying in was significantly stained, warning Rylie to lift her with extra care. Once the dog was in her arms, she turned for the back door.

"Can you get that for me?" she asked Noah.

Without comment, he slammed the car door shut and pressed the remote lock on the key. Then he jogged the few steps to open the steel-and-glass clinic door.

Inside, Rylie led the way to the nearest stainless-steel operating table. The fluorescent lights remained on, and it made the room as bright as midday. Whispering soothingly to the little dog that was trying to burrow her head into Rylie's armpit, she eased Bubbles onto the table.

"Poor friend. What happened here, huh? Gonna let me see so I can make it better?"

"You're authorized to do this?" Noah asked, coming up beside her.

Without taking her eyes off the wound, Rylie said, "I'm at least capable of seeing how badly she's hurt. Did you manage that much?"

Noah admitted, "No, and neither did Ramon."

"Were you present when the accident happened?"

"I was pretty much the cause of it." At Rylie's startled glance, he continued. "Mother was annoyed with me. I was supposed to be working later than she expected. After changing, I came downstairs and caught her trying to have more wine than is safe for her. With her nurse upstairs preparing her bath, and our housekeeper outside in the garden, she thought she was alone."

"You startled her."

"I did," he said, regret deepening his voice. "She doesn't have the strength she thinks she has despite the therapy she gets, and the bottle and glass slipped from her grasp. A moment later, upset at the commotion that followed, Bubbles got into the mess, and the rest you can see."

It was apparent by the way Noah looked everywhere but at her that he was either embarrassed, or ashamed, or both. Rylie had heard enough to understand that it didn't matter how much money you had, a condition like Mrs. Prescott's was difficult for more than the patient.

"I'm very sorry," she said with the utmost sincerity. "I promise that won't go any further, and I hope she wasn't cut, too?"

"Externally, no. However, you can imagine what it did to her emotionally to see the hurt she'd caused her *baby*."

"I suspect *you* will always be her baby," Rylie assured him. "The thing is that Bubbles is who she's allowed to coddle. If you can learn to look at it that way, it might not annoy you so much. Besides, you don't strike me as a man who would enjoy being stroked and petted relentlessly."

"It depends on who's doing it."

The throaty reply made Rylie grateful to have the dog to focus on. It would seem that the county's assistant D.A. wasn't quite the cold fish he pretended to be. That was information her imagination didn't need.

"It's okay, sweetheart," she assured Bubbles. "I'm just going to… Yeah, there it is. There's a shard about the width of a large sewing needle between her toes. It did some slicing before getting lodged where it is now."

"Will she have to be sedated?"

"No, which is also good news because we can do this without waiting on Doc."

"Are you authorized to take care of this?"

"I have more schooling and skills than most certified technicians, plus the common sense to know it would be good to get this over with quickly. However, if you want to leave this little girl in pain, it's your call. Or you can help me keep her still while I use tweezers and take out the glass." All the while that she spoke, she kept her tone soft and soothing, and her expression pleasant to reassure the whimpering dog watching her with trepidation. While it seemed to have a positive effect on Bubbles, Noah remained a hard sell.

"Fine. I guess. As long as Dr. Sullivan is told about what you've done."

"I wouldn't have it any other way."

Aware that any frustration or annoyance with him would transmit itself to Bubbles, Rylie started humming a lullaby her mother had often sung to her as a child, as she carried the dog with her to the cabinets to get what supplies she needed. Once she had the tweezers, cotton balls and antiseptic, she returned to the table. Finally, she set down the dog, still keeping her arm around her.

"Casually move over to the other side of the table to face me, and with your hands, brace her hips to keep her still," she told Noah. "She'll squirm and kick, so be prepared, but only be firm, not rigid. I'll be as quick as I can."

As soon as he complied, she deftly plucked out the splinter.

Bubbles made a slight yelp and then barked at her.

"Yeah, fooled you, didn't I?" Rylie quipped. "But guess what? You're going to be feeling better and better by the second." She soothingly stroked Bubble's tummy, only to connect with Noah's fingers. Surprised that he hadn't already released his hold, she looked up at him, only to find that he was staring at her. That close scrutiny and the physical contact created a circuit that sent a strong wave of something hot and heavy through her body. "You…can let go now."

He glanced down and appeared surprised himself,

but recovered quickly. Taking a step away from the table, he allowed, "You are fast."

His raspy admission had her smiling as she carried Bubbles to the sink, where she got a stainless-steel bowl and filled it with warm water. Then she set the dog carefully on the counter and coaxed her to put her foot into the warm water.

"Let me get the blood off," she told Bubbles, her tone all reassurance. "We can't send you home all messy."

As soon as she was through, she wrapped the dog in a clinic towel and collected more items. Then she returned to the surgery table to treat the wound.

"Does she need to take antibiotics?" Noah asked.

"Not unless she comes down with an infection. She's a healthy girl, so I'm not looking for that to happen. I'll put Betadine on her—"

"What's that?"

"A great antiseptic. Part iodine. It's widely used in hospitals. If the wound happens to reopen, you could use Neosporin, too, and save yourself a trip back here."

"Ramon thought of hydrogen peroxide."

"In a pinch, okay, but that can be harsh on skin."

"What else?"

"That's it. Tell your mother to try to keep her quiet for a day or two. If she shows signs of prolonged limping, or licks the wound too much, bring her back. Go ahead and give her a low-dose aspirin when you get home. It should help keep down any fever and might help her sleep."

"Sounds easy enough. One more question."

"Sure."

"Why do you have more education than a certified technician?"

Oops. One thing she would say for Noah Prescott, he listened well. "As I said," she replied with a shrug, "I've been doing this for years." She all but held her breath, hoping that rather evasive answer satisfied him.

Although he looked as if he was going to continue probing, he just frowned and asked, "What do I owe you this time?"

Rylie shook her head. "Forget about it, I was already here, and we didn't do anything major. Just give your mom my best." From Noah's unsatisfied expression, she concluded that it made him uncomfortable to be beholden to her, and that made her grin wickedly at him. "What's the matter, A.D.A. Prescott—worried that you might have to be nicer to me now? Don't strain yourself, or *you're* the one who might end up needing stitches."

He grunted his opinion of that, and yet a hint of amusement lit his brown eyes. "I just knew there was a touch of smart-ass in you."

"Shocking," she replied, her tone playful.

For the next minute, she worked on gingerly drying off Bubbles's paw and then applying the Betadine. As expected, Bubbles didn't think much of that, but the slight stinging eased quickly. "Sorry about the bit of yellow staining, but this way you know it's keeping her safe from infection."

When she was through with that, she got a fresh towel to wrap Bubbles in, explaining to Noah, "Tell your mother that I'll soak hers and return it the next visit. Don't worry about this one." With a nod to indicate her intent, she started for the door.

As they exited the building and walked to his car, Noah sped up to look her in the face. "I should have said it sooner, but I do appreciate this, especially since it's after hours."

Sweet, Rylie thought. If only that frown didn't continue to mar an otherwise handsome face. "You're most welcome."

Once Noah opened the BMW's passenger door for her, she just stood there looking at him. He caught on immediately.

"Right." He rounded the sedan and climbed in, not only starting the engine, but also turning the air conditioner on high to cool off the car quickly. "Happy now?"

"Practically speechless with it." Rylie eased Bubbles onto the floorboard. Stroking her reassuringly, she said, "You're going home now. Be a good girl and no more owies."

Although she thought she hid it well, she was sorry to see Noah drive away. She knew that intimate moment by the surgery table was the cause…second only to seeing that she'd made him smile. At the same time, it saddened her to hear there were some serious issues going on at Haven Land. The accident was three years past, but life wasn't running smoothly for Noah, any more than for his mother.

He sensed you understand that.

"Oh, stop the mental contortions," she muttered to herself as she returned to the clinic. "He's still way out of your league."

And probably always would be. At twenty-five, she had lived a busy, full life so far, but had yet to fall in love. Heaven knows, she had opened her heart in invitation. She had plenty of friends and acquaintances, and up to the moment when she put California in her rearview mirror, her social life was as active as anyone her age who enjoyed people and school. However, although she'd had only a handful of relationships, two that she wrongly thought could be the real thing, neither of those men—boys, really—had managed to make her feel what seconds in Noah's presence did. The encounter this evening proved that, after a mere graze of flesh. How unbelievable was that?

As she pondered that, she wiped down and disinfected everything with even more gusto. By the time she got MG out of the RV and went to put the kenneled dogs on leashes, she was ready to dismiss the experience as an anomaly.

"I'm being ridiculous, MG," she said to her dog. "If I start breaking into song like I'm in a Broadway musical, bite me."

The long-legged retriever-mix pranced beside her, happy to be with her again and about to get some exercise. Having full awareness of what the word *bite* meant, she barked, ending her commentary with a throaty growl.

Rylie laughed. "I knew I could count on you."

He would have said something. Even as he went to work on Tuesday, Noah continued to dwell on how yesterday had ended at the clinic. He'd been left… unsatisfied.

Rylie slammed the car door in your face!

Okay, he amended, so she'd shut it without giving him a chance. The point was that he would have at least thanked her again, to further prove that he wasn't the curmudgeon she seemed to believe he was. Why were they rubbing each other the wrong way? Such…friction was new to him. Usually, he had no problem getting along with people. Granted, he tended to be measured, cautious, but then he had his family name to respect and protect, and now his position with the D.A.'s office. But he wasn't inaccessible, let alone mean-spirited or cruel. He was someone who kept up with fraternity brothers from college and classmates from law school, for pity's sake!

Entering the courthouse, he already knew that Vance would be out of the office again. His boss had called while Noah had been driving to town to confirm that he was still feeling poorly, even though he'd been to see his doctor. That meant Noah would be fielding calls and handling several matters on behalf of the D.A.'s office, including having lunch with a civic group that had been scheduled months ago. That would be no problem, since he had made similar presentations before. This was a great opportunity to make more residents of the area aware of who he was.

Even with all that on his plate, Rylie's face appeared in his mind. Noah all but groaned in frustration.

It's because you touched her.

The contact had been clinical, inevitable due to the need to keep the dog still. There was no reason for him to read something sensual into the experience, but tell that to his body. It had responded as though he'd walked face-first into a furnace, and he'd remained thrown off balance long into the night, until he'd indulged in a second shower for relief. Thank goodness his mother's car was back in good shape, and Ramon would take over these clinic trips again. Clearly, he needed to protect himself from his own imagination.

After starting the coffee machine, Noah went to his desk with his collection of newspapers that were stacked daily on the hallway bench outside the office door. But as he sat down, the computer's dark monitor screen was what captured and kept his attention. It stared back at him in bold daring, a portal to…what?

Your best opportunity to find answers. Go ahead. You know you want to.

He checked his watch. The empty office would stay quiet like this for another half hour at most. Temptation won.

Noah booted up the machine. *Just one more search,* he told himself. He didn't want to dream about her again tonight. Yes, she was cute, yes, she was a new experience to him, but was it sane to become obsessed with a woman who lived in an *RV!*

As soon as that censorious thought formed in his mind, he felt shame, only to get defensive. Experience had taught him that few people had the Teflon skins attributed to some Washington, D.C., politicians that they could survive scandal or the weight of relentless gossip. If he was going to run for office, the shortest distance to that goal was to choose your society with circumspection. He needed some information, any excuse to get Rylie Quinn out of his head.

Try the social networks.

Although he grimaced at the thought of venturing there, Noah knew as friendly as Rylie was, she probably lived every free moment on Facebook and Twitter. It didn't take but seconds before he logged in to his own account—a tedious requirement for him per office policy to make the public feel connected—and typed her name in the search box. Her page came up within seconds.

There was no ignoring the jump in his pulse as he clicked through her photo album, seeing that at her high-school graduation, she'd had waist-length hair. His next thought was that she had a ton of friends, including guys still carrying a crush, and a very proud family, he thought after seeing her parents gaze at her in each photo with love and adoration. Noah would never do the profiles or answer the idiotic questions they asked, but Rylie didn't seem to have a problem with them. Some, anyway. Actually, she had a contagious sense of humor, he thought, as he caught himself smiling, and then chuckling a few times. At other times, he was left transfixed.

She'd thought about joining Cirque du Soleil before heading for college to become a veterinarian. Being an athlete and cheerleader in high school explained why. In college, she'd continued with the cheerleading and had been the highflier. Noah suspected that's also what came with being the smallest in the group. Having witnessed her questionable balance, though, he wondered if she'd spent more time on crutches and in slings than on the practice floor.

She loved potatoes and gravy, wildflowers, pears in rum sauce, and confessed to craving steak too much to become a vegetarian. Nevertheless, she vowed she would jump at any chance to be on someone's fishing boat, and found lightning both terrifying and hypnotic.

Her dislikes were questions about dislikes. She didn't want to focus on the negative; every day was a new opportunity to her.

Just as you thought, the original optimist—or an eternal kid.

Then why were there secrets in her eyes?

"Good morning!"

Judy Millsap entered, bringing with her the scent of lavender and doughnuts. Since many sheriff's deputies, bailiffs and clerks passed their open door numerous times a day, Judy liked to bring a box of doughnuts to place by the coffee machine on the counter. Goodwill to all who passed. In her own way, Judy was the older rendition of Rylie—without the impishness—the ambassador of their office. At least Judy was a realist and mostly did it because—as she put it—"You get more flies with honey than vinegar."

"Morning," he called back to her. If his heart wasn't entirely in the greeting, it was because he knew he would now have to get focused on his day job. "Everything okay on your end?"

"It will be after another big mug of caffeine. I was up half the night ridiculously transfixed on listening to coyotes. Say something nice to me before I take off these sunglasses and offend you with the feed bags under my bloodshot eyes."

"You run the best office in East Texas," Noah replied, truthfully.

After a moment's hesitation, Judy slid off the glasses and gave him a pained look. "For an attractive and intelligent man, you are truly clueless, Noah Prescott."

Startled, Noah sat back in his chair. "What?"

"You don't have a clue, do you?"

"I just complimented you."

With the smile of a patient mother, Judy replied, "You complimented what I do. That's not who I am."

He groaned inwardly. Women. Surely, Judy didn't believe the two were separate. Not at this juncture of her life. She had been with the office for over twenty years, and there had been few eight-hour days, even in a small department like theirs.

"Have you been watching old Errol Flynn movies or that Don Juan something or other with Brando and Depp?" he asked, suspicious.

"*Don Juan Demarco*—as a matter of fact, I did. Last night because that horrible howling does bad things to my imagination. And even though I watched in the living room, would you believe Dwayne said the flickering lights coming down the hall and the audio—though set low—ruined his sleep, too?" From a singsong voice, she went almost feral. "Why couldn't he just say that he missed having me beside him? You men never say what you mean."

He thought he had. Noah suggested with more care, "You could always move. Away from the coyote problem, I mean."

Judy rolled her eyes in disbelief. "You of all people have no business saying anything like that, Noah Prescott. Could you leave Haven Land?"

His first impulse was to remind her that he had done so. Before the accident that left him with responsibility too great to delegate to others. But Judy had lived in Cherokee County her entire life, and had never wanted to go anywhere else. She'd earned her business degree through a combination of the community college, online and via UT Tyler. Nothing wrong with that if it was what you wanted. He, on the other hand, hadn't felt as though Haven Land soil was somehow intrinsic to his heart and liver function. Fate, though, seemed to be insisting otherwise.

Instead, he said, "I'll catch the phones while you have your coffee." With regret, he shut down the Facebook page. He would have gone on to the next idea/source, since he'd learned Rylie was from some small town around Palm Springs, California. Palm Springs gave him the hunch that there was a good reason why she could afford that RV. No wonder she hadn't been star-blinded by his family name, or his mother's friends. She had to be used to wealthy clients. That raised the question, what else was she used to?

"I'm used to a lot, and I'm game to try more."

Rylie had been armpit-deep into a pregnant cow's womb often enough not to hesitate trying to help Gage with a pygmy goat having a difficult labor due to tangled kids inside her. It was six hours after closing. She'd been in bed, asleep, for an hour when Doc had called her asking if she was up to helping with the emergency he was coming in to tend to. Now they were in the brightly lit clinic, and Gage had failed to get his big hand in far enough to remedy the problem.

"I know you're borderline on time," she added, "and need to do a cesarean soon or risk losing all of them."

"That's right," Gage replied, "and you have the smallest hands, so you're likely to be the least intrusive for the poor doe. Now we'll see if you have the dexterity and strength. I'll give you one try, and then I'm going to be forced to call this."

"Yes, sir."

Giving the animal's owner—Vicky Turner, a long-time customer—a reassuring smile, she went to work, reaching in to feel what Gage had already discovered for himself. "Ah… I see what you mean," she told him, keeping her eyes closed to rely on the most important sense right now—touch.

"Three, right?"

"Give me a second." Hoping she was right in separating the twist of legs, Rylie suddenly felt a yielding, and slipped out the first baby, slick and slippery. From the protesting movements, it was apparent this one was alive.

"Great," Gage said, immediately using a little suction bulb to make sure the mouth and nostrils were clear. "We have one pretty strong boy," he said, laying the firstborn by the mother's head.

She immediately set to licking him clean, and Vicky moved to that end of the table to make sure the infant didn't inadvertently fall or get knocked off the table.

"He's probably the biggest, so maybe the others will be easier." Rylie reached in again. Sure enough, while the puzzle of body parts continued, she was able to pull out a second baby in half the time. "Hurry, take this one," she said to Gage. "The next one is acting like this is a sprint to the finish line."

Gage scooped up that baby and proceeded to give it the same treatment. "Hopefully, that's it," he said. "Mama's wide, but not a big girl herself. Isn't three her standard, Vicky?"

"No, this is Wink's third litter, Doc. While she had three her first time, she had four last time," the anxious woman reminded him.

Sighing, Gage stroked Wink. "Don't you know you're supposed to stick with two?"

"Well, Mrs. Turner, I have a feeling that's what's

going on this time, too," Rylie said, delving into the womb again. "Why else did a pretty girl like this try to emulate a small aircraft carrier?"

Just as the wife of the grocery-store manager laughed, the third baby emerged. Trying to catch the wet thing was like trying to grab a fish. Thankfully, she managed. This one was about the same size as the second baby. "Looks like we have two girls and a boy," she announced.

"Excellent. Girls tend to be easier to sell," the woman replied.

"Better check a last time," Gage told Rylie. "You're starting to make a believer out of me."

Once again, Rylie eased her hand into the mother and gasped. "Oh! There is one more. Poor little thing was pushed way in back." Rylie grinned as she learned through touch what was happening. "I guess with finally having some room, she's content to stretch out and enjoy herself for a while."

"Do you really feel movement?" Mrs. Turner moved the third cleaned baby to the mother's teats. "It's not just a birth reflex? I've lost a few of the ones that have to struggle for space."

Gage nodded to Rylie. "Get it out. The sooner we get them all a good dose of colostrum, the better."

Rylie knew the "first milk" from the mother needed to occur within the first hour of birth to help build immunity. Searching again, she finally got a safe hold and drew it out. As soon as the tiny creature emerged, it started wailing lustily.

"Ha!" Rylie chuckled. "Nothing wrong with her lungs."

Vicky's eyes welled and Gage grinned.

"Good job," he said, automatically making sure the infant's mouth and nostrils were free of mucus. Then he gave the baby to the mother. "Here you go, Mama. Three girls and a big boy. Wish they gave awards for that."

Vicky told Rylie, "Thank you for saving me a surgery bill, too. I really appreciate that."

"You're very welcome. I was thrilled to assist." And she was. However, she was also feeling bittersweet, aware that this still wasn't the same as being the doctor-in-charge making that life-or-death decision whether to do the cesarean or not.

Giving herself a mental shake, she continued to help, until they had all four kids in a carrier kennel in the SUV. Then they put the mother in the second one. Dawn was still hours away as they waved to their happy client while she drove off.

Side by side at the deep stainless-steel double sinks, they soaped up and started scrubbing. Standing on his right, Rylie could feel Gage's scrutiny.

"I'll bet you're ready to crash," she said. There had been so much overtime lately—and Gage's schedule had already been virtually nonstop when she'd first arrived in Sweet Springs. "I hope you unwind enough to get a few hours' sleep. Feel free to add an extra hour. When Roy arrives later this morning, we can split the usual chores between us."

"What?" Gage protested. "You want me to give up this sleep-deprived look? It's getting me plenty of sympathy from my bride."

"I can imagine, but you can't keep up this pace, so please, please, please, feel free to let me help whenever you want."

After a short silence, the tall, gentle-mannered man said, "I just can't keep silent any longer, Rylie. You're a natural at this. What happened that you couldn't get through a few more months of school?"

Rylie worried her lower lip, trying to think of another evasive answer to buy herself more time; however, she was growing more and more fond of him—as she was everyone here. That was making it difficult not to be completely forthcoming. In the end she could only offer, "I promise to tell you one day soon, Doc. I'm not hiding anything that will embarrass or upset you. I'm just not ready to talk yet."

Although he looked disappointed, Gage replied, "Okay. Ask my wife if I have patience. It took a lot of mental fortitude to outlast Brooke's determination to get back to Dallas and resume her career, not to mention to make her see me as the guy she was going to fall in love with."

Appreciating the playful note in his voice, Rylie chuckled. "I'm glad she saw the error of her ways."

"Me, too, since she's carrying my baby!" Then he grew serious again. "If it helps, all you need to know is that you're an asset that I don't want to lose. I'm all the more convinced we need to get you your technician's certification as soon as possible. How do you feel about that?"

"Wow. I knew you were suggesting that we'd be working toward that, but I thought I needed to prove myself over a sixty-or ninety-day trial period. Thank you, sir!"

"For heaven's sake, will you please call me Gage?" He glanced over his shoulder. "Unless someone with a badge is present and I need to look like a serious authority figure."

Rylie nodded, grinning. "That's not a problem you'll have to worry about with me."

"I'm so relieved that you were here," Gage continued. "As great a helper as Roy had been, his hands aren't much smaller than mine. Sleep loss aside, I'm also glad this didn't happen during regular hours when you had a grooming appointment. That's not to take away from what you're achieving with your business. I'm aware of the clientele you're taking from Rusk as a result of word getting out about you."

"Mrs. Prescott alone saved me plenty on advertising costs."

"Well, keep it up. I'm working on getting us more help."

Although she was doing better dealing with the abrupt turn in her career path, Rylie couldn't ignore a sinking feeling. "Have you settled on anyone yet?" She was aware that he'd talked to a few people, but no one had come in for a tour and meeting yet.

"I'm afraid not. Does that make me seem too particular?"

"Not at all. I can't imagine having to try to fit personalities and abilities to their best effect."

"Thanks. You don't by chance have a twin with your talents? We could use another technician, too."

Rylie knew her uncle was happy in the reception area and managing the stock and storerooms, but she couldn't help but wish more for him. "You can't change Uncle Roy's mind about working toward his certification?"

Gage shrugged. "He's willing to help in an emergency, but he said he thought it was time to get some younger help to handle the more physical stuff. I can't completely regret that—he's excellent and honest to a fault when it comes to the paperwork side of things."

"That's a wonderful compliment, but I can't help wishing more for him."

"Well, I'm sure I'm not sharing any secret," he drawled, "but he feels the same about you."

Once again she saw how Gage was perfect for this work, and why he was so well liked in the community. He had an ability to at least appear laid-back and able to go with the flow. However, she had seen enough to know he missed nothing and was on top of everything at all times. No wonder he'd had the patience and savvy to outwait and outmaneuver Brooke.

Rylie couldn't help but eye him with growing affection. "You sure seem happy despite the workload, Doc. *Gage*. How's Brooke doing? Any more morning sickness?" He had shared the news about them expecting their first child, and that the baby was due in the late spring.

"No, thank goodness, she's about done with that, I hope. But she's starting to look like she might cry every time she goes to the doctor and has to step on the scale. To keep her from obsessing, I've locked up the one at home."

Rylie chuckled. "Now that is being a *gentle*man."

"Yeah, well, if she's carrying a boy, he's likely to take after me. The sooner she forgives herself for every few ounces she gains, the better for everyone within hearing distance."

Rylie thought how wonderful it would be to have someone whose every thought was about *you*. "Have you started thinking of names?" she asked, as they headed toward the back door, where he would lock up.

"A little bit. I got 'the look' for suggesting Gager, which I thought was a clever avoidance of Gage Jr. I think we're narrowing things down to Mitch, short for Mitchell after my grandfather, and she gets to choose if it's a girl. Her Aunt Marsha never cared for her name and warned her not to do anything nostalgic on her behalf."

"I visited a few minutes with Mrs. Newman at the assisted-living center yesterday," Rylie told him as he held the door open for her to pass into the quiet night. "She's doing so well."

"I'm glad you think so. Brooke still has moments of guilt for moving her in there, despite it being on the doctor's directives. Marsha seems to be having fun, though. She's among friends, she still gets to see Brooke as much as she wants, and she's no longer burdened with business and property concerns. Old age should be a time when you enjoy the fruit of your labors, or do other things you've been thinking about with the experience and skill you've worked a lifetime to achieve."

"She does seem to be blooming. While I was making the rounds with MG, she was in the atrium with the dominoes players, and the way they were carrying on, you'd think it was New Year's in Times Square."

"I'll be sure to pass that on to Brooke." Gage slid his key into the dead bolt. "So MG is liking her therapy work?"

"Mostly." Rylie felt a wave of sadness momentarily block her voice. "There's a patient—Mr. Wagner—he's in bad shape after cancer surgery and isn't dealing with his radiation well. MG crawled up on the bed with him—with the nurse's permission—and just lay there quietly until he had no more strength to stroke her." She had to clear her voice to continue. "She's so patient and compassionate with people, Gage. I love that, but it also breaks my heart, too. She had a bad dream later."

Testing the door, Gage turned to her, frowning. "You think there was a connection?"

With a one-shouldered shrug, Rylie said, "I can only say that it's not like her. She's only had a couple of troubled dreams since I've had her, nothing this disturbing or prolonged. And when I woke her, she snuggled closer against me as though relieved that I understood, or that she wasn't alone."

"She's an intelligent, sensitive dog," Gage replied. "But if you think she's taking on too much, I wouldn't blame you if you wanted to rethink using her as a therapy dog."

"I would hate that for the patients' sakes—and as social as she is, I think she would be disappointed, too."

"You know it could be that her first owner was an elderly person and that's brought back sad memories."

"I hadn't considered that."

"Let me know if the dreams continue." Rocking his head to get the kinks out of his neck, he nodded to her RV. "Get yourself inside and lock up, so I can head for the house for some shut-eye."

"Yes, sir!"

Chapter 3

After that abbreviated night, Rylie thought she would be dragging by lunchtime—after Gage generously bought breakfast, she sure wasn't hungry—but she found that she was too wired to even put up her feet for a ten-minute power nap, so she borrowed her uncle's truck to "run an errand," as she explained it to him.

It was time, she decided. If Gage was going to use her more, she would have fewer free moments than ever to take care of getting herself permanently settled in as a resident of Sweet Springs, Texas. A trip to the county DMV in Rusk was needed to transfer her driver's license. The only reason she refrained from explaining that was her fear that something could go wrong, so with Roy agreeing to watch MG and Humphrey, she took off.

Autumn was finally arriving in Central East Texas,

and the skies were growing cloudier by the hour, the winds stronger. Strong thunderstorms were in the forecast for the evening, when a front would bring plummeting temperatures. She took great care driving to the county seat, and had no problem finding the courthouse. Having ascertained by her laptop that the Department of Motor Vehicles would be within walking distance, she pulled into the first parking spot she could find in the busy heart of town.

Locking up her uncle's truck, she crossed the road and then started down the street, only to hear, "What are you doing here?"

For a fraction of a second, she almost believed she'd conjured him; after all, this was *his* territory, and she had been thinking of him more and more as she approached the city. Even so, her heart pumped harder once she spun around to see Noah Prescott slamming the door of his BMW and taking loping strides to reach her. With only a wallet to clutch, since she rarely bothered with purses, she hugged herself despite the eighty-degree temperature.

As usual, he looked suave and confident in another tailored suit—this one navy blue. No athletic hunk, which was fine with her, he had this smooth-drink-of-water look that would make him perfect to play a highly educated, prodigal son of some organized-crime figure, most dangerous when he smiled, as he did now. In comparison, she felt like a member of the janitorial service at Guantanamo in her Day-Glo lime T-shirt and jeans.

"Hello, you," she managed, hoping she sounded wryly amused. "How's Bubbles?"

"Almost as good as new. Mother was most relieved—and grateful," he added with a hint of a bow.

He was on his best behavior, which just made her feel all the more nervous. She offered a weak, "Small world."

He shook his head, all confidence. "My territory this time. What's your excuse?"

"Oh... I'm... I need to transfer my license." After that confidence stumble, she shrugged to suggest the chore was no big deal. Unfortunately, the truth was that there were going to be complications. "You all—excuse me, *y'all* are more tolerant than in California, but I figured the sooner I did this the better."

"They're closed for lunch."

Rylie told herself that this would be a good moment to check her watch if only to stop staring at him, but she didn't wear jewelry. Working around upset and injured animals and every type of farm and clinical equipment was dangerous enough without inviting injury. That left her with only the option to grimace. At least he couldn't know that her disappointment was more about their ill-timed meeting than his news. "I guess I'll go grab something to eat and try to be first in line when they reopen."

"You don't have to rush back for an appointment?"

"My next one is at two o'clock, but I'll definitely call and let them know what happened, in case Doc needed me sooner."

Noah studied her for another few seconds and suddenly said, "Come with me. I know the lady who operates that facility, and she usually brings her lunch from home. I'll ask her to make an exception for you and give her an IOU for lunch."

The latter part of his solution had her feeling almost sick. She could just picture an Angelina Jolie–type being offered lunch with Noah Prescott, an image that helped her uncharacteristically floundering ego nose-dive to Dismalville. As it was, anyone looking at Noah, then her, would not see much reason for him going out of his way to gain her favor. In the vast international range of beauty, she thought herself as cute on a good day when life wasn't coming at her at a hundred miles per hour. This was not one of those days. At least she wasn't wearing her maroon clinic smock that hid any sign that she had breasts and hips, such as they were.

With an adamant shake of her head, she replied, "No, really, I appreciate the thought, but I don't want any special treatment."

Behind his sharklike smile and brown-eyed gaze was a speculative glint. "It's the least I can do for Mother's favorite dog groomer."

I must be projecting. Stop projecting.

She knew from her years of work with animals that words were often unnecessary to communicate and that he was sensing her discomfort, and it was making him all the more intrigued. What was going on with the man? Usually he couldn't wait to get away from her.

"You know what?" she said, glancing toward her uncle's truck with longing. "I'll just come back another day."

As she started her escape, Noah followed her up the sidewalk. "After coming all this distance? That's a wasted trip, not to mention gas."

"Well, with the weather about to change, I'm glad to have been outside for a bit. Thanks for the offer, though. Tell your mother that I said—" As she pivoted on her right heel, she clipped her shoulder hard on the stop sign's post. "Ow!"

"Are you all right?"

Idiotic question. Gritting her teeth and gripping her shoulder, Rylie rode out the worst wave of pain. She knew never to turn right without more care, but being right-handed, it was still her instinctive choice.

"You know, they tend to put these signs at every cross section of roads."

If he hadn't had the decency to look at least a tad concerned, she would have gladly replied with something totally unladylike. At the least, he deserved a dry-cleaning bill for that insult-upon-injury remark. Instead, she reached for her usual self-deprecating humor. After all, this area was not just her new home, it was Uncle Roy's and Gage's, and she needed to set a good example for them, as well.

"Glutton for punishment that I am," she quipped, "I was trying to add to my collection of scar tissue."

"Take my arm," he said, all Southern charm. "Before you forget there's traffic, too."

Being thought of as an amusing klutz hurt worse than being disliked, she realized, even if she'd more or less invited the perspective. Feeling her eyes begin to burn from tears, she muttered, "Hilarious. Now would you please go away and—and *persecute* someone who deserves it!"

What the hell...?

Rylie's words startled Noah, and as he watched her drive away in the red pickup truck, they began to gnaw at him like a haunting wound. Nothing was as it seemed with her. The embarrassment he understood well enough; she really was an awkward little thing, but why on earth the tears and accusation that he was persecuting her?

She must have hurt herself worse than he thought, or maybe it was a second blow to an old injury? He thought again about the cheerleading. That could be it.

No, she was upset from the moment she saw you, and it got worse when you offered to get her into the DMV office.

As he returned to the office, Noah saw that Judy was busy on the phone, so when he settled at his desk, it was all but inevitable that the first thing he did was start typing California Department of Motor Vehicles into the search box. But just after the site came up and he began to type in Rylie's name, he caught a motion across the room.

Judy was waving at him. "It's Vance. He wants to talk to you about the Condon case. I'm off to get these affidavits logged with the county clerk and then help Ann in the file room."

Resigned that his detective work would have to wait yet again, Noah exited the page he'd been on and picked up his phone. "Yes, sir? How are you feeling today?"

"As the saying goes, 'Better than the other guy.'"

Gage's words replayed in Rylie's mind as she jumped out of bed. Friday was also starting too early, although not as much as Thursday had. At minutes before five o'clock, her cell phone started playing the theme from *The Lion King,* and she automatically knew it was Gage. Grabbing for it, her response had been, "Are you okay?"

It turned out that he was asking her to be ready when

he arrived within the next ten minutes. There was a dog that had been hit by a car at the southern perimeter of the county. Dairy farm she suspected, considering the hour.

She grabbed for clothes. Fortunately, she was learning to keep a clean set handy for this kind of situation. As for her usual morning shower, that would have to wait. She knew Gage lived close and would move fast, giving her enough time only to brush her teeth and throw water at her face to finish waking up.

When she emerged from the RV, she was greeted with fog. Perfect autumn conditions for stagnant air masses. The front hadn't pushed through all the way. If there had been storms, she'd slept through them. No wonder there had been an accident. As thick as this stuff was, the driver probably had never seen the dog until he—or she—was right upon it.

Restricting MG to only a quick potty break for now, she locked her back in the RV. "I'll come get you as soon as the emergency is over," she assured the good-natured dog.

Just as she came around to the side door, Gage turned into the parking lot. Even though they'd come from different directions, not far behind him was a white pickup truck. As they drew nearer, Rylie saw a young teenage boy in the bed of the truck. When the driver stopped behind Gage's vehicle, she went to look at the dog lying between the boy's legs on a blanket. There was no blood, thank goodness, but the canine was alternately licking its leg and the owner's hand, then whimpering, clearly in pain and trying to communicate the injury and desire for help.

"Hey," Rylie murmured to the sleepy-eyed, anxious boy. "How's he holding up?"

"Not too good. I think the leg is broken." Nodding to the blond-haired youth, who looked no more than thirteen, she thought if that was the case, and there were no major organ problems, there was no place better equipped to help the poor animal—if the father okayed the expense. "I'm Rylie. Who are you?"

"Bryce. This is Jackson."

"Jackson is one of the most beautiful chocolate Labs I've ever seen. He looks…maybe two?"

"Next month. Hopefully."

Hearing the worry in the boy's voice, Rylie knew it was time to get him to thinking more positively. "Celebrating his birthday early, huh? Is that why he was in the road at this hour?"

Bryce almost smiled. "We were working our dairy cows and usually Jackson listens to me, but he spotted a red fox. He'd never seen one before and he just couldn't resist going after it. The newspaper-delivery guy tried to miss him but didn't quite make it." He gave her a sheepish look. "He did annihilate our mailbox, though."

"Ah." Rylie nodded with sympathy. She glanced up to see Gage had the clinic door unlocked. "Just a second while we get the lights on and we'll be out to help get Jackson inside."

She nodded to the father as she went to help Gage get things set up. "Morning," she said to her boss.

"Sorry again for another early call," he said.

Since he sounded as if he was barely awake himself, she decided to help him with a little humor. "You should be. You ruined my best dream in months. Brad

Pitt had just walked away from Angelina Jolie to ask me to dinner."

Gage snorted. "Only dinner? Woman, the guy can afford to buy you your own restaurant. We need to have a talk about wasting good sleep."

After grinning, she offered what she'd gauged so far. "The Lab's name is Jackson. Beautiful chocolate Lab. On first, minimal glance, it looks like a clean fracture. He was lured away from the boy by a red fox."

Gage's gaze shifted briefly to her own red hair. "It's the only color that will grab attention in fog like this."

"Jackson's a good-size two-year-old. Maybe we should put him on a cart?" Rylie asked.

"Nah, that'll only stress the poor guy even more. I know big babies like that. I'll go carry him in. Just get the X-ray machine ready—and if you get a second after that, putting the coffee machine to work would be great, too," Gage said.

"Consider it done."

Less than an hour later, Rylie helped Gage put the dog into an enclosure with a half wall and cushioned bed to finish sleeping off the anesthesia. Jackson's leg was wrapped securely and protected by a splint that would ease the pressure on the limb when he was ready to stand.

Bryce looked unsure about this so-called "help" for his dog. "How's he going to get around?"

"At first, he's not supposed to, but he'll learn to hobble on three legs," Gage told him. "That's seventy-five percent of his usual power compared with your fifty percent if you were the one hurt."

Bryce grunted. "I guess so."

"We'll keep him in this enclosure instead of the kennel as he wears off the sedation, so he'll stay calm," Rylie added. She knew that was the next question coming from the boy. "If we put him in the kennel, the other dogs' barking would be a bit much for a guy with a hangover."

"Can I stay with him, Dad?" Bryce asked his father. "There's nothing going on at school today."

Daniel Black glanced at Gage and Rylie with a wry expression. "It's only the first full month of school and there's nothing happening." To his son, he added, "You're going to classes, and maybe by the time you get home, Jackson will be ready for us to visit for a minute."

"Not to worry," Rylie assured the crestfallen boy. "We take good care of our friends in recovery. And my dog, MG, will happily lay in there with him to keep him company if he's feeling lonely. She's a therapy dog."

The boy brightened. "She is? Wow! I heard about them. Can I meet her?"

"When you come see Jackson."

Daniel Black nudged his son toward the door. "Thanks, Doc. Rylie. I appreciate all that you did— especially considering the hour."

Once they left, Rylie breathed a sigh of relief. "I was afraid Mr. Black wouldn't okay the expense of treating Jackson."

"I should have told you that they have three other pets that are older," Gage replied. "But there wasn't the discreet opportunity. Their long-term commitment to their animals is a given."

Pleased, Rylie said, "Well, I don't know about you,

but I'm ready for another dose of caffeine. What a week it's been."

They were still on daylight saving time, and day-break was more than a promise. There was no chance for either of them to return to bed, although Gage would have to go get Humphrey.

"I'm ready," Gage said. "You'll find me logging this procedure into the computer."

"As soon as I get you yours, I'll go take MG out. Would you like me to get you something to eat from my freezer? I can offer you a nuked sausage and bis-cuit or a day-old bran muffin."

Gage shook his head. "So it's true, you and Brooke are the two least useful women in a kitchen?" he teased.

"If I could look as elegant as she always does, I'd call that a compliment." Rylie gestured helplessly. "I can give Uncle Roy a call and have him pick up some-thing more than the usual doughnuts on his way in."

Gage shook his head. "I'll take care of breakfast for us when I collect Humphrey. It's the least I can do when you're not getting much more sleep than I am."

By the time they regrouped, the old-timers were camped out at their corner table and a third pot of cof-fee was being brewed. MG kept nudging Rylie's leg, wanting to repeatedly check on Jackson.

"What a good girl you are, MG," Gage said, fol-lowing them to the enclosure to check on Jackson's progress himself. "Yeah, we have a different kind of patient, don't we?"

MG sniffed, then licked Jackson's bandage once and then quietly lay down beside him. Except for the "pa-tient" being canine, it was typical behavior for MG, but Gage was impressed.

"If she wants to stay in here with him," he told Rylie, "I wouldn't mind. Let me know if her attitude changes to where you think she's troubled or concerned for him."

"Are you worried something isn't right?"

"Not at all. I'm just wanting her to use her obvious talents." His stomach growled and he rubbed it sympathetically. "There's something that doesn't need interpretation. I'm off to get Humph and breakfast."

By the afternoon, everyone was doubly grateful that it was Friday, although they would be open half of the day tomorrow. There was no chance to bother trying to run to Rusk in the hope of getting her license transferred; besides, she'd learned through some online research that she could go to any of the other DMV offices in the area, and she had about convinced herself that was what she should do to avoid another run-in with Noah. It was also a good thing that they'd had an opportunity for a big breakfast because there was barely time to take a bite of their sandwiches at lunchtime.

Rylie was chewing fast when Roy passed her with boxes the UPS man had delivered. He pressed his lips together trying not to laugh.

"Go ahead," Rylie said, holding her hand in front of her mouth. "Call me Chipmunk Cheeks."

"If you promise not to throw the rest of that sandwich at me, I was wondering if MG and Humphrey tripped you and tried to lick you to death, or is that hairstyle an homage to the punk look?"

Although Rylie often styled her hair into a spikier look, she knew what he was referring to—earlier, she'd had to wrestle one of the kenneled dogs into his pen after his outside time, and the goofy Great Dane— every bit as tall as she was—had shown his affection by licking her head repeatedly. Because they'd been non-stop busy, she'd forgotten about the incident, until now.

With a sigh, Rylie put down her sandwich and crossed to the bathroom, where she opened the door to look in the mirror. "Oh, jeez." She combed her fingers through her short, stiff hair with no results. Nothing short of sticking her head under the sink was going to help the situation, which she didn't have time to do. To resolve the situation and keep from being teased by the old-timers when they spotted her, she grabbed one of the white-and-maroon baseball caps that Gage kept for staff by the coat rack at the back door and slipped it on, tugging it low over her forehead.

"Thanks," she told her uncle. "I swear, this has been a day for the books."

"Can I do anything so you can finish your lunch?" Roy nodded toward the front of the clinic. "We're quiet up front for the moment."

"I so appreciate the offer, but I don't think you're up to putting metallic-pink nail polish on Annabelle Leigh." The toy poodle belonged to the Leigh family, who owned a car dealership in Rusk and Tyler, and she was sitting patiently in her kennel in the first examination room, acting very satisfied with her wash and trim. All that remained was the polish and matching bow, and she could go home with Mrs. Leigh, who was picking her up within an hour.

Roy made a face. "You're right. I'll end up with more polish on me than on the dog, and then never mind those guys out there teasing *you*. They'll laugh me out of Texas."

"What you could do is take out Humphrey. That would be a big help, since the little fire hydrant just gulped down half a bowl of water. MG is okay. She's still with Jackson."

"Poor Humph. Dumped for a big, strapping Lab," Roy teased, going to collect the basset hound.

Minutes later, just as Rylie finished Annabelle and returned her to her kennel, Gage came from the opposite side of the clinic. "I hate to bother you, but if you could give me five minutes, I could use your help with a Manx needing inoculations in Room Four. While I have no problem with most cats, that one acts like she wants to rearrange my face."

How odd, Rylie thought. "I always believed that breed was considered the sweetheart of the feline world. Do you think you have too much canine scent on you?"

"No more than you, but—" he glanced over his shoulder to make sure the examination room door remained closed "—frankly, her owner is a pretty tough customer, too, and I think the cat picks up her negative vibes toward me."

Rylie was doubly surprised and intrigued. Gage was a 24K darling, and if you couldn't get along with him, you probably needed psychiatric care. "Lead on. I have your back, boss."

Although prepared for anything, Rylie hesitated one step into room—not due to any concern for her or Gage's safety, but rather for the unusual pair waiting for them. The Manx and owner were both attired in a smoldering gray, the cat endowed with luscious long fur, the woman, maybe in her late thirties, wearing a leather vest over a matching T-shirt and jeans. Of average height and build, the cat's owner sported red hair, too, except it was a shade that could be achieved only via the help of chemistry. It also appeared that she cut her own hair, and not necessarily while looking into a mirror. However, considering her recent bad luck in the hair department, Rylie just adjusted her cap and continued inside.

"This is Rylie. She's going to assist me and hopefully reassure your pet."

With a smile, Rylie approached the table while calmly analyzing the situation. It was impossible to ignore the array of tattoos and body piercings adorning the woman. While they weren't excessive, there were more than she could ever perceive of wanting. She couldn't help but wonder where the hidden ones were located.

Closing the door behind them, Gage finished the introductions before busying himself with getting the inoculations ready. "Rylie, this is Jane Ayer."

Rylie was sure she'd heard incorrectly. "Excuse me. Did you say—"

"Yeah, yeah," Jane said with equal parts weariness and sarcasm. "Spare me the jokes. Not *that* Jane Eyre. Spelled with an A. What's more, the last time I was in a petticoat was in the seventh grade when I wore it with boots and a bustier to the junior-high dance that I was ejected from."

"Okay, point taken." Usually when she met people with all of the body art that Jane sported, they tended to be fairly comfortable in their own skin. But Jane seemed on the defensive side, or at least sensitive. Hoping to ease that, Rylie focused on the tattoo on her forearm. "Love the panther. My brother has one coming over his shoulder like that. Your artist did a good job."

The woman had been staring hard at her, but Rylie's observation seemed to at least trigger some curiosity. "Thanks. What does he do?"

"Restores old houses. Up in New England."

Nodding thoughtfully, Jane stroked her cat on the examination table. "This is Rodeo."

Rylie tilted her head as she considered the gorgeous cat with her short torso and strong hindquarters. Of all the names she would have guessed for such an exotic breed, it wasn't that. "Rodeo, huh? She's a fair-size female, but she still looks a little delicate to be a bull rider."

At first, Jane looked as though she was going to rebuff her attempt at humor, but she finally said, "I named her that because of how she plays with the mice she catches."

"An alpha girl. I'm all for women handling their own vermin extermination." Aware that Gage was taking an inordinate amount of time to make notations on the cat's record sheet, which Roy would put into the computer, she added, "My favorite fable about how the Manx ended up with no tail is that they were on the slow end of getting to Noah's ark and the door closed on them."

"Ha—not this one," Jane replied. "She can smell when it's going to rain for two days out. She's not too fond of water, but then I rescued her from the rain barrel her previous owner had thrown her into. No telling how long she'd been paddling around in there trying to get a good grip in order to climb out."

Rylie looked sympathetically at Jane and then the cat. "How awful. But what a relief that you happened to be there to rescue her." She was used to seeing welcome and good humor in this breed's big eyes, but Rodeo was all caution, like her mistress. No doubt Gage was right about Jane giving the cat some unwanted signals—it happened with dogs all the time. But she'd believed cats were far too independent to be easily influenced—until now. "How does she prefer to be approached?"

"Not at all. But she looks like she's starting to be interested in you. Maybe it's the hair."

Not a lot of it was showing. Rylie removed her hat, hoping her hair had been flattened enough by now not to look too ridiculous. If the cat thought redheads were okay, then that's what she would use to gain her acceptance.

Sure enough, the cat made a guttural sound not unlike a human saying, "Huh," as in "Go figure."

"I think," Rylie said to Jane, "if you wouldn't mind shaking hands with me, I'll be able to reassure her by having some of your scent on me. Unfortunately, I've just come from a poodle, and that can't be welcoming news to her refined senses."

After a slight hesitation, the woman nodded and extended her hand. "Why didn't you think of that, Doc?" Jane asked Gage.

Ever the unflappable one, he finally glanced their way. "Because this is only your second visit and I didn't know whom to be more afraid of, you or Rodeo."

Jane finally managed a real smile, though a reluctant one. "If I didn't approve of you, I wouldn't have come back."

Gage said to Rylie, "Jane brought in Rodeo a short time before you joined us, but Alpha Girl, as you call her, was having nothing of this place and Jane had to leave. I'll admit that we had more dogs in the building that day. I recommended that she give Rodeo a few days to recover and try again. Baby steps and all that."

An almost palpable easing of tension spread throughout the room. Grateful, Rylie shook hands with the woman and then let Rodeo smell her before stroking the cat's dense coat. The Manx gave what could have been a warning sound, only to flop onto her back and starting to play with Rylie's fingers as though taunting a mouse before the kill.

"Is this really play or am I about to become dinner?" Rylie mused.

Jane snorted. "She's not going to bite you. She's just making sure you're worthy of her grooming you. In other words, you're okay. Like I said, she belonged to some jerk before I got her. He ran a gas station up north. To get her out of harm's way, I lit up the paper towel dispenser in the ladies' bathroom to get his attention. We've been together ever since."

"Jane drives a Harley," Gage offered as though he was reporting the weather. "Rodeo rides in a kennel on the backseat secured by a bungee cord."

Rylie whistled softly. "A Harley, huh? I would have to bench press this examination table for weeks before I could manage one of those. I'm very impressed," Rylie told the no-nonsense woman.

Rodeo started licking her fingers, drawing her attention back to the cat. "Well, you are one of a kind, aren't you? Thanks for the affection." She noticed that Gage was ready. "I'm sorry that we're about to make you doubt your goodwill, but as the saying goes, it's for your own good."

As Gage approached them with the first needle, he gave Jane a tentative look. "Go for it. It'll be fine now," Jane assured him. "If I'm okay with you, she will be."

That turned out to be exactly right. Rylie easily got a comfortable hold on the cat. Then Gage did his usual, admirable job in giving the shots quickly and with such minimal pain, Rodeo barely reacted.

"It's been real," Gage said to the cat, as he retreated toward the door. "Rylie will get Roy up front to log this information and get you your tags," he told Jane.

"That wasn't too bad, was it?" Rylie asked, ruffling the cat's fur, while being careful to avoid the tender spots. "You just like to call the shots, don't you?"

"We both do," Jane told her, all but sighing. "It sure would be nice not to have to."

Sensing a lonely soul, who was probably also hurt badly at some time, Rylie offered, "Stop by for a cup of coffee sometime when you have the time. You'll find everyone here is pretty laid-back and accepting. People come and go all the time to shoot the breeze with the guys," she added with a nod toward the reception area, "or to ask one of us if we know someone when they're looking to find a pet or they're hoping to locate a new home for one that they have to give up."

Jane didn't look sold on the idea. "I'll think about it. I stay pretty busy as it is."

"What do you do—if you don't mind my asking?"

"I'm helping out at the dairy farm on the east side of town. Rodeo likes that I get free milk whenever she wants it."

"Lucky kitty. Hard work for you, though." Gesturing

to the door that led back into the reception area, Rylie said, "Let's get you finished up. Have you actually met my Uncle Roy? He's been here for several years. I'm relatively new. He handles all of the front-desk stuff."

"I guess he's the one who put us in this examination room and told us to wait on Doc. He's kind of gruff."

"Oh, he has a deep voice, all right, but otherwise what you noticed was shyness. Except when he has to keep the guys in the corner straight. Then you'll see how protective he is of ladies—not that they'll say anything. They're a sweet bunch, just ornery between themselves."

"I wondered what that was all about," Jane said. "I guess it was so busy that I didn't see them the last time I was here."

Leading the way to the counter, she waited as Roy handed another customer his receipt then came over to reach for the patient chart before Rylie could even say a word. Rodeo hissed and swatted at him, causing her uncle to recoil quickly.

"Hey, pretty girl," he protested. "I'm not the one who gave you those vaccinations."

As Rylie stroked the cat's head, she quietly explained to her uncle, "Rodeo's previous owner was abusive."

"Aw. Thanks for telling me. There should be a special hell for people like that—right next door to those who hurt kids." Roy sighed. "She's a real pretty specimen," Roy said to Jane, only to give the chart a quizzical look. "You've been here before? Sorry. I must have been tied up with a delivery, Mrs. Ayer."

"Ms." Jane glanced at him from under her short, unpainted lashes. "Rodeo here is the only family I have."

Roy nodded outside at her bike. "That's a grand bit of machinery."

"Do you ride?"

"Not in years."

Rylie tried not to gasp as his words jarred memories. "I'd almost forgotten, Uncle Roy." When he all but ignored her, she looked from him to Jane and thought she saw something happening. *Go figure,* she thought. How often had she tried through the years to find out why there was no one special in his life, and here he was sending out signals. What's more, Jane was sending her own back at him!

"Now that I think about it," Jane ventured, "I've seen you at the car wash from time to time scrubbing on your truck's hubcaps."

"You probably did. I'm guilty of liking my vehicle looking like it did when I first drove it off the lot." He started typing data into the computer. "I don't guess I saw a bike like that while I was there, though."

"No, I take care of it at home. But I take my 1957 Chevy Impala to the car wash."

Roy's gaze lifted from the screen in record speed. "The red one? Man, that's a gorgeous machine. Did you happen to restore it yourself?"

Jane acted as though she'd just been told she was the most beautiful woman on two continents. "I did, thank you. Everything on it is original."

Roy's stare reflected his astonishment—and admiration. "Well, I am proud to meet you." Cautious of Rodeo, he extended his hand, which Jane accepted. "So you like restorations?"

"I like things well put together."

"Okay," Rylie drawled, catching Jane give her uncle

a slow once-over. "So I have a poodle going home in a minute, and I have to go prepare a ticket. Good meeting you, Jane."

"Oh, you, too, Rylie. And thanks!"

Rylie decided she was the one who should be thanking Jane. She'd never seen her uncle show this much interest in a woman. Fascinating, since Jane's style was a bit "out there," and not the kind of look she would think her uncle responded to, but so much for her hunches. She sure wouldn't mind if someone looked at *her* the way Roy was looking at Jane.

Correction...not "someone." Noah.

No, she thought sadly. She'd pretty much ruined any possibility of that fantasy coming true after the way she'd run from him the other day. And slamming into that post had cinched things. Now more than ever, Noah undoubtedly thought she was too easy to resist.

It was minutes before closing time, and Rylie stood up front with Gage and Roy double-checking that today's patients' files had been thoroughly updated on the computer. In between they were joking with the guys in the corner, who'd just finished a game of dominoes and were packing up to leave. Gage was in a hopeful mood, thanks to the phones remaining quiet. With no emergency calls, he was going to make it home before dark for a change. As for Rylie, she was debating how to spend her evening.

"Come to the VFW hall with us," Roy told her. "It's fish and chips night."

Before she could answer, Pete Ogilvie called, "Incoming," and everyone's attention was drawn to the parking lot.

The sheriff's SUV was pulling in. Occasionally a deputy came by to ask to put a dog in quarantine for having bitten someone, or to ask for help in getting a dead animal checked for rabies, but never Sheriff Marv Nelson himself.

"What's he doing here?" Roy asked. "He doesn't have to campaign for another two years."

That won him a few chuckles, but they all kept their eyes on the vehicle as it parked up front. There were clearly two men inside, and when Noah Prescott emerged from the passenger's side, Rylie felt a tightening in her chest. She also self-consciously ran her hand over her hair. She'd had a chance to quickly wash her short hair, but not much more. At least it wasn't acting as if she'd gone headfirst into a tub of wall plaster.

"Did you have a break-in that you didn't tell us about, Doc?" Warren chided from the corner. "Get some drugs stolen?"

"Not lately," Gage replied, his eyes narrowing as the men entered.

Sheriff Nelson nodded to Gage and barely glanced at the others before his gaze settled on Rylie. "Miss Quinn?"

"Yes, sir," she said cautiously. Although he was an impressive man in height and girth, it was impossible not to look from him to Noah, who followed him inside. The look on Noah's face was one of anger and distaste. "What's going on?"

"I have a warrant for your arrest."

Chapter 4

Sheriff Nelson's incredible announcement had Rylie reduced to staring at Noah. Now she understood his excessive interest in her the other day, and it had nothing to do with attraction. "What have you done?" she whispered.

He would have to have been totally blind not to see her utter shock and despair, and he momentarily had the grace to look somewhat unsure of himself. But he rallied well enough. "Are you going to deny that you know what this is about?" he asked stiffly.

"I suppose I can make a ballpark guess."

"Rylie!" Roy sounded as astonished as she was resigned. "What on earth…?"

Reminded of the many eyes on her, she aimed her reassurance at her uncle and Gage. "It's nothing like what you might be thinking. It had been my hope to get all of this taken care of before I explained. In fact I just sent the money for two of the tickets last week. There's probably some delay in the processing," Rylie added to Sheriff Nelson. "I can get you a copy of the checks. And I'm certain that I'll have the other paid for by next month."

At that news, Gage frowned and crossed his arms over his broad chest as he eyed Marv and Noah. "Seriously, gentlemen? You want to let them haul her back to California for a couple of traffic violations?"

"Technically, one was a parking violation."

"I'm still learning how to drive the monster," Rylie told her uncle and Gage. "Parking is a whole different story."

"The last one was an accident," Noah intoned.

"A fender bender!" Rylie was determined to protect at least a modicum of her unraveling reputation before it was distorted into something unrecognizable. "And the reason I'm late with paying the tickets is because I paid for the other driver's paint repair out of my pocket. I didn't want my insurance company to drop me."

"I can say that there was no evidence of intoxication or drug use," the sheriff pointed out, as if trying to be of help to her—or at least be fair. "But apparently she also got stopped in Arizona for having an expired license."

"The officer never wrote me a ticket," Rylie countered. "I'd explained that I was moving to Texas and was trying to avoid duplicating the procedure. In the midst of that, the officer had another emergency come over the radio and, when I assured him that I would stop at the RV park just ahead and call a friend to finish the drive for me, he let me go with that warning.

That's exactly what I did—you saw yourself that Cliff got me parked here," she reminded her uncle. "And he told you that he was going to see family in Austin before heading home. That's the other reason I'm late with paying my fines. I had to buy him a plane ticket back to California."

Roy nodded his confirmation to the sheriff. "I saw the young man with my own eyes. Very polite. His sister picked him up the next morning."

Although Sheriff Nelson nodded, his expression remained regretful. "It does appear that you're trying to get your problems resolved, Ms. Quinn, but the authorities in California don't seem satisfied, what with you operating a vehicle that seems above your abilities to handle."

Rylie slid Noah a bitter look. "No doubt confirmed by Assistant District Attorney Prescott, who believes that I'm incapable of walking and breathing at the same time."

"Are we supposed to wait until something serious happens here?" Noah asked.

"But she hasn't driven anywhere in the RV." Roy stepped forward to put his arm around her shoulders. "Look, there has to be a good explanation. My niece has always been a conscientious and safe driver." He gave Rylie's shoulders a squeeze. "Tell them, honey. You hadn't had any tickets until this. Lots of kids get two or three before they graduate from a permit to a full license. Not Rylie."

"Uncle Roy, it's okay." Realizing that she'd run out of time, she turned to him and Gage. "I should have told you both everything from the beginning, but it was important to make you see me as normal first."

"Of course you're normal!" Roy declared, reaching for her again. "What a thing to say."

"Well, not exactly," Rylie admitted, gently resisting his hug. Taking a deep breath, she took hold of his hands and gripped them, relaying her need for him to let her say what she needed. "This is about why I couldn't continue with vet school, too. It turned out that I discovered I had a tumor behind my right eye, just as I was starting my final year of veterinary school. Long story short, I'm fine now, but... I've lost my sight in that eye."

Murmurs of shock from the old-timers buzzed behind her, and she saw the sheriff and Gage hang their heads, while Noah suddenly looked positively ill. Rylie stood tall seeing her uncle's eyes fill with tears. "Hey," she whispered. "None of that."

"But sweetheart..." Roy had to clear his throat to regain his composure. "I can't believe this. You look—I mean it looks—"

"Like I can see. It's okay to say it, Uncle Roy." Rylie totally understood. Heaven knows she'd spent her share of time—too much time—looking into mirrors wondering if anyone saw the subtle changes that she saw, which she thought belied the doctors' assurances. Fortunately, or unfortunately—depending on one's perspective of human nature these days—most people were too preoccupied with their own lives to have noticed.

"That's the good news. I've retained muscle movement. You probably remember when Sandy Duncan had this happen to her. She's successfully continued her career in show business. I think all of her high-flying as Peter Pan onstage has been after the fact."

Of all people, Sheriff Nelson murmured, "I remember that. My wife took the kids to see the show."

"'After the fact'?" was all Uncle Roy said.

Giving Gage a "help me here" glance, she continued. "Yes, and that relates to me because you need your peripheral vision when working around larger animals. You can slap all of the extra bubble mirrors on a vehicle to make sure you can see the traffic around you, but you can't safely manage a horse or cow—any large animal—without two working eyes, any more than you can with a missing limb. Besides, it wouldn't be right to endanger whoever else is around you, either, or the animals."

"It's a matter of safety, yes," Gage admitted. He gave her a soul-searching look, and then reached out to squeeze her shoulder. "I'm so sorry. That was a lousy turn of luck." Hearing her uncle choke, Rylie grimaced and rubbed his back. "He's remembering how I got the nickname Lucky. Hey, I still am fortunate, Uncle Roy. As I said, cosmetically, nothing's really changed."

"But you've wanted to be a veterinarian since you could speak. I was there the day you came home from kindergarten with your first drawing of a dog with half his body bandaged and a big red heart painted on it."

Touched by his recollection, Rylie offered a philosophical shrug. "So I couldn't fulfill that ambition. But I wasn't going to waste all of that schooling and time. You know that not being around animals isn't an option for me, so I knew what I had to do."

Roy wiped his eyes only to interject, "Wait a minute. Your parents never told me a thing about this."

Hoping he would understand, Rylie said, "I had the procedure done near school and recuperated at a friend's apartment. My folks still don't know, Uncle Roy."

He shook his head, rejecting the possibility. "They were shattered when you dropped out...and disappointed."

Remembering too well, Rylie repressed her own misery to explain. "Letting them think I'd let them down was preferable to them convincing themselves that I needed to be nursed and hovered over 24/7 like some invalid."

"Are you telling me they believed that you had your heart suddenly set on being a dog groomer?" Roy demanded, incredulous.

Her uncle was nobody's fool, and her answering look admitted to him that things didn't go smoothly between her and her parents for a while. "At least I proved quickly enough that it's a lucrative market when I sold my truck and bought the RV."

For once Roy wasn't buying her glass-half-full perspective. "This is me, sweetheart. I know you, and I know this business. You had to have about killed yourself after serious surgery to manage the pace that you did to come as far as you have."

"The family had high expectations, Uncle Roy. *You* had high expectations...and I had dreams."

"You don't have to give them up," Gage said. "You could have discussed the matter with your instructors and professors. You could still specialize in small animals and do routine surgeries."

Rylie smiled. "My ego stumbled. That didn't seem like enough. Then, hearing that I'd have to learn to adapt my balance and everything, I thought a definitive time-out was necessary. Look, I don't know if I'll ever be so resolved or stubborn again, but in this case, determination and stubbornness worked for me. I'm *fine*."

Roy, on the other hand, was still having a hard time taking this in. "You should have called me. My God... there was no reason for you to handle this all alone."

Hating that this conversation was taking place in front of Noah and Sheriff Nelson, Rylie was starting to feel the months of hard work take their toll. The news of the warrant still had her shaking, which showed her how emotionally tired she was.

"You are helping me," she reminded him. "You have helped, more than I can tell you. As for my parents, who would have gone back into debt for me... Uncle Roy, you know they've made a comfortable living for themselves with their antique-and-salvage business, but they're not wealthy. Even so, with me grown and Dustin off creating his own life, they're thinking about adopting again or trying foster care."

"Adopting—at their age? Why am I the last to hear of any of this?"

Rylie kissed his cheek. "That's Dad. Why linger on important details when you can laugh with your big brother on the phone? Uncle Roy, you know he worships you—his veteran-hero brother. The thing is that I didn't want them to sacrifice something as wonderful—and helpful—as adoption by taking on my financial minefield. Really, it was almost under control until...this."

Gage turned to the sheriff. "This is so clearly a case of simple misunderstanding. Can't we work this out without the flashing lights and handcuffs?"

Sheriff Nelson looked torn. "Forget the flashing lights nonsense, but, Doc, a warrant is a warrant. I'll admit that from what she's said, Ms. Quinn has been an admirable member of society—a little naive about the handling of such a big vehicle, but I admire her independence and conscientiousness. However, I can only act on behalf of the State of California's edict. I'll have to take her in, until we can see how California wants to handle this."

"That's nuts," Roy declared. "I'll cut you a check for whatever you need right here and now." He pointed with his thumb over his shoulder. "I always keep a spare check in my wallet. It's in the safe in the storeroom."

"If he can't cover all of it, I will," Gage added.

From the corner of the room, Warren Atwood declared, "You can count on us for whatever you need, sweetheart!"

Rylie pressed her hand against her chest. "Guys… everybody, stop. You're going to make me cry." She struggled to steady her breathing. "I don't know what to say."

"Well, I know what I have to say," Roy told the sheriff. "This is all a joke. You don't have to take her. It's not like she's a flight risk."

Sheriff Nelson said, "I agree. But considering how politics are being played on virtually every front page of newspapers these days, I'm not taking any chances. This job is enough challenge without politicians and newspaper editors making it worse. Ms. Quinn, you are going to have to come back to the office with me, but I swear, we'll get on the phone with California straight away to clear this up. For my part, I'd take your check or whomever's gladly, but I don't even know what the total is. So what do you say that we get this resolved?"

"That would be a relief," Rylie said, although not at all confident that luck would ever be on her side again.

"Well, then I'm coming, too!" Roy declared, scowling at Noah. "Why are you in on this? Your mother relies on Rylie's work. Do you even have a clue as to what will happen if my niece is formally arrested? Gossips don't care if they have facts straight. It's all about the adrenaline rush that comes with *maybe, could be, possibly.* What's the matter, you can't stand for her to even have half a dream?"

Trying to make eye contact with Rylie, but failing, Noah replied, "I had no idea it would come to this. All I did was do some checking online."

"What?" she gasped. "You investigated me? On what grounds? Because I *annoyed* you?"

Noah's bowed head told her that she was close enough to the truth not to need an answer. With a sound of disgust, she asked Gage, "Please, watch MG for me in case I don't get back tonight?" She dug her keys out of her jeans pocket and handed them over to him. "You'll need these."

"You're coming home," Roy declared, staring hard at Noah. "I'm following you to Rusk and we'll get this resolved in no time."

"In that case, you'll be needing my services," Warren said, rising.

Both the sheriff and Noah looked uneasy as the former D.A. of Cherokee County joined the group. As the other veterans applauded their friend, Marv Nelson pinched the bridge of his nose. "Folks, we don't need to make this any harder than it already is."

"Yeah, well, you're the one taking her away from us, Marv. We all served so everyone could have a fair shake at justice," Stan Walsh, Rylie's Porthos, declared. "This doesn't smell like justice to me."

"No, it reeks," Jerry Platt muttered.

Still anxious, but heartened by this show of support, Rylie extended her hands to the sheriff. "Do you need to cuff me?"

Sheriff Marv Nelson grimaced and waved away her offer. "Quit that. But you do have to give me your word that you won't attempt bodily harm to our assistant D.A. here as we drive back to Rusk—not that I would blame you if you tried."

"As tempting as the idea is," Rylie assured him, without sparing Noah so much as a glance, "I have no desire to waste any energy on him." Rising on tiptoe to give her uncle a last kiss, she led the way out.

"Don't worry, baby, we're right behind you!" Roy called after her.

In the privacy of her own mind, Rylie hoped so! Because inside she was shaking like a gelatin salad in an earthquake and couldn't believe she was still able to stand on her own two feet. Discipline had always been her "go to" remedy in times of challenge, but this situation might be too much. Betrayed by the man she'd wanted to—

To what?

It didn't matter now, she decided. Hoping that Noah took note, she went straight to the sheriff's car, but to the passenger door on the driver's side, making good her assurance that she wanted no other contact with him. Sheriff Nelson opened the door for her and waited for her to fasten her seat belt before shutting it.

Once Noah got in on the front passenger side, he turned to speak. Unlike the other department vehicles, this one had no metal grid separating them, which disappointed Rylie. From here on, she wanted all of the distance and barriers from him that she could get.

"I thought you were acting suspiciously," he began, sounding more than a little regretful. "The other day when you were in a hurry to get away—I thought you were hiding something. It never crossed my mind that it could be a medical problem."

"Please shut up," she muttered, turning to look out the passenger window. "You've caused enough trouble and humiliation to last me a lifetime. To never have to speak to you again would be a gift." Tears of humiliation blinded her, and all but garbled her words.

"Rylie, once the authorities in California understood where you were, I had to at least follow through and bring in Sheriff Nelson before this blew up into something we couldn't keep out of the news."

"Why couldn't you have thought about that beforehand?" She covered her face with her hands. "Oh, my God, there may be reporters? Do you realize you're going to hurt Doc's practice, too? He'll have to fire me just to protect his business!"

Settling into his seat, the sheriff raised a calming hand to Rylie, but he spoke to Noah. "Call ahead to your people. I already warned mine that no one better notify the press."

"They just knew I was out on a call with you, not the reason," Noah assured him.

That proved to be the first good news for Rylie. More followed, but it was over three hours before she could leave the sheriff's office a free woman with a clear record. When she did, she was framed by Uncle

Roy and Warren. She had never been so relieved in her life!

The authorities in California had, indeed, been willing to accept payment—with a penalty for their time invested on the case and legal expenses. Before Roy could reach for his check, Noah had his checkbook in hand, scrawled the amount, signed his name and handed it to the sheriff.

Although startled at first, Rylie quickly snatched it and ripped it to shreds. "How dare you," she whispered. "This may clear your conscience, but it doesn't undo what you did as far as I'm concerned."

"Believe me, I understand. But it's the least I can do."

"I think you need to leave," Roy said, handing his own check over to the sheriff.

"You might take that under advisement," Sheriff Nelson told Noah, looking none too pleased with him, either.

Noah did leave and Roy muttered as he glared after him, "I'm going to get Gage's permission to make sure that so-and-so never comes to the clinic again."

Rylie grabbed his arm. "Uncle Roy, think. Mrs. Prescott is a lovely woman. She probably doesn't know anything about this."

"I hope not. You deserve her business more than ever—and that of her friends."

"Well, you're free to go, Ms. Quinn," the sheriff told her. He smiled, although he looked almost as tired as she felt. "I guess I don't have to tell you that I'm as relieved as you are. You're a brave young woman, and I admire your determination not to inflict expense or worry on your loved ones. You shouldn't have trouble getting your license, but if there's anything I can do to help you in the matter, let me know. Just promise me that you won't be driving that monster RV of yours too much."

"No, sir, I know I have plenty of help around if that's necessary. Uncle Roy has also let me borrow his truck if I need to go somewhere, until I can afford my own, and I always put on extra side-view mirrors."

"How come I never saw any?" Roy asked, scratching the back of his head.

She gave him an impish smile. "Probably because I removed them just before I got back to the clinic."

Roy scowled. "Well, just leave them on the thing now so when you need to borrow the truck, it's ready for you. Wait—you know what's a better idea? The truck is yours. I'm going to treat myself to a new one."

Stunned, Rylie cried, "Uncle Roy, it's barely two years old."

"Yeah, but I sure like the new models they had at the county fair."

"You didn't get to go to the fair this year. You told me that you were too busy at the clinic and missed it." Rylie gripped his arm. "Uncle Roy, I love you for this, but I can't let you do it."

"Why not? You're my only niece. Why shouldn't I spoil you if I want to?"

"Because you love that truck. You were just saying as much to Jane."

Her uncle shrugged and gave her a sheepish smile. "So I'll love the new one even more. It's not like I have anything else to spend my money on."

Rylie hugged him fiercely. "What would I do without you? You're the dearest uncle ever!"

"What does that make me, a grapefruit?" Warren complained, feigning a scowl.

Rylie quickly hugged him, as well. "No, sir! You are a darling, too."

They were laughing as they exited the building and went to the truck. On the drive back to Sweet Springs, Warren couldn't contain himself.

"So that seemingly clumsy trait every now and then is you still learning to adjust, huh?"

"Shucks, you did notice." Rylie sighed, disappointed that apparently she hadn't successfully fooled anyone. They'd all thought she was less than graceful, not the unfortunate victim of situations beyond her control. "Yes, sir. That was another reason I stayed with friends while I was getting through this. I didn't want my parents panicking every time I misjudged spacing and bumped myself, or have them trying to do things for me that I needed to relearn how to do for myself. It's been hard enough to get through the emotional and psychological aspect of this."

"I can imagine," Roy mused.

"Do you think Gage is going to let me stay?" Rylie asked, as some of her doubt returned.

"Why on earth wouldn't he? You not only have helped business, but you make our jobs easier."

All but confirming his words, as they pulled into the clinic's parking lot, Rylie was astonished to see not only Warren's vehicle still there, but everyone else's, too, including Gage's pickup truck. "Oh, my gosh," Rylie whispered. "They stayed?"

"You are loved, sweetheart," Warren told her. Once they entered, he was the one to announce amid the applause, "Everything is resolved and fine." As cheers erupted, he added with glee, "I thought the sheriff was going to throw Prescott out of his office."

At the mention of Noah, Rylie felt a deep pang. Granted, she was foolish to feel anything but loathing, but that was the human condition—sometimes illogical, especially where matters of the heart were involved. How much sweeter it would have been if he'd liked her, admired her or at least approved of her.

"Congratulations, honey!" the men said in near unison, drawing her out of her introspection.

Gage held out his arms and gave her a hug. "That's from Brooke as well as me. I hope you don't mind that I called her. I needed to explain why I was expecting to be ultralate getting home."

"Of course not—and thank you." Rylie looked at him with chagrin. "I know I should have been straight with you from the beginning—"

"I understand, believe me. And now that we know what's going on, I'm doubly impressed with you. I wish we could clone you. Your dedication and determination are second to none."

He made her feel as though this horrible experience had almost been worth it. "That's so much nicer to hear than, 'You're fired.'"

"You say something as crazy as that again and I'll let the air out of your RV's tires."

Everyone around her laughed.

"Now we're definitely going to get your certification on the front burner," he added. "And Monday, you take off and get that license business done. I don't care if we have a clinic full of Manx cats snarling at me. Well, check that," he said, as though having second thoughts.

This time Rylie joined in on the laughter.

"I'll drive her so Roy can keep his truck here in case of an emergency," Jerry said.

Warren snorted. "You'll keep your lecherous self away from her. You're still on probation after your last so-called helpfulness with you-know-who. Besides, Roy here is buying himself a new vehicle over the weekend, so she won't have a problem in that department—and if she does, I'll take her."

"Jeez, guys," Rylie said, once again pressing her hand to her heart, "my cup runneth over."

Noah dreaded the drive home, knowing what awaited him. He would have to explain everything to his mother. She was going to be seriously upset with him, considering how she'd reacted to his fussing over having to take Bubbles to Sweet Springs. This was a dozen times worse; he'd almost been responsible for putting Rylie behind bars.

It's not like you wanted it to go that far.

No? Then what?

To find something wrong with her so that you could stop thinking about her. To make her go away.

"Congratulations," he told himself with disgust. "You almost succeeded."

In the process, he'd also made himself the laughingstock of the county. It would be a miracle if the sheriff ever took him seriously again. But it was his mother he was most worried about. If she didn't have a stroke—after she verbally disowned him—it would be a miracle.

After parking at the house, each step up the walkway left him feeling as though he was the one about to get ill. Thankfully, no one was around when he first walked into the old plantation-style dwelling. Most of the lights were off, and considering the hour, that was no surprise. His mother should already be in her bed, although if she was asleep, it was only to doze. She wouldn't turn off her lights until he poked his head in to tell her that he was home. That was a habit she'd begun since the accident, now that he was all she had left in the world.

Setting his briefcase at the foot of the stairs, he went to the living room, where he intended to pour himself a stiff drink. He had the lead glass in his hand and the stopper off the crystal bourbon decanter, when he heard a scurrying, and then Bubbles ran into the room and barked at him.

"Same to you, dust mop," he muttered. "Why aren't you upstairs?"

"Why are you so late?"

Closing his eyes, Noah said, "Evening, Aubergine."

"Phones not working at the office? Your mother's been fretting herself sick."

"I apologize. I'll go up in a second."

"Did you eat? If you did, you look like it isn't agreeing with you."

"It's not that, and I don't think I could keep anything down, but thank you for asking."

Aubergine scowled. "You getting sick? Then you stay out of your mama's room, hear?"

"I'm not sick, just—" He shook his head, unable to continue, and concentrated on putting several ice cubes into his glass. "Is Livie in her room?"

"That's right. Waiting on you, so she can tuck your mother in for the night."

Nodding, Noah poured the bourbon. "Good night,

then." As Aubergine left, he took a fortifying sip, and then another. The stoutness should have made him shudder, but it didn't. Another bad sign. He was so numb with the bruising he'd taken that near-straight alcohol had almost no effect on his usually discerning taste buds.

"Let's get this over with," he told the little dog that stood by staring at him.

With a low growl, Bubbles hurled herself up the stairs ahead of him. Noah suspected that if the dog could talk, she would be ratting on him well before he reached his mother's room.

"If it wasn't for your high-maintenance self, I would never have met her, and this mess would never have happened," he said, picking up his briefcase and following the animal.

At the top of the stairs, he set down the briefcase again, since his rooms were on the west end of the house, while his mother's were to the far end of the east wing. They were not his childhood rooms, but they provided the privacy and independence he'd insisted on to make this move back.

The moment he entered his mother's bedroom, she asked, "Are you being ugly to my baby girl again, dear?"

As usual, too short-legged to jump onto the high bed without help, Bubbles had used the tiered method, leaping up onto the chaise longue at the foot of the bed, and then using pillows on it to make it the rest of the way. She now lay tucked comfortably at her mistress's side and gave him a "What are you going to do about it?" look.

"She started it," Noah said, before taking another sip of the potent drink.

The mauve, ivory and gold room smelled like gardenias—his mother's favorite scent—and at sixty-seven, she still looked like the blonde actress in that old TV series about dynasties, with her ash-blond hair—a lovely gift from nature yielding to silver, but still styled in a perfect pageboy. As always, she was cocooned in silk, satin and enough pillows to stock a boutique. Not all of that was aesthetics; his mother's body needed the support so her lungs could continue to work adequately.

Bending over to kiss her cheek, he marveled, as always, that she had almost no wrinkles; her skin was as smooth and soft as a child's. She remained a beautiful woman, thanks to great bones in her triangular face and warm, cognac-colored eyes.

"When are you going to stop waiting up for me when I'm running late at the office?"

"When it's a woman. Better yet, a woman you love making you late." Audra frowned as she studied his face, and she touched the back of her hand to his forehead. "You look ghastly."

"I feel worse, but then I deserve to."

"Bad day at the office?"

"That's the understatement of the year. Maybe since I passed the bar."

Eyeing his drink, she said, "It sounds like I'm going to need a drink, too. If you were a good boy, you'd pour half of that in my water glass."

"You're on medication," he reminded her, as he often had to, "and I'm not up for the joint retaliation by Olivia and Aubergine."

"A half glass of white wine with lunch and dinner

isn't my idea of being fair. It's practically European austerity."

While taking another drink, Noah yanked his navy-blue-and-silver tie, then opened the top two buttons on his pastel-blue shirt.

Looking increasingly concerned, Audra closed the book she'd been reading on a white leather bookmark. "All right, you have my full attention."

Instead, Noah frowned at the book. His mother read everything from romances to suspense, to sagas and history, with plenty of nonfiction in between. He thought her one of the best-read women he'd ever met and would claim so even if they weren't related. "Why aren't you using the tablet I gave you at Christmas?"

"Because this is a borrowed book, and because I still prefer a binding and paper to a screen. I'm on the computer enough. I can't see how all of these screens can be healthy for one's eyes."

"Probably not." Noah thought that he deserved to go blind for all of the problems and hurt that he'd caused via an electronic screen.

"Good grief, darling, you're turning green. Sit down and talk to me."

"Maybe I should get out your old riding whip first. You're going to be tempted to use it on me in a minute."

As expected, his mother's eyebrows lifted as she grew intrigued—and worried. "That bad?"

"Mother—" unable to look at her as he said the awful words, he yielded to the need to pace "—I hurt and humiliated Rylie Quinn today. If there was any way to take back the last several hours, I would. I would do anything not to keep seeing her shock and pain in my mind, but I know it's nothing less than what I deserve."

"What have you done?" Audra whispered.

"That's exactly what she said, how she sounded, when I brought the sheriff to the clinic to arrest her."

"You *what?*"

Noah watched her cover her mouth with her right hand. Her diamond wedding and engagement rings twinkled in the lamplight. It had taken her an entire year before she'd had the heart to move her rings from her left hand to the symbolic widow designation on her right. Tonight it was just another reminder to Noah of how all she had known these last years had been grief and pain, and it devastated him to add to that.

"Noah, what on earth?"

"If I'd known it would trigger so much curiosity in California, I would have been more careful about how I probed into her background."

"What right did you have to do that?"

That was the question that would yield the most condemning answer. "Because I wanted her out of my mind. Because she seemed too good to be true." As soon as he spoke those words, he took another drink.

"That's the most ridiculous thing I've ever heard."

"Yes."

"Ramon says she's cheerful and like—what did he say?—a Fourth of July sparkler. What in heaven's name is wrong with that?"

"I thought she was playing everyone, including me. I thought it was all pretense." Of course, now he knew some of it had been, but for a totally noble reason.

"She's a businesswoman," Audra reminded him. "It's important to remember to be polite to people, even people who may not be deserving of it, or whom we feel have wronged us."

"I *know,* Mother." Noah regretted his edgy tone, but what she was telling him wasn't anything he didn't already know. "I know," he whispered again, his pained look beseeching her not to torment him more than he was already doing to himself.

"Tell me the rest," she demanded, her expression already tightening with disappointment and disapproval.

Unable to bear that, he returned to his pacing. He was going to be blunt, but that would reflect only on him, not Rylie, as it should. "Long story short, the reason she'd gotten all the tickets that precipitated in an arrest warrant being put out on her was that she had a tumor and lost the vision in one eye. That was also why she dropped out of veterinary school."

"Oh, Noah! That poor dear!"

"Yes."

"To want something so challenging and admirable, only to have it snatched away. Her heart must be broken. Is there no way she could fulfill that dream?"

"Would you have let a one-handed surgeon operate on you?" he challenged, only to wish he could take back those words. Damn his survivalist legal training.

His mother gave him a reproving look. "If you remember correctly, I'd have been perfectly content not to have been operated on at all."

Noah's grip on the glass was so tight it should have shattered, but the damned thing was just too thick. "I was supposed to let you lie in E.R. screaming?" For days afterward, he'd wakened sweating, feverish as he remembered those sounds.

With a calming motion of her hand, Audra said, "I shouldn't have said that. Go on."

Noah explained the peripheral vision challenge, and

how Gage had agreed with Rylie as she'd explained it to
her uncle and the rest of them. "It's my understanding
that women are already professionally challenged by
large animals anyway—it's the whole size-and-weight
thing factoring in with a woman's inferior strength to
that of a male vet. Add a high-strung horse or an ornery
or downright mean cow or bull, or whatever creature
they have to deal with, and you're facing the threat of
injury or even death. Gage did say that she could still
be a vet, but with primarily smaller animals. She acted
like that was a Miss Congeniality award to her."

"Yes, I see," Audra said, nodding slowly. "What an
awful situation for her. I suspect she was also left with
medical bills on top of her college expenses, so even
the hope of the lesser license wasn't of much reassurance. Could her family not help?"

"She didn't tell her parents in order to keep them
from using their savings."

"Oh, Rylie," Audra whispered. "What a big, generous heart you have." She looked at Noah, her expression incredulous, but also admiring. "So to stay
near the animals she loves and honor her debts, she's
become a groomer. What an incredible but inspiring
story. I'm so glad to have been told about her. Now
more than ever I want her to keep caring for Bubbles."

"Dr. Sullivan is assisting in getting her certification as a technician, as well. She'll be able to do quite
a bit—give shots and do some care, as long as the vet
is on the premises." Having heard some reference to
that between Warren and Roy, he'd looked up the job
description online.

"I haven't met Gage Sullivan, but I already know I
like a man who would try so hard to help an employee."

What she'd left unsaid, Noah thought, enduring a new wave of shame, was that in comparison, he had acted in the exact opposite way.

"Now, about these tickets. You've covered them for her, I hope?"

"I tried to, but she ripped up the check." However, Noah felt compelled to defend himself on at least one point. "Doesn't it bother you that she could have caused a more serious accident being behind the wheel? You of all people have paid a high enough price for someone's bad judgment. Good grief, she even tried to drive that big RV of hers from California to here."

Rather than agree with him, Audra asked, "Why did she need to leave California? Did she know there was a warrant out for her?"

"I don't know that there was one at the time. She just didn't want her parents smothering her with good intentions and trying to make her dependent on them."

"Well, I for one think we were blessed when she made her decision to come here, but Noah... I'm deeply ashamed of you."

"I'm pretty sick of me, too."

"What has happened to the brave and compassionate boy and man I used to know?"

What indeed? It was one thing to get chewed out by a boss, or a mentor, but his mother was the person he respected and loved most on earth. For her to find him morally and ethically wanting was another blow that had him downing most of what was left in his glass to where he thought about excusing himself to get a refill.

"Don't you go sneaking off on me."

Suspecting that she was picking up on his body language, Noah countered with, "If I'd wanted to avoid you, I would have stayed away until I was certain that your door was closed and your lights off." But when he sat down on the foot of the bed, he did sigh wearily. He would listen for as long as she wanted to berate him, but he didn't have to enjoy it. He did, however, feel it was his duty, since he was also hoping for a woman's perspective.

"I don't think I've ever seen you quite this way before. The accident—that changed you."

"It changed both of us."

"Of course. I think we're both still dealing with anger issues on top of our huge sense of loss." Audra nodded slightly. "Maybe that's why your first reactions to Rylie seemed so strange. Everyone else thinks she's a doll, and she just made you more bristly. And now you look…hunted."

Maybe he wasn't up to advice yet.

"Why don't we give voice to what the truth seems to be?" Audra prodded when he didn't respond. "You're attracted to her…. Maybe it's already become more than that?"

"But I don't want to be." There was no reason to try to pretend or try to keep anything from her. She knew him too well. And clearly, he wasn't as good an actor as Rylie was an actress.

"Because animals are her life and you have no use for them?"

"I don't really have a problem with that—as long as people remember they have four legs, not two," Noah added drily.

"If that's supposed to be another hint that I spoil Bubbles," his mother countered with equal dryness, "maybe that's partly your fault. I fear any possibility of grandchildren will come after I'm too far gone to enjoy them."

Noah wasn't ready to visualize her condition degenerating any more than it already had, so he took on the next-hardest hurdle. "It's not her work. It's just *her* that's the problem."

"No, she's not your usual type, is she? My friends tell me she's very pretty, energetic and charmingly unpretentious. Let me see…she has no piercings, not even in her ears? That's almost delightfully old-fashioned in this day and age."

Noah gave her a mild look, completely aware of what she was doing. She wanted *his* description of Rylie. It was too easy to do, and it would give away too much. However, to refuse would be even more obvious.

"She's built like a dancer—petite and slim. Long legs and arms, rather than a gymnast's sturdiness. Indoors, her hair appears the color of cinnamon. No, what's that spice that Aubergine puts on my favorite dishes that I've asked about before?"

Audra smiled. "Paprika."

Noah snapped his fingers. "That's it. But when outside the color is…well, it defies real description."

As she lifted her artfully tinted eyebrows, Audra asked, "And her eyes?"

That was more difficult yet. "A frustrating gray-green."

"You might mean *beguiling*," Audra mused, "if you have to try so hard that the simple question leaves you annoyed."

"They're green, okay? But in certain light the shade of green takes on a smoky tint."

"How interesting, and expansive for someone you've only met twice."

"It's been five—no—six times, counting yesterday." When his mother didn't reply, he glanced up from his preoccupation with the increasingly naked ice cubes in his glass and saw amusement. "Go ahead and say it."

"I was only going to correct myself. You aren't falling for her—you've fallen."

"Well…that's not a good idea."

"As though what's wise or preferred has anything to do with whom our hearts and souls link themselves with."

Noah managed not to groan. Barely. "Feel free to stop at any time."

"What I don't understand is why can't you let yourself feel what you're feeling?"

"Because she's never going to forgive me, let alone trust me again, and even if she could, she's all wrong for the life we live, what I expect for my future."

That wiped every sign of pleasure from his mother's face. "You can't be serious! Why? Because she's not a society princess? You tried one of those, remember? And from such a fine family that her father is in federal prison, and she's contracted an agent to scout for a spot on a reality show, while her mother is trying for a book deal to share more of the family scandal. Such humility, such principles," Audra scoffed. "Rylie could only dream of living up to such high expectations."

The reminder of his close call with tainting the family name wasn't necessary for Noah, but he did wince at the memory of his brief but colorful time with the Houston debutante. True, she'd been a fun girl, yet he'd hit the elevator down button fast after his first and only dinner with her family and "man-to-man" chat with what was meant to be his future father-in-law.

"It's not as though we were ever engaged," he reminded his mother.

"No, however, she didn't take 'goodbye' gracefully, did she?" Audra shuddered delicately. "I would never have been able to show my face in public again if we'd needed a blood test to prove a child's paternity." She fussed with Bubble's bow. "You did get yourself medically checked afterward, I hope?"

"Mother...yes."

"Thank you." As he rolled his eyes, she continued. "Your father and I came from decent, hardworking stock. That is what you benefited from, and that continues to provide our privileged lives now—not to take away from your success before coming back here. All I'm saying is that from what little I've talked with Rylie on the phone, I've found her to be professional and articulate. Heaven knows she would be a huge asset with the livestock."

"It takes a little more than that to hold your own against the movers and shakers in this or any community, and you know it. Vance's wife and the mayor's went to SMU together—I've watched them turn a perfectly nice person into sushi before the poor soul knew what had happened."

"Those two self-starving, surgery-loving mental patients are exactly what we don't need around here, and it's about time they were replaced with people with common sense and wholesomeness. And by the way, I hold the men just as accountable as their women. If you saw or overheard something any of them said that wasn't right, and didn't immediately stop it, then you're as bad as they are."

"Vance is my boss, Mother."

"He's a servant of the people, too." But as quickly as her indignation flared, Audra grew forgiving. "At least you've given me something to get excited about. You've been acting like a monk rather than a child from your parents' loins for too long."

"Mother." His parents had been a romantic couple, and he didn't need the reminder. Even though he'd arrived late in their marriage, he'd witnessed plenty of displays of affection while growing up to know they'd shared a healthy sexual life.

"Oh, excuse me. I'm not supposed to mention s-e-x." Audra tried to lean forward to reach for his glass. "Give me that. I want a sip."

"Impossible. I know what time it is, and Livie is about to come give you your last meds for the night." He rose to go knock on the nurse's door. He knew it was the only way his mother wouldn't try to wear down his defenses.

"Judas," Audra whispered.

"I love you, too." As the door opened, he met Olivia Danner's ghostly, makeup-free face, framed by equally washed-out hair. One glance at her shrewd gray gaze and Noah knew that she'd heard every word of his conversation with his mother. Belatedly, he remembered that by this hour, Livie had the intercom on that sat on his mother's bed stand. Its partner was on Livie's nightstand. "Tuck her in, General," he muttered.

As he crossed the room and began pulling the door shut behind him, his mother called, "I better not learn that Bubbles is no longer welcome at the clinic."

Noah leaned back into the room. As Livie—dressed in flannel pj's and robe—drew her stethoscope from around her neck and put the plugs in her ears, he said, "You know that's out of my hands."

"No, it's not. And penance *is* necessary."

What could possibly be enough? Noah wondered. "Flowers?"

"At the very least. Dr. Sullivan's wife has a shop in town. Go talk to her."

Noah thought he'd endured enough glares from residents in Sweet Springs. He suspected there were plenty more "friends of Rylie" whom he hadn't met yet. "Why can't I just call?"

"Because you could use an advocate. She's undoubtedly fond of Rylie and will be the best bet to know her tastes. Find out what you can."

"Married to Doc, she also probably knows about what's happened. What if she doesn't want my business?"

Audra gave him a "spare me" look. "You are my son. You're named after a man who managed to get two of everything on a ship for a flood that everyone insisted wasn't going to happen."

"I thought I was named after your father?"

"Smart-ass. Are you going to tell me that you've become suddenly tongue-tied and socially incompetent?"

"Merely humbled by the depth and breadth of my stupidity."

"Use that." Audra smiled. "It has its own charm. A woman loves to see a man squirm with regret as much as with unrequited love."

Seeing Livie glance up from logging pulse and blood pressure figures to look over her shoulder at him, Noah felt about sixteen and replied to his mother, "You're embellishing."

"And you're going to make me give Olivia upsetting numbers." She waved Noah away. "You have all of the information you need. Now off with you."

Chapter 5

By nine o'clock on Saturday morning, Noah was in downtown Sweet Springs. He had been here only once before since returning home, and that was for a civic function on behalf of his boss. Otherwise, he hadn't been in this area since his high-school days. Things had changed quite a bit. There were many more and new businesses, and most of the old structures had undergone serious face-lifts, including Newman's Floral and Gifts. The whitewashed brick with the artsy copper-and-brass sign along with the green awning was classy. He hoped that what awaited him inside was as inviting.

Chimes rang a cheery welcome as he entered, and a perky blonde restocking a shelf from her perch on a short ladder looked down to greet him.

"Hi! Happy Saturday!"

The greeting was so like something Rylie might

say that he had to chuckle. The young woman did look close to her age. He wondered if she knew her, too.

"Good morning." He glanced around. "There's a lot to look at in here."

"We do our best. I didn't think I'd seen you before. I'm Kiki. Can I help you find something?"

"Actually, I was looking for Brooke. Mrs. Sullivan."

The young woman nodded over her shoulder toward the back, where the two woman stood conferring. "She's with Hoshi going over some orders. We have a wedding tomorrow."

Noah nodded, having attended enough of them to have a clue as to what an undertaking that was—at least for the brides. Then his gaze fell on a crystal cross on a stand and he paused. The etching was fabulous, and the way the light played off the piece made him think of his mother and how she liked to sit in the sunroom for hours at a time watching the sun change the shadings on all of the plants inside and out. The cross would look beautiful in there between her many plants.

"Thank you," he said, his gaze lingering, as he headed down the long main aisle.

He realized that Brooke Sullivan was a blonde, too. She was a few years older than Kiki, and petite. Maybe even an inch or two shorter than Rylie. She moved with a natural grace yet confidence, which was evident in her initial smile.

"Hello," she said as he approached. "Did I hear my name?"

"Yes, I was hoping you could help me. I'm Noah Prescott."

Brooke's welcoming countenance froze. "Oh. I see."

Noah knew if he ever needed that charm his mother

spoke of, it was now. He exhaled heavily and hung his head. "So Dr. Sullivan told you."

"I'm afraid he did."

"Mrs. Sullivan, the last twenty-four hours have been some of the worst in memory—and I've been through a few, as you can imagine if you know anything about my family."

Some of the ice melted in Brooke's demeanor. "I admit I did ask Gage more questions after he told me about what you did to Rylie. I'm very sorry for your family tragedy."

He nodded his thanks. "Then perhaps you'll have the generosity to understand how badly I feel about the humiliation and pain that I caused Rylie, and you'll agree to help me. I need to make a gesture worthy of my regret to her."

"You want to send her flowers?"

"I was thinking that would be a good start."

"Do you want to deliver them yourself?"

He gave her a doubtful look. "I'm a thick-headed man, not suicidal."

That won a slight smile from her. "When would you like to have them delivered?"

"As soon as possible—although I understand that you have a big event pending."

Although she nodded, Brooke said, "We have that under control. Besides, if it involves our Rylie, I'm not about to send you to my competition. What were you thinking of?"

"I don't exactly know. Roses seem appropriate gesture-wise, but they don't exactly seem like *her,* do they?"

"I like the way you're thinking already. No, she

wouldn't be moved by the long-stemmed variety, and it would be a rather blunt display of affluence. On the other hand, pink baby roses in a pink round vase—" she pointed to the selection of roses in the cooler to his left and then to the vase on the second shelf of a display beside the cooler "—that shows thought, and we could add a little humor…or romance…with a bow or balloon, or teddy bear."

It struck Noah the instant he saw the two items that Brooke understood what he was trying to do. The arrangement would be charming, even endearing, considering the size of the cute flowers—petite like the person receiving them. He also wondered if Brooke had added the word *romance* because of something she knew, or was she simply fishing?

"I think I like the baby roses, definitely."

Brooke reached for an order pad. "To do this right, we should use two dozen due to the size of the vase. We'll put baby's breath in between to create a fuller, dreamy effect."

Noah reached into his camel-colored sports jacket for his billfold. The jacket, worn with khaki Dockers and a white silk shirt, minus a tie, was as casual as he got when away from the privacy of home. "Whatever you think serves the situation best." He glanced over his shoulder again. "There is one more thing. The crystal cross…it caught my eye as I entered."

Brooke's demeanor went all soft and tender. "Isn't that lovely? We only got that in yesterday, and I haven't been able to stop looking at it."

"Then will I upset you if I take it, as well? I mean take it with me. For my mother," he added at her confused look. He could tell her first reaction was that it was also for Rylie. "She's confined to a wheelchair—"

"I've met Audra. We keep the foyer flowers fresh at Haven Land."

Tapping his left temple, Noah sighed. "I actually know that, since I oversee all of the bookkeeper's reports for the estate. Pardon my memory glitch." He decided that he was going to have a few words with his mother, as well. The sneak had made the suggestion to come here as though it had simply been a hunch. That would teach him to check only the totals in the book-keeper's monthly statements. If he'd inspected actual receipts, he would have saved himself yet more embarrassment. "Well, then you know the sunroom she loves to spend time in. I thought the cross would look wonderful on one of the tables."

"It would, and how thoughtful of you. Let me get it safely boxed and wrapped. Is this a special occasion?"

"Another apology...or thank-you."

Brooke looked pleased. "We have some stunning autumn wrapping paper that I'll use. It's almost as gorgeous as the gift itself."

"That sounds perfect. As you probably know, Mother takes art classes, so everything down to the wrapping does mean a great deal to her. She's all about texture, color and visual sensation."

"She's very talented. I've always admired creative people. I'm afraid I tend to be too left-brained to be more than a mimic." As she set to work, she asked, "So have you adjusted to being back in East Texas?"

"Sometimes more graciously than at other times," Noah admitted, and then remembered what his mother knew of her situation. "You were used to the faster-paced corporate world, too, weren't you?"

Brooke nodded, humor deepening her dimples and bringing a new sparkle to her warm, brown eyes. "But you can't pout for too long around Gage. Now I can barely imagine living to work sixteen-plus hours a day. Besides, we have an addition to the family to focus on, as well."

Noah glanced down as she laid a protective hand over her almost flat tummy. Only then did he realize she was wearing a rather loose poet shirt. "You and Dr. Sullivan are expecting? I didn't realize. My warmest congratulations."

"They are warmly accepted."

Once Brooke had the cross packed and wrapped, and the order for the flowers written up, she ran through his credit card and handed him the receipt to sign.

"What about a card?"

"Ah." There was another clue that this whole experience was throwing him completely off his axis. At Brooke's suggestion, he chose one of little note cards, only to stare at the blank space. In the end, he said, "I'd better let the flowers do the talking," and put back the card.

"Do you want me to call you when the delivery is made?" Brooke asked gently.

"Only if there's a problem."

"I understand. Usually, we have Charles—our deliveryman—handle things, but in this case, I think I'll do it myself. I haven't seen Rylie yet this week, and we need to catch up."

Feeling as though he'd passed some test, Noah was grateful. "I do appreciate that." He reached for his billfold again for one of his business cards. "This is my office number." He scrawled his cell number on the back. "And my private number."

"I'll be in touch. In the meantime, thank you, again. On behalf of Gage and myself, good thoughts to your mother. She's a very brave woman."

"She is, and will appreciate your kindness, as well. She said some very nice things about you, too."

Despite the compliments she'd been receiving all morning—from customers as well as from her uncle and Gage alike—Rylie struggled to maintain her usual cheerful demeanor. She was almost grateful that this was one Saturday when the old-timers weren't gathered at their table for their usual coffee klatch. It was difficult enough to see and feel Uncle Roy's and Gage's concerned gazes as they all took care of clients and daily chores; however, a buddy of the musketeers' was in the hospital, and they were keeping vigil with him.

"I think we should go do something different after we close up," Roy said to her moments after she sent off a cocker spaniel that she'd groomed. He knew that Toby was her last appointment for the day, so any other work she had was whatever Gage needed her to do. "You like fishing. You want to go to the town lake with me after we close up? I hear there's been some good catfish caught on the north side of the lake."

Although she gave him a grateful look, Rylie said, "I'd have to get a license, and it's almost year-end," she told him. "That's sort of a waste of money, and taking a risk fishing without one isn't something I want to gamble on, given my luck lately. The last thing I need is to be ticketed again, even for something as innocent as having a line with a hook in the water."

"Well, then let's find someplace new to have dinner. I haven't been up to Longview in a long time. Want to see what's happening there? We might even take in a movie."

Rylie couldn't help but give her uncle a disbelieving glance. "What was it that you'd recently said to Pete? The last movie you went to see was *Jaws,* or was it *Rocky?*"

"Which proves that I need a change of pace, too."

"In that case, why don't you mosey over Jane Ayers's way and see if she's available? Maybe she'll take you for a spin on her Harley."

Roy's coloring wasn't conducive to blushing, but what he lacked in that department, he made up for in getting tongue-tied. "I don't want to—I mean, I can't—aw, I just wanted to spend some time with you. Shoot the breeze a little. I have a hunch there's a lot more going on with you that I don't know about."

Rylie momentarily paused at sweeping up the dog hair in the reception area left by the morning's shedding clients. "I appreciate your intentions, but I'm fine. Stop worrying about me."

"You say. If what happened to you happened to me, I would want to box that Prescott jerk's ears until they were as big as the space in between."

"Nice," she drawled. "Violence resolving vindictiveness. But aside from letting you vent, I don't think we'll venture down that road. I've scared Doc enough, not to mention almost caused him serious trouble. Oh, look…"

Roy looked up at the car entering the property. "Say,

that's Brooke. She's going to be disappointed when she learns that Doc's out on a farm call."

True enough, Rylie thought. Brooke didn't come to the clinic often, what with her own business interests expanding even faster than the clinic was. Plus, there were doctor appointments and a nursery to plan for. When Rylie usually saw her, it was apt to be at the assisted-living center, or when Brooke and Gage invited her and Roy to dinner, so when she saw her boss's wife circle her Mercedes and pick up something out of the passenger floorboard, she instantly knew it wasn't going to be a dog emerging. After all, Humphrey was too heavy for her—besides, he was here napping with MG in back.

"Uh-oh," Roy said.

Brooke was carrying a gorgeous arrangement of pink baby roses in a pink glass orb that looked like a princess's crystal ball. It took both hands to manage it, forcing her to close the car's door with her hip.

"Think that's for you?" she asked her uncle.

"Ha! If it is, I'm going to stop worrying about you and start worrying about me. Could be a nice gesture from Doc and Brooke," Roy mused, going to get the door for Brooke.

"He's already given me too much by letting me hook up out back, not to mention fast-tracking me to get my certification," she replied, setting aside the mop. "Hi," she said, as Brooke entered. "Lost?"

"Not at all. This is yours."

As quickly as Rylie came to greet her new friend, she backed away, clasping her hands behind her. "Noah?"

"How many other sexy-but-conflicted lawyers al-

most turned your world upside down?" Brooke held up
the arrangement in the fluorescent light to admire it.
"He came to the store this morning. You have to admit,
the man does have good taste."

It was the first part of that comment that left her
openmouthed. "He drove to Sweet Springs?" Her gaze
was drawn to the windows as though she half expected
him to be parked up the service road to watch the reception his gift would receive in order to gauge his
next move.

"He did. He was quite humble, too. Extremely concerned for you and totally a gentleman." Once again
Brooke tried to hand over the arrangement.

"Oh, Brooke, they're lovely, but I don't want them."

"Will it help to know that my heart sank when I realized who he was? I didn't want to take his order, but
I have to confess he grows on you. Fast."

"Wait until Gage hears that."

Smiling at the obvious, though weak, tease, Brooke
continued. "You don't think he's sincere?"

"Of course, but I still can't take them." Rylie stuck
her hands into her back pockets to keep Brooke from
trying to force the gift on her.

"You mean you won't." Brooke's demeanor grew
sympathetic. "I feel awful for what happened, too,
Rylie, and I let Noah know he wasn't well thought of
for doing what he did, but he didn't need my input. He
looks pretty miserable, and ashamed."

"He should," Roy snapped.

Letting that pass, Rylie said to Brooke, "He's made
it clear that he's disliked me from the moment we met."

"I think quite opposite is the case. He picked this
himself. A person just going through motions because

of guilt that someone told him he should feel would have sent a dozen roses via the phone or online. Noah was painstaking. While in the store, he also found a lovely gift for his mother that seemed to affect him, as well. The man's not all cold strategy with feet of clay."

"That's reassuring to hear, but the person I remember wasn't so commendable. He enjoyed making me feel…inadequate."

From behind them, Roy puffed up. "He did *what?* Well, I guess I still have a few things to say to that stuck-up—"

"No, you won't. I said all there is to say. Now it's over." Rylie returned her attention to Brooke. "I just want to move on. Please, give those to the assisted-living center. They'll look wonderful in the main living-room area."

Although she looked regretful, Brooke didn't argue. She did, however, shift the arrangement in order to give Rylie a hug. "I hope you don't mind that Gage told me about your vision."

"Of course not. It's actually a relief to not have to pretend anymore. I'm not usually a secret keeper— about myself, I mean. I like life simple and honest."

"Well, you're doing beautifully, if that's any reassurance."

"It is, thanks. And I think I am getting better at balancing and adapting by the day." But eager to get off the subject, Rylie pointed to her new friend's tummy, hidden by the gauzy material of her blouse. "How's my future babysitting assignment?"

Brooke grinned. "Growing fast. If this isn't a boy, my poor daughter is going to have to deal with the confusion of looking down at her mother by the time she's

ten, yet still having to obey me." She eyed the flowers again and gave Rylie a final wistful look. "Please
reconsider and accept these? I think I'm a good judge
of character, and while I admit Noah made some huge
mistakes with you, in hindsight, I could see that as a
monumental compliment. You've quite gotten to him,
and he's at a loss as to how to deal with his feelings."

If she had heard that shortly after their first or second meeting, Rylie could have found the generosity
to overlook a great deal and be patient, as Gage had
been patient in winning Brooke's love; however, Noah's dogged determination to be right about her being
flawed was crushing.

"I'm sorry, but I don't know if I could really trust
him again," Rylie admitted.

Nodding, Brooke winced. "That's not something I
ever had to worry about with Gage. Well, then… I'll
just tell them at the center that this is your donation.
Expect to be hugged a lot when you and MG next visit."
At the door, she paused and glanced around. "Speaking of…where's Humphrey and MG?"

"Oh, in a kennel outside while I mop up in here. If I
let them have their usual run of the place, they would
see this as a game and I'd never finish."

Nodding, Brooke said, "That I understand. I can't
believe the difference in Humph since you and MG
arrived in his life. He's a totally different dog at home
now, and when we open the gate, all he wants to do is
get into the truck to get here." With a wave, she headed
back to her car.

No sooner did she exit than Roy stood his ground.
"I think you should have taken the flowers. Not be-

cause I want you to forgive Prescott, but because you deserved them."

Rylie shook her head, unable to tell him that the thought of looking at them day in and day out would be almost painful. "No, I don't. There are people dealing with a lot worse injustices than I did. Now, if it turns out that the rest of my vision gets compromised, we can talk pity party, but my doctors said that this was just a fluke and I should be safe from worry. So I'm ready to move on."

"Well, put up that mop and figure out what we're going to do this afternoon."

Voicing an impulse, Rylie said, "What would you say if I called Jane and the three of us went to the barbecue place in town this evening for music and good food?"

Roy's chest shook with his restrained laughter. "You not only want to fix me up with a date, you want to chaperone? Let me handle things in the Jane department, okay?"

"I just wish you would—handle it." Rylie took a deep breath. "Okay, then…we'll go truck shopping for you. Don't think I didn't see you checking the newspaper ads earlier."

"Now you're talking!"

"That's not what I expected to hear," Noah said. "Correction, what I'd hoped to hear." When Brooke Sullivan called him shortly after noon, he grabbed for his cell phone like a man waiting for an organ-donor call. But Brooke had little good news to share, and when she told him where she'd ended up placing his gift, he'd been deflated. "I suppose I should have anticipated this outcome," he told her, "but I'm disappointed nonetheless."

"I understand," Brooke told him. "But you're not giving up, are you?"

Noah stopped in midstep as he paced along the outside of the pool at Haven Land. The afternoon was gorgeous, with just enough autumn coolness, but none of that helped his melancholy mood. "I...don't want to. At the same time, I don't want to continue upsetting her."

"Without betraying a new friendship, I can tell you that she was torn over what she was doing. She thought the flowers were glorious and the gesture good of you. She just wasn't ready to embrace your generosity."

"Because?"

"In the end it's always about trust, isn't it?"

"I guess that's a subtle improvement over all-out loathing."

"I would say *subtle* is significant."

Noah took heart from that. "So we'll try again. But...what? Flowers again?"

"Gage and Rylie use a lot of repetition with animals to build trust, but does she need that in her personal life? I don't think so. She hears what you're saying. It's your job to convince her that you really mean it."

Noah figured at some point, he would owe Brooke a huge gift of her own for getting him through what he realized was totally foreign territory for him. He'd never had to pursue a woman in his life! "What do you have in mind? I'm guessing no arrangement at all?"

"We handle chocolates now. Locally made fudge, to be exact. Maybe we'd put a nosegay on the package? It would have to be Monday, though."

"Sure. A nosegay? They still do those things?"

Brooke laughed softly. "You're right—it's almost an archaic word and there's no real call for them except as a bit of whimsy, or for smaller, informal weddings. I did read that they're usually made of the most fragrant flowers, which, duh, explains the name. So much more appealing than a bow on top of the box, and she could then put it in a small vase, which I could provide, giving her what amounts to three gifts in one."

Noah wasn't certain. "Rylie didn't strike me as the kind of woman to be so…"

"Feminine?"

"She's very feminine." He frowned at the mere idea of anyone not seeing that. "Just not…fussy."

"I promise, it won't be remotely fussy," Brooke replied, a smile in her voice.

Relieved to sense Gage's wife continued to approve of him, he added, "Be generous with the chocolates. It's obvious calories slide right off her."

On Monday during his lunch break, Noah returned Brooke's call that he'd missed due to being in court. His trepidation turned out to be warranted. "She didn't accept that, either, did she?" He could tell by the tone of Brooke's voice message, although she'd said only, *"Please call me at your convenience."*

"No. And she was embarrassed that all of the guys at the clinic saw it. But I was discreet and drew her to the back to actually try to convince her to change her mind."

"I appreciate your efforts. You're my sole ally, except for my mother." How to gauge if there really was hope after all? he wondered. "So she's still opposed to giving me at least the benefit of the doubt?"

Brooke made a soft musing sound. "We're looking at a bit of stubbornness now. But part of that could have been a reflex for having the audience at first. I should have known better, so I owe you this next try, because given her expressions when we were alone, I do think she appreciates that you're still trying, and some of her resistance is crumbling."

"I don't want surrender or resignation," Noah said, turning his back to the room, afraid that Judy or Vance, who was feeling better and was in deep conference with his secretary, saw his own emotional turmoil. "I just want to be able to talk to her again. Where does she want you to take this gift?"

"A young girl in Sweet Springs who'd survived a cancer scare. You probably read about her in the local newspaper. She's barely eleven, Noah. It's a dear gesture."

"Yes. Of course, and I did see that." Noah ran his free hand over his hair, at once admiring Rylie for her thoughtfulness, and on the other hand trying to figure what it would take to make her want to keep something from him. "What do you suggest next?"

"We have some great fragrances that Kiki developed herself. They're becoming quite popular in the area."

"But I don't know what Rylie would prefer—or that she even wears a fragrance." He wasn't going to admit he thought he'd caught the hint of something tropical and flirty once when standing near her. Peach? He'd figured it was a result of a shower gel, not an actual fragrance she'd sprayed on.

"I don't suspect she does too often, considering that she wants the dogs to get used to her natural scent, but it's always nice to have something for special occasions. I'm thinking forward," Brooke told him, her tone conspiratorial.

"Thinking forward would be nice, but I'm not the optimist I used to be. What else could you recommend?"

"We have some cute stuffed animals."

He remembered seeing a nice display in one corner of her store. "I think I would rather go with that. I saw a kangaroo…"

"I sold it shortly after you were here."

Disappointed, Noah tried to think of what else had caught his eye. "The giraffe?"

"Um…the giraffe that's almost her height?"

"I know it's probably the most expensive thing in the store, so I insist you put it on my bill. You can tie a note in the shape of a heart on ribbon around the neck that reads, 'I'm stretching my imagination to convince you that I have one.'"

"Noah, I'm impressed," Brooke replied, laughing softly. "And I can do better than snipping at construction paper. We have pretty lace doilies that will work beautifully."

"Good, very good, because that about used up the one creative gene in my DNA."

"But, Noah, about the giraffe…it's cute and would probably make her laugh—"

Noah could hear her moving around the store.

"—here it is. I have a sweet mini schnauzer. It's white and I could make an equally dainty basket of flowers to stand beside it. That seems more her size, and the heart would work even better, if you ask me. It is my favorite of the stuffed animals, and I think she might like to use it in her clinic display advertising her grooming services."

"That sounds like the winner to me. Okay, thanks, Brooke." Since their initial conversation, she had insisted he call her by her first name.

For the next few hours, Noah waited, barely able to concentrate on his work. When he returned from court and Judy blocked his way to his desk, saying, "A Brooke Sullivan is on your line," he all but lifted her to move her out of his way and get to the phone.

"Yes, Brooke," he said, unable to keep the anxiety and hope out of his voice.

"Well, she didn't send it back with me."

"You mean she accepted it?"

"I'm hoping that's what she's doing."

"Well, what did she *say?*" His voice sounded so tight and foreign to him that he had to check himself. He couldn't remember when he was more eager to hear something positive.

"She stared at it a good while and finally said it looked very lifelike. Then she asked if she sent this back, would you keep ordering things? I told her that was probable."

"How did she react to that?"

"She was quiet for a moment and then she thanked me for bringing it."

Noah didn't try to hide his relief. "Thank you, Brooke. I sincerely appreciate all that you did."

"I just hope something good comes from this. My opinion of you has changed—if that makes any difference."

"It means a great deal."

But now what? Noah thought after he hung up.

* * *

She just didn't know what to do.

On Tuesday afternoon that dilemma preyed on Rylie's mind. Her first impulse yesterday had been to return Noah's gift to Brooke again, but she knew Gage's wife was right—he would only send something else, and she didn't want him wasting his money on her. Okay, so she was somewhat flattered that he had done everything he had so far, but there was no future in it. They were apples and oranges—more accurately Dom Pérignon and diet soda. By closing time, she asked her uncle for a favor.

"Do you suppose they were wrong about your new truck not being in until later this week?" On Saturday, they'd had fun shopping the dealerships in the area and then having dinner to celebrate Roy's deciding on one. But the silver extended-cab Chevy wouldn't be delivered from its current location at the Port of Houston until tomorrow or even Friday.

"I've dealt with them before. The interior package that I wanted was hard to find without special ordering, so, yeah. I'm not expecting a call until then. Why?"

Knowing he was too sharp not to read into what she was going to say, she said, gently, "May I drive you home and borrow the truck for an hour?"

Roy—and everyone else—had already picked up on Noah's latest gift, and that she'd kept it. Therefore, his narrow-eyed stare was less intimidating than it might have been.

"What are you going to do?" he demanded.

"Go talk to him."

"I don't like that idea."

"Well, it needs to be done."

"I'll drive you."

"No, you won't. I'm twenty-five, not fifteen. Either you'll lend me the truck or I'll figure out something else." She hadn't yet gotten her license changed, as planned. Regardless of everyone's good intentions to get her there, Monday had been crazy and Tuesday's scheduling turned out to be not much better. At least now she wasn't worried about being bothered by the police.

"Staying put is the idea I like best," Roy grumbled.

Rylie tried gentle persuasion. "I just want to make sure he understands that I only accepted his gesture because I wanted him to stop."

"That can't be said over the phone?"

"Important things should be done in person, Uncle Roy."

In the end, her uncle relented, only to insist on waiting in the RV for her to return. He would be comfortable watching MG as he kept up with the latest baseball playoff game on TV. Rylie had reminded him that there was beer and the rest of the pizza from lunch in the fridge, and had driven off.

Now, what if Noah was out for the evening? she wondered while en route to Haven Land.

When she pulled into the estate with the grand stone entrance where the electronic gates were open, she almost lost her courage. She'd passed the place a few times now on her way to Rusk, and the acreage was every bit as stunning as the stately white-pillared mansion. *A modernized Tara,* she thought, eyeing the sunroom on the left side overlooking a pool every bit as large as the one in the city park.

Her confidence turned into full-fledged nerves

when she spotted Noah in front talking to a shorter and darker man whom she quickly recognized as Ramon. As she drew closer, she saw a series of mounds near the driveway, which was probably what had Noah concerned.

As she came around the circular drive, Ramon's eyes widened with surprise. Then, with a wave of his Western hat—he was clearly on yard duty at the moment—he hurried off toward the barn with the spray canister he had been toting.

As Rylie parked and approached Noah, she tucked her hands into the back of her slim jeans and asked as though they'd just talked minutes ago, "Showing Ramon what a fire-ant mound looks like?"

The mild sarcasm was a subtle reminder of his tone with her during their first meetings. Noah's self-deprecating smile indicated that he remembered only too well.

"As usual, he's four or five steps ahead of me. I was only worried that Mother would come out in her chair to admire her roses and accidentally roll into the ant nests before she realized they were there. I should have known that he'd already been mixing the poison. Thankfully, he's patient with me." Noah's tone then grew far more tender and husky. "It's so good to see you. Words are inadequate."

Rylie studied him in the late-afternoon light. He looked less browbeaten than Brooke had suggested, but there were undeniable shadows under his eyes and he was a bit paler than the last time she saw him—undoubtedly losing himself in his work more than ever. She wished she could take some satisfaction out of that, but she'd never been that kind of person. It was time to just say what she meant and get this behind them.

"I didn't come here looking for compliments. I came to thank you for the gestures, but to ask you to quit. That's why I accepted your last gift. You need to know that I've put what happened behind me, so you can, too. Stop, I mean."

Still wearing the white dress shirt and gray pants from the suit he'd obviously been wearing at work today, Noah looked as underdressed as was probably possible for someone like him. Nevertheless, he retained the power to make her pulse do crazy things. In comparison, she was in a turquoise T-shirt and jeans, but at least she'd ditched the maroon lab jacket, and the four-legged critters had been easy on her clothes today. Given the compliments she'd received now and again, the turquoise seemed to do nice things with her hair and eyes.

Noah looked stymied by her directive. "Stop…? I don't know that I can."

Was he kidding? He was the assistant D.A. of Cherokee County, probably the next D.A. He'd been groomed to convince, coerce, chide, mock, herald and warn off in nuances a mockingbird would envy. Where was the difficulty for an orator in canceling an ongoing flower-shop order?

With curiosity getting the best of her, she asked, "Why not?"

"I'm on a mission. What's more, just because you're generously putting this—what I did—behind you, that doesn't mean you've really forgiven me. That's what I need to be convinced of."

"You're forgiven, okay? It's done."

Shifting his hands on his hips, he shook his head. "No, it's not."

His stance might look bold, but his words weren't arrogant. They were simply, quietly spoken. "What difference does it make to you anyway?" she replied, feeling a little desperate now. Her resistance was crumbling under the power of this somber, intense Noah.

As soon as she uttered those words, she wished she could take them back, because he started to walk toward her. The expression in his gorgeous-but-compelling brown eyes had Rylie backing away, completely forgetting the truck behind her, until she bumped into sunset-warmed metal. From bra line to hips, she felt the heat; however, that was tepid compared with what his look stirred inside her.

When Noah was toe-to-toe with her, he framed her face with his hands. "Only this," he whispered against her mouth.

For a man with so much brooding going on within those intelligent eyes, his hands and lips were incredibly tentative and gentle, inviting and appealing. His touch seduced, as well, as he caressed her skin, exploring her cheekbones, her jawline. He treated her as though she was made of the fibers of a sweet dream, and all the while his lips moved over hers with the ardor of a man who was willing her to hear the words trapped in his mind.

At first, Rylie gripped his wrists, only to freeze on the impulse to push him away. But, his kisses were already too potent. She could no more resist what he was offering, and asking of her, than she could remember why she should remember the need to protect her emotional welfare. She could only absorb.

His tender appeal almost brought tears to her eyes. By the time he paused to catch his breath, or steady some wave of emotion within him, she felt as though she'd been through a tumultuous, but brief summer storm, as well. So when he simply rested his forehead against hers, and closed his eyes, she swallowed against the ache in her throat.

"It's a relief to discover you can be reasoned with," she said between shallow breaths.

His attempt at laughter brought a soft caress of air against her lips. "I can't believe you let me touch you, let alone kiss you. This goes way beyond my fantasy."

"If fantasizing is what you're doing, you could have dressed me better."

"You're delectable. But what I'm really trying to see is what's in your heart."

Rylie remained bewildered—in an amazing way. "I don't understand you," she admitted.

"You will." His voice held the velvet vibrato of promise. "The way I behaved, have been behaving—I was lost in anger, and emotionally AWOL. This is me, Rylie. This is me."

He kissed her again, a deeper kiss this time, which had her releasing her hold on his wrists, only to slide her hands up his chest and wrap her arms around his neck. Here…on his family's driveway, under God's sky. She couldn't write poetry, she rarely read it, except when she downloaded lyrics for a song she loved and wanted to learn. She knew it existed all around her in nature—at birth, and death—but this was the first time she'd tasted it and ached to imbibe it.

For a precious space of time, life's pain and unfairness lost its hold on them. Rylie's entire being basked in the aura of being totally present and in tune with the universe. She realized that she'd just been blessed—she was not going through this life without knowing something like this existed.

When Noah finally ended the kiss to gently, quietly wrap her in his arms and hold her against his pounding heart, Rylie could only whisper, "Noah…this is surreal."

"Yes."

"And pretty crazy."

"Crazy was fighting this. Denying what I was feeling."

"I have just enough sense not to share what I'm feeling right now. As it is, I'm not sure I remember how to get home."

That confession earned her a pleased look from Noah as he tightened his embrace in a quick, urgent hug. "That's probably the best thing anyone has ever said to me. And you can't go home yet. Come inside and say hello to Mother."

His invitation yanked her back to reality faster than a sudden downpour could have, and she abruptly slid sideways to escape his embrace. Go inside? After practically begging him to make love to her? "Oh, no! I'd be too embarrassed."

Before she could take another step backward, Noah took hold of her hand. "Listen—that's Bubbles barking. She's spotted you—probably from the sunroom window." He gestured to the left side of the house that was width and length floor-to-ceiling windows. "Mother's in there painting, so it won't be long before she drives her chair to see what the fuss is all about. Actually, I'll bet she's already watching us." He caressed the soft inside skin of her wrist with his thumb. "Rylie, there's nothing to be embarrassed about. She's on your side."

If true, that was a relief. Rylie had enjoyed the few times they'd conversed on the phone.

"You'll see," Noah said when she looked at him for verification. "She's been thoroughly disgusted with my behavior." His gaze searched her face and lingered on her right eye. "I'm so sorry for what happened to you," he added, his voice husky. "Does it help at all if I swear that it doesn't show?"

"The doctors said that, and some nurses. Most of the time, I figure people are just being nice."

"You can believe me—and in what's between us, as well. This isn't going to only be about sex."

Her humor stirred back to life. "There's going to be sex?"

He burst into laughter. "After kissing me back the way you did, there damned well better be." As quickly as the moment grew lighthearted, he got serious again. "I've never reacted to anyone the way I have to you. You've knocked me a galaxy away from my constellation of preconceptions, never mind my comfort zone."

As he started to draw her up the sidewalk, Rylie wasn't sure all of what she'd heard was a compliment. "So handsome, brilliant you feels something for little, insignificant me, huh?"

Halfway up the sidewalk, Noah paused, visibly startled. "That can't be how you see yourself. Little, maybe, but you have the heart of a giant. Life threw you a hell of a curveball—that happens to plenty of people— but what did you do? Instead of embracing the support you know would be there from your family, you exuded a superhuman effort not to worry or burden them. In the meantime, you've built a new career and paid off a small mountain of debt.... You call yourself insignificant? There are CEOs of Fortune 500 companies who would like to tap into your perseverance and discipline." Noah shook his head. "My God, woman, you're amazing."

Before she could respond, he resumed his eager escort toward the house. Rylie was still basking in the delight of his words when they passed the threshold into the mansion, only to have to deal with a new assault on her senses.

"Mercy. I didn't think that it could be even more stunning inside."

The foyer was a rectangular space of light, which was interesting since there were no visible windows except for the two that framed the front door. But the buttercup-yellow walls and the ivory chairs and tables set around the room created an atmosphere of merriment and welcome. In the center of all that was a round white marble table on which sat a flower arrangement that Rylie suspected was every bit as tall as she was, concocted of seasonal flowers, branches and dried seed pods from plants she didn't believe grew on this continent.

"Where's the light coming from?" She hadn't meant to whisper, but the stateliness of the place seemed to demand the respect.

"A skylight we put in at the top of the stairs. Mother didn't like the big chandelier over the arrangement competing with the flowers."

"That explains it," Rylie said with a nod as she continued taking it all in. "My parents would writhe in envy if they knew I was in a place like this. They would know with one glance what the stairs are made of and what era the chairs are from."

Noah cast her an apologetic look. "You said something about their work—no, your brother's. I'm sorry that I don't remember who does what."

"Dustin renovates seriously old and historic homes on the East Coast. In California, my parents are the people whom people like you call when something breaks and you need to either repair or replace it—or you're looking for something that's one of a kind. They reclaim old things and store them for when a decorator, contractor, renowned builder or even an independent rehab aficionado needs them, which is what I would be if I ever bought myself a place."

"I would think that takes a good eye—and tons of patience. It would drive me crazy to see a doorknob sitting on a store shelf for two years just collecting dust."

"Frankly, me, too. In that case, you also have craftsmen working for you, as my folks do. You can turn something like that doorknob into a birdhouse foot grip. Or if you need impromptu storage or hanging space in an apartment, you fasten the knob to a rustic board or shutter, and it becomes a hanger for a jacket, or robe…maybe the house and car keys."

"Mother is going to love pulling stories out of you." Placing a hand at the small of her back, he directed her to the left, where they entered an equally lovely room about four times larger than the large entryway, resplendent with darker woods, tall majestic hutches, perhaps a mile of bookcases, a piano and a very large flat-screen TV built into one of the cases. The upholstered furnishings in here were a mix of leather and velvet, pewter and burgundy.

Rylie didn't get a chance to comment on any of it because Bubbles came charging out of the sunroom yapping happily. As Rylie scooped up the canine version of a greeting card, Noah sighed.

"Hello, you cutie," Rylie said, cuddling the young dog. "Good to see you, too. I see that foot isn't giving you any more trouble."

As the dog licked at her chin, Noah led Rylie into the sunroom, where Audra Prescott was sitting at her easel, paintbrush in hand. Her excited expression told Rylie that Noah had been right. She'd looked to see why Bubbles was acting up and had realized it was her.

"Rylie—my dear!"

Although they'd never been face-to-face, apparently Noah, or even Ramon, had described her enough to take an educated guess. "Yes, ma'am. I'm sorry to intrude."

"Nonsense. I'm overjoyed that you could bring it upon yourself to speak to this rascal again." After giving Noah a wry look, she reached out her arms to Rylie. "Come give a lonely old lady a hug. It's so wonderful to finally meet you."

Warmed by the welcome, Rylie did lean over to do that, but she couldn't help teasing her, as well. "At least I know where Noah gets his gift of blarney. 'Old lady' is seriously stretching the truth. The compliments I've heard don't do you justice."

"Oh, my friends are kind because they know I'm never going to compete with them for their cosmetic surgeon's time. But I did want to thank you for taking such good care of my Bubbles, especially after that wound she suffered. Noah said you were so calm and good with her."

As Audra grasped her hands, Rylie realized where Noah had inherited the shape of his from. She, too, had the long, elegant fingers and the pianist's reach. It hadn't been surprising to glimpse the grand piano in the far end of the living room by the fireplace. And Audra's nails were impeccably cared for. In comparison, Rylie had hands the size of a child's, only the skin was a bit tougher from wrestling with animals and machinery and having to wash so much. That didn't make her self-conscious, though. Audra was too accepting and warm to make her feel uncomfortable.

"Bubbles is a delight," Rylie assured her. "One of my best-behaved clients."

"Wait until I brag to my friends."

"Most of them have darling pets, too."

"Which doesn't? Oh, I know you won't tell me," Audra said, with a wicked smile and wink. "But I had to ask."

She was fun and it left Rylie with a bittersweet feeling to know she was a shadow of the woman she'd been when her husband was alive. She couldn't imagine losing the person who made your life whole. Without needing confirmation from Noah or anyone, she believed that was the kind of relationship Audra had shared with her husband.

Rylie turned her attention to the work on the easel and was enchanted at the watercolor in progress. "That's what you see when you look out these windows? I definitely need to go see my ophthalmologist. How lovely!"

As Audra chuckled, Rylie admired the autumnal scene—still weeks away by the East Texas weather schedule—where amber and russet-colored trees framed a quiet pond where a family of wood ducks swam in absolute contentment.

"That's actually the pond where I grew up. Noah's father proposed to me there. It's easy to paint it from memory."

Noah must have heard the emotional hitch in her voice as Rylie did, and he stepped forward to ask, "Can I get you a glass of wine, Rylie? Mother, here's your one chance."

"You know you don't have to ask me twice," Audra replied. "I'd love a chance to celebrate and get to know Rylie better."

"I shouldn't." Rylie saw Noah's mother deflate and reassured her. "This was meant as a quick trip. I do need to get home, since my uncle is watching my dog and waiting for his truck back. Besides, it will be getting dark soon and I'm not yet familiar enough with the roads to risk driving with only half of my vision."

Audra nodded, her look sympathetic. "But Noah can lead the way, can't you, dear?"

"It would be my pleasure," he assured Rylie.

Chapter 6

"So what did you say?"

It was the following Friday and the week had passed in a busy, but happy blur. Certain that Roy would be talking to her parents soon, Rylie had called her folks during the lunch break to tell them the truth about everything. She'd meant to do it sooner, but either they were tied up with clients, or she was helping Gage on an evening emergency call.

Naturally, her parents were shocked and upset. Her mother had even begun to cry over the fact that her daughter had carried the weight of everything on her own. Their one reassurance was that Roy was there to represent them.

As for the matter of Noah and the warrant scare, they were indignant on her behalf, until she explained that she and Noah had made peace, and were "officially" seeing each other. There was a little commentary on that, but Rylie assured them that they needed to give Noah a chance, as she had. It helped to brag about Haven Land and Audra Prescott's warmth and hospitality.

"Yes," she said now. "I stayed for a drink and Mrs. Prescott, Audra, was lovely." Afterward, Noah had followed her home like a true gentleman, but she'd stopped out front to make sure he left at that point. "Uncle Roy is back there," she'd explained to him. "He's still having issues with all of this."

"If you kiss me good-night, I'll go without protest," Noah had said.

Thinking about the kiss, she barely heard her mother now say, "It sounds like he's sincere—and his mother clearly likes you."

Rylie could only smile to herself and touch her lips that had held the tingling sensation of Noah's hungry kiss until she'd fallen asleep. "I think so. My only concern, Mom, is that they're as well-to-do as some of your Hollywood clients. They might not be of the oldest Texas aristocracy, but they mingle in circles that I don't."

"Who's going to turn up their nose on a young woman who knows almost as much about animals as a licensed vet does? You're a professional even if you didn't achieve your ultimate goal. Clearly Dr. Sullivan is seeing your worth. Wait a second, your father is adding his two cents…. Oh, he says it's not like you to turn chicken."

Rylie had to smile. Leave it to her father to try to get her back up. "Okay, okay, don't use reverse psychology on me. I promise to be open-minded about this."

"And call your brother to tell him what's happened," Denise Quinn instructed. "You know he was crushed when you dropped out of school, too."

So much so that he'd kept his distance for months. That had hurt Rylie, but she couldn't forget they'd been as close as "blood kin," as Uncle Roy would call it, until then. "I will," she assured her mother. "He's next on the list, but as I said, we've been swamped here. Speaking of…it's time to prepare for my next client. Talk soon. Love you, bye."

As she pocketed her phone and returned inside with MG and Humphrey, who'd been enjoying the respite out back, she saw Roy coming through the breezeway from the front. "I just spoke with Mom and Dad as you urged, and they send their love."

With a satisfied nod, he asked, "How did they take the news?"

"About as you would expect, but with you here, they're not as upset as they might have been."

"You think Dustin is going to take it as well?"

Her adopted brother was only five years older, but he could act three times that. "Nope. So I warned them not to say anything until I have the time to call him myself."

At the busy inference, Roy said, "That's why I came looking for you. Gage needs you in Room Two. I'll receive your next appointment and get things ready for grooming."

And so went the afternoon. Fortunately for her, she got to breathe a little easier when they locked the doors at five o'clock. But while she could finish up some things, Gage was already out on calls.

When her cell phone rang, she was relieved and

delighted to see it was Noah. "I thought you'd still be in court."

"I'm about to be. We've been waiting on a jury to come in with a verdict and just got word that they've reached one. On that good news, I wanted to see if I can talk you into dinner."

Rylie would pretty much drop anything for him—short of helping Gage if he'd asked for her assistance. "But you know you have at least another hour before you're free," she reminded him, "and I'll be cleaning up in here that long, too, and then need a shower." Their schedule had been that way since they'd last parted. But they had talked every day and often just before bedtime, and their conversations were growing more and more flirtatious and intimate.

"Imagine me washing your back. Then your front. All of you."

Feeling her body heat in response, Rylie whispered, "Noah! I hope you're not where someone can hear you."

"Barely." He cleared his throat. "I meant dinner tomorrow. If memory serves, you're only open a half day on Saturdays."

"Oh." She really was dead on her feet, but the idea of having to spend one more day without seeing him was a disappointment. "Yes, that's true."

"I thought I would come get you at three and bring you to the house for that tour Mother wanted you to experience last week. Then we could have a leisurely early dinner with her, and finally have some time alone."

"That sounds wonderful," she said. Particularly the alone part.

But only seconds after she hung up, her nerves

kicked in. "Okay…" she said to herself. "So what do you wear for an occasion like that?"

Noah's heart was pounding with excitement on Saturday afternoon, and he kept catching himself going over the speed limit on his way to Sweet Springs. Thankfully, he reached the animal clinic without seeing a police vehicle, and he drove around to park beside the RV. For the past twenty-four hours, he had been thinking of little else besides the pleasure of Rylie agreeing to see him again. He felt like a high-school kid going out on his first date. True, he hadn't exactly dated much since returning here, but he knew that had nothing to do with what he was feeling. This was all about the *whom,* not the what.

He'd barely shut off the car's engine when the RV door opened and Rylie descended. Noah's throat went dry. She was dressed in an emerald-green sheath with a silk shawl in shades of blue, purple and green draped casually around her for the coming coolness of the early October evening. But as she began to close the door, MG squeezed her way outside, too.

"No, MG. You know you have to stay here this time. Get back in."

Instead, MG planted herself at Rylie's feet and gazed up at her with adoration. When that didn't get her the response she wanted, she raised her paw and offered a soft, "Woof."

"Looks like she wants to go, too," Noah observed as he emerged from his vehicle.

"I know. Sorry. That's what comes from letting her go almost everywhere with me," Rylie replied. "Give me a second. She's usually very good about obeying. MG—"

"Bring her along." The words were out before Noah realized he'd said them; however, he felt rather proud of himself that they came so naturally.

For her part, Rylie could only stare. "Have the pod people replaced you with an alien? Open the trunk! I know my curmudgeon is in there probably stunned by a ray gun."

Accepting her teasing, he explained, "Mother loves animals, not just Bubbles. She was an excellent horse-woman, and being restricted as she is has denied her the company of other creatures, as well. She used to ride the pastures to enjoy seeing the new calves. Any-way, I've seen enough of MG to know she's a well-be-haved dog. She's certainly been good around Bubbles." He leaned over and asked MG, "You don't even care that Bubbles has a title and you don't, do you?"

MG uttered something throaty that sounded agree-able and with impressive civility offered her paw.

Noah smiled up at Rylie. "See? We're in agreement."

Crossing her arms, Rylie replied, "Cute. What about your expensive leather seats?"

He had already noted that she kept MG's nails trimmed. "I overreacted with Bubbles, you know that. If you have a blanket or towel we could set down for her in back, that should take care of things."

"I do. Just a second."

When she reemerged with a thick flannel blanket, he was at the door to take hold of her waist and help her down. Any excuse to get near her now. But her high heels gave him pause. "I guess you forgot that we were going to take a tour?" he asked, although he liked the taupe slingbacks on her. Her feet were as slender and small as the rest of her.

"I don't expect you to take notice of the purse," she said, nodding to the taupe shoulder bag on her shoulder. "To know me is to know I have to be crossing state lines to carry one—or going farther yet. My sneakers are in there."

Satisfied, Noah took the blanket from her and escorted her and a prancing MG to the car. If he'd been wondering how to win over Rylie's four-legged companion, he received his "pass" quickly. She was delighted to climb into the backseat, and even seemed to realize the gesture by the way she daintily sat down on the blanket, a big smile on her face, followed by a soft growling sound, clearly meant to hurry them up.

Once he and Rylie were seated and fastening their belts, she said, "You'll get comments when the people who detail your car notice the nose prints and saliva spots on the back windows."

Although that gave him a moment's pause, Noah mentally shrugged it off, as well. "This will be a good test to see if they're doing everything I pay them for."

"You know I'm only teasing you about being fussy, don't you? Brooke told me she was the same way about having Humphrey in her BMW. That's how Gage arranged to see more of her—he insisted on bringing Humph to the clinic every day in his truck, so she could focus on the shop and her aunt."

"They seem to have built something special between them."

Rylie looked at him with new respect. "I like that—built, not found. It's true that relationships take work.

That's part of what makes the results all the more precious."

Nodding again in agreement, Noah shifted into reverse. "I'm late in saying it, but you look beautiful."

"I don't know that I'd go that far."

He found her near shyness endearing. "You want to argue? Already?" Noah kept his tone teasing, but he was curious, too. "You always look fresh and appealing. Tonight you're a Rylie I've never met, and she's even more intriguing."

She dropped her gaze to the hands clasped in her lap. "Thank you."

"Surely you've been told you're beautiful before?"

"It's my brother's favorite word to me. But he's clinically prejudiced."

"Sounds to me like he knows what he's talking about. How much older is he?"

"Five years. My parents had tried to get pregnant for the first ten years of their marriage and nothing was happening. Only weeks after adopting Dustin, my mother discovered she was pregnant with me. We've been as close as blood relatives—in some cases more so, considering what some friends and classmates told me about squabbles with their natural siblings."

"My mother kept miscarrying," Noah replied. "She was almost thirty-seven when she became pregnant with me. Her doctor point-blank ordered her to bed. He said if she wanted to carry me to term, she needed to stay there, and that's exactly what she did."

"I'm sure she didn't regret one day of that."

He glanced at her profile to note her serene expression and saw that she was wearing more makeup beyond the touch of sable-brown mascara and lip gloss that she usually restricted herself to. The smoky eye shadow and liner made her eyes more mysterious, and the slightly darker-toned lipstick enhanced the tempting bow of her mouth. That she had great bone structure, he already knew. That she had the cutest nose, he'd only just realized.

"Do you want to pull over and let me drive?" Rylie asked, although she didn't take her eyes off the road.

Noah grinned. "Okay, I'll be patient. Just don't complain once we get to the house and I don't want to take my eyes off of you."

"Please don't embarrass me in front of your mother."

Dear God, she made him want to pull over and haul her onto his lap this second to kiss her until she said yes to anything and everything. "I suspect that's impossible," he drawled, "unless you disrobe at the table and dash in your birthday suit for the pool."

"Considering that I know you have staff, I wouldn't do that even if I thought we were alone."

"What I'm saying is that she's utterly delighted that you're coming," Noah continued, unable to stop smiling himself. "She could barely settle down enough to take her nap, what with all the excitement, and believe me that's heartening, because while she puts on a good show when someone other than myself or staff is in the house, she struggles to show any genuine enthusiasm for anything."

"Can you confide what her prognosis is?" Rylie asked. "I'd like to be as supportive as I can, but at the same time not stick my foot in my mouth."

"She broke her back in two places and almost her neck. By rights, she should have died in the accident, too. She'll never walk again, and although we try to buy her time with the pool therapy and massages, there's chronic pain, and there's no expectations that she'll reach the normal life span for a woman. She has days when she wishes it was all over. That's when Livie and I—Olivia Danner is Mother's live-in nurse—have to be extra watchful of her alcohol intake." After a pause, he added, "And we never, ever keep her medication where she could get at it herself."

Rylie sucked in a sharp breath. "Oh, Noah, I'm sorry. That's a challenge for all of you, not just her. Now I'm doubly glad that your mother has Bubbles, and tries to stay interested in her painting."

Noah couldn't resist the impulse to reach over and cover her hands with his. "You'll be good for her. You're an optimist as much as a nurturer."

"I suppose I am, given my preference to work with animals. I haven't really thought about it. I just know that I don't like contention for silly or immature reasons. That happens easily enough without manufacturing it."

"I wasn't being exactly mature in my reactions to you at first."

"Or with Bubbles," Rylie added, with an impish smile.

His answering groan was only half-affected. "My four-legged baby sister."

When she laughed spontaneously, he felt as if something burst open in him and bloomed. She had a lovely, musical lilt that pleased the ear and heart. If she broke into a helpless, full-fledged, tears-down-the-cheeks laugh, he supposed that would be it for him. He would have to fall head over heels in love.

At the house, when Noah escorted Rylie up the sidewalk, he noted how MG walked serenely beside her. "She's really an amazing animal."

"Oh, she quite agrees with you," Rylie drawled. "Her reaction to everyone's surprise at how well she behaves is, 'What's not to love?'"

Noah was still chuckling as they entered the house. "We're here!" he called as they passed through the threshold.

"We got eyes. You don't have to show off for your little lady," Aubergine huffed from the kitchen, her intimidating alto voice surprising on someone not much taller than Rylie. But the plump sixty-year-old had a torso that a century-old oak would admire. Her skin was a flawless rich caramel, and her eyes were as black as the cotton tunic and pants that she wore as a uniform, along with her sensible black orthopedic shoes. Usually as stern as the tight bun pinned to her nape, she did possess a wicked and dry sense of humor, something Noah tried to excavate as often as possible.

"Aubergine Scott is our housekeeper," Noah explained, "but the truth is she's the majordomo of Haven Land. Aubergine, the 'little lady' is Rylie Quinn, who deserves any and all credit for keeping the dust mop looking halfway decent."

"I know who she is. Hello, child." The woman stopped before her and sized her up with unapologetic interest. "You better be hungry because I got a glimpse of you a few days ago, and I intend to feed you. There won't be any pushing food around the plate, either. We don't use forks as hockey sticks in this house."

Rylie put her left hand in the air and her right over her heart as though taking an oath. "Miss Aubergine, I eat like a Clydesdale. And having heard so many enviable stories about Southern cooking, all I can say is bring it on."

That had the woman looking at Noah with haughty approval. "Thank the Lord, you ain't brought home a food pecker." Before Noah could reply, Aubergine looked down upon MG. "And what do we have here?"

MG was sitting obediently beside her mistress and Rylie said, "Say hello to Aubergine, MG."

The dog lifted her right paw.

Aubergine looked long into the retriever-mix's eyes before bending to accept her paw, and said softly, "Well, you are an old soul, aren't you? Welcome, darlin'," she cooed. "I'll bet you'd like your own dish in the kitchen, wouldn't you?"

"You'd guess right," Rylie assured her. "You won't have any trouble with either of us when it comes to cleaning our plates."

Suddenly there was a yap and then Bubbles came scampering from the direction of the living room. At the sight of MG, she threw herself at the bigger dog's feet and rolled onto her back in welcome.

MG gently nuzzled the little dog for a moment before Rylie scooped up the merry bundle of white fur.

"Hello, happy girl," Rylie said. "Are you ready for MG to give you your exercise for the evening?"

Aubergine considered the difference in the sizes between the two dogs. "This should be interesting. Y'all go in and say hello to Miz Audra. Noah, are you going to take care of drinks?"

"I will, thank you. Can't let you prove straight off what a superwoman you are and put me to shame."

"I reckon she'll find out soon enough."

Winking at Rylie, he led her into the living room,

with the dogs following. When he noted her continued awe at the size and splendor of the room, he leaned closer to her ear and whispered, "It's just home."

"You say. They could play an NBA game in here."

As they entered the sunroom, Audra was sitting in eager anticipation. She was wearing a favorite ice-blue caftan that zipped in the front, with matching blue ballet slippers. Rylie started to extend her hand, only to have Audra draw her closer for a hug.

"No more of that. Remember I told you that I'm a hugger, and I'm so happy to see you again. Oh, and how lovely you look."

"Thank you for the invitation, as well. This is my dog, MG, which is short for Mommy's Girl. I hope you don't mind her tagging along. Noah seemed to think it would be okay. MG, say hello to Mrs. Prescott."

The graceful dog sat down before the wheelchair and politely raised her paw. Naturally, Audra was delighted.

"What a beautiful girl. I heard Aubergine say she was an old soul. I see that in her eyes, too. How did she come into your life?"

"Pretty much the usual way for strays. She was someone's throwaway. My prize of a lifetime." Rylie quietly directed her dog, "Hug, MG."

The dog put her head on Audra's knee.

"Oh, what a heart stealer," Audra told her, stroking her silky head tenderly.

"Did Noah tell you that she's a therapy dog?" Rylie asked. When Audra shook her head, she explained, "We visit the local assisted-living center and nursing home regularly."

"How marvelous for the inmates. I've heard of such

patient and giving creatures, but never met one. What a treasure you are, MG."

MG gave her two soft woofs as though thanking her.

As Audra petted her for that, Rylie said, "You'll get exhausted doing that before she gets tired of compliments, Mrs. Prescott."

"Again, it's Audra, please."

With a nod of thanks, Rylie looked around in wonder even though she'd been here briefly only days ago. "It's simply breathtaking in here. I would sit here, too, especially if the weather kept me indoors." Her gaze happened to settle on the cross. "Oh, that's lovely."

"It was a recent gift from my son," Audra said with a twinkle in her eye.

Rylie glanced over at Noah. "So this is what I heard you also found at Brooke's? You have good taste."

"And it's improving by the minute," he replied, his look intimate.

"You will let Noah show you around this time, won't you?" Audra asked.

"That would be wonderful. As long as you don't let me intrude on your schedule," Rylie told her.

"I get entirely too much rest as it is," Audra replied. "Noah, we should have drinks now. What would you like, Rylie?"

Rylie gave Noah a questioning look.

"Wine? White? Red? Sweet? Dry?"

"White and dry would be perfect, thank you."

"Talk away," he told them, slipping off his navy blue, light wool sports jacket. "I can defend myself from the bar."

It was good to hear laughter in the house…and conversation that wasn't about dosages, pleading for cooperation or assurances that things would get better. Rylie clearly had as good an effect on humans as she did on animals.

After he set the jacket over the back of a chair by the chess table, he rolled up the sleeves of his white silk shirt. He wanted Rylie to feel as comfortable as possible; that's why he'd worn dress jeans instead of a suit. As he poured the wine—red for himself and his mother—he listened as Rylie moved around the room taking in the minijungle of plants, water fountains and pieces of sculpture, some of which were his mother's own work. He heard his mother give a name and explanation of whatever Rylie apparently pointed to that she especially liked.

"You'll have to tell me when I talk your ears off, but I do love to share my plants, my books, *my* interests. I'm totally selfish in that way," Audra said.

"Go right ahead," Rylie encouraged. "Part of the fun of doing what I do is also learning what people's passions are. I don't read as much as I should these days, but I love plants. I hope to sell the RV and buy a little piece of land one of these days so MG and I can have a garden and flowers, too. We would spend most of our time outside if we could."

"Noah tells me that you're from California. You still have family there?"

Rylie briefly explained what she'd told him earlier about her parents and her adopted brother. "Unfortunately they're on opposite sides of the country. I'm grateful for today's technology. Otherwise I'd miss them far more than I already do. Would you like to see a sample of my brother's work?"

Noah was returning with their glasses as Rylie

showed his mother pictures on her iPhone. "This is Dustin's restored project in Massachusetts. It had belonged to the son of one of the signers of the Declaration of Independence and now it's owned by a former soap-opera star. This one is in Vermont—he helped convert it into a successful B and B. This is the one he's currently working on in Maine that belongs to one of the state's top chefs."

"Well, we know who to call if we're in need of assistance," Audra said, all admiration. "He does painstaking work…and he's quite handsome in a darkly romantic way."

It was true, Noah thought, catching a glance of the guy over Rylie's shoulder. He'd been picturing a bulky lumberjack, but the guy in the photo was tall, lean and looked as if he drank cognac and read Byron instead of King or Conrad. As Rylie closed the app, Noah distributed the glasses, and then raised his in a toast. "Here's to more opportunities to learn via eavesdropping."

It was a scrumptious dinner. Aubergine wasn't merely a fine cook, but she was also forever aware of Audra's health, and after a fresh garden salad, her stuffed salmon with Haven Land's own vegetables steamed over broth with wild rice was mouthwatering. The whole-grain rolls were also homemade, as was the cheesecake with the warm cherry sauce. Rylie couldn't have eaten one more thing and was grateful when Noah offered her the tour. She was ready to walk off some calories.

Noah suggested they start upstairs first because, he'd explained, his mother would be turning in soon. Once Rylie ordered MG to stay at the base of the stairs, they headed up. She got a better idea of how large the house was when they reached the second floor and she realized there were two full wings of bedrooms. Noah led her to the right first, taking her all the way down the hall.

"This is Mother's suite," he said, beckoning her through the opened door.

The room faced the back with a great view of the grounds. Rylie loved the romantic balcony and the bay window that also allowed for sitting indoors and enjoying the view. There was a huge bathroom that had been adapted for a handicapped person's needs, and the king-size bed had an ethereal canopy. The main color scheme of mauve, gold and cream seemed regal yet soothing to her.

A side door opened and a tall, toned woman entered with prim confidence. Somewhere in her fifties, her short, straight brown hair swung with each energetic step belying her age. She was dressed in a white nurse's pantsuit and nodded at them with a tight-lipped smile. "Excuse me. Good evening."

"Rylie, this is mother's other real-life angel—Nurse Olivia Danner. Livie, this is Rylie Quinn, Bubble's groomer."

"Ah." Livie's thin lips became less pinched. "How do you do?"

Her formality had Rylie starting to retreat from the room. "We're in your way…"

"Not at all. I'm just going to turn down the bed before I go down to bring up Audra. By the time she has her bath, she'll need to get under the covers to avoid catching a chill."

"We missed you at dinner, Livie," Noah said.

That earned him a double take from the all-business nurse, and she melted a bit more, almost allowing a crooked smile. "Audra needed some time with you two, and I wanted to take advantage of this weather and have a brisk walk, before the next front blows in tonight. But thank you. Next time, perhaps."

After they were down the hall a few steps, Rylie asked, "What was that all about?"

"Livie and Aubergine dine with us. I wanted her to know that there's no reason for that to change."

Rylie touched his shoulder, but then kept walking. "What?"

"You surprised me...in the nicest way," she said softly, aware voices carried easy in this tunnel-long hallway. She didn't think he could have said anything else that would have made her trust in him more.

Noah caught up with her and entwined his fingers with hers.

They looked at two of the four bedrooms on this wing. Each was luxurious without being fussy and included queen-size beds, ready for guests at a moment's notice, and separate bathrooms. Aware that Noah was an only child, she wondered how much company they had.

"Does Aubergine have help keeping up with all of this?" Rylie asked. "This is an insanely big house, even if most of the rooms are rarely occupied."

"She does bring in Ramon's wife and daughters on Mondays for a cleaning of our rooms and most of downstairs, then twice a month they do the rest of the rooms."

He led her down the opposite hallway to the very end, where a shut door led to a room that obviously faced the front of the house. As he opened it, he murmured near her ear, "Enter if you dare."

The shiver that ran down her spine had nothing to do with concern; rather it was the warm hand that was at the small of her back, and the fact that he'd barely taken his eyes off her since she'd stepped out of the RV. Every touch and look was a communication that he wanted to do more, and so did she.

"Does that line work with the others?" she asked softly as she stepped into the room.

"You know there haven't been any others up here."

"I believe you." She saw his chest expand as he drew in a deep breath and knew it was the best thing she could have said to him. This was like a first dance. They were both tentative, but they had the same goal.

As she felt her pulse dance like raindrops on fragile petals, she tried to focus on the decor. It was a handsome room. They both seemed to be drawn to blues, his preferences mostly indigo and peacock with brown and bronze accents. It was masculine, but quietly elegant.

She stroked the bedspread, a design like waves in a deep sea, and breathed in his scent. It was more defined here and made her mouth water, even though she had only just eaten. Initially, there were the woodsy, deep male layers, but then came the surprises of chocolate and coffee bean.

"I believe you," she said again, "because if anyone inhaled this yummy scent, it would take a crowbar to get them out of here."

He came up behind her and slowly caressed her bare arms. "You think I'm yummy?"

Hearing the smile in his voice, she turned to face him, and he immediately enfolded her against his body.

This was the first time they'd been this close since Tuesday, and she was instantly under his spell. "Much too soon to tell you. You'll get a swollen head."

"Not with you. I'm too grateful for any crumb of kindness from you." As he spoke, he ran his lips down her neck, his warm breath as much a caress as his words. "God, I want to lay you down and make love to you here. Right now. I know it's supposed to be too soon, but it's what I feel, so to hell with reason."

"It's the same for me, but I have too much respect for your mother to behave in a way that would offend her on her own property."

"We'd shut the door."

She had time only for a brief laugh before he kissed her, a kiss that almost made a liar out of her. She could lie down with him here and make love. Ached to. He was allowing her to see more of his hunger, and also that his control wasn't what it had been. As he deepened the kiss in search of the tongue-tangling dance and probing exploration that made her ache to take his hands and bring them to her breasts, or her hips, she couldn't stop a soft sound of yearning.

"Me, too, darling. Me, too."

Rylie looked up into his eyes. "I'm glad you're not who I thought you were."

"I'm glad you gave me another chance." His gaze lowered to her mouth. "Now help me get you downstairs before I lose the battle with my good intentions."

"How does your mother get upstairs?" she asked, striving to regain her composure as they descended the stairs.

"Right there." As they reached the foyer again, he

pointed to the gated door to her left. The elevator was partially hidden by a tall palm plant.

"How clever—and a relief for her." She leaned over to accept MG's happy greeting. Bubbles stood by eager to get her share of attention, too.

"I had it installed while she was still in the hospital. Let's take the dogs outside, so they can burn off more energy. I'll show you some of the grounds. If you thought the sunroom was something, wait until you see the vegetable and cutting gardens."

As stately as the front of the property appeared, the back was breathtaking. Roses, gladiolas, peonies, zinnias, sunflowers…there was an abundance of offerings in the full acre of blooming beauty. "You didn't need to go to a florist," Rylie said. "You could have brought me a bouquet from here. It would have been equally special."

"Then next time I will," he assured her.

He was right about the beauty of the rest of the grounds, as well. It was resplendent with fountains, a stocked pond, stables and hundreds of acres of pasture where cattle grazed leisurely. "Who manages the animals?" she asked.

"Ramon's brothers. Impressive *caballeros*. Every once in a while, we'll have a bull here, or one of the neighbors' animals take down a fence and the boys will load their horses, jump into their trucks and race off. Before you know it, the renegade animal is back where it belongs, and they have the fences repaired. Ramon runs a strict operation here, and I appreciate that. I'd be lost without him."

"Do you ride?"

"I can—you can't be a Prescott without being able

to sit on a horse—but my father was more hands-on.
I think I'm better at managing the financial side of
things."

"You didn't want to come back here, did you?"

Noah's expression exposed his struggle. "It's home.
It always will be, but this was my parents' passion. I
thought I would create my success in a different direction."

No wonder he'd seemed bitter and like a caged animal when she first met him—edgy, restless and re-
sentful, despite his love for his mother. And here she
thought she'd just set off something negative inside
him. Rylie touched his arm. "Can't you do both?"

He took her hand and raised it to his lips. "I'm beginning to feel that I want to."

Reassured, they walked on. The dogs enjoyed themselves, playing well together, until it was clear that
Bubbles had exerted herself trying to keep up with MG.
"We'd better head back," Rylie told Noah. "I have to
be heading home anyway. There are still chores to do
and tomorrow will come soon enough."

"But it'll be Sunday."

"Your people here work on Sunday to some degree
or other—feeding, cleaning stables or whatever. Besides, Gage presented me with my own key today. I'm
definitely going to buy him a sleep-in morning and
tend to the chores in the kennel and stables myself.
Barring an emergency call, it'll get him most of the
day off. It's the least I can do after all of his support,
as well as his and Brooke's kindness to me."

"Want some company?"

Rylie couldn't believe he'd actually offered. "Seriously?"

Once again, he reached for her hand and laced his fingers through hers. "At some point you're going to believe me when I tell you that I want to spend time with you. We both have demanding jobs and hectic schedules. Is an hour for dinner here and there enough for you?" His gaze grew intent. "It isn't for me."

"Not me, either." Despite the admission, she continued to look dubious. "You're sure? Vet work is physical and messy."

"I grew up on the estate, remember? Dad made sure I spent evenings and summers working side by side with the hands. What's more, I understand that animals are a part of your life and always will be, so warning me off is a waste of energy."

Finally convinced, Rylie teased, "Okay...only please don't come dressed in designer jeans and Italian loafers, or I'll think you forgot everything you ever learned."

"Come here and apologize," he growled, drawing her into his arms.

She did, repeatedly, and it was several minutes before they caught up with the dogs, who by then were napping at the patio's French doors.

The next morning when Rylie unlocked the back door of the clinic at minutes after seven o'clock, she felt as though she'd had one mug of caffeine too many, she felt so jittery with excitement. It wasn't only that Noah was coming back this morning, but before he'd left her last night, he'd kissed her again.

"To get me through the long, lonely night," he'd told her.

He'd taught her that there was a world of difference between kissing a boy or a man with a one-track mind, and a man who saw it as important to please as to be pleasured. It amazed her that she'd been able to sleep at all; her body had been left humming with awareness and need.

She'd barely started working on the animals inside when she heard him pull up in back and park by her RV. There was no repressing her smile of joy as she went outside to greet him. Then it widened as she took in the well-worn jeans and boots he wore with a jeans jacket over a simple white T-shirt for the cooler weather.

"What did you have to pay Ramon for the clothes?" she asked, her tone wicked, as he leaned over to pet MG, who ran to him in welcome. Her own jeans were stuffed into knee-high rubber boots for hosing down the kennels and mucking stalls, and her black T-shirt bore the UC Davis emblem for the veterinary school out of San Diego, which she wore under a navy blue windbreaker.

"In rare form, I see." His own narrow-eyed gaze roamed over her with a mixture of pleasure and possessiveness. "How can you be all bright-eyed and bushytailed when I didn't sleep after I left you last night?"

"I'm younger, more resilient." After his bark of laughter, she nodded inside. "There's coffee."

"You're an angel." But when she led the way, he stopped her a step beyond the door and drew her against him. "That's it? That's my welcome?"

"You're right," she said, wrapping her arms around his neck. "Good morning. I'm so happy you came."

His arms became tight bands around her, and his bold kiss told her that his appetite wasn't just for coffee. "Better," he said against her lips. "If I could look forward to this every morning, I wouldn't need as much caffeine."

"My, you are turning leaf over leaf," Rylie purred. But needing to slow things down before she lost her head, she asked, "How's everyone at the house? Did you leave before your mother was up?"

"No, she was already downstairs having coffee with Aubergine and Livie at the kitchen table."

"Aubergine...now there's a romantic and dramatic name."

With an affirmative murmur, Noah pressed a kiss on her forehead, and went to get the coffee. "She has a sister named Sapphire pronounced the French way, *Sa-feer.* She lives in New Orleans."

"I'll bet those two have some stories between them."

"They must well have. Aubergine recently mentioned her only once and fleetingly, after she'd finished a tiny glass of absinthe on what was her sixtieth birthday. The bottle and dainty glass had come from New Orleans the day before. I haven't seen either since. Knowing Aubergine as I do, she's likely buried everything in the vegetable garden somewhere in the hopes of gaining points with God or seducing the garden fairies."

"Ah...*absinthe*..." His droll humor triggered some memory about the liqueur. No, she amended, remembering sugar wasn't added, meaning that technically it was a spirit. A very strong spirit. "I've heard of it. It experienced some resurgence a few years ago, and some of the kids in school were talking about trying it. Wasn't it once banned in France and said to be a hallucinogen?"

With a slight shrug, Noah replied, "As potent as it

smells and tastes, it could well have been. Fortunately, I tend to be a boring stick-in-the-mud when it comes to my alcohol preferences. No testimony on truth in advertising."

"Was the family surprised when you told them where you were going this morning?"

His expression turned wry. "I now have a keen understand of the expression 'deafening silence.' I'm sure hilarious laughter followed as soon as they heard the front door close behind me."

"I'll bet you're wrong."

After giving her one of his intimate looks, Noah gestured with his mug. "What can I do?"

"I'll be easy on you to start, but finish your coffee first. Then get a leash—" she pointed to the dozen or so hanging by the door next to the coat rack "—and take Dumpling for a walk in the pasture out back. He's one of our two larger boarded dogs, in the other building between here and the stables. I'll deal with Pacino as soon as I'm done tending to the smaller animals in here."

Noah frowned. "Start me off easy? You don't think I can handle both of them?"

Rylie gave him a sympathetic look. "Pacino is blind, like the character Al Pacino plays in *Scent of a Woman.* His owner is a police-dog handler who rescued him from being put down after he was injured in the line of duty, and she's at a seminar out of state until tomorrow. It's taken me since day one to earn his trust. I don't want you to suddenly find yourself on your back with a hundred pounds of German shepherd standing on your chest just because you said the wrong thing."

"Dumpling it is," Noah replied, holding up his free hand in surrender. Then he asked, "What breed is he?"

"A sheepdog. He's a big sweetie."

"Thank goodness Ramon isn't here to witness me cooing, 'C'mon, Dumpling,'" Noah muttered.

"Oh, believe me," Rylie replied, "that's the least embarrassing thing that's apt to happen to you when working at an animal clinic."

Chapter 7

"Take that picture and I won't be responsible for my actions."

Although Rylie couldn't help but laugh at Noah's expression as he sat in the middle of the spilled contents of the wheelbarrow, she was only teasing about recording the moment for posterity on her iPhone, and tucked it back into her jacket pocket. Then she shut the stable door before the chestnut mare decided to add injury to insult.

"I was only kidding, but I did warn you to watch Lady B's head. Now you know what the *B* really stands for besides Barbra from Bentwood Farms. Be glad she's a head butter and isn't inclined to kick." Of course, Rylie would never have sent Noah in there if the horse had been mean rather than mischievous.

The mare with the attitude had been there a week,

and was another animal going home tomorrow when her owners returned from a trip to a family wedding out of state. While Rylie had cleaned the messier pens in the cow barn, Noah had done Lady B's and had just put her back into her stall, only to be knocked back out the moment he let down his guard.

"Are you okay?" Rylie asked, with sincere sympathy.

"The body is intact, but I think my pride is terminal. Thanks for talking me into putting my keys and wallet in your RV. I'd hate to have to dig them out of this stuff."

Extending her gloved hand, Rylie said, "Let's get you out of that."

"Sweetheart, you don't need to join me down here."

"I'm stronger than you'd think," she replied. "It's a job requirement to be able to wrestle with all sizes of animals. Come on." She did succeed in helping him to his feet, only to shake her head in regret. "I really am sorry. You almost made it through the morning in good shape."

"Do you have about ten plastic garbage sacks that I can spread over my car seat? I sure can't get into it like this."

She had no intention of letting him do that. "Aubergine will take one look at you and bolt the doors. We'll hose off your things and you can shower in my RV while I throw your clothes in the clinic's heavy-duty washer and dryer. You'll be as good as new in a couple of hours."

He leaned over to right the wheelbarrow and Rylie stopped him. "I'll get that. Go on and get those boots off by the RV door, then strip down to your shorts and leave everything on the concrete."

"My fantasy was that I talk you out of *your* clothes." He cast her a wry look. "You're sure? I can call Ramon to bring me something."

"No doubt the poor man has plenty enough to do before he gets to enjoy Sunday with his family." She gave him a challenging look. "What's the matter, Prescott, afraid I'll come in for a free peek?"

"If you don't, I'll be seriously disappointed."

His look sent Rylie's pulse skipping as much as his invitation. As he headed for the RV, she drew a deep breath.

So it's come to this.

She couldn't have been more touched or grateful as he'd worked with her these past few hours. Never could she imagine the Noah Prescott she thought she knew several weeks ago doing all they'd done getting the pens and stables in shape and the animals fed. He'd not only been a good sport, but he'd teased her as much as she had him—and flirted twice as much. As she heard a whistle, she glanced over her shoulder and saw that he was still at it.

He had his boots and socks off and his jacket and T-shirt. Smiling in invitation, he began a slow, provocative striptease as he unzipped his jeans.

For a man who claimed he preferred a courtroom to ranch labor, he had an impressive body, broad shoulders and narrow waist and hips with enough muscle tone to make her fingers itch to explore every inch of him, as well as the soft nest of hair tapering down his chest and into his briefs. Then she saw that her staring was having a powerful an effect on him.

"Get inside before you cause a wreck on the inter-state," she called to him.

As he did that, Rylie finished cleaning up, and then went to deal with his boots and her own. She could ac-tually feel her pulse growing stronger. She knew she was going to him in a few minutes, but in the mean-time, she welcomed the anticipation. Once she had his clothes taken care of and in the washer, she turned to MG.

"I'm going to get you a treat for being a good girl, and you can nap while the washer runs," she told her beloved pet. MG would be fine while the machine was running, and if she woke before Rylie came back, there were dogs in the inside kennel to check on and keep her entertained.

Done, she locked the back door and sat on the RV stairs to remove her boots and set them beside Noah's clean ones. Stepping inside, she heard the shower water still running.

Removing her windbreaker, she set it on the hook by the door and slipped off her socks on her way to the back. By the time she reached the bathroom, she had her T-shirt over her head and was working on her jeans.

"Are you going to leave me any hot water?" she called to him.

"Not unless you hurry."

Grinning, she barely got her jeans off before the door opened and he snatched her around the waist and lifted her inside.

"You're crazy!" She still had on her underwear, which became plastered to her skin within seconds.

"No, starving," he replied, as he claimed her mouth for a kiss that proved it.

Rylie wrapped her arms around his neck and gave herself up to the moment. It was perfect. *He* was. Among the longing, the hot water pummeling them, her sensitized body and his hard and aroused one, she was instantly elevated to a new experience in pleasure.

As Noah drank in her throaty moan, he rasped, "That's sexy, and you take my breath away."

He'd begun caressing and exploring her only seconds into their first kiss, and before she knew it, he'd removed the last bits of her clothing, and what had been covered in silk was now being caressed by his lips and tongue. Rylie let her head fall back and lifted her face to the water as warm liquid transported her from above, and sensual man from below.

Those hands she'd admired before deserved a new designation—lethal, she thought as he threatened to be her undoing. Wherever he caressed her, she kept being thrust to what she thought was her climax, only to be drawn back, and then flung close again. He discovered the same thing, as his fingers probed the ultrasensitive, sleek place between her legs.

Unable to help moving against his hand, she groaned, "Oh, damn."

"Go ahead. Do you know what it does to me to know I can make you feel this way so quickly?"

When he replaced his fingers with his mouth, she didn't have a choice. His gifted touch shot her straight over the edge, dragging a sharp cry from her. Pleasure vibrated through her body in wave after wave, until she thought her legs would no longer hold her up. Seeming to sense that, Noah rose to clutch her tightly against him.

His body hard with tension and desire, and his heart

pounding like a runner's, he rasped, "I have to get my billfold."

Remembering that it was way back on the dining table, she said, "Try the right-hand drawer of the vanity. There's an unopened box."

"Unopened, huh?"

There was no missing the satisfaction in his voice, or the adoration in his gaze, before he stepped out to get them.

Once he was back, and quickly ripping the cellophane, she said, "Thank my brother. It was in his care package when he heard I was moving. Otherwise I wouldn't have even thought about getting some. 'To be kept within reach whenever around smooth-talking cowboys,' is what his note said."

"Fooled him, didn't I?" Noah drawled.

"Oh, I don't know," she replied, loving the chance to finally explore his body as he had hers. "Haven Land is half ranch, and with this body, you can't tell me you sit at a desk all day and night researching and prepping for your next trial."

Instead of denying or confessing, he grew serious as he framed her face with his hands. "Angel, I want you to know, I've never had unprotected sex."

"Neither have I," she said, a bit sad that such things had to be discussed these days when every fiber in her being told her that she could trust him. "And I'm on the pill, in case you were worried about that side of things."

"My only concern is that I'm not going to get in that sleek, little body soon enough. God, Rylie," he groaned, lifting her into his arms. "Come here."

Even as she wrapped her legs around his waist, he

began the careful probing. He watched her face for any sign of discomfort.

"Are you going to be my lover or my gynecologist?" she teased, bemused at his intent study of her every facial nuance.

"Both this first time," he said, his voice showing the strain his patience was costing him. "You're tighter than this latex, but damn, you feel like heaven. Kiss me."

She did, and he continued to claim a place for himself inside her. She'd never felt safer, more cherished— or more feminine. Noah was introducing her to what adoration felt like, and she blossomed under his tutelage.

"I think we're running out of hot water," she gasped, every breath laborious now.

"It's okay. I'm running out of endurance." His voice was all strain, and his vise-tight embrace told her even more about how close he was to climaxing. "It's your fault for feeling too damned good."

If she could have found her voice, she could have said the same about him. Human nature was strange that way. Anatomy was just that—bone, musculature, skin, nerve endings…but how incredible that when two certain people came together, the results could create such magic. Rylie was glad that it was happening with this man.

They were so in tune that no more words were necessary. He increased the momentum of his thrusts and she tightened her embrace outside and in, until their kisses took on a near wild abandon.

In the last moment, Noah pressed her against the fiberglass wall and gave her every bit of himself that he could, a harsh cry breaking from his lips. At the same time, Rylie sobbed helplessly, as a climax more powerful than the first shook her entire being.

The water sluicing off them was now only tepid, yet Rylie could feel Noah continuing to pulsate within her. "You're lasting a long time."

"That's all you, darling. What you do to me." He kissed her shoulder and said, "I want to do this again in bed—where I can use both hands."

"Oh, yes, *please*."

He chuckled softly and shut off the water, then reached for the bath sheet on the rack to dry them both. Rylie didn't think he stopped touching her once, and by the time he lowered her onto the bed, she was aching to have him inside her again.

He already had another condom packet between his teeth and quickly put it on. "I wasn't even in such a hurry when I was sixteen," he admitted, wryly.

"Poor girl. I hope she wasn't a virgin."

"Believe me, she wasn't, and hadn't been for several years."

Taking hold of her wrists with one hand, he drew her arms over her head and with his other hand, he stroked her slender length from arm to knee and all of the sensitive places in between. "Believe me," he rasped, sliding between her thighs to seek a home in her again, "I've never wanted anything more than I want you."

"It's the same for me," she whispered.

"Since it's been some time, you might be sore."

"Uh-uh."

"I have a serious appetite."

"So there's no need to list today's specials?"

"Heck, no. I'll take the whole menu."

And as he claimed her mouth for a deep, thirsty kiss, Rylie abandoned herself totally to the experience.

Long afterward, they lay replete in each other's arms, absorbing the subtle sensations that trickled through their bodies. This time their skin was slick from exertion and determination to get every ounce of pleasure they could from each other, and Rylie felt a pleasant ache in muscles rarely used even in her physical job.

"You don't want to nap?" Noah asked, his tone musing as he traced circles over and around her puckered nipples.

"Not possible with you doing that. Besides, your clothes aren't going to dry if someone doesn't get them into the dryer. I can also hear MG telling me that she's been locked inside long enough. I could close the bedroom door so you can sleep, though."

As she got up to get new panties out of a drawer, she felt Noah's possessive gaze follow her every move. She'd been around nature and had been studying anatomy for too long to be self-conscious about her body or anyone else's, but that didn't mean she was desensitized. On the contrary, she reveled in the knowledge that even momentarily sated, he didn't want to take his eyes off her.

"Get back in this bed and I'll show you who's tired," he drawled.

Rylie chuckled but slipped on her panties and clean jeans, and then a T-shirt, leaving off the bra. The lack of lingerie was going to be obvious the way he was staring at her, but she figured she wouldn't be wearing it all that long anyway. "Thirsty?"

"Dry as an old tree stump. I could handle a beer."

"I'm going to have wine. This was too special for beer."

"Special, huh? Make it wine for me, too. I want to taste like you do, so you'll want to keep kissing me."

"I don't think you'll have a problem there."

"And you don't mind if I'm in no hurry to leave? You're not tired of me yet, are you?"

That was so incredibly opposite of what she was feeling that Rylie laughed all the way into the clinic.

By Thursday, Noah knew he was in trouble. He was glad he and Rylie had spent all of Sunday together because he hadn't seen her since, and they'd barely had a chance to talk, except in the evening when they were both pretty worn out from the demands of their work. It was lunchtime and he was buzzing her cell, hoping she wasn't having to work through lunch. Considering that more and more her assisting Gage was overlapping with her grooming appointments, that was entirely possible.

"Hottie Central," came her lilting voice after the second ring.

Sitting back in his chair, Noah grinned. "Yeah, you are. I take it that you're alone?"

"In the RV with MG and Humph, trying to have a calm few minutes before we return to the circus inside. How's your day going?"

"It's less physically demanding than yours, but also high theater. Hung jury on the Slattery case."

Rylie offered a sigh of commiseration. "I'm sorry.

People can't see that lowlife for what he is? They need to throw the book at that slick con man, who found it easier to rip off old people and widows than actually work for a living."

Noah knew that she'd followed the trial in the news enough to grasp the essentials of the case. "I told Vance it was a mistake to put those younger people on the jury panel. They think it compromises their religious beliefs to stick him in prison with such a hefty sentence when the victims are old anyway, and it's only money."

Rylie yelped in indignation. "That's their reasoning? Obviously, they haven't had to work to make car payments or pay rent or tuition. I don't know how you're keeping your cool. How do you reason with ignorance like that?"

"I remind myself that they're Vance's choices. He'll have to live with the results." Then Noah said, "Let's not waste another precious second on that. Say something soft and sexy. I miss you."

"I miss you, too. It's starting to feel as though Sunday was a figment of my imagination."

Noah frowned, not liking the inference of what he'd heard. He knew their relationship was in its fragile, early stages when outside influences could still steal her away. "We have to do something about that. Is there a chance we can have dinner tonight?"

She uttered a regretful sound. "I'm staying late to do two dogs. There was no way to fit them in otherwise. And Gage had asked me to do a dairy-farm call to do inoculations, so it would go faster, but Uncle Roy is filling in for me instead."

"What about after your appointments? I could be

coerced to spend the night…bring a change of clothes
and head for work from your place in the morning."

"Determined to send tongues wagging, are you?"

Noah was heartened by the smile he heard in her
voice. "Frankly, my dear, I'd be proud to," he said, hoping he sounded at least remotely similar to suave, who-
gives-a-damn Rhett Butler. "I'm all for doing whatever
it takes to make it clear that you're taken."

"Then I'll see you later," she said softly, only to utter
an apologetic groan in the next instant. "But if you're
hungry, you'll have to pick up something on your way
down. My fridge is empty except for beer, wine and
pickles. I haven't even had time to think about the gro-
cery store. If Gage didn't carry dog food, MG would
be begging for pizza and hot-link dinners from the
musketeers."

"I'll handle the food," Noah assured her. "Call you
when I'm on my way."

"Don't call, just come. No cell phones while driving."

"So I'll text you before I head out there. This way
you can start thinking of me kissing you—all over."

By eight o'clock that evening, a cold front was pushing through. Strong winds with driving rain were bat-
tering East Texas, and temperatures were expected to
drop thirty degrees. It was the first real precursor of
things to come, a signal to wildlife that hunting season had arrived, and that geese would be seen and/or
heard for the next week or so as they headed south for
the winter.

The dropping temperatures had Rylie's teeth chat-
tering by the time she locked up the clinic and waited

on MG to do her business a last time. As soon as she got into the RV and towel-dried the dog, she ran for a hot shower.

She'd just changed into clean jeans and an oversize sweatshirt that she used as a sleep shirt and thick socks, when she saw lights play around the edges of the mini-blinds. Not lightning, she realized, as Noah parked his BMW as close to her stairs as possible.

Quickly opening the door for him, he shoved a huge bag of takeout and a bottle of wine at her.

"Take that and I'll get my suit bag," he yelled above the howling wind and driving rain.

Worried that she would lose her hold of everything, she gave up trying to keep the wind from slamming the door against the RV's outer skin and ran to dump her armload on the dinette table. By the time she returned to the door, a thoroughly soaked Noah scrambled up the stairs and yanked the door shut behind him. MG barked her approval of that move.

As he hung the clothes bag on the door frame so water would only drip on the rubber mat, Rylie ran to get him a towel. "You shouldn't have been driving in such weather," she called back to him. "The roads must have been treacherous."

"There are some trees down," he admitted, shrugging out of his soaked suit jacket. He hung it over the back of an iron barstool. By the time Rylie handed him the towel, he had his tie off, too. As he mopped his face and hair, he added, "I heard on the radio that sections of the county are without power."

"At least the tornado warnings are about to expire," Rylie replied, "otherwise, I'd insist we ride this out in the clinic. Did you check on your mother?"

"She and her two attack-dog guardian angels were ready to get into the storm room." Noah had shown it to her, behind the pantry, when he'd given her the tour. "And if they lose power, Ramon knows how to get the generator system operating." He gave her a tender look. "She was equally concerned for you."

"How sweet." She accepted the towel back and hung it in the bathroom. "Can I have my hug now?"

"I'm still drenched," he warned, working on the top few shirt buttons and the ones on the cuffs.

"That's how I like you best."

With a deep-throated sound of pleasure, he enveloped her in his arms and kissed her eagerly. "God, what a relief," he said between eager kisses. "I've missed you."

"Me, too, you."

"This is nuts. The weather…our schedules…"

"At least we don't have to be concerned that we'll get bored with each other anytime soon."

That earned her a one-word expletive from him, and his next kiss was meant to prove that there wasn't going to be any talk about boredom as long as she was in his arms. Even when MG nudged his thigh, wanting some recognition for herself, Noah wouldn't break the kiss; he only reached down blindly to pat her.

When he finally took a moment to catch his breath, Rylie planted a kiss in the V of his opened shirt, only to discover his skin hot to the touch. "You aren't coming down with something, are you? You're practically feverish."

"I should be. I was in foreplay mode driving here, aching to touch you and feel your hands and mouth on me." His gaze was as intent as his touch was urgent.

"Are you absolutely starving, or can you wait fifteen minutes before we eat?"

With a graceful leap, she wrapped her legs around his waist. "How's that for an answer?"

With a husky, "Bless you," he took the few strides necessary to reach the bedroom, and kicked the door on MG. From the other side came the dog's indignant "woof."

"She'll pay you back," Rylie said, as Noah laid her amid the pillows. "We may emerge from here to find whatever you brought already devoured—or splattered around the room like a Pollock painting."

"A small enough price to pay for this." As he peeled off his clothes in record time, he clearly enjoyed watching her watch him. "You're adorable in that getup."

"Pinocchio. At best I look shower fresh. You got here before I could at least put on some mascara."

"With lashes like that you don't need it…but you are still wearing too many clothes." Naked himself, he went to work on getting her out of her things. In the process, he kissed and tasted every inch of satin-smooth skin that he exposed, until she kicked off her panties to speed up things.

"God, I'm crazy about you." He pinned her against the bed with the lower half of his body. "Kiss me again before I explode."

She did, eagerly giving herself up to this spontaneous reunion. As long and hard as the day had been, she felt renewed in his company. She also liked that she could reduce Mr. Cool and Confident to a state that was anything but. Having such power over a partner had never mattered to her before, but if you were going to turn to mush whenever you were anywhere near the man whom you couldn't put out of your mind or heart, it was a huge relief to know that he felt the same way about you!

As he ran his hands over her, she arched into the caresses, and when he duplicated the journey with his lips traveling down her throat and over her breasts, then her stomach, she raked her short nails over his back, his tight buttocks and hard thighs. It was she who reached for the condom and slipped it on him. Outside, the massive front continued to push through, but inside she and Noah created their own force to be reckoned with.

When he entered her, Noah moaned near her ear. "Baby, you're going to hate me for how fast this is going to be over. But I want you so badly. I can't—"

"It's all right," Rylie whispered, bending her knees and digging her heels into the bedding to aid him. "As long as it's you, it's good."

He uttered an indecipherable something, and then his thrusts grew harder and faster. "I promise to make it up to you," he uttered between gasps.

"I promise to remind you," she whispered, tightening inner muscles around him.

With a raspy oath, he lost control and found his release.

It was almost ten before they ate. By then they were beyond ravenous. Sweetly forgiving MG had behaved, and her good manners and calm demeanor earned her a few slivers of Noah's steak. Rylie watched, looking amused and pleased that her beloved pet wasn't seen as a nuisance to him.

"I think you're a fraud," Rylie chided, when he gave

MG his last bite of meat. "You like dogs. You probably had one when you were a boy."

Taking a sip of his wine, Noah thought back to those days. "There were a few cow dogs on the place—still are—but they've always lived with the hands. Ramon's uncle had the job back then. My father wasn't big on animals in the house." Seeing her disappointment, Noah reached across the table and took hold of her hand, stroking the soft back with his thumb. "I had a great childhood, a privileged life. No regrets. Traveled through two continents, and Japan. There isn't much that I couldn't afford if I wanted it."

"But if your father hadn't died, you wouldn't be here. We would never have met."

Noah hated that her usually optimistic attitude had stumbled on that thought. Sitting forward so he could bring her hand to his lips, he kissed each finger before saying, "I have a feeling that on one of my visits home, I would have come upon you with a flat tire in front of the house, and I would have noticed that irresistible little tush as you stubbornly tried to put on the spare yourself. No, no, too mundane. You'd be driving this monster and accidentally cut me off as you tried to pull over to recheck your directions to the clinic. I'd be so beguiled by your sexy self, that I would borrow one of Ramon's dogs as an excuse to come see you."

"You wouldn't need an excuse," she said quietly. "Not if you came smiling the way you are now."

Noah shook his head. He couldn't get over how quickly her sweetness and honesty went straight to his heart, and groin. Pushing aside his glass, he rose and drew her to her feet as well, then lifted her into his arms. "Say good-night to MG."

"Night, pretty girl."

It was midnight when they made love the last time. Using his shoulder as a pillow, Rylie had slipped off into a deep, contented sleep, but Noah was still reveling in what they'd shared—and listening to the wind continue to blow in cold air.

Hearing another sound, he saw the door ease open and MG quietly approach Rylie's side of the bed. After observing the situation for a moment, she hopped up and curled in the V created by her mistress's bent knees.

As he felt himself drifting off to sleep, Noah reached over to fondle the dog behind her ears.

"If no one needs me, there's something I need to do on my lunch hour." Friday morning was proving to be as busy as Thursday had been, but Rylie made her announcement just before noon, determined to take care of an important matter. "Uncle Roy, you're okay with monitoring MG and Humphrey, right?"

"Sure, sweetheart. But is it anything that I can do for you, instead? You're looking a little tired. Did the storm keep you from getting much sleep?"

He wasn't fooling her for a second. Uncle Roy had arrived this morning just as Noah was leaving, and he had acted disappointed in her ever since. She knew he felt she should hold a grudge against Noah, just as she knew he understood that any fatigue she exposed had little to do with last night's storm. At least Rylie could take comfort in the fact that they were in the back of the clinic and the old-timers weren't hearing any of this.

"Shame on you," she replied, albeit gently. "If I'm not allowed to ask about Jane Ayer, you're not allowed

to needle me about Noah." Rylie had been itching to bring up the redhead's name ever since Brooke happened to mention observing Roy and Jane entering the grill across the street from the flower shop last Saturday. During the quiet hours between lunch and dinner, when it was least likely that that they'd run into anyone they knew, Rylie suspected. She was dying to know how their date went and when her uncle would ask Jane out again. He deserved to be happy.

"Okay, okay," he groused. "Just be careful."

"Driving?" she asked, her expression all innocence. "You know I will be. Now that you have your truck, the bubble mirrors are permanently fastened on mine."

"Wise guy," he muttered.

"You know I appreciate your generosity very much," she added, dropping her teasing tone. She had gotten her driver's license transferred and the truck title changed into her name on Tuesday afternoon. "And your concern about everything else."

"Anything for you," he said with a sigh. "You know that. All I'm saying is that you've been through enough disappointment for someone of your tender years."

"I love you, too," Rylie said, kissing his whiskered chin. "I won't be long. It's just that Noah's phone fell out of his pocket and he's stuck at court."

"Mr. Big Shot needs it so much that he can't send an underling to collect it for him?" Roy sniffed. "He sure is romantic—not to mention concerned about your welfare."

"Since he helped me clean the kennels and barns on Sunday," she announced, "I thought this was the least I could do to reciprocate."

Roy all but gaped. "He was here Sunday, too?"

"Oh, Uncle Roy, he's a good man."

"And considering how preoccupied he was that he almost clipped me leaving this morning, I'm guessing that he's been rewarded plenty for that," Roy muttered.

With a gasp that he'd actually been so frank, she swatted his arm. Then, exchanging her clinic smock for her windbreaker, she left.

Her uncle's worries aside, Rylie was delighted with the chance to see Noah for even a minute. She grinned all the way up to Rusk, as she remembered how he sounded on the phone when he realized what had happened as a result of his drawn-out love play before he'd forced himself to head for the office.

"See what you do to me?" he'd moaned, when she'd confirmed that she found it had slid farther under the couch than they'd checked.

She did have to deal with one worry, though. The incident about the warrant could still be fresh on some peoples' minds. It would be embarrassing if she crossed paths with someone from the sheriff's office, or the courthouse, who looked at her with continued suspicion or censure. As much as she wanted to put the matter behind her, the memory of what a close call she'd had couldn't quite be forgotten. As a result, when she pulled into the courthouse square and didn't see Noah outside waiting for her as they'd agreed he would do, she drove around and around the building, thinking she'd mistaken which door he would be at. Finally, she pulled into an empty slot and hurried inside. Like it or not, she had to get back to the clinic.

Thinking that he may have been called back to court, she decided she could only hand off the phone to whoever was at front desk in the department. To her amazement, she found the room empty—except for Noah speedily collecting papers on his desk, and then turning around to glance through the miniblinds.

Relieved to see that he hadn't forgotten about her, she playfully scoffed. "Too late, Mr. Assistant District Attorney!"

He wheeled around, and his expression was a priceless mixture of worry-turned-surprise-turned-pleasure. In the next instant, he was rushing across the room. Momentarily ignoring the iPhone that she offered him—he hugged her, rocking her in his arms. "I'm sorry that I wasn't outside. I was waylaid by the defense attorney on this case."

Perfectly willing to forgive him the small inconvenience, she handed over the phone. "I'll bet you felt lost without this. I sure missed your text messages."

He chuckled. "I missed sending them. The rest of the time, I felt naked without it."

"Interesting," she mused, and slowly ran a finger down his red tie. "I haven't noticed you being shy about nudity around me."

With a glance over his shoulder to check the doorway, he took hold of her upper arms and started walking her backward.

"Noah...?"

He didn't stop until they were in a small, secluded space made up of file cabinets and supply shelves. "I can't let you go without at least one taste of you."

He locked his lips to hers and drove his tongue deep. Almost instantly, Rylie felt his body harden against hers. She moaned softly, helplessly leaning into the kiss.

Then, like that dreaded and cruel bucket of cold water, someone cleared his throat.

They jerked apart like kids caught necking in a parked car. "I'm so sorry," Rylie whispered to Noah. Before he could respond, she rushed for the exit, keeping her head ducked as she passed District Attorney Vance Underwood.

Just as she reached the hallway, she heard, "Noah? Wasn't that the trailer-park girl? The one Marv Nelson had trouble with a week or so ago?"

"No trouble, sir. A misunderstanding easily enough resolved. And there's no trailer park. Her RV is quite a machine."

"What was her name?" Vance went on, clearly ignoring him. "Quince?"

"Quinn. Vance, you're wrong—"

"Now you listen to me, Noah," Vance continued, an edge entering his voice. "I didn't imagine that an out-of-state warrant existed, did I? And from anyone on the outside looking in, she got special treatment and never spent so much as an hour in jail."

Frozen in place, Rylie couldn't have left if she wanted to. Not only did she find his censorious tone offensive, but he was acting as though the sheriff had done the wrong thing in letting her pay her fine and go home.

Noah remained civil, but firm. "There was no such thing as special treatment. The matter was discussed with all parties involved and—considering the mitigating circumstances—we saw no reason to make a huge production out of something that would cost taxpayers needless expense. Ms. Quinn has satisfied her debt to the State of California and has otherwise been a model resident in our county. I should confirm, this had the sheriff's blessing."

"Maybe," Vance replied, in his subtly droning, nasal voice, "but the whole thing has the unpleasant after-taste of favoritism, Noah. I appreciate your youth and virility. You work hard and deserve your playtime, even if I question where you're shopping for it."

"That will be enough. Sir."

"No, this is enough," Vance whispered, his *s*'s sounding like a serpent's hiss. "You don't embarrass *my* office. I don't care who you do what with in your free time. You remember that you want and need my endorsement to become my successor. That's not happening if she's part of the package."

Stunned and sickened by what she was hearing, Rylie couldn't stand to hear any more. All but running from the building, she barely dodged an elderly couple coming up the sidewalk and overcompensated, slamming her forearm into a U.S. Mail drop-off box on her right side.

"Sorry, sorry," she cried, blinded by pain.

It was a relief to reach her uncle's truck and get away from there. The tears that flooded her eyes were as much from emotional pain as the physical kind.

The D.A. had all but called her a slut! Trash! She knew that her pedigree was nothing like that of a Prescott—she honestly didn't know anything about Vance Underwood's family tree, but it didn't matter considering his position. However, he'd had no right to besmirch her family's good name. They were humble and hardworking people who'd built their own success one customer at a time! And what was the D.A. threatening to do to Noah's future? Her heart ached. He'd already given up so much of his dreams by leaving his position in Houston. Now he was in danger of even losing a post that Rylie knew was beneath his abilities.

She couldn't let that happen.

How she made it back to the clinic, she didn't know. Wishing she could run into the RV and bury herself in the pillows where she and Noah had made love last night, she forced herself to enter the clinic. Her forearm was throbbing and she thought some cold tap water would help.

She was holding her arm under the faucet when Gage came out of his office with a stunningly beautiful, Amazon-tall woman. Naturally, ever sharp-eyed Gage took in her situation and frowned.

"What happened?"

"You know me. Miss Clumsy."

"Uh-huh." Gage turned to the raven-haired goddess. "This is Rylie, who I was telling you about."

Hearing undercurrents she wished she didn't, Rylie shut off the water and quickly patted her arm dry before grabbing up her clinic jacket. The last thing she needed was a guest looking at her with pity.

"Rylie, I want you to meet Dr. Laurel Lancer, a recent graduate of Texas A&M's veterinary school. She's finishing up an internship south of here for extra certification and wants to do another here. I'm hoping after that we can bring her in as a partner."

Having given herself a pep talk that things couldn't get worse, Rylie realized she'd been a fool. "How—how wonderful for you, Dr. Lancer. Welcome." As she summoned a bright smile, she felt a new pain—as if someone was taking out her appendix using only fingernails.

"I've heard great things about your talents with animals, and your rapport with the locals," the young woman replied. Her onyx gaze dropped to Rylie's injury. "That's going to be some bruise, and it's already swollen. Are you sure you didn't break it?"

"Fortunately, I don't have the weight to combine with speed to create enough velocity to do anything thoroughly," she quipped. "It's just another bump to add to the collection."

Rylie didn't know if it was the woman's superior height, her stop-you-in-your-tracks beauty that appeared to be partly credited to some Native American heritage, her enviable degree and future, or that she was simply so close to Rylie's age that she represented everything Rylie would never be…but it didn't matter. Dr. Laurel Lancer was here on the tailwind that had already kicked Rylie off of her dreamy trajectory. Enough was enough. She was cashing out on everything. The Amazon was going to be a partner, and Rylie had to leave.

As though from another dimension, she heard Gage say, "Most of her family is up in Montana."

"Oh," Rylie replied, suddenly frowning. "Um…isn't yours…?"

"That's right, it turns out our families know each other slightly."

Great, Rylie thought.

"Laurel's father and some brothers are ranchers, and another brother is in oil."

So what was she doing in Texas? Rylie thought. They didn't have veterinarian schools in Montana? Belatedly, she forced herself to extend her hand. "Mine is mostly in California. They're in building, dust and rust."

Laurel just studied her as though she was a lab project, while Gage choked back a laugh. Feeling like a bigger fool than before, Rylie said, "You'll have to excuse me. I... I have a Pekingese waiting for me up front, who, like Mick Jagger, has a face that only a mother can love. It'll take every second I can spare him to get him in shape."

Could things get any worse? she wondered.

At least Dr. Stunning was gone by the time Rylie was done with the Pekingese, Wokie, as his mistress called him. But at soon as they were gone, Rylie's uncle appeared, acting like a mosquito buzzing around her head.

"You look terrible. What's happened? Did Wokie bite you?"

"Of course not." Rylie showed him her hands to prove as much, but it was a mistake. Her bruise was now a lump the size of a kiwi, and about the color of the fruit's seeds. Not something that Uncle Roy could miss.

"How the hell did you do that?"

"It's Senior Citizens Day. You see one, you automatically throw yourself at the nearest mailbox in celebration."

"Oh, baby." He sighed. "The right eye again?"

She gestured, signaling that talking about it wasn't worth his energy or hers. "I guess you met Dr. Lancer?"

"Yeah. Wow. I knew Doc was talking to someone, but I didn't expect...that."

Keeping her back to the old-timers and her voice low, Rylie said, "It's okay, Uncle Roy. You can say 'gorgeous.' Great pedigree to go with the capital investment. Add an actual license qualifying her to make independent ranch and dairy calls. What did I leave out?"

"Your feelings are hurt."

Rylie didn't hear him come up to the front. But in her current frame of mind, which was anything but reliable, she chose to be less than honest and shook her head stubbornly as she turned to face Gage. "I'm good. And God knows, you need someone to have your back, Doc. But I've been thinking…with another doctor, things are going to get a little crowded in here. If you need me to clear out, I'll totally understand."

Gage looked flabbergasted. "Are you kidding? I'm trying to build up the clinic, not whittle it down to the smallest common denominator. And there's plenty of room yet in this building. When there isn't, we can expand." He tilted his head, trying to get a better look at her face. "I thought you were happy here."

Feeling as though her heart was taking a torturously slow turn through a shredder, Rylie whispered, "Oh, Doc… I am. I was. I just…." She swallowed, determined to put the best face on the situation. She loved everyone here and wanted them to understand that.

"I've been a fool," she said with a self-deprecating shrug. "It's not just about what you're doing. I understand it. I may not be head-over-heels thrilled, but I'm a big girl, I get it. It's just that it's been one of those revelation days, you know? It's made me see that maybe it's best for everyone if you go with a whole change of scenery."

To his credit, Gage kept his usual calm demeanor and waited for her to say what she really meant.

"I'm not a good fit here," she told him. "And I'm

not right for someone like Noah Prescott, either." She laughed mirthlessly. "The irony is, he needs someone like…like… Dr. Lancer."

Chapter 8

Wondering if closing time would ever come, Rylie was relieved when she could finally retreat to her RV. While it was evident that Gage had wanted badly to continue their discussion, considering her out-of-right-field outburst, life—in their case, business—intruded. The reception room started filling up as if there was an epidemic. Then came news of an overturned cattle truck several miles up the interstate, which had forced Gage to apologize to those with pets still waiting to be seen and hurry to that emergency.

Rylie's uncle Roy had gone, too. She was relieved. She didn't want to answer questions, and she desperately needed time alone to think. Then, of course, there was Noah.

He started sending her text messages shortly after she'd left the courthouse. For the first time since they'd started to indulge in that method of communication, she didn't respond. Later the calls started, and she ignored them, too. It was no surprise, then, when, only minutes after she retreated to the RV for the night, she saw car lights coming around to the back of the clinic.

With her heart working like a Triple Crown contender, she forced herself to open the door to him. He looked the same—handsome, concerned, polished. The "can do" guy. And he would succeed if she had any say in the matter.

"Thank God," he said, jogging up the stairs. "Did your phone go out on you? When you didn't answer my calls, never mind my texts, I got really worried." He paused only long enough to take in first impressions of her standing there, her arms wrapped around her middle. "You're sick?"

He wasn't totally wrong. She'd showered and brushed her teeth twice, hoping she would stop feeling as though she'd spent the afternoon losing what wasn't in her stomach, only none of that had worked very well. However, going with the affirmative would still be lying by evasion. "It's just been a long day."

"They all are for you these days."

"A particularly long one." For him, too. Was he going to tell her? He didn't look much better than she did, but he had a better grip on his self-control than she did. That gave her an ugly thought: maybe what she was going to do would end up being a relief for him.

"I heard about the accident on the interstate," he said slowly. "I'd hoped Doc wouldn't take you out there."

"No, my uncle went."

"Because of that? Sweetheart, did you get it x-rayed?"

He'd noticed the bruise. "No need. But I'm sure it had something to do with that." Rylie watched MG try to get Noah's attention, and when he failed to realize that, Rylie made things easier for him. "MG, down. Not your time."

Her tone was one she rarely used. It brooked no nonsense and, looking crestfallen, MG went to the couch and curled up in the corner of it and hid her face in the cushions.

Perfect, Rylie thought, hating herself for hurting her sweet friend. With a sigh, she gestured to Noah. "I was going to have wine in the hope that it would make me sleep. Would you like a glass?"

She prayed that he would decline. She was losing her nerve to go through with this, and hoped in his worry about her needing rest, he would leave. But that wasn't happening. Watching her as though he was still analyzing what was going on, he nodded at her offer.

"But I'll get it. Sit down."

As he took off his jacket and poured the wine, she chose to sit in the recliner by the door. He was less apt to try to draw her into his arms there. Tucking her bare legs under the sleep shirt, she hugged herself again and tried to make sensible small talk. Maybe the more normal she sounded, the sooner he would be willing to leave.

"How did the rest of your day go?" she asked, hoping her smile didn't look as false as her voice sounded to her own ears.

"I have to admit, long, too."

The grim note in his voice told her that he was thinking about Vance's nasty remarks again. Now he would tell her, she thought.

"It's better now that I see for my own eyes that you're safe, if not one hundred percent." He brought her glass and waited for her to sip a little.

Noah leaned over her to kiss her gently. "You're awfully preoccupied."

His observation gave her a branch, something to grip on to. Maybe it could still make things easier than the truth. "Doc interviewed for a partner today."

"A partner?" Noah's dark eyebrows drew together then lifted as he took stock of that idea. "I thought he was just looking for help, not someone to share in the business with him."

"That surprised me, too. Worse yet, she only graduated a while ago."

"Ouch." Scowling, Noah reasoned, "That has to be a painful reminder. What was Gage thinking? He couldn't find someone with a little more experience?"

Rylie shrugged and took a sip of her wine, although her stomach warned her that she would pay for it. "It isn't in his makeup to intentionally cause anyone embarrassment or hurt. Dr. Lancer is undoubtedly as special as she is qualified."

Rylie thought that the woman may have squeezed him into her itinerary at the last minute. Maybe she'd been disappointed wherever she'd interviewed previously. Maybe that's why Gage hadn't given them more warning. The list of possibilities kept growing. Whatever the case, Gage couldn't be faulted. Things just happened the way they did.

"You know what you need?" Noah said, taking her glass and putting it down on the side table along with his own. "You need to stop thinking so much." With that he lifted her into his arms, only to sit down himself, setting her onto his lap. Then he began kissing her, gently, repeatedly, first only on her mouth, then over her eyes, her chin, between her eyebrows and the hollow at the base of her throat.

This was something they could agree on, Rylie thought with bittersweet emotions, making each caress feel all the more poignant. One last time...

Her decision made, she wrapped her arms around his neck and kissed him back with everything in her heart. Noah immediately responded with a welcoming murmur and tightened his arms. He slid his hand into her short hair to keep her close and feasted on her lips and urged her on with his tongue.

Beneath her hips, she felt his quick arousal. She rocked against him and brushed her breasts against his chest.

"Are you sure, sweet? Because my self-control isn't at its best tonight," he told her, his breath starting to grow shallow.

"That's what I want. Make love to me, Noah."

Without another word, he carried her to the bed.

The room was lit only by the light coming from the other side of the RV, which was a relief to Rylie. She didn't want Noah to study her with his usual intensity for fear of what he would see. For her part, she closed her eyes and just gave herself up to the moment.

"You know what keeps taking my breath away?" he whispered against the side of her neck as he worked on unfastening his clothes. "It's how fast you've become a necessity to me." He began spreading kisses down her chest, at the same time drawing up her shirt, until he reached bare skin. Then he slipped the fabric over her head. Next he slid his palm down over her silk-clad

mound, directing his fingers between her thighs, and
planted a kiss on the bare skin just above it. "I think
about this all the time—how perfect you are. How you
respond to my touch."

Rylie knew what he intended, but she couldn't bear
it—not tonight. This was going to be hard enough without that intimate gift. Writhing free, she urged him
onto his back, slipped off her panties and finished releasing him from his clothes. "I just want you inside
me."

Her urgency released, and then fed Noah's, and he
shucked his pants while she spread his shirt wide to
where she could kiss him all over. Only when she began
taking him inside her, he hesitated. "Protection...?"

"I told you, I'm on the pill." And she wanted to feel
all of him, just once.

Noah wanted it, too. She knew from the way his
hands trembled slightly as he took hold of her hips and
urged her closer, and deeper.

Tears burned behind her closed lids as she rocked
against him, urging him on in the eager dance that
was quickly going out of control between them. As
delicate muscles contracted around him, she felt him
spasm, then pour into her. It brought her own ecstasy,
and she collapsed against him, letting the pillows absorb her tears.

As the silence between them grew, Noah remained
almost motionless except for stroking Rylie's hair. He
had the strangest feeling—as if he was waiting for
something that he knew wasn't coming.

Finally, he eased her onto her back, so he could see
her face in the dim light. He knew she was awake by

her breathing, but she kept her eyes closed. Even so, he could swear there was moisture under her lashes. He stroked the delicate skin beneath her right eye and it came away wet.

The worry that had been growing all day was now a tight band around his chest. "What's wrong?" he asked, wiping the moisture from beneath her other eye.

"Nothing," she whispered. "It was perfect."

Every time was perfect with her. "I'd be the happiest man on earth if I knew those were tears of joy."

Rather than voice that lie, she covered her eyes with the back of her hand. "Noah, don't ruin this."

The band tightened to where he could barely drag in another breath. "What's that supposed to mean?"

"I can't do this anymore."

Do what? he wondered, each beat of his heart a worsening pain. Make love with him? But she'd asked him to. Or was that only her parting gift to him?

"That sounds like…goodbye."

"It is."

"Why?"

Her lips moved, but no sound came out.

"You're leaving," he said, voicing the only thought that came into his head. "Gage didn't fire you. He wouldn't."

"I'm making it easier for him."

"Where are you going?"

"I don't know yet. Just somewhere better suited to me. Somewhere where I'm better needed."

"You're needed here. *I* need you here."

She finally opened her eyes. They shimmered with new tears. "Noah, I heard what the D.A. said to you today. I'm sorry—I never meant to eavesdrop, but the moment he began criticizing you, I froze."

He groaned and leaned over to kiss her forehead. "Baby, I'm sorry. He was being an ass—and a hypocrite. His wife may be a former congressman's daughter, but she's on so many prescription drugs, most of the time he has to hide her car keys to keep her from hurting herself or someone else. He has no business lecturing anyone about anything."

"He knows the voters. I'm not right for where you're going. You deserve someone who will complement your life."

"I'm looking at her."

With a sound of frustration or desperation, she sat up, reached for her shirt and tugged it over her head. "You're not listening to me. We grew up in a two-bedroom house with one tiny bathroom. When I was too old to sleep in my parents' room, I was moved to the couch. It wasn't until I was thirteen when they turned half of the garage into a bedroom for Dustin that I had my own room. Sure, by the time I was fifteen, we moved into a bigger house, and my parents have a comfortable life now, but I still remember those days when Dustin outgrew his T-shirts, they became my pj's and play clothes because there was no money for buying us both new things. I've worked since I could give change for a dollar, five dollars, a ten and a twenty. And I never even went to the prom, Noah, because I was working two jobs, scared to death that I wouldn't have enough saved for college tuition."

Noah had already learned enough to know that their pasts were polar opposites, but that didn't matter. What mattered was what you did with what you had.

"The fact that you got through college despite all of that is beyond admirable," he declared. "Then most of vet school. I know I acted like a jerk when we first met, but you forgave me for that."

"Of course. I told you."

"And no one will ever be able to accuse my mother of being a snob."

"Noah!" Rylie cried. "You can't win the D.A. seat without Vance Underwood's endorsement."

"Who says?" He framed her face with his hands. "Rylie, I'm in love with you. The rest doesn't matter... unless you don't feel the same way?"

He never expected the words to come out—not that way. She deserved better. He'd intended to do this right, to create a moment, a moment she would never forget. Instead, he watched everything disintegrate in front of his eyes as she bowed her head.

"I'm sorry," she whispered. "But I don't."

"Have you lost your mind?"

Rylie didn't know how much more that she could take. Of all people, she thought that Uncle Roy would be relieved that she'd sent Noah away and wouldn't be seeing him again. Noah's reaction last night— the stunned silence as he'd dressed, and the way he'd walked to the door, paused and then uttered a hoarse "Goodbye," without looking at her—had almost been her undoing. Now her uncle was clearly going to finish breaking her heart because of the rest she'd told him— that she was going to leave Sweet Springs.

Wearily, she shifted the three-quarters-full coffee-pot to the extra burner and started the second pot. "You heard me. Please don't yell. I'll explain."

"What's to explain? I have ears. You're walking away. From this." He swept his hands to encompass the clinic.

Rylie pressed her hand against her stomach. Aside from not getting any sleep last night from all of the upheaval, she felt sick. There was proof that upbeat people didn't handle the downfalls of life better than anyone else.

"I think it's in the best interest of everyone," she began. "Gage has a great opportunity with Dr. Lancer."

"But why does that mean you need to leave?"

"Because now I'll have two bosses, and I'm not sure one of them will be thrilled to have me around. It's also better if she has input on the staff here."

"She will," Roy replied. "For those coming next. But I know during that closed-door meeting that Gage showed her what's in the computer. He would have to for someone taking in a partner. So she already knows what an asset you are. And Doc confirmed it several times over as he gave her a tour of the place. I heard your name mentioned repeatedly in reference to ideas you'd suggested, and improvements in operations." Taking a stabilizing breath, Roy shook his head and poured himself a mug of coffee. "I knew something was wrong yesterday when you got back from Rusk. You looked like—" He stopped the mug halfway to his lips. "Well, crap. This isn't about Dr. Lancer at all."

"Oh, really, Uncle Roy," she replied with a shaky laugh, "she's part of it."

"Bull. This is all about Prescott."

"What's all the hollering about?" Stan Walsh complained as he shuffled down the side entrance to join them.

Roy hooked a thumb at Rylie, his expression disgusted. "She says she's leaving."

Stan squinted at her as though he couldn't see her, let alone grasp the idea. "Seriously?"

She gestured helplessly, having no energy to start from the beginning again.

"Aw. That's not right," Stan said.

"What's not right?" Pete Ogilvie demanded as he entered the room.

"Rylie here says she wants to leave."

"She doesn't *want* to leave," Roy all but snarled. "She's got issues." He cast Rylie a speaking glance as if to suggest that was as far as he was going to defend her—or buy her time before she had to say more.

"Is one of them the life-size doll who was here yesterday?" Jerry Platt asked as he arrived. He paused at the box of doughnuts Roy had brought, eyeing them, even though he patted his still-trim belly. "I love you bunches, Rylie, but I'd consider adopting a pet if it would get me an appointment with her."

"Oh, put a muzzle on it," Stan snapped. "The only animal you should be allowed to adopt is a porcupine." He squeezed Rylie's shoulder, his expression growing tender. "She seems like a nice lady," he told her, "but you'll always be our number one. Besides, you accepted us right away. I got the feeling that she didn't cater to us being here."

"Aw, Stan, that's sweet," Rylie told him, rising on tiptoe to kiss his weathered cheek.

"Where's Warren? Isn't Warren here yet?" Jerry asked, glancing around. "If anyone can talk you into staying, he will."

"Warren won't be coming this morning," Gage said

as he entered through the back door. "His wife died during the night."

As Rylie gasped and the others murmured words of regret and concern for Warren Atwood, Gage shared what he knew. Apparently, the chief of police had called him first thing this morning to say he'd just come from the nursing home himself, and that Warren was at the funeral home with the body.

Bernadette Atwood, "Bernie," as Warren and everyone else who knew and loved her had referred to her, had spent the past few years in the Sweet Springs facility as Alzheimer's took control. They all knew that he visited her every morning, before coming to join his *compadres* at the clinic, and ended his day sitting with her. But it had been rough on him, as Bernie had spent a few months now between this world and the next. Now that devoted watch was over.

As everyone grew silent, Rylie pressed her hand to her mouth, thinking of how awful this had to be for poor Warren. He was a strong man, and a tough man, but the disease had been his Achilles' heel, the way Bernie had been his heart.

She felt a hand on her shoulder. Turning, she saw Gage tilt his head toward his office.

"Let's talk."

As conversation resumed, Gage poured himself a mug of coffee, then led the way down the hall to the paneled room. He waited for her to pass, and then shut the door behind them.

"I won't beat around the bush," he told her as he motioned for her to sit down. "When I first walked in I heard someone talking about you leaving and something about Laurel not wanting you around. Let me just confirm that nothing could be further from the truth. I wouldn't consider her if she couldn't blend in with everyone here, and I do mean everyone."

"I appreciate that," Rylie replied, grateful for the chair. She hadn't even bothered getting any coffee yet, unsure that it would stay down. "The guys...don't really understand. Neither does Uncle Roy."

"Neither do I," Gage said drily as he settled in his seat behind the cluttered desk. He took a sip of the steaming black coffee, then set it on a clear spot on the blotter and rested his forearms around it as he leaned toward her and studied her with tenderness and concern. "Why don't you explain it to me? The fact is, we can't afford to lose you, Rylie. This whole idea was to enhance, not to detract from your presence here. Good grief, you've increased our revenue by twelve percent just in the short while you've been here. That's not counting that you've relieved me to do more that I needed to do. And don't tell me that you couldn't work with Laurel. You could charm the tusks off a wild boar. Now, I appreciate that she represents a painful reminder of what you've given up. My heart aches for you, and Brooke's does, too. We consider you like a little sister already. That said, I believe that you're just too fine a person not to be able to work through whatever feelings you might have against her."

"Please stop," Rylie said, rubbing at the tension headache threatening to split her skull wide open. "You're being way too kind and generous. I admit, I wanted to dislike her on sight, and when you said 'partner,' a part of me was crushed."

Although he nodded in understanding, he said, "But you won't let it because you're not a quitter."

She rolled her eyes, but a hint of a smile twitched up one corner of her mouth at his high opinion of her. It meant the world. "I don't want to be a quitter... only sometimes things happen that make you realize it would be better for the other person if you weren't around."

Gage narrowed his eyes, his gaze speculating. "We're not just talking about Laurel, are we?"

"I guess not." she admitted softly.

"Is there anything I could do to help?"

She knew he and Brooke had discussed that, too. "I think I've done enough. At least, I know I've hurt Noah too deeply for him to ever want to speak to me again."

Gage looked skeptical. "He practically got you thrown in jail and you somehow worked through that."

"Let's just say, I couldn't let him sacrifice what he would have to for me."

Taking that in, Gage nodded slowly. "You have to love someone a whole lot to be that sacrificing."

This time she was able to smile, but it was a smile of sadness. "I'm glad you understand. Only, this conversation is just between us, okay?"

"Provided you give me a full two weeks' notice?" he countered. "Heck, it'll take Laurel a month before she has her business settled, gets back to Montana for a quick visit and gets back here."

"Of course. I owe you more."

"Don't tempt me," he replied with a determined look. "And don't think I won't use every single day of that time to reason you out of this decision."

The next two days were all about Warren, and the mood around the clinic was solemn and sad. For the first time in almost a year, Uncle Roy told Rylie, the round table had a missing member for more than one day.

Gage closed the clinic for the morning of the funeral, and an evergreen wreath with a black ribbon was put on the door below the note explaining the reason for the temporary inconvenience to customers. Having lost a son in Iraq several years ago—the highest-ranking officer to be killed there—Warren had no immediate family left and he asked Rylie to sit beside him at the service. It was both a proud and painful experience, as he held her hand between his throughout the service.

The rest of the day passed in a blur, the shortened business hours creating a packed waiting room for over an hour after closing time. When Rylie finally made it to the RV, she was so emotionally and psychologically spent, she collapsed on the bed and fell into the deepest sleep of her life.

She woke up the following morning feeling as if she was rising out of a coma, and it took her several moments to realize where she was and to remember all that happened yesterday. Coming quickly on the heels of that was Noah, and her heart wrenched anew. Somehow she had to not think about him. There was too much to do, and she needed to be able to function.

"Oh, jeez," she groaned, as her gaze landed on the clock on the nightstand. It confirmed what the daylight around the miniblinds also did. She was going to be the last person at the clinic, not the first—and MG had to be in total discomfort.

Thankfully, she'd passed out still dressed in her black T-shirt and jeans. She ran into the bathroom, telling MG, "Give me one minute more. Thank you for having an iron bladder the size of a watermelon."

She brushed her teeth and didn't even run a comb through her hair. While MG did her business, she would poke her head into the clinic and explain and apologize, then get a quick shower.

Wondering why no one had knocked on the door or buzzed her cell phone to wake her, she yanked on her windbreaker and opened the door to let MG out—only to shriek in surprise, before clapping her hand over her mouth.

Oh my—

Laughter and cheers erupted through the crowd. Someone yelled, "Surprise!"

Surprise nothing, she thought. She was in the process of having a heart attack. Everyone she knew was out there—Gage, Brooke, Uncle Roy, Jane, the musketeers…

"Jane?"

As MG barked and trotted down the steps, her tail wagging as though she thought all of this company was for her, Rylie tried to make sense of what was happening. Then her heart skipped a beat as her gaze locked with Noah's.

If the brisk morning air didn't cause her to shiver and clutch the windbreaker tight around herself, she would have been convinced that she was dreaming. But, no, there was Audra in her wheelchair with Ramon gripping the handles, and Aubergine and Livie framing her like human bookends.

As her gaze returned to Noah, Uncle Roy stepped forward to offer his hand to help her down the stairs. "It's an intervention, Sunshine."

"It's something, all right," she muttered, belatedly realizing that she hadn't showered or washed her hair and the makeup she'd put on yesterday must be long gone.

"Come on down out of there so we can all watch this. I can't see."

Who was that? Rylie wondered, finally taking her uncle's hand and descending the stairs. Then she saw more people—their mailman and the chief of police, Bob Burnett—whom she'd barely spoken to beyond saying "hello"—and about a dozen more. But once again her gaze was drawn to Noah. She couldn't help herself, or keep from letting him see how wonderful it was to see him again, regardless of what she'd told him.

"I don't think she gets it yet," Audra said, beaming.

"It's shock," Livie said matter-of-factly.

Audra squeezed Noah's hand, only to push him forward. "Get to work, son. Make me proud."

He made his way to Rylie. Dressed in a navy sports coat and jeans, he looked his usual charismatic self. But his hand was shaking as he took her cold left hand in his, and he lowered himself to one knee.

"Oh, my God," Rylie whispered. Suddenly, her hand started shaking as much as his.

"Sweetheart, you already know how I feel about you. You burst into my life and through my defenses like nothing I'd ever experienced before," he began. "You lit a fever in my heart that was numb from neglect and bad choices. I wake needing to see you, and go to sleep aching to hold you. No one and nothing can come before that. Marry me, Rylie. You're as precious and necessary to me as my next breath."

Unable to deny what she was feeling, or the yearning burning in his eyes, Rylie could manage only to nod. However, that was enough for Noah to draw a ring out of his pocket and slip it onto her finger. Then he stood and crushed her against him to the sound of cheers and applause. The ruckus got even louder when he kissed her.

"You don't have to say it so loud that everyone hears," he whispered near her ear. "But you'd damned better say it to me. I can see the truth shimmering in every inch of your face, and feel it in the arms hugging me back."

She threw her head back and laughed with joy. "I love you!" she declared. "You, you, you. From the first, it was you!"

Epilogue

November

"It's time to cut the cake and go, my love."

Rylie leaned back against Noah's firm body and covered the hands tenderly holding her at the waist with her own. "I'm ready."

She had been Mrs. Noah Jamison Prescott for almost two hours, and she had yet to be alone with her husband for one minute. She only had to turn and look into his glowing brown eyes to see passion waiting to be unleashed.

They had been married in the Prescott family's church—Sweet Springs Methodist—and the reception was at Haven Land. Even though over one hundred were in attendance, it was generally easy to make their way to the dining room, where the cake was set up.

Rylie loved the bouquet Brooke had made for her, a happy autumnal collection of chrysanthemums, some of which almost matched the warm glow of her hair. She also loved how her gown whispered with every step. It had a lace bodice with a straight cut, Audrey Hepburn neckline, V-back and full satin skirt. Noah had remembered her sadness over never having worn a gown and convinced her that she have a one-of-a-kind dress for the wedding. He'd also insisted on flying in her parents and Dustin, and they had been staying upstairs in the guest rooms for two days now.

As they passed Dustin, Rylie stopped to give him another hug. They would be leaving on their honeymoon for a week in Ireland right after they changed clothes, and she didn't know how long it would be before she saw him again. She cupped his darkly handsome face in her hands and kissed him on both cheeks.

"My, munchkin, you clean up fine," he said, his dark gray eyes saying much more.

He'd been as upset as her parents had been with the news about her partial blindness, and when he'd first gotten off the plane, he'd swept her into his arms and hugged her so fiercely, she'd thought she was going to end up with a cracked rib.

"I'm so glad you approve—and that you came."

"I had to see for myself that you were really happy." Dustin released her to shake Noah's hand. "See that she stays that way," he added, with a mock narrow-eyed glare.

The two of them had hit it off almost immediately and, laughing, Noah hugged him easily. "Count on it. And don't be a stranger. There's always a room for you here."

Next they stopped to say a few words to her parents and Uncle Roy, who were still catching up on news. Rylie had told her uncle to bring Jane, but he'd confessed that there would be so much family talk going on that she would be bored. Rylie hoped that was all, and that the budding "couple" hadn't actually hit a road bump.

"I'm so excited for you," her mother whispered to her as they embraced.

"And proud," her father added, kissing her forehead.

It was good to see the musketeers, especially Warren, who was looking better in the past weeks since Bernie's passing. Rylie kissed each one, and Gage and Brooke, who stood nearest to the cake.

Brooke looked radiant in her royal-blue matron-of-honor dress with her baby bump now unmistakable. Best man Gage kept his arm around her waist, his fingertips never far from the gentle swell of her abdomen. They were going to keep MG at their place while the newlyweds honeymooned, since MG and Humphrey were solid pals.

Although they had been invited, Vance and his wife sent their regrets. When Noah announced he felt he should resign, Vance quickly apologized for his remarks, and had been decent if not warm and fuzzy ever since. It was clear that he knew who the best candidate for the office was, and smart enough not to cost the county Noah's service.

Laurel had been invited, too, but she was still in Montana one last week to spend Thanksgiving with her family before starting at the clinic.

Rylie and Noah posed for several pictures of the

cake cutting for the photographer, and then stopped to kiss Audra on their way upstairs.

"Don't party so much that you tire yourself out," Noah warned her.

Rylie echoed his concern. In the weeks since she'd sold her bus to Jerry Platt—who planned to treat his buddies to a trip to Vegas, while the newlyweds were on their honeymoon—she'd been staying in the spare bedroom across from Audra's, and they'd enjoyed getting to know each other better.

"I won't, darlings. I know if I'm not on top of my game, you'll deprive me of all the stories about your trip when you return."

Once up in Noah's bedroom and the door was shut, Noah reached for Rylie. "Oh, God, I need this," he said, claiming her lips for a long, deep kiss. "Whose idea was it to spend so many hours in a plane?" Being circumspect, he had done without her company for nearly a month, and the strain of being in opposite wings in the mansion had taken its toll.

"Yours. Be glad my ancestors don't come from Australia," she teased, turning in his arms so he could unzip her gown. "And at least we have tonight in the airport hotel before our flight in the morning."

"I'm not sure I'll even last through that drive," he said as he exposed bare skin, and the daintiest lingerie. He groaned as he cupped her lace-covered breasts. "Sweet heaven," he said, pressing a kiss to her bare shoulder. "You're sure Aubergine is going to have your things moved in here by the time we get back?"

"The moment the furniture store delivers the extra armoire. Why you thought we needed another, I don't know. My clothes will fit perfectly in the closet."

"It's for all the sexy undies I plan to buy you," he said, caressing her until her nipples were taut nubs. Then he grew serious. "Love, I know we've talked and already made tentative plans about school, and all, but I was wondering…"

Rylie turned to face him. He'd made her cry when he'd insisted on paying off her college debt and suggested—with Gage's encouragement—that she return to school to finish her veterinarian training. She might not be able to handle every case, but she could specialize in small-animal care—and Gage said he would welcome her as a partner, as well.

"Ask away. Anything," she said, meaning that. She loved him so much, if he asked her to wait a year before returning to school, she would.

"I just wanted Mother to have the strength to hold a grandchild in her arms. It would break her heart if she grew too weak."

"No, you're right," Rylie said, moved that he was being so considerate. "So… I'll leave my birth control pills behind?"

Exhaling shakily, Noah touched his head to her forehead. "You know Aubergine will tell Mother when she finds them."

With a wicked grin, Rylie said, "Maybe even before my parents head back to California. That'll be our going-away gift to them all—and more incentive to your mother to stay strong."

"Thank you, my heart. It's been ages since this house has had the sound of children's laughter flowing through it." After a reverent kiss, he added lightly, "What a relief and blessing to have married a woman whom I see eye-to-eye with on the important things."

"Correction, many...many things," Rylie whispered, drawing him closer until they shared the same breath and she could tease him by brushing her lips against his.

"Oh, yes," he murmured, and kissed her with hunger and promise.

* * * * *

Christyne Butler is a *USA TODAY* bestselling author who fell in love with romance novels while serving in the US Navy and started writing her own stories in 2002. She writes contemporary romances that are full of life, love and a hint of laughter. She lives with her family in central Massachusetts and loves to hear from her readers at christynebutler.com.

Books by Christyne Butler

Harlequin Special Edition

Welcome to Destiny

Destiny's Last Bachelor?
Flirting with Destiny
Having Adam's Baby
Welcome Home, Bobby Winslow
A Daddy for Jacoby

Montana Mavericks: 20 Years in the Saddle!

The Last-Chance Maverick

Montana Mavericks: Rust Creek Cowboys

The Maverick's Summer Love

Montana Mavericks: Back in the Saddle

Puppy Love in Thunder Canyon

Visit the Author Profile page
at Harlequin.com for more titles.

PUPPY LOVE
IN THUNDER CANYON

Christyne Butler

To the ladies at WriteRomance,
the best critique partners in the world:
don't know what I would do without you!

And to Susan, Charles and Jennifer...
you all know why.

Chapter 1

"Do you understand everything we talked about during the drive here?"

Annabel Cates pulled into an empty spot in the Thunder Canyon General Hospital parking lot. "I know these visits are routine by now, but it's important we cover the dos and don'ts every time."

She cut the engine, turned to the backseat of her practically new lime-green VW Bug and was rewarded with a sloppy kiss.

"Smiley!" Annabel pushed at the wet nose of her three-year-old golden retriever, her constant companion since she'd brought him home from the local shelter when he was just a pup. "You could've just nodded!"

An excited bark was her pet's answer.

"Yes, I love you, too." Releasing her seat belt, Annabel grabbed her purse and Smiley's leash and got out of her car, pausing to hold the driver's seat up to allow her dog to exit.

Kneeling, she latched the leash on to his collar then straightened the bright blue bandana around his neck, her fingers lingering over the black lettering on the material. "Just think, buddy, a dozen more sessions and we can switch this In Training bandana for one that reads Certified."

Smiley did the exact thing that earned him his name: he smiled. Many told her it was the natural curve of his mouth, a trait common in golden retrievers, but Annabel could tell when her fur baby was happy.

Which was just about all the time.

Smiley's outgoing, friendly personality, to both humans and other animals, made him a great therapy dog. The two of them had completed the required training, registration and certification over the past few months, but the American Kennel Club required fifty visits before being awarded the title of AKC Therapy Dog.

And Annabel wanted that title for Smiley, which didn't explain this particular visit.

"But this one is special, isn't it, boy?" Annabel gave Smiley a quick scratch to the ears then rose, and they walked across the hospital's parking lot.

Once inside, she stopped at the directory near the elevators. The geriatrics and children's areas were the most familiar to her and Smiley, but today they were headed for a specific doctor's office.

Smiley padded along beside her, staying right at her knee, despite the comments, grins and hellos that greeted them. Then a little boy sitting alone on a bench came into view and Annabel felt the familiar tug on the leash.

Almost by instinct, Smiley was drawn to those who were injured and hurting, but not all injuries were visible. A low whimper and the quickening of his wagging tail made the little boy look up. The beginnings of a smile crossed his face. Annabel slowed and allowed Smiley to work his magic.

After a few minutes visiting, Annabel continued on her way, energized by the boy's improved mood and excited chatter to his mother. They stopped outside the elevators and she eyed the hospital directory on the wall.

"Can I help you?"

Annabel turned and found a pretty nurse standing beside her dressed in scrubs, a short-sleeve shirt and loose cotton pants featuring a dizzying pattern of colorful flip-flops. Perfect for a warm August morning in Montana. "Yes, I'm looking for Dr. North's office."

The woman's eyebrows rose, disappearing into her perfect straight bangs. "Dr. Thomas North?"

"If he's an orthopedic surgeon, then yes, he's the one."

"Is Dr. North expecting you?" Her gaze shifted to Smiley for a moment. "Both of you?"

Living by the motto "it's better to beg for forgiveness than ask for permission," Annabel smiled. "We're here to visit with one of his patients."

"Oh. Well, his office suite is on the second floor, far left corner. I could show you if you'd like."

"That would be great, thanks."

The elevator dinged and seconds later the door opened. Annabel and Smiley waited for everyone to depart before they followed the nurse inside. Once on the second floor, they turned a few corners and moved into an office area. At the end of the long hallway Annabel finally spotted the nameplate for Dr. Thomas North.

"Hey, Marge. I've got a visitor for you."

The older woman sitting behind the desk was obviously Dr. North's secretary. Annabel smiled, not missing the glances between her and the nurse or the way her eyebrows rose in matching high arches, as well.

It was okay. She and Smiley were used to it.

"Can I help you, miss?" Marge asked as a beeping noise filled the air.

"Oh, shoot. I've got to go." The nurse checked her pager and smiled. "I so wanted to stick around and see this. Let me know what happens, okay?"

Marge gave her a quick wink and nodded.

A bit confused, Annabel offered her thanks. The nurse waved it off and then disappeared.

"Miss?"

Annabel turned back to the woman. "Oh, I was wondering if Forrest Traub has arrived for his appointment with Dr. North yet?"

"And you are?"

She opened her mouth to reply, but a low, measured voice came from over her shoulder.

"What are you doing here, Annabel?"

She whirled around, surprised to find the man she'd asked about had somehow snuck up on her. Not usually easy to do with Smiley close by. Annabel then noticed her dog remained sitting at her side, perfectly still, not even his tail moving as he stared intently up at Forrest.

And there was a lot to look at.

Tall, muscular, dark hair and the coolest light brown eyes. Yes, he was very nice to look at. Annabel was sure her sisters would use words like *yummy* and *sexy*.

Even the two recently married ones, one of whom was the bride of Forrest's cousin, Jackson, would have to admit good looks ran strong in the Traub family tree.

Too bad the man did nothing for Annabel. No spark, no fizzle.

But that was fine with her. Annabel wanted more. She wanted true love.

The kind of love that came at you like a bolt of lightning and left you dazed, confused and tingly all over. She'd never felt that way in her life, but darn it, after a dry dating spell that had been going on for three years, she was ready for it!

"Hello?" Forrest leaned heavily on a cane with one hand while waving the other in her face. "Annabel?"

"Oh, sorry!" She blinked hard and chased away her dreams. "I…um, I'm here to see you."

His mouth pressed into a hard line as he looked down at Smiley. Annabel did the same, noticing how her pet returned the man's stare with a simple tilt of his head.

She wasn't sure who was sizing up whom.

"How did you know I was going to be at the hospital this morning?" he asked.

Her cheeks turned hot. "I overheard you talking to Jackson at the family barbecue yesterday."

He opened his mouth to say something, but Annabel kept talking. "I know you've been through so much since you got back from overseas. Even before then. And after all that time you spent at Walter Reed Medical Center to still need…well, I thought we could help."

Forrest sighed and directed his gaze to the secretary. "Would it be okay if I—if *we* waited for the doctor inside his office?"

A thrill raced through Annabel. It wasn't a complete victory, but it was a start.

"I'll take full responsibility for them being here," he continued. "And I really need to sit down."

The woman's blue eyes flickered toward the chairs in the corner of the room, but then she said, "Of course, please go in. The doctor is running late, but he should be here soon."

Forrest gestured toward the open doorway with a wave of his hand. Annabel gave a quick tug on the leash and entered the office, Smiley at her side. Forrest followed, and the doctor's secretary stood to close the door behind him.

It was a large room, with a wall of windows behind tightly closed blinds. Two chairs sat in front of a large desk with a more comfortable-looking leather couch along one wall.

Annabel stayed off to the side, not wanting to get in Forrest's way as he dropped into the closest chair. He jammed the cane she didn't remember him using yesterday into the armrest and closed his eyes. His right leg stuck out straight. The bulk of the brace underneath his jeans pulled the worn denim tight around his knee.

This time Smiley tugged a bit at the leash and Annabel released the slack, allowing the dog a bit more leeway while keeping a tight grip on the looped handle. Just in case.

Smiley had been with her yesterday at the barbecue, but he and Forrest didn't interact at all. Considering her pet's reaction to the man a few minutes ago, Annabel wanted to be sure she could pull him away if needed.

Seconds later Smiley was at Forrest's side, instinctively resting his furry head on the man's uninjured leg. Then a deep sigh echoed in the dog's chest.

A full minute passed before Forrest's large hand came to rest behind Smiley's ears, his fingers digging into the dog's thick coat.

Annabel titled her head back slightly and rolled her eyes, upward, pretending a sudden interest in the tiled ceiling. She'd learned it was the fastest way to stop the sharp stinging in her eyes.

Tears, or any sign of pity, were the last thing most people wanted.

The last thing Forrest Traub wanted.

He'd made that very clear while talking to his cousin yesterday about the reason he was in Thunder Canyon for the summer.

"So, Dr. North's secretary seemed a bit hesitant about us being in here." Annabel wanted to talk to Forrest about Smiley being a part of his upcoming medical treatment, but she couldn't just jump into the topic. Not when she'd taken it upon herself to be here instead of waiting for an invitation. "Me and Smiley, that is. Don't tell me your doctor is a stodgy, old curmudgeon who considers his office his inner sanctum?"

"He's not—"

"I'm only asking because the more senior the doctor the more they tend to think the only good medicine is the kind that comes in a pill or from the sharp end of a scalpel." She glanced around for clues, but wasn't close enough to see the graduation dates on the medical degrees hanging from the wall. "Wow, look at all those awards and certificates. Pretty impressive. Then again, this place could use some brightening, a splash of color. Everything in here is brown."

"Annabel—"

"No family photos on his desk. There's not even a plant," she pushed on, afraid if she shut up Forrest was going to kick her and her dog out. "His secretary practically has a jungle around her desk. You'd think she'd put at least one green leafy thing in her boss's office."

"Annabel, stop."

Forrest's soft, yet firm command included an unspoken request for her to look at him. She obeyed, while holding her breath.

"I know why you're here," he said.

She waited a moment, then air became a necessity. "You do?"

"I know all about the work you and your dog do."

"Smiley."

"Excuse me?"

"My dog's name is Smiley, and how do you know?"

"Your sister is very proud of you...and Smiley." Forrest looked down at the dog, continuing to scratch him behind his floppy ears. "But I don't think he can help me."

Annabel had heard those words, many times before and from many different types of people. Young children fighting diseases they couldn't pronounce, the elderly fighting to hold on to their memories and their dignity, and those fighting for the most important thing of all, hope.

"How do you feel?" she asked. "I mean, right now?"

Forrest shook his head. "Forget it, Annabel. I'm not going there."

"I'm not trying to psychoanalyze you." She moved closer. "And I know there's nothing medically we can do—"

"Good. That's my job."

Annabel whirled around at the very deep, very male voice coming from the open doorway.

She immediately cataloged a pair of men's shiny black shoes, dark slacks with a sharp crease down the center of each leg, a cobalt-blue shirt, striped tie and white lab coat.

Dr. Thomas North.

Before her perusal could get past a nicely chiseled jaw, Smiley bounced across the office, pulling his leash to its full length.

Offering an enthusiastic greeting that included a playful bark, her pet rose on his back legs and planted his front paws on the man's midsection.

The move knocked the doctor back against the door frame and sent the paperwork in his hands flying everywhere.

"Smiley!"

Horrified at her pet's unusual behavior, Annabel rushed to help. A quick tug on the collar and Smiley dropped back to all four paws on the ground, but the tail continued to wag up a storm.

"I'm so sorry!" She quickly wound the dog's lead around her palm, pulling him back to her side. "He usually doesn't act like this. I have no idea—" She then focused on the mess on the floor. "Oh, here, let me help you!"

Dropping to her knees, she started grabbing the loose pages and the manila folders, but the man in front of her mirrored her actions. Their heads collided with a resounding crack.

"Oh, fudge nuggets!" Annabel swore and fell back-

ward, landing on her butt. She rubbed hard at the stinging at her temple hoping to erase the pain.

Darn, that hurt!

Suddenly, the warmth and strength of male hands,
one capturing her rubbing fingers and the other cupping her jaw, caused a shiver to dance over her skin.

"Look at me. Are you all right?"

Annabel blinked hard as her world tilted. She could
swear she saw a dizzying array of stars.

Forcing her gaze upward, she found icy blue eyes,
serious and probing and perfectly matching his shirt,
staring intently back at her.

Forget the stars.

This was a full-blown meteor shower.

Thomas North knelt on the carpet, cringing at the
wrinkled paperwork beneath his feet.

The last thing he'd expected when he hurried into
his office, cursing himself for being late thanks to his
weekly breakfast date with his grandmother, was to be
attacked by an overgrown hairy beast.

Or by the woman who was obviously its owner.

"Hello, miss? Did you hear me? Are you okay?"

"Y-yes, I think so."

Ignoring how her breathy words warmed the inside
of his wrist, then transformed into a tremor that raced
up his entire arm, Thomas focused on her pale blue
eyes. They seemed clear and bright, but her speech
was a bit slow.

He waved his hand, holding up three fingers in front
of the woman's face. "How many fingers do you see?"

"Two."

Hmm, not good.

His own head still smarted from where they'd come together with a hard *thunk,* but he didn't have any problem directing Forrest Traub back into the chair he started to rise from or to see the beautiful blonde on the floor in front of him.

Not to mention another blond, with four legs and a wet nose, who was getting in his way.

"And a thumb."

"Excuse me?"

"You're holding up two fingers, index and middle, and your thumb." She laid a hand on the dog's snout, where it tunneled into her loose waves at her shoulder. "I'm okay, Smiley. Please, sit."

The dog obeyed the woman's command, just barely, as its backside continued to shimmy, helped by the rapid wagging of its tail.

Thomas took the paperwork from the woman's grip, added it to the pile he'd shoved back into the top folder. He handed it all to his secretary, who stood over his right shoulder. "Can you put this back into some semblance of order, please?"

"Wow, how did you know she was standing there?" the woman asked, drawing his attention back to her.

"He's got eyes in the back of his head," his secretary quipped as she stepped around them and headed for his desk. "It's something they must teach them in medical school."

Thomas did what he always did when Marge got mouthy. Ignored her. She'd come with the office, having worked for his predecessor for a dozen years, and knew the inner workings of the hospital like the back of her hand. Thomas had only been at TC General two years and he'd be lost without her.

Concentrating on getting the woman back on her feet, he rose and held out one hand. "Do you think you can stand?"

"Of course I can."

She grabbed his wrist with a surprisingly strong grip, and pushed to her feet. He couldn't help but notice the dark polish on her bare toes, the snug fit of her jeans over curvy hips or how the loose ruffled neckline of her blouse had slipped to reveal one bare shoulder.

"Annabel, are you sure you're okay?" Forrest asked.

She turned her head, sending long waves of blond hair flying, covering that shoulder. "Yes, I'm fine."

Thomas swallowed hard and pulled from her heated touch, refocusing his attention on his patient and the reason he was here.

"I don't mind your girlfriend being at your appointment, Mr. Traub—" he moved to sit at his desk, not surprised to find Marge had already left the office, closing the door behind her "—but a dog is a different matter entirely."

"She's not my—"

"Oh, I'm not his girlfriend." The woman dropped into the second empty chair. "Forrest and I are practically family. I'm Annabel Cates."

Thomas tucked away the news these two weren't involved, and why he even cared, to concentrate on finding out what exactly was going on. "Then what are you and your dog doing in my office, Miss Cates?"

"Two reasons, moral support and a proposition you can't refuse."

Chapter 2

"Oh, and please call me Annabel. This is Smiley."

Thomas watched the oversize furball move to sit between her and his patient, ears flopping as it looked back and forth between the two. Then the mutt leaned toward Forrest. Thomas was about to call out, until he saw how the dog rested its chin lightly on Traub's uninjured knee.

"Smiley is a certified therapy dog," she continued. "As his owner and handler, I've been trained and certified, as well. Because of Forrest's injury, and his ongoing treatment, I thought Smiley might be able to help."

He looked back to the woman. "Help how?"

"Therapy dogs are used to assist patients in dealing with the stress and uncertainty that comes with medical issues."

Thomas didn't put much stock in therapy dogs—or

meditation, or aromatherapy, or any number of other alternative therapies that floated around out there.

All he believed in were cold, hard facts. And science.

"Miss Cates, I really don't have time for this. Your visit today is not authorized, by me or, I'm guessing, Mr. Traub, and is distracting to say the least."

"Oh, I don't mean to be any trouble—"

"You've already been that." Thomas dropped his hand to the folder in the middle of his desk, drumming his thumb repeatedly on the cover. An action her dog apparently took as a cue to perch its large front paws on the edge of his desk and swat its large, fluffy tail at the shoulder of Forrest Traub.

"Smiley, stop that and get down." She gently tugged at her dog's leash. "I'm so sorry, Dr. North. I promise you he never acts this way. I guess he must really like you."

"I doubt that."

The dog sat again and returned its attention to Forrest. Miss Cates did the same. "I guess this wasn't such a good idea. Maybe you can spend time with Smiley another day."

"I'd like you to stay." Traub laid his hand back on the dog's head. "Both of you."

Surprised by his patient's request, Thomas studied him closely, silently admitting the animal did seem to be having an impact on the man.

He and Forrest had only met twice before, the last time being a week ago when Thomas had performed a thorough examination of the ex-soldier's injured leg. Forrest had been withdrawn and testy, speaking only when asked a direct question.

In the subsequent reading of his military medical records, Thomas had found the former army sergeant had good reason for his surliness, having gone through hell after a roadside explosive destroyed the Humvee he was riding in during his last tour in Afghanistan.

He'd been in and out of hospitals for the past year and still had not regained full use of his leg. Today though, he seemed more relaxed, a hint of a smile on his face as he continued to scratch the animal's ears and neck.

Of course, this had to be temporary. Depression was common in veterans, as was post-traumatic stress, and Thomas couldn't see how patting a dog could counteract such difficult conditions. The only real cure for Forrest was in the skilled hands of a surgeon.

At any rate, the man clearly enjoyed the dog's company, so Thomas had no choice but to let the mongrel—and Miss Cates—stay.

"Fine." Thomas flipped open the folder. "We planned to discuss my findings and go over recommendations for further treatment. Are you comfortable discussing your condition in front of Miss Cates?"

"Don't worry about me. I've been present at doctor-patient consults before. Confidentiality isn't an issue," the blonde spitfire said with a wave of her hand. "I know how to keep a secret."

Thomas ignored her and waited for his patient to reply.

"Yeah, go ahead," Traub said.

"The results are a bit complex and cover a lot of technical jargon—"

"Get to the bottom line, doc."

Thomas did as requested. "You are going to need surgery. Again."

He waited, but Forrest's only reaction to the news was the fisting of his free hand while the other continued to dig deep into the dog's fur. Thomas glanced at Miss Cates, but her focus was on his ceiling as she blinked rapidly.

"How soon?" Forrest asked.

Thomas looked back at his patient. "The sooner the better. We can schedule you for next week."

The conversation continued for several minutes as Thomas outlined the presurgery preparations, what he planned to accomplish with the delicate procedure and the post-care that would be required.

"Okay, then. I'll see you next week." Forrest finally released his hold on the dog and grabbed his cane. Pushing to his feet, he held out his hand. "I'm betting on you to work your magic, doc."

Thomas rose and returned the man's firm grasp, determined to bring all his skills and knowledge to the operating room, like always. "You can count on it, Forrest."

The man returned Thomas's gaze for a long moment before he released his hand and turned away. "Annabel, I'll walk you to your car if you and Smiley are heading out?"

"That would be great, thanks." Rising, she held out her hand. "Dr. North, it was a pleasure. I would appreciate the opportunity to discuss the possibility of us working together in the future."

Thomas took her hand, the warmth and softness of her skin against his again creating that same zing of awareness he'd felt earlier. "Thank you, but I don't see that happening, Miss Cates."

"I'm sure we can come to a meeting of the minds, not quite as literally as we did this time, I hope." Her full lips twitched and then rose into a playful grin. "Besides, I'm known to be very persuasive when I want something."

For some reason, Thomas believed her. "My schedule is pretty full."

"A half hour." Her fingers tightened around his. "What harm can I do in thirty minutes?"

Thomas cleared throat and released her hand. Seeing her again would be crazy. His mind was already made up. To him, dog therapy was nothing but…fluff. Still, the chance to spend time with this bewitching woman was something he couldn't make himself pass up.

No matter how much his logical side told him it wasn't a good idea.

"Okay, thirty minutes. You can call my secretary to set up a date and time. But be warned, I rarely change my mind."

Once a decision had been made, Thomas stuck by that decision. No matter what. It was something the hospital staff had learned about him in the two years he'd been here.

But agreeing to meet with Miss Cates?

Thomas had seriously reconsidered allowing the meeting to take place many times over the past week.

Thunder Canyon General wasn't a large facility, but thanks to the financial boom that came to town a few years back and the hard work of the hospital administrators—including his grandmother Ernestine North until she finally retired a year ago—the facility lacked for nothing.

Including a thriving gossip grapevine that, until recently, he'd never been a part of. An accomplishment Thomas had worked hard at since accepting his position.

He'd come home to Thunder Canyon determined not to make the same mistake twice. Oh, he knew the staff talked about him. Even after twenty-four months he was still considered the "new" guy around here.

His reputation as a skilled surgeon, and a success rate that was all the more impressive here at TC because of his age, followed him from his previous position at the UCLA Medical Center in Santa Monica.

Thank goodness that was the only thing that had followed.

He also knew some at Thunder Canyon General considered his bedside manner a bit…cold, at least to those who confused emotional involvement with professionalism.

A mistake he wouldn't make again.

But thanks to Annabel Cates and her dog he'd found himself the recipient of even more stares, whispered conversations that ended when he appeared and a few hazing incidents, some subtle and others not so much, starting the day after her visit.

The sweater Marge had worn the other day covered in miniature poodles had been a delicate jab, but the not-so-quiet barking his fellow surgeons and residents engaged in whenever he walked into the doctors' lounge was not.

The old-fashioned glass apothecary jar filled with dog biscuits and tied with a bright bow he'd found on his desk just the other day had been a nice touch. There'd been no card and Marge hadn't said a word about it. Deciding that leaving it in the break room for someone who actually had a pet would only add more fuel to the fire, he'd tucked the jar into the bottom drawer of his credenza.

All of which had to be the reason why Thomas found Annabel on his mind so much over the past several days. While he could admit, at least to himself, there'd been a spark of attraction, she was definitely not his type.

If he had one.

It'd been a while since he'd dated anyone. The women he'd gone out with in the past, when he found the time or desire, were professionals focused on their careers, much like him.

Of course, his last attempt at a serious relationship had dissolved into such a fiasco he ended up having no choice but to seek another job as far away from Southern California as he could get.

Which meant returning home to Thunder Canyon.

Besides, Annabel seemed…well, a bit flaky, idealistic, pushy. They could not be more opposite. Yet when he reviewed his calendar each morning he'd found himself looking for her name.

It wasn't until after Forrest Traub's surgery two days ago that it appeared with the promised thirty minutes blocked out for Thursday afternoon.

Today.

Annabel—and her dog—should be here any minute.

Not wanting a repeat from last time, Thomas sat behind his desk and tried to edit his latest article for a leading medical journal, but after reading the same paragraph three times he was glad when familiar tapping at the door came.

"Come in," he said, recognizing his secretary's signature knock. "Marge, I'm out of red markers. Could you find me a few more, please?"

"Sorry. I come bearing gifts, but not a red marker in sight."

Thomas looked up and found Annabel Cates standing in his doorway. He immediately noticed she wore her hair pulled back from her face in a ponytail. It made her look younger, though the curves presented in her simple bright yellow top and denim skirt said otherwise. He found himself wondering just how old she was.

He stood, his gaze drawn to her bare legs and toes, thanks to her sandals, this time the nails sporting a matching neon-yellow shade.

Details. Thomas was known for being a man of details, but he realized he'd taken in her entire outfit before he noticed the large, leafy green plant she held in her hands.

And the fact she was alone. No dog in sight.

"Don't tell me my secretary is baby—err, dog sitting."

She smiled and it lit up her entire face. Another detail he remembered from the last time she was in his office.

"Nope, it's just me this time. Disappointed?"

"Not in the least. Please, come in."

She did, closing the door behind her before she walked to his desk and held out the plant. "This is for you. It's a Peace Lily."

"Are we at war?"

"No, but I thought the name was fitting and this place needs a bit of color. Also, they're known for tolerance for low light, dry air and are great indoor air purifiers."

"Well, thank you." Surprised that she went to such lengths to pick out the offering, Thomas took the container, pausing when his fingers brushed over hers. He placed it on the filing cabinet next to his desk. "I can't promise I'll remember to water it."

"I kind of figured you were a busy guy, so I included an aqua globe. See?" She walked around the desk and moved in behind him, pointing out the green shaded globe barely visible among the leaves. Heat radiated off her body and he suddenly felt naked without his lab coat. "You just fill it, turn it upside down and jab it in the dirt. It'll water your plant for two weeks before you need to refill."

"Ah, that's…that's a good idea." Damn, he sounded like a schoolkid nervous to be talking to the prettiest girl in the class. "Why don't we sit down and get started?"

"Sounds great." Annabel stepped back but instead of taking one of the chairs in front of his desk, she moved to the couch against the wall. Skirting the coffee table, she dropped to one end and patted the spot next to her.

Thomas cleared his throat, but joined her, making sure to keep an empty space between them. Not that it mattered. Annabel simply scooted closer.

He fought against the automatic reaction to lean back and rest his arm against the back of the leather sofa. Instead, he scooted forward and braced his forearms on his knees, his hands clasped together.

"I left Smiley at home because I wanted to be able

to talk without any furry distractions." She grabbed a large book from an oversize bag at her feet. "You don't have to feel bad or think you're not an animal person because the two of you didn't hit it off. You just haven't met the right one yet."

His shoulders went stiff. "I never said—"

"Most people love Smiley, which makes him so good at being a therapy dog," she continued, opening the book and laying it flat across her lap. "I started this scrapbook to document our training and all the work we do. There are a number of tests that Smiley had to pass before being certified, such as acceptance of a friendly stranger, walking through a crowd or sitting politely."

Thomas cleared his throat. It then closed up completely when Annabel laughed and reached out, giving his arm a gentle squeeze. "You're a special case."

Her heated touch seemed to sear his skin through the smooth material of his shirt. His fingers tightened against his knuckles until she released him. "Ah, that's good to know."

"Smiley was also tested for basic commands and how he reacted to being around other dogs, children and medical equipment and so on."

"I'm guessing all the animals in this program are required to provide health records?"

"Of course. They have to be tested annually and maintain a good appearance. Grooming is a must." She turned the page and pointed to certificates in both her and her dog's names. "We passed every test with flying colors and have been doing this kind of work for the last six months. I document every visit we make, sometimes with photographs, as we are working toward the American Kennel Club's Therapy Dog title. Smiley's been to schools, group homes, clinics and nursing care facilities. Not to mention a couple areas here at TC General."

Annabel gently brushed her fingertips over the pictures on the next page of a young girl lying in a hospital bed, her head covered in a colorful head scarf and Smiley stretched out beside her. "This is Isabella. She was the sweetest thing. When we arrived to visit with her she asked me if Smiley was an angel. When I asked why, she said she'd just dreamed that an angel was coming to take her home."

Thomas watched as Annabel paused, pressing her fingertips to her lips, and glanced upward for a moment before she went on. "Her mother told Isabella she was too sick to leave the hospital just yet and the little girl said she wasn't talking about their home. That the angel was taking her to God's house. She died six weeks later, just days after her tenth birthday. That last week Smiley and I were there every day."

He had to ask. "Why do you do that?"

She looked at him, her blue eyes shiny. "Do what?"

"Roll your eyes that way. You did it during the appointment with Forrest when I was discussing his surgery and again just now."

"I wasn't rolling my eyes. Not in the traditional sense."

"Meaning?"

"Meaning I'm not bored or exasperated. You see, I tend to get a bit emotional, especially in some of the situations Smiley and I find ourselves involved with. It's a trick I picked up from another dog handler to stop the tears."

"It works?"

Annabel nodded. "My mom told me that tickling the roof of my mouth with the tip of my tongue will do the same thing, but I'm usually too busy talking—" She stopped and bit down on her bottom lip. "Well, I guess you've already figured that out."

Yes, he had. What he couldn't figure out was why he liked that about her.

"Should I go on?" she asked.

As if he could tell her not to. "Please do."

Annabel turned the page and his gaze was drawn to the photo of a teenage boy holding himself upright on parallel bars, a prosthetic where his right leg should have been. "This is Marcus Colton. He lost his leg last winter in a snowmobile accident. Like most teenagers, what he did best was give his physical therapists a hard time."

"Let me guess. Smiley changed that?"

"We were at the clinic one day when Marcus was being his usual charming self, demanding no one would get him to make a fool of himself by trying to walk, even though he'd been doing pretty well at his rehab for a month by then."

She pointed to the next picture showing her dog sitting calmly at the opposite end of the bars, Annabel just a few feet away holding his leash. "Smiley allowed Marcus to pet him for a few minutes and then he went and sat there, almost daring Marcus to come to him."

"And he did."

"Not the first visit. Or even the second, but Smiley proved to be every bit as stubborn as Marcus. The boy finally relented and now he's making great progress."

She went on, telling him stories of senior citizens

who had no one to visit them but Smiley, of the patients attending their dialysis sessions who welcomed the distraction petting a dog brought and schoolkids finding it easier to practice their reading when their audience was a dog.

With each story came more looks upward, a couple swipes at the tears that made it through and a sexy husky laugh, all of which struck a chord deep in Thomas's gut.

"I'm guessing all of this is to convince me to allow Smiley to work with Forrest during his rehab, if my patient agrees," Thomas said when she finally finished. "But why do I get the feeling you are looking for something else from me?"

"Hmm, now that's a loaded question." She closed her book, a pretty blush on her cheeks. "Yes, working with Forrest was my original plan. I still want to now that he's home from the hospital and ready to start his physical therapy, but what I'd really like is to set up a weekly support group here at the hospital. One that's open to any patient who wants to come, no matter what their illness."

While Thomas still had doubts about her work, he found himself enamored of Annabel's spirit. What surprised him even more was the fact he wanted to see her again.

And not just here at the hospital.

"I'm still not completely convinced, but I'll agree to at least consider your idea."

"Really?" Annabel's smile was wide, her blue eyes sparkling up at him. "That's wonderful!"

"There's just one condition." He could hardly believe the words pouring from his mouth. "You agree to have dinner with me."

Chapter 3

Stunned, Annabel didn't know what to say. Anyone who knew her well would say it was the first time she'd ever been at a loss for words.

Especially after she'd spent the past half hour hogging the conversation with a man who'd put those dreamy and steamy television doctors to shame. Without the standard long white lab coat he'd worn the last time she was here, his purple dress shirt and purple, gray and black striped tie brought out just a hint of lavender in those amazingly blue eyes.

Not to mention what the shirt did for the man's broad shoulders.

He wore his dark hair short, but it stood up in spiky tufts on top, as if he'd been running his hand through it just before she arrived. The sharp angles of his cheeks and jaw were smooth-shaven despite it being late in the afternoon.

Her breath had just about vanished from her lungs when he'd joined her on the couch, his woodsy cologne teasing her senses. Thank goodness she'd remembered the scrapbook so she had something to do with her hands.

Besides attack the good doctor, that was.

"Annabel? Did you hear me?"

She blinked, realized she'd been staring. "You want to go out?"

"Yes."

Considering how hard she'd tried not to sound like a sap with her endless chatter about the therapy dog program, Annabel now found it hard to put her thoughts into words. "With me?"

"Yes, with you. We can talk more about your program. Unless there's a reason why you can't?"

Was "too stunned to reply" an acceptable answer?

"Do you have a boyfriend?" His expression turned serious again. "I didn't see a ring on your finger, but I don't want to presume you are free—"

"No." She cut him off. He'd actually looked to see if she wore a ring? "I'm free, totally free. Free as a bird."

"Is that a yes, then?"

She nodded. "Yes, dinner sounds great."

"Tomorrow night okay?"

Something to do on a Friday that didn't include her dog or a sibling? Tomorrow night would be perfect. "I work until six, but after that I'm all yours."

Thomas cleared his throat and stood, rising to his feet in one smooth motion. "Where do you work?"

"At the Thunder Canyon Public Library." Annabel

mirrored his actions, grabbing her bag and slipping it over one shoulder. "I'm the librarian in charge of the children's area."

He waved a hand at her scrapbook. "So, all the work you do with therapy dogs is strictly volunteer?"

"Oh, yes. I don't get paid for any of my visits, other than Smiley sometimes getting a doggy treat or two." She hugged her book to her chest, peeking up at him through her lashes. "But I love the work. The therapy program is one of my many passions, along with books and my family. I guess I'm just a passionate person by nature."

His eyes deepened to a dark blue as their focus shifted to her mouth. A slight tilt of his head, a restrained shift in his body that brought him just a hint closer.

Her tongue darted out to lick her suddenly dry lips. She couldn't help it. Not that she dared think he might—

Yes, she had thought about the man, probably too much, over the past two weeks. She'd been looking forward to this meeting for more reasons than convincing Thomas to allow a therapy group here at the hospital. One she would be in charge of.

Annabel could admit, at least to herself, she'd wanted to find out if the quivering sensations she'd experienced when they'd first met had been all in her head.

They weren't.

"I know a great Italian bistro, Antonio's, over in Bozeman. Where should I pick you up?"

She blinked again, breaking the spell the doctor seemed to weave around her. Antonio's? A dinner there cost more than she made in a week. "Oh, we don't have to go that far. Any place in town would be fine by me."

"My treat, so I get to pick the place."

His tone was persuasively charming, so Annabel simply rattled off her address. And her cell phone number. "You know, just in case."

Thomas nodded, then gestured in the direction of the door with one hand, signaling the end of their meeting. "Until tomorrow night, then."

Annabel stepped in front of him, sure she could feel the heat of his gaze on her backside as he followed her. She turned when she reached the door, but found those blue eyes squarely focused on her face.

"I'll pick you up around seven?" he asked.

She smiled. "I'll be waiting."

She waited.

And waited and waited.

Palming her cell phone, Annabel paced the length of her bedroom, her bare toes scrunching in the soft carpet. Smiley lay at the end of her bed, watching her stride back and forth like he was a spectator at a tennis match.

She'd changed out of the sundress with its matching knitted shrug and into a cropped T-shirt and yoga pants an hour ago, kicking her cute kitten heels back into the bottom of her closet.

After she'd accepted the fact Thomas had stood her up.

She'd really been looking forward to tonight. Yes, the chance to talk more about her idea of a weekly therapy session with Smiley at the hospital was a big draw, but darn it, getting to know Thomas better appealed to her even more.

"It's after nine thirty," Annabel said softly, eyeing the clock on her bedside table. "Why hasn't he called?"

Smiley offered a sympathetic whimper and lowered his head to his paws until a quick knock at her bedroom door grabbed his attention.

Seconds later, her sister popped her head in. "Hey! We're about to start a Mr. Darcy movie marathon now that Dad has gone off to bed. You coming downstairs?"

Annabel gave Jordyn Leigh a forced smile, knowing the "we" she was referring to was herself, their older sister, Jazzy, and their mother, all of whom shared a deep affection for the beloved Jane Austen literary character.

As did she.

"I don't think so," she said. Not even Colin Firth's portrayal of the dashing hero could lift her disappointment—or erase the tiny flicker of hope she still held.

"You know, Mom said she can't believe the three single Cates sisters are all home on a Friday night." Jordyn Leigh nudged the door wider and leaned against the frame. "Of course, you taking a pass on dinner tonight had us all thinking you had other plans."

"I did."

Her sister eyed her outfit. "Dressed like that?"

Annabel sighed and glanced at her phone again. "I decided to change after he didn't show. Almost three hours ago."

"Yikes. Hoping for the old 'if I get into my sweats the jerk will call' effect, huh?"

"He's not a jerk." Her defense of him came easily, even if she had no idea why.

Her sister frowned, but only said, "Why don't *you* call *him?*"

Annabel had thought about it, but the only number she had for Thomas was his office. The last thing she wanted was to leave a pathetic voice mail for him to find first thing Monday morning.

"I don't have his number," she finally said. "He's got mine, at least I'm assuming he does. I mean, I gave it to him, but—"

"But he didn't write it down or put it in his phone right away?" Jordyn guessed. "So you're thinking he forgot?"

Her number? Their plans? All about her?

Annabel didn't know what to think.

"Well, you know where we'll be if you decide to join us. Mom's insisting we start with the black and white version of *Pride and Prejudice* featuring Sir Laurence, so you have plenty of time before our favorite Mr. Darcy appears."

With that, her sister vanished and Annabel flopped down on her bed, immediately bestowed with a sloppy kiss from Smiley, who'd crawled next to her.

"Oh, buddy, what am I going to do?" She scratched at her dog's ears. "Maybe I should go back to work. Goodness knows I got zero done this afternoon thinking about tonight. Or do I stay up here and drive myself crazy wondering why—"

An odd chiming filled the air. It took a moment before Annabel realized it was coming from her cell phone. Not her usual ringtone that asked a cowboy to take her away.

She sat up and read the display. Caller unknown.

Her fingers tightened around her phone. One deep breath and she pressed the answer button. "Hello?"

"Annabel? It's Thomas."

"Oh." She paused. "Hi there."

"I'm sorry. I didn't mean to be a no-show tonight."

She released the air from her lungs, while the ache in her stomach that she'd insisted was due to lack of food eased. "Did you get lost?"

"I never left the hospital." His voice was low and a bit husky. "I was called into an emergency surgery this afternoon and didn't have time to try to get ahold of you. I didn't expect it to take this long, but there were complications."

Stuck at work. She'd never even considered that. "Was the surgery a success?"

"Yes, it was." He sounded surprised. "Thanks for asking."

"Are you still at the hospital?"

"Sitting in the men's locker room. I called as soon as I got out of the shower."

Trying not to picture Thomas standing in front of a locker dripping wet and wearing nothing but a towel was as impossible as stopping Smiley from hogging the bed at night.

So she didn't even try.

"You must be exhausted," she said. "I can hear it in your voice."

"I am, but it's a good fatigue, sort of like a runner's high after completing a marathon. I feel like I could run ten miles." He sighed. "Not really, but that's the only comparison I can think of."

An idea popped into Annabel's head, so crazy it

just might work. "So, I'm guessing you didn't have a chance to eat dinner either?"

"I'll probably grab a burger at a drive-thru on my way home—wait, did you say 'either'?"

"How about meeting me at The Hitching Post? Say in about twenty minutes?"

"The what?"

"The Hitching Post. It's on Main Street in Old Town. You know the place, right?"

Silence filled the air. Annabel crossed her fingers. On both hands.

"Ah, yeah... I mean, yes," Thomas finally said. "I know where it is."

Annabel jumped up and began rifling through her closet. "Great! I'll see you there!"

Thomas slowed his silver BMW to a full stop at the curb, surprised to find an empty parking space so close to The Hitching Post on a Friday night.

He'd never been here before, but he'd heard his co-workers rave about the local hangout. Once owned by a lady with a questionable past, the place was now a restaurant and bar, a modern-day saloon right in the middle of Thunder Canyon's Old Town, an area that proudly retained its Western heritage.

A section of town Thomas rarely spent time in. Then again, he rarely spent time anywhere other than his condo or the hospital.

Stepping out of his car, he thumbed the button to lock the doors and set the alarm, then headed for the sidewalk.

He hated to admit it, but his plan had been to take Annabel someplace outside of Thunder Canyon where the walls didn't have ears and the gossip didn't travel at the speed of light.

Things at the hospital were finally quieting down, but to be seen together here tonight... Who knew what kind of rumors would fly?

Asking her out in the first place had been crazy enough. Agreeing to meet her here? That he blamed squarely on the fact she'd surprised him by not being angry at being stood up.

And the fact he wanted to see her again as soon as possible.

He started for the front door then realized the place was completely dark.

Geez, how late was it?

He glanced at his watch and then noticed the sign stuck in the front window. Closed for Renovation. What the heck was going on—

"Hey there!"

He turned and found Annabel standing on the corner, cradling two large paper bags in her arms. She was dressed casually in jeans and a distressed leather jacket, her hair in loose golden waves.

Thomas again felt that familiar zing at the sight of her. "Hey, yourself. Looks like this place is shut down."

"Oh, I knew it was closed. At least temporarily. My uncle Frank and my cousin Matt have been overseeing the renovation for Jason Traub and his new wife, Joss, who are the new owners. I only named it as a meeting place."

Meeting place for what? He must be more tired that he thought. "What's with the paper sacks?"

"Dinner!" Annabel beamed. "A care package chock-full of ribs, chicken and steak fries from DJ's

Rib Shack. Come on, I've got the perfect place for us to eat."

He joined her, not knowing what smelled better, the food or that sexy floral scent he'd noticed the first time they met.

"Here, let me take those," he offered.

Annabel handed over one of her parcels. The heat from the cooked food warmed his hands. They headed up the street and Thomas was curious as to where they were going. His first thought had been her place, but she'd given him an address that was on the southeast side of town.

At the end of the next block she crossed the street and walked toward a large two-story stone building.

"The Thunder Canyon Library?" He read the sign as they walked past the front steps. "We're eating here?"

"My second favorite place in town."

"Pardon my ignorance, but isn't it closed, too?"

"Don't worry. I have a key." Annabel smiled and led him around the corner to a tall wooden fence. He followed her directions to open the gate. "Latch that behind us, okay?"

Thomas did as she asked and they entered a shadowed courtyard. Thanks to a full moon, he could see a grassy area to one side with trees and benches and a wooden jungle gym on the other. Straight ahead was a wall of glass doors covered with blinds.

"This is the back way into the children's section. Don't worry, a security light should come on—" A bright spotlight shined down on them, illuminating the area. "And there it is. Come on, this way."

Annabel punched a code into a hidden keypad and pushed open the closest door. She held the blinds to one side and Thomas followed her, watching as she then did the same thing with another keypad on an inside wall. "The outside light will go off in a few minutes."

"Are you sure it's okay for us to be here?"

"What's the matter, doc?" She turned, that same saucy smile on her face. "Haven't you ever broken a few rules?"

Yeah, an unwritten one about dating a coworker's ex-wife.

Not good, especially when he found out the lady hadn't yet told her husband she'd filed for divorce. The fact that the man had been a senior surgeon while Thomas was fresh out of his residency only added to the mess.

"It's not something I make a habit of."

"Well, you're not doing it now, either. This is my domain, remember? I'm allowed to be here anytime I want and I often work after hours." Annabel hit a light switch, bathing the large room in a soft glow. "Ah, almost like candlelight. No need to go with all the lights just for dinner."

It wasn't the intimate setting like a private corner booth at Antonio's, but Thomas had to admit it was close.

"This used to be a storage area before I took it over three years ago," Annabel continued. "I had the place completely gutted and rebuilt from the ground up, including the wall of glass to the outside area. Now the kids have a place to come where they don't have to be quiet like upstairs. Well, not as quiet."

Thomas looked around, taking in the floor-to-ceiling bookcases, the scattered tables and chairs, most sized for patrons under four feet tall, as well as several large pillows, comfy armchairs and knit rugs covered hardwood floors.

Posters of children's authors and book covers decorated the walls. A curved wooden desk that must be original to the building stood against one wall, and above it hung a framed headshot of a grinning golden retriever that had to be Annabel's dog, with a placard that read Honorary Mascot.

"Come on, grab a piece of floor."

He turned to find Annabel kneeling at a child-size table, removing a couple of water bottles from the paper bag. She paused to peel off her jacket, revealing a faded Johnny Cash 1967 concert T-shirt that hugged her curves in all the right places.

Thomas had to swallow the lump in his throat before he asked, "You plan on eating right here?"

"Of course." She pushed aside a couple of miniature chairs and grabbed two large character-decorated pillows. "Here, you can have Dr. Seuss, in honor of your profession. I'll take Winnie-the-Pooh."

Shaking his head, he joined her on the carpet, their hips bumping as they worked to empty the bags of their dinner. Thomas edged away, determined to keep this night light and easy. "So, how did you become a librarian?"

"Freshman-year biology."

That got his attention. "Excuse me?"

Annabel opened one of the containers and the spicy tang of barbecue filled the air. "As a kid I was always the one bringing home stray cats or injured birds. I even stole a horse from a rancher who was using inhumane training techniques on the poor animal. My family thought I'd grow up to be a veterinarian or maybe even a doctor. But when I got to high school and was told I had to dissect a defenseless little frog…" Her voice trailed off as she shuddered. "I just couldn't do it."

Thomas grinned. "You do know the frog was already dead, right?"

"Yes, I knew that, but I still didn't understand why we couldn't learn what we needed without killing…cutting—anyway, I organized a protest which pretty much ended my science career. So I got my bachelor's degree in English from San Jose State University, stayed on to get my master's in Library Sciences and here I am."

He was surprised to hear she'd gone to school out of state. "You went to college in California?"

"With the size of my family a full scholarship made it an easy decision." Annabel filled two plates with ribs, chicken and fries. "I loved it. The bay area is so beautiful."

"And yet you came back here afterward?"

"Of course, Thunder Canyon is my home." She pushed a plate in his direction. "This smells heavenly! Let's eat!"

It was a far cry from the refined dinner he'd originally envisioned, but the food was terrific. They ate picnic style with Thomas trying his best to work with the plastic silverware and keep his meal out of his lap.

"You know, messy is the only way to go." Annabel took a barbecued chicken leg in her fingers and attacked it with a large bite. "Mmm, so good."

Thomas smiled. Her lack of pretense impressed him. Most of the women he'd dated seemed to refrain from eating altogether. Annabel approached her meal the same way she approached the rest of her life—with gusto.

Messy gusto.

"And you do know the caveman method to dining will always result in more sauce on your face and hands than in your mouth, right?" Thomas asked, then smiled even wider at the exaggerated indignation on her face. "You've got a large dollop on your cheek."

His breath caught the moment her tongue snaked out, trying to capture the evidence. It should look comical, but Thomas was captivated. "Ah, other side."

She repeated the motion, but still missed.

"Here, let me help…"

He leaned closer, brushing at the side of her mouth with his thumb the same moment Annabel tried again, and was stunned when the quick lick against his skin sent shock waves through his body.

Her blue eyes widened and he couldn't stop himself from dragging the moist digit over her full bottom lip.

Three dates in the past two years, longer than that since he'd even wanted to feel a woman's mouth beneath his, but right here, right now, there was nothing Thomas wanted more in the world than to kiss Annabel.

And damn the consequences.

Chapter 4

For the second time in two days, Dr. Thomas North had left her utterly speechless. Breathless, too. Heck, the only way Annabel knew she was alive was the hot flush burning across her skin and the way her heart was about to jump out of her chest.

Then again, her heart had been rocking and rolling to its own crazy beat from the moment he'd agreed to her spontaneous dinner invitation earlier tonight.

Less than an hour ago, she'd skidded to a stop in her favorite black ballet flats as he'd eased out of his shiny sports car, looking relaxed despite hours spent in surgery, and especially yummy.

His white dress shirt and khaki pants were still fresh and polished. The only concession to his long day were the shirtsleeves folded halfway to his elbows. Even the loafers on his feet gleamed in the streetlights.

She'd used the few moments it'd taken him to notice The Hitching Post was closed to reassure herself that her idea of a take-out meal at her home away from home was a good idea.

Especially after he'd joined her and she'd seen the deep lines of fatigue bracketing his eyes.

Now, however, those icy blue eyes were bright and alive, the exhaustion replaced with longing as they stayed locked on her mouth. The heavenly back and forth friction of his thumb against her bottom lip had her wondering just how amazing it would be to kiss this man.

Should she or shouldn't she?

Despite her flirty and confident attitude, Annabel had no idea how Thomas would react if she threw caution to the wind, closed the short distance between them and pressed her mouth to his.

The barest taste of him lingering on her tongue from where she'd licked his thumb wasn't nearly enough. She wanted more. Did he? The way he continued to touch her, his fingers brushing her neck—

"I'm sorry." Thomas jerked his hand away. Grabbing a napkin, he thrust it at her while managing to effectively put space between them without moving an inch. "That was— I'm sorry."

"No need to apologize." Annabel wiped her mouth, dropping her gaze to the alphabet-patterned rug. Was he sorry about touching her? Almost kissing her? Not wanting to know, she purposely misunderstood his regret. "Messy eating and barbecue go hand in hand, I guess."

"No, I mean I'm sorry about tonight. This isn't exactly the meal I had planned when I asked you to dinner."

"Plans change." Annabel put the chicken leg back on her plate while offering what she hoped was a casual shrug of one shoulder. "Besides, sometimes the best things happen when we least expect it."

"Maybe so, but I'm the kind of guy who likes to have everything fall neatly into place."

That didn't surprise her. He seemed the type who liked to have every *i* dotted and *t* crossed, as her father often said.

Her?

Not so much. Most of Annabel's life had been a crazy, mixed-up mess of spontaneous opportunities and gut decisions that either worked out better than she hoped or provided a much-needed life lesson.

Hoping for the former, she decided to steer the conversation to a safer topic. "I guess your surgery today didn't go as planned either, huh?"

"No, that was another surprise." He took a long draw on his water. "What should've been a simple lumbar spinal fusion went totally out of whack when we discovered more damage to the spinal cord than we originally believed. Then the allograft was rejected even though a positive match had been achieved beforehand, resulting in us having to take bone from the patient's pelvis—"

Thomas suddenly stopped speaking, the self-conscious grin on his face making his chiseled cheekbones even more pronounced. "I'm sorry. Again." He braced an arm on a bent knee and waved his hand in the air as if to erase his words. "I tend to get carried away when I talk about work."

The change in him was amazing. He'd grown relaxed and animated at the same time. "Oh, please, tell me more." Annabel tucked her legs to one side. "I think it's fascinating."

He did as she asked, going into great detail about the remarkable work he and his surgical team had accomplished today and the more he talked, the more those amazing dimples appeared. Most of the technical stuff went right over her head, but it was fun to listen anyways.

"I'm guessing you didn't have any problem with slicing and dicing back in high school?" Annabel asked.

Thomas's featured softened. "Never even hesitated."

"So how did you end up here in our little corner of paradise?"

"Thunder Canyon is my home, too."

Now that surprised her. She guessed him to be in his early thirties, which would've put him a few years ahead of her in school, but she found it hard to believe someone as good-looking as Thomas had missed being caught on the radar of her older sisters. "Really?"

"Born and raised. Well, born anyway. I started attending private schools when I was around ten. After that it was summer camps or trips abroad until I went to college at seventeen."

"Considering who I'm talking to, I'm going to assume you skipped a year or two in high school and not the more common late-year birthday?"

"I completed high school, college and med school in nine years. Most people take the standard twelve."

Wow, she was impressed. "So did you follow the family business?"

"No, my parents are lawyers. They have a law firm

here in town." He looked away, but not before she saw a muscle jump in his cheek. "They probably expected their only child to follow in their footsteps, but I've known what I wanted to do with my life since I was seven years old."

"That young? I was still undecided between being a princess or the presidency." Annabel read the seriousness in his gaze when he turned back to her. "What happened to create such a deep conviction?"

"My grandfather lost both his legs in a car accident that year." Thomas paused, pressing his lips into a hard line. When he continued his voice held a quiet intensity. "He changed after that. Sank into a deep depression that as a little boy I didn't understand. Even though Grandpa Joe lived almost another twenty years, he was never the same man I knew and loved."

A warm, protective feeling came over her. She blinked hard to erase the stinging in her eyes. "Oh, Thomas."

"I remember telling my parents if I was a doctor I could have saved my grandfather's legs. After that, there wasn't any question about what I planned to do with my life."

"And from what I've heard, you do your job very well."

His gaze flew back to hers. "What you've heard?"

"From you. Tonight. When you talked about that surgery I could tell how much you love your work and how good you are."

"Ah, yeah…thanks." Thomas glanced at his watch. "Wow, look at the time. It's almost midnight."

Okay, she could take a hint. "And you've been at the hospital since before dawn."

One brow arched in inquiry.

"You know what a small town Thunder Canyon is." Annabel shrugged and started to clear up the remains of their meal. "I've heard your name bantered about. Nothing but good things, of course. Like your tendency to work very long days."

"Yes, well, I've heard a few things about you, too." He joined her, collecting the empty containers. "You and your dog are a popular topic at the hospital."

"It's all Smiley. He makes an impression everywhere he goes."

"How did you two get involved in that line of volunteer work?"

"I had a guest speaker here at the library earlier this year who spoke about the special work dogs do, from assistance for the blind and physically challenged to the therapy dog program. I knew right then my sweet little bundle of fur would be great at it."

"That dog isn't so little."

Annabel laughed and headed for her desk. She was glad they were talking about Smiley. Until now she hadn't even thought about her plan to use this time to persuade Thomas to give the go-ahead for her idea. "But he is sweet, gentle and kind. He also instinctively knows when someone is in pain or needs a good dose of unconditional love."

"What my patients *need* is excellent health care, which comes from scientifically proven methods and top-of-the-line medicines."

"I agree." She ducked behind her desk and, hidden from his view for the moment, stuck out her tongue at his lofty tone. Not mature, but it felt good just the same.

"But sometimes they need someone who will listen when they talk and love them without expectations."

"Annabel, I don't want you to think I'm a total jerk—"

"I don't think that." Rising, she found Thomas standing in the middle of the room, his hands shoved deep in his pockets. He should've looked out of place, surrounded by miniature furniture and bright colors, but his serious expression made her want to bring back the relaxed one from earlier. "Not totally. At least not yet."

One side of his mouth rose into a half grin. She'd take it.

"Thanks, I think. I'm just not sure that petting a dog can have much effect on a serious medical condition."

"I don't see how it can hurt."

Hmm, silence from the man. Score one for her and Smiley.

"Okay, I'll give you that," he said.

"How about giving me something more?" Annabel offered a sincere smile as she walked back toward him, shaking out a garage bag. "As in a chance to test your theory? Let Smiley and me work with some of your patients, Forrest included, on a trial basis, and we can see how it goes."

"Annabel—"

She pressed her index finger to her lips, the librarian's universal signal for silence. "Just think about it."

It took a lot of willpower, but Annabel allowed her request to hang in the air as they worked together to fill the bag with their trash and headed for the exit. She reset the alarm, locked the door behind them and pointed out the Dumpster on the far side of the building.

Once they were back on the sidewalk, a cool breeze sent a shiver though her. She started to pull on her jacket, but Thomas gently took it from her.

"Here, let me help."

Turning her back to him, Annabel smiled as she slid her arms into the sleeves, enjoying the gentlemanly gesture.

Tugging her hair free, she peered backward at him. "Thanks."

"My pleasure." The weight of his hands rested a moment at her shoulders then they were gone.

As they headed back toward Main Street to their parked cars, Annabel knew this was the end of their evening, and she wanted so much to ask again about the therapy group. But she'd told him to think about it, and pressuring him wasn't giving him time to think. Still she had to capture her bottom lip between her teeth to stop the words from blurting out of her mouth.

Of course, that move only made her think back to the almost kiss.

Would Thomas want to brush his lips across hers as he said good-night? How would he react if she kissed him instead?

"Which car is yours?"

Thomas's question surprised her and she stopped short. They were back in front of The Hitching Post, but on the other side of the street.

Well, she guessed the saying good-night part was already here.

Annabel pointed toward her vehicle. "The little green Bug. Straight ahead."

Thomas headed toward it and Annabel hurried to catch up with him. "Oh, I'm fine. You don't have to—"

"Annabel, don't argue." He motioned for her to continue moving. "Just walk."

She did, digging her keys out of the bottom of her purse. Hitting the button to unlock the driver's side door, she reached for the handle only to have Thomas's hand shoot past hers first.

He opened her door and she stepped off the curb into the space between the door and the driver's seat. Thomas moved in behind her, his close proximity distracting her for a moment.

Should she turn around? If so, would he still be standing on the curb making him appear even taller?

Darn, why hadn't she slipped on her wedged sandals instead? They would've put her at the perfect height to lean forward, balance herself by lightly placing her hands on his chest before she'd lay a quick kiss on his—

"It'll probably take me a few days to secure a room for your group. How about you start two weeks from today?"

She spun around, his words setting off tiny bursts of sparkling happiness—almost as sweet as the kiss she'd been imagining a second ago—that reached all the way to her toes. "Oh, Thomas! Really?"

He stood, one hand braced on the door and the other on the roof of her car looking down at her with a smile that turned those miniature fireworks into a full-blown explosion. "Yes, really."

Kiss him!

Fighting off the internal command to throw her arms around his neck took all of Annabel's strength.

She clasped her hands together and held them tight to her chest, just in case.

He took a step backward, his hand coming off the roof. "My secretary will call you with the details. We'll put the word out about your group, but I can't guarantee anyone will agree to come. Or how many sessions you'll have. That all depends on the patients' reactions and your dog's behavior."

Trying to feel grateful he'd saved her from making a fool of herself, again, she concentrated instead on the good news. "I understand. Don't worry. Smiley will be on his best behavior. This is too wonderful for words. I really don't know what to say, but thank you so much!"

"You're welcome."

Deciding to end the evening on an upward note, she dropped into the driver's seat and started the car's engine. She then reached for the door, but Thomas's voice stopped her.

"Thanks for tonight...for dinner."

The pause when he spoke made her look up at him, but he'd moved farther back on the sidewalk, his face in the shadows. "Thanks for meeting me. I had a lot of fun."

He gave her a quick nod in return, then crossed in front of her headlights to his own car on the other side of the street. Pulling out into the road, Annabel stopped at the red light. In her rearview mirror she watched as Thomas made a quick U-turn in the middle of the empty street and headed in the opposite direction, his taillights disappearing into the night.

The light changed to green and Annabel headed for home. As happy as she was about Thomas giving her therapy-group idea a green light, she had to admit his reaction to her reaction did sting a bit.

Had he been able to tell how much she wanted to kiss him?

Heck, he'd started it with wiping the barbecue sauce off the side of her mouth. She'd only been responding to the vibes he'd put out in the cozy setting of the library. Just because she'd been told in the past, by more than a few people, that she tended to leap before she looked, didn't mean she was to blame.

Pulling into the driveway at her family's home, Annabel parked alongside the collection of other cars that belonged to her parents and siblings. She was greeted by a happy, tail-wagging Smiley as soon as she stepped into the darkened kitchen and her victorious feeling returned.

Kneeling, she gave her baby a hug and a treat from his special biscuit jar in celebration. "I did it, sweetie. We're all set for you to work your magic. Provided you follow the rules and do what you're told."

Smiley offered a cheerful bark in return and Annabel hugged him again. So what if her date—if one could even call it that—hadn't ended the way she'd hoped.

"I got what I really wanted tonight," she whispered to herself as much as to Smiley. "That's what counts."

"Hmm, not sure if I like the sound of that."

Annabel's head jerked up at her mother's voice. Evelyn Cates stood in the doorway that led into the family's oversize dining room, flanked by Annabel's sisters.

Jordyn Leigh snapped on the overhead light. "I don't know, Mom, it sounds pretty good to me. So how was Mr. Better-Late-Than-Never?"

"He was fine. I mean, it was fine." Annabel stood. "I told you Thomas got held up in surgery. That's why our plans changed."

"Yet you left and returned with the same sappy grin on your face." Jazzy winked as she headed for the sink with a handful of empty glasses. "And it sounds like you had a better-than-average time on your date, the first one in…what? How long has it been?"

"Refresh my memory." Annabel opened the refrigerator and stuck her head in for no other reason than to escape her sisters' prying eyes. "Which one of us actually had plans tonight?"

"Oh, sis, she's got you there," Jordyn Leigh said, then laughed. "Come on, let's get back to our movie."

"Why do I get the feeling that line 'the lady doth protest too much' fits somehow?" Jazzy shot back. "Hmm, I smell another romance brewing."

"Oh, please. We've already got two bridesmaids dresses hanging in our closet. The last thing we need around here is another wedding."

Annabel jumped at Jordyn Leigh's parting words as her sisters left the room.

Wedding? Who said anything about a wedding?

Grabbing a soda she didn't want, Annabel closed the door. Her mother had stayed behind, her blue eyes filled with the same loving concern she'd shown for all her children over the years.

"Mom…"

"Can I at least ask what it is you got tonight that you're so happy about?"

Annabel explained her plans for Smiley and the therapy group. "This is something I've wanted to do for a long time. Talking about the group and how I want to help Forrest, and anyone else who might come, is the main reason Thomas and I met tonight. I really think Smiley can make a difference."

"I'm sure he will, honey." Her mother smiled. "But I do think your sisters might be right. You haven't been this happy about a date in a long time."

"I'm happy about getting the approval for my therapy group," Annabel said, refusing to allow the memory of the way Thomas had touched her mouth and the desire she'd seen in his eyes come back to life. "Tonight was no big deal. Goodness knows I've had enough missed connections and false starts when it comes to men in the past. I doubt I'll be spending any more time with Dr. North outside of the hospital."

"Okay, dear. If you say so." Her mother leaned in and gave Annabel a quick hug. "I'm going to wash up those dishes before I head to bed. You joining your sisters?"

"No, I think I'll go up to my room. Good night, Mom."

Annabel headed for the stairs, Smiley at her side. She knew her sisters' good-natured teasing was all in fun, and with two recent weddings in their family, Annabel supposed she couldn't blame them for seeing romance where none existed.

She had to admit that Thomas North wasn't anywhere near as stuffy and uptight as she'd first thought. In fact, he was smart, caring and downright sexy. And if asked, and there was no reason why anyone should, she'd also admit the barest hint of his touch sent zingers to all her girly parts.

However, when he had the chance to kiss her tonight—more than once, in fact—he'd backed off.

So what did any of it mean?

Frustrated, she placed the unopened soda can on her dresser and once again flung herself down on her bed and stared at the ceiling. Was the attraction all in her head?

Or was the hunky doctor very good at keeping his feelings under wraps?

Chapter 5

Thomas pushed the button that activated the garage door as he turned the last corner in the condominium complex. When he moved home two years ago he'd been one of the first people to buy in the gated community and had chosen an end unit in the last row, hoping for as much privacy as possible.

At the time there had only been a couple dozen of the two-story condos in the development. Now there were fifty units along with amenities that included a gym, pool and club house, not that Thomas ever found the time, or the inclination, to use them.

He preferred to take his daily runs in private, usually on the many trails crisscrossing the hills behind the complex or the treadmill in his spare bedroom.

Damn, it felt like forever since he'd done his usual five miles this morning.

After pulling his car inside and shutting down the engine, he locked his BMW and closed the garage door. Heading upstairs, he entered the open living/dining room and went straight to the kitchen.

Tossing his keys next to the pile of mail on the granite countertop, he yanked open the refrigerator and pulled out a cold beer. The cap released with a simple twist and he tilted his head back, downing half the bottle without stopping.

Then he dropped his head back against the wall with a resounding thunk.

Nope, she was still there.

Two more thunks and one empty beer bottle later didn't help.

Annabel Cates, with the most delicious mouth he'd even seen on a woman, was still front and center in his head. Not to mention his other body parts that remembered and appreciated her soft curves, the spicy vanilla scent that clung to her skin and the way she got him to open up and talk about himself as if they'd known each other their entire lives.

He'd even told her about Grandpa Joe.

Tossing the empty bottle in the recycling bin, Thomas grabbed a bottle of water and made his way upstairs, pausing to set the security alarm and turn on a couple of table lamps in the living room. He'd learned the hard way to leave the low lights on all night. The chrome, glass and leather furniture he'd chosen was sleek and modern, but it also hurt like heck when walked into while fumbling around in the dark during those times he needed to leave in a hurry.

He entered his bedroom, stripping as he went. Leaving an uncharacteristic trail of clothing behind him, the last thing he did was put his cell phone, wallet, and the water on the bedside table before crawling naked between the cool sheets.

The clock read 12:35 a.m., meaning he'd been awake for twenty hours, fifteen of them spent at the hospital. He should be exhausted, but closing his eyes didn't help.

All he saw was Annabel.

The way she almost glided when she walked, as if her feet barely touched the ground. The way her lips curved upward in a mischievous grin when she'd asked him about breaking rules. The pride in those amazing pale blue eyes of hers as she showed off where she spent the majority of her waking hours.

Pride that melted into kindness and compassion when he'd revealed how a childhood tragedy shaped his entire life.

Damn, it was going to be a long night.

Thomas groaned, remembering his cell phone needed charging. He plugged it in, took it off vibrate and punched up the volume of his ringtone. Just in case.

His fingers paused when he saw the missed-call icon. He pressed the code for his voice mail, breathing a sigh of relief it wasn't the hospital when he heard the voice of his buddy in Hawaii who'd left a disjointed message, mixed with the sound of crying babies, that ended with Reid's usual "I hate talking to these damn things" tirade.

Grinning, Thomas pressed the button to return the call, figuring out it was only nine-thirty in the Aloha State. Besides, his roommate through medical school and five years of residency had said Thomas should call because he was spending his Friday night—

"Dr. T!"

Thomas smiled at his friend's greeting. "Dr. Gaines, I presume. It's been a while since I've heard from you."

"Well, you know. The life of a busy doctor."

Yes, Thomas did know about that.

He also knew Reid somehow made time for his beautiful wife, a nurse he met a year after graduating from medical school who'd convinced him to return to her native hometown of Honolulu after they'd married. Now Reid was the father of twin eight-month-old boys who he was constantly sending Thomas pictures of via text messages, and the owner of three prized surfboards.

The former San Diego surfer had found his own slice of paradise.

Wasn't that what Annabel called Thunder Canyon earlier?

Maybe for her. But Thomas often wondered if he would've ever returned to his hometown if not for making the biggest mistake of his life—one that forced him to leave behind everything he'd worked so hard for.

"So it's already Saturday in Montana." Reid's voice filled his ear. "Please tell me you were not at work this late."

"Is that any better than what you're doing tonight?"

"Hey, me and the boys, who finally crashed, thank goodness, are watching my beloved Angels getting their butts handed to them by the freaking Red Sox while the baby mama is out with her posse of girlfriends," Reid shot back. "Hopefully the twins will stay asleep until after she strolls in. Then we'll have some real home-run action going on."

"TMI, buddy." Thomas pushed himself up against

the padded headboard, refusing to think about the fact he'd passed up the chance to even get to first base tonight. Twice. "Since Gracie was practically a third roommate back in the day, I already know more about your sex life than I ever wanted."

"At least tell me yours has improved since we last spoke. I think you said something about a lawyer who caught your eye?"

It took Thomas a moment to figure out what his friend was talking about. "Yeah, that was almost a year ago."

"Okay, so it wasn't the last time we talked. Sue me. You still seeing her?"

"No."

"Because…"

"Because our careers kept us too busy." The lie fell so easily from his lips. Thomas grabbed the water and took a long swallow. "Doctor. Lawyer. Long hours all around."

"You are the worst liar I've ever met."

"It once served me well."

His friend sighed. "Dammit, you haven't let go of that yet? It's been almost three years."

This time Thomas knew exactly what his friend was talking about. Reid had had a front-row seat to his stupidity and ultimate humiliation after he'd gotten involved with the wrong woman.

The worst possible woman.

Another man's wife. And to make matters worse he'd actually fallen in love with her.

Except he had no idea at the time she was married, with no plans to change her status.

Not that Thomas had been inexperienced in matters of the heart. He'd dated through high school and college, but most girls wanted more of his time and attention than he was willing to give. His studies had been his main focus, especially during medical school, and that focus switched to his work while living the crazy life of a new doctor knee-deep in his residency.

Then he'd met Veronica, in the parking lot of a hospital function no less, which should've been his first clue. But he'd been riding a high after getting his board certification and acceptance into an orthopedic surgery fellowship right there in Santa Monica.

When the gorgeous redhead thanked him for fixing a flat tire by tossing him the keys to her Aston Martin convertible and insisting they drive up the coast until they ran out of gas, he'd been hooked. By the time he'd returned home after spending the entire weekend in bed at a "friend's" beach house, he'd agreed to keep their romance a secret, which had made it even more thrilling. Of course, he'd thought it was great that she didn't try to monopolize his time and understood his long working hours.

Until it all came crashing down on him less than a year later, when they'd gotten caught by her husband.

Thomas soon found their affair the talk of the medical center and any job prospects there had quietly disappeared despite his outstanding record. Thankfully, his grandmother had pulled enough strings to get him an interview at TC General, for the job he now held.

"Victoria Meadows is history, man." Reid's voice jerked Thomas from his memories. "You got played by a coldhearted witch who used you to make her old man jealous. A man she's still with and who made chief surgeon earlier this summer if I read the news correctly."

Yeah, Thomas had read that, too. "Thanks for the history lesson."

"Look, I know your grand plans of making the staff at UCLA Medical flew out the window after everything came out, but you said you were enjoying your work in Thunder Canyon."

"I am." There was no hesitation in his voice and Thomas realized just how true the words were.

Yes, his grandmother had come through with a job for him, but he'd worked harder than anyone on the staff to earn the position. TC General might operate at a slower pace than UCLA, but the work they did was just as important. "Things are going well here."

"Any pretty nurses on the staff?"

Thomas sighed. "You never give up."

"Hey, buddy, I just want you to be as happy as I am."

Reid's words caused the image of blond wavy hair and blue eyes to slide through his head, fully formed and in color, as if he'd had a photograph of her in his hand.

And just like that he was remembering how drawn he'd been to Annabel's warm smile and infectious nature.

He wanted to be irritated that she kept coming to mind, but he had to admit tonight had been more fun that he'd had in a long time. An improvised experience he usually stayed far away from whenever his set plans changed, but something in Annabel's voice had been hard to say no to when he'd called to apologize for messing up their date.

And later he'd seen the bright burst of desire in her gaze making it clear that if he'd wanted to kiss her she would've welcomed his mouth on hers.

If he'd wanted? Who was he kidding? His hand fisted the sheets as he remembered how it'd taken every ounce of discipline he had not to take things to the next level tonight.

Annabel was unlike any woman he'd ever met, nothing like—

Thomas cut off that thought.

Getting involved with someone who'd be a presence around the hospital was the last thing he wanted. And she would definitely be around, now that he'd actually given the okay to put that crazy idea of hers into action.

A mutt that could make sick people well? Who was he kidding? Wait until the hospital gossip grapevine got a hold of *that.*

Thomas scrubbed at his eyes, his bones aching with exhaustion. Chalking up his reaction to Annabel Cates and her dog therapy plan to being overtired was easy to do.

Maybe sleep would be easy now, as well.

"North, did you pass out on me?" Reid asked. "It got real quiet all of a sudden."

"No, still here, but fading fast. I should go."

"Okay, I'll hang up. Oh, but before you drift off to dreamland I'm going to text you a picture of the newest member of the family."

Thomas must be more tired than he thought. "What? You and Gracie have another kid I didn't know about?"

"No, we agreed to foster a dog from the local animal rescue center a couple of weeks ago, but she's the sweetest pup and fit so well with the Gaines clan we had to keep her."

"Let me guess." Thomas closed his eyes and again

dropped his head, the headboard muffling the sound this time. "A golden retriever?"

Reid chuckled. "How the heck did you know that?"

Over the past few days Thomas swore he'd dreamed about dogs every time he closed his eyes.

Being chased by a Great Dane during his daily run. His take-out lunch scarfed right off his desk by a basset hound with ears so long the animal had tripped on them while making his getaway. Performing a knee replacement on a police K9 unit dog, a German shepherd who'd been hurt in the line of duty. These were just a few of the crazy scenarios that invaded his sleep.

He had no idea what all that meant, but he figured it had something to do with the fact Marge had surprised him on Monday afternoon when she'd announced she'd found a meeting room for Annabel's sessions and that they were ready to start this week.

Or maybe it was because over the weekend Thomas had started to do his own extensive research on the results achieved by dog therapy programs. He told himself it had nothing to do with Annabel and everything to do with his responsibility as a staff member at the hospital to know all he could about a program he'd indirectly offered to his patients.

Yeah, right.

So why had he been standing here in the hall on Wednesday afternoon, watching through the open doorway for the past fifteen minutes while Annabel and her dog worked the crowded room? He really needed to get back to his office.

"Dr. North?"

Thomas turned and found a trio of nurses from his surgical team passing him by in the hallway. "Ladies."

"Hmm, that's a new look for you, Doctor." Michelle, the newest of the three and fresh out of the army, had only been at TC General for a month. "Blue is your color."

One of the other nurses quickly elbowed her and the three hurried away, but not before Thomas saw the smiles on their faces.

Glancing down at the standard blue surgical scrubs he wore, Thomas silently acknowledged they were far from his usual attire of dress slacks, shirt and tie. The outfit, complete with thick-soled sneakers that were perfect for long hours on his feet, was comfortable and familiar. He'd practically lived in scrubs during his residency, but now they were something he was never seen in outside of surgery.

Until today.

Now that he thought about it, he'd gotten more than a few stares and smirks since he'd donned the clothes an hour ago. He'd planned to head to his office to change into the spare suit he kept there, but not until he'd completed his rounds.

Then he'd purposely taken a route that brought him right by this meeting room with the idea of observing Annabel for just a moment—

"Dr. North." This time his name was spoken as a statement, not a question and by a voice that held the familiar rasp of maturity and authority Thomas had known his entire life. "I assume there is a fascinating explanation for your current attire."

He turned back and there stood a wisp of a woman at just over five feet tall with steel-gray hair pulled back into a perfect chignon and the same icy blue eyes as him.

"Hello, Grandmother."

She didn't return his greeting as her chin rose a degree while her gaze traveled the length of him.

Thomas straightened his shoulders and stood a bit taller. Force of habit. Despite celebrating her eightieth birthday a few months ago and, more recently, her retirement from her position as a hospital administrator, Ernestine North was still a force to be reckoned with within the halls of TC General.

"And your choice of foot apparel, as well," she finally said with a hint of a smile. "Please don't keep me in suspense."

"I had a patient who had an…er, adverse reaction to his medication while doing my rounds. This was the only choice for me to change into at the time." Thomas relaxed and crossed his arms over his chest. "And I like your shoes, too."

His grandmother leaned on her cane and lifted a foot, offering him a better display of her red-and-white polka-dot shoe with tiny white bows at the ankle peeking from the hem of her navy blue pantsuit. "Yes, they are adorable, aren't they?"

"And a bit too tall. I thought your doctor said no more high heels."

"I'm old. I don't have to listen to him. Besides, the heel is less than two inches." She set her foot down and waved the cane at him. "I don't really need this. I just use it to make myself look authoritative."

More likely because the cane had once belonged to his grandfather, until he had no use for it after his accident. She'd started using it the day of Joe's funeral and

Thomas had never seen her without it since. "You're retired, Gran."

"Yes, but many of the staff still fear me in my honorary position. I like it that way."

"Gran—"

"But we weren't talking about me. Did it ever occur to you to keep an extra suit in your office?"

"Of course." Thomas grinned, enjoying the banter. "I'm headed there right now to change."

"No, what you are doing is standing here. Why?" She glanced around, the double take when she spotted Annabel and her dog was slight, but Thomas saw it. "Ah, the dog whisperer."

"She's not a dog whisperer. Annabel Cates is certified in dog therapy and she's doing a weekly session here at the hospital for anyone, including staff as you can see, who wish to stop by."

His grandmother remained silent, the tilt to her head saying more than any words could.

Damn. Had he actually been defending her?

"Yes, I know who Miss Cates is. I read your memo and wanted to stop by and see how things were going." His grandmother stepped closer to him and out of the way as people started to exit the room. "Apparently, I'm not the only one who thought to do so."

Annabel's sweet laughter spilled from the room and Thomas found it impossible not to look.

She knelt in front of a young girl who couldn't have been more than three years old. The child tried to wrap her arms around the furry neck of Annabel's dog, who sat quietly in front of her, his wagging tail the only part in motion. Annabel laid a hand on the dog's shoulder and he bowed his head. The child completed her hug;

the woman behind her who was doing her best to hold back her tears had to be the mother.

Annabel smiled when she accepted a hug, as well. She then turned, as if she'd felt his gaze on her, and sent him a quick wink he felt all the way to his toes.

"Thomas?"

It took more effort than it should, but Thomas gave his attention back to his grandmother, not realizing she'd stepped a few feet away to speak with a hospital volunteer. The woman in the pink smock walked away, but Ernestine stood there, a single arched brow that told him she was waiting for an answer to a question he hadn't heard.

"I'm sorry, Gran. What did you say?"

"You seem different, Thomas. Where is that straitlaced, perfectionist grandson I know and love?"

Thomas fisted his hands for a moment, her words delivering a light blow he didn't like. Because it was a direct hit?

"I am not straitlaced."

"Of course you are. It's a family trait. And I asked if you plan to attend your parents' dinner party tomorrow night."

Her question had him wanting to tighten his grip even more, but he relaxed it instead before his grandmother's sharp gaze spotted his reaction. The woman was already well aware of the distance between him and his parents, thanks to having grown up more away from home than with them, but he'd go to their dinner party because his grandmother wanted him there. "Yes, I'll be there."

"And please—" she paused, her lips pursed as if she was holding back a smile "—at least wear a tie."

Unable to hold back his own grin, Thomas didn't even try. "At the very least."

She nodded once, turned and walked away, her steps graceful as always. He watched as she made it as far as the nurses' station halfway down the hall before getting into an animated conversation with another staff member.

"Oh, I love her shoes."

Annabel's soft voice carried over his shoulder, catching him off guard. For a moment Thomas wondered if he should've left when his grandmother did, but Annabel had already seen him. He probably shouldn't have stopped by at all. Being seen with her would only fuel the gossip.

A quick greeting and then he'd leave.

He faced her, noticing the meeting room was completely empty now. A couple of steps and he crossed the threshold before a slight nudge at his knee, followed by another more insistent bump, had him looking down at the dog at his feet.

"Smiley insisted on coming over to say hello."

Thomas considered the dog's expression and damn if the mutt didn't look like he was smiling, before shifting his attention to its owner. "Did he now?"

"Well, I wanted to talk to you, too." Annabel's eyes sparkled. "Because I realized, despite that first meeting in your office, you and my best bud here haven't ever been properly introduced."

"Annabel, that's not really necessary—"

"Smiley, I'd like you to meet Dr. Thomas North." Annabel gave a gentle tug on the leash as she spoke to her dog. "He's the one responsible for us being here and having such a great first session. Please say hello."

The golden promptly sat and lifted one paw.

Thomas couldn't hold back his laughter as he bent over, accepting the offering with a quick shake. "It's nice to meet you, Smiley."

As he knelt down before the dog and took its offered paw, he was struck by a realization. He, Dr. North, was on his knee shaking a dog's paw. And enjoying it. Just like he enjoyed the dog's unpredictable owner.

Chapter 6

It was silly, but Annabel had to blink back the sudden sting of tears biting her eyes as Thomas interacted with Smiley.

Happy tears, for sure.

Today had been wonderful with all the people who'd come by to meet her and Smiley at their introductory session, but Thomas stopping by to see them made the day perfect.

She'd been so worried no one would show, but then Madge, Thomas's secretary, had called this morning and told her about the buzz the notices for her sessions were generating.

She and Smiley arrived this afternoon to find a half-dozen patients waiting and, as the hour passed, even more stopped by. Not everyone stayed for the entire session, but Smiley had made sure everyone got some much-needed attention.

Even a few of the hospital staff had wandered in, out of curiosity or looking for a bit of comfort or stress relief, an aspect of dog therapy Annabel hadn't even considered until today.

"Did things go as well as you expected?" Thomas asked as he straightened. "I only caught the last few minutes of your session."

Annabel grinned, watching from the corner of her eye as Smiley heaved a deep sigh that signaled his contentment before he lowered himself to the floor, paws stretched out over Thomas's shoes. "Things went better than we could've hoped for."

"You know, I was worried it might be depressing, so it surprised me at how uplifting and hopeful the session seemed to be."

"Thanks. I think."

He blushed and Annabel's insides fluttered like a mass of butterflies taking flight. She loved it.

"No, that's not what I meant. I was just concerned—"

"Hey, I was only teasing." She grabbed his arm and gave him a quick squeeze. The heat of his bare skin against her fingers set off those tingles she'd missed over the past five days. "I was worried, too, but today was more like a meet and greet. To give people a chance to get to know Smiley a bit and see if regular sessions are something they might be interested in."

Thomas pulled from her touch and folded his arms, stretching the cotton material of the scrubs tight across his chest. His fingers rubbed at the spot where she'd made contact with him. Was that good or bad?

"Well, it looked like you had all the age groups covered," he said. "Who was that last little girl I saw you with? She wasn't wearing a patient band on her wrist."

"No, her little brother was born two months premature and is still in intensive care. Their parents came by to check on the baby and the mother thought her little girl would enjoy meeting Smiley."

"She certainly seemed to."

"I'm glad they stopped by. Of course, the one person I was really hoping to see today was Forrest Traub. Do you know if he was notified about the session?"

A shadow passed over Thomas's blue eyes. "Yes, I saw him on Monday and mentioned it."

Her excitement deflated a bit. "He didn't want to come?"

"He's left town, Annabel."

Confusion swamped her. "What? Why?"

"Something came up at his family's ranch in Rust Creek Falls and he decided to return home."

"But what about his leg?"

"I've done what I can, for now. He's still healing and he assured me that scheduling private sessions with a local physical therapist is one of his priorities."

Annabel didn't like the seriousness of Thomas's tone. Although she was glad Forrest would continue to work toward his full recovery, she was worried about his mental well-being.

"You're concerned about him."

"Aren't you?"

Thomas sighed and nodded. Knowing he couldn't discuss a patient's care in any detail with her, Annabel didn't ask, but made a mental note to check in with her sister and the rest of the Traub family.

Maybe a road trip would be necessary? Rust Creek Falls was only about three hundred miles or so from Thunder Canyon.

Setting that idea aside for now and turning her thoughts back to all the good things that happened today was easy. At least four of today's visitors had expressed interest in coming back on a regular basis and two of those were veterans who'd recently served in Iraq. She was determined to find a way to make those sessions happen.

"Did Marge mention she reserved this room for me for the rest of the week?" The surprise on his handsome face answered her question. "Oh, I guess not."

"You plan on being here tomorrow and Friday? What about your job at the library?"

"It'll take some creative scheduling, but I'll make sure Smiley's sessions don't interfere." Annabel tightened her grip on the leash when the pet responded to his name and rose to his feet between the two of them.

"Once I get a better idea of who's interested in attending, I'm thinking of having two sessions a week. One will be like today, more casual, where people can stop by and stay as long as they feel they need to. Maybe I'll even invite some of my fellow volunteers to stop by." The ideas flowed as she spoke. "The other session should be more private with a limited number of attendees. It's amazing how people open up and talk when their attention is focused on something else."

"Like petting a dog."

"Exactly." She looked down, realizing she'd been scratching Smiley behind his ears this whole time. "See what I mean?"

"Somehow I don't think you need anyone's help to open up."

Annabel laughed then said, "I do tend to talk a lot. The curse of trying to be heard in large family, I guess."

"Sometimes that's hard to achieve no matter the size of the family."

Intrigued, Annabel wanted to ask him what he meant, but the busy hospital sounds from the hallway grabbed his attention and he took a step backward. "I should head to my office. I want to get out of these clothes."

Need any help?

Annabel managed to hold back the words, but took the moment to enjoy the view of how the loose-fitting top and pants still managed to show off Thomas's strong arms. "Oh, I don't know. I think scrubs look really good on you."

"Ah, thanks." A beeping noise filled the air. He reached for the pager at his waist. "Sorry, I need to answer this. Are you two heading out?"

Smiley's tail started wagging vigorously, batting both their legs.

"That's a yes in Smiley speak," Annabel said. "We'll get out your way now."

"You're not in the way. Come on, we're both heading in the same direction."

Annabel tightened her grip on the leash as they exited the room and started down the corridor. The whispers and stares that followed them were pretty standard, Smiley always drew his share of attention, but Annabel noticed how Thomas's demeanor changed with every step.

Gone was the easy banter between them and that wonderful smile of his. They were stopped twice by people asking about the sessions and by the time they reached the elevators, she could almost sense his relief.

"Well, here's where we part ways, Miss Cates," Thomas said, his attention focused on the button to call for the elevator.

Miss Cates?

Surprised by his formal tone, Annabel forced her feet to keep moving. She kept her reply breezy and refused to look back. "Thanks, Dr. North. See you tomorrow."

Annabel slid her sunglasses on, to ward off the bright sunshine in the hospital parking lot and to hide from her sister's sharp gaze.

"Okay, spill," Abby said. "You've been tight-lipped about the handsome doctor since Wednesday night. Have you seen him in the past two days?"

"Yes, I saw *Dr. North* yesterday."

Abby took Smiley's leash from Annabel's hand. "So, how did it go?"

"Oh, so well he's pulled a complete vanishing act today."

"Do tell!"

Darn! Annabel should've known she'd regret confiding in her youngest sister. They'd shared a private chat Wednesday after a family dinner while enjoying a glass of wine on the front porch.

Her emotions had been flying all over the place ever since she'd left the hospital—excited about the sessions, confused by Thomas's behavior—and all it took was a simple "what's wrong" from Abby for everything to come pouring out.

"Well, running into him yesterday wasn't planned." Annabel moved to one side of the sidewalk to let an elderly couple walk by. Smiley followed her, of course, and so did Abby. "We'd finished up our second session, and unlike Wednesday afternoon Thomas hadn't show up at all."

"But you'd said you thought he wouldn't after the way he dismissed you the day before."

"I know." Annabel hated that she'd been right. "Anyway, we were getting ready to leave when one of the nurses stopped by. She told me about a patient up on the second floor who she thought could use a personal visit from Smiley."

"The patient didn't come to the session?"

"Mr. Owens broke his hip and leg in three places and is bedridden. He's also a widower with no children, almost ninety years old and, according to the nurse, as mean as the devil."

Abby smiled. "And you just couldn't resist."

"Of course not. So, Smiley and I used the stairs as his room was at that end of the hall. I could hear loud voices coming from his room while we were still in the stairway. Heck, everyone on the floor probably heard him arguing with his doctor."

"Oh, no."

"Oh, yes. You know me, I didn't even hesitate. Thinking Smiley could take the edge off any situation I just waltzed in, and there stood Thomas."

Her sister's eyes widened. "What did he say?"

"He ignored me at first. Well, not really ignored." Annabel lowered her voice, her gaze on the large expanse of grass and flower beds that led to a low stone wall. The tables and chairs of the hospital cafeteria's outdoor eating area sat scattered on the other side of the wall where a few people gathered, enjoying the late summer afternoon. "I doubt either of them stopped arguing long enough to even notice I was in the room."

"Until Smiley made his presence known."

"By making a beeline straight for Thomas."

"Smiley has always had a good instinct about people," Abby said, giving the dog a quick smile. "He must like Thomas."

"He does," Annabel agreed. "So do I, but the good doctor made it clear he wasn't happy to see either of us. Even after his patient stopped grousing the moment Smiley walked to his bedside and said hello. Of course, I followed to make sure things went okay. The next thing I knew Thomas had disappeared."

"And today?"

"Are you kidding? The man probably took a sick day just to avoid running into— Oh!"

"Oh what?"

The moment he stepped outside, Annabel's eyes were drawn to his steel-gray dress shirt and solid black tie, a calming beacon among the sea of colorful scrubs.

Thomas walked with sure strides to the far corner of the patio and sat alone at a table shaded by a large tree, never once looking up from the paperwork in his hand.

"That's him, isn't it?"

Annabel turned and found her sister openly staring. "Yes, that's Thomas North, M.D., but hey, don't be shy. Just go ahead and gawk at the guy."

"Well, he certainly is something to gawk at." Abby looked back at her and grinned. "Go talk to him."

"What?"

"You like him, Annabel. You just said so and after the way you gushed about meeting him for the first time, your impromptu date at the library, the way he filled out those scrubs—"

"Hey! I wasn't gushing."

"Yes, you were, and don't even think about blaming it on the wine." Her sister waved a finger at her. "Believe me, if anyone knows how hard it is to get a man's attention, it's me. I had to practically throw myself at Cade before the guy finally noticed me."

What her sister said was true, even though Cade Pritchett had been a friend of the family's for years and was now her sister's very besotted husband. "But you two knew each other a long time before things got romantic last year."

"Which only made it harder to get the man to see me as anything but the youngest of the Cates girls. Take my advice, I know what I'm talking about."

With five sisters, Annabel had heard that line many times before. "Famous last words."

Abby laughed. "Trust me."

Unable to stop herself, Annabel gazed across the lawn. "Just jump into the deep end?"

"With both feet and a big splash." Abby blew her an air kiss and crossed her fingers. "Thanks for letting me borrow Smiley. I'll drop him off at the house later. Good luck!"

Annabel stood on the sidewalk as her sister and Smiley disappeared among the cars in the still-crowded parking lot. Checking her watch, she saw it was almost six and Thomas was still here.

Sitting at a table, alone, with his back to everyone.

Giving a tightening tug on her ponytail, Annabel wished for a cuter outfit than her pink cotton blouse and wrinkled khakis, and headed for the stone path that led to the dining area.

She paused when she reached his table. "Hi there."

Judging from the way his head jerked up, she'd surprised him. He stared at her, but thanks to the dark lenses of his sunglasses, she couldn't read anything in his gaze.

"Am I interrupting?"

He closed the folder. "No, of course not."

Without waiting for an invitation, Annabel dropped into the chair opposite him and went cannonball style with her opening line. "I'm sorry for my unannounced visit to Mr. Owens's room yesterday. It was wrong of me to bring Smiley to a patient without asking for permission first. It won't happen again."

Thomas sank back into his chair.

Annabel wasn't sure how to take his relaxed posture. The hard line of his mouth didn't help and she wished desperately he'd remove the sunglasses, which probably cost more than her entire outfit, so she could see his eyes.

"It's just that after I heard about his condition and his attitude, I thought—"

"How did you find out about him?"

Why did she think he already knew the answer? "One of your staff mentioned him to me at the end of Smiley's session. I guess because he's a patient of yours, she felt it was okay to recommend a private visit." Annabel then remembered her own sunglasses and shoved them up onto the top of her head. "I didn't know he was your patient until I walked into the room, but still…that's no excuse."

He stared at her, as still as a statue. It was like playing the "who will blink first" game and Thomas didn't know it, but Annabel was the family champion. She'd wait him out if it took all night, but she wasn't leaving until he accepted her apology.

Yanking off his own sunglasses, Thomas rubbed at his eyes with the back of his hand before tossing the glasses on the table. "Annabel, I—"

"Hey! It's Smiley's mama!"

Annabel jumped when a cool, sticky hand landed on her arm. She turned and found the little girl whose brother was still in the ICU standing there.

"Well, hello to you." She smiled at the girl, loving her twin ponytails of curly blond hair. "Where's your mother?"

"Suzy!"

Annabel spotted the child's mother waving from across the patio. Rising, she shot Thomas a quick look, surprised to see the slight grin on his face. "I'll be right back."

He nodded.

Taking the girl's hand, Annabel walked her back to her mother and visited for a few moments. She wanted to get back to Thomas, to find out what he was going to say to her, but it felt like an eternity passed before she could. Every time she started moving in his direction, she was stopped by people wanting to talk about Smiley and her program.

She glanced over to make sure Thomas hadn't pulled another disappearing act, hoping his attention was at least on his paperwork.

Each time his attention was on her.

She didn't know if that was a good thing or not, but she liked the warmth that spread throughout her, especially when they made eye contact when she was finally able to rejoin him.

"Whew! Sorry about that, but it is nice to know we're making an impact."

"So, where is Smiley?"

His question surprised her. "That's what everyone else asked me. My sister Abby came by to pick him up earlier. She's taking him to hang out at ROOTS."

"Roots?"

"Haven't you ever heard of it? ROOTS is the hang-out down on Main Street for local teens. They have all kinds of programs year-round, but the summers are especially busy. Abby works there while she's pursuing her master's degree in psychology."

"Is she a trained volunteer in dog therapy, too?"

"Smiley's not there in an official capacity. He's just hanging out with whoever might be there on a Friday night."

That got Thomas to smile again. "So he can unofficially work his magic? Like he did with my patient?"

Annabel's breath caught in her throat. "He did?"

Thomas leaned forward, his gaze intent as he laced his fingers together over his paperwork. "I owe you an apology, Annabel. Yesterday was a…difficult one, which seems to be the norm for Mr. Owens since his surgery." His gaze dropped away. "I handled your arrival…badly."

The pain in his voice tugged at her heart. She reached out and laid a hand over his. "He reminds you of your grandfather, doesn't he?"

"Mr. Owens is like many of my elderly patients, obstinate and scared. But today he actually smiled at the nurses and took his medication without issue." Thomas flipped his hand over and captured her fingers in his. "And when I met with him this afternoon he asked when that beautiful girl and her pup were coming back to see him again."

Annabel gasped, surprised at the man's request. "Oh, I'm sorry we didn't get up to see him. Smiley has an appointment at the vet in the morning, but I can come after— Oh, there I go again!"

Thomas's smile widened. "If you can rearrange your schedule I'd appreciate it if you, and Smiley, came back to visit with him again."

"We would love to." Those familiar bursts of tingling happiness that always seemed to happen whenever she was with him filled Annabel's chest. "Thank you, Thomas, and until Mr. Owens is capable of joining us in the regular meeting room, I'll make a point of stopping in to see him afterward. As long as his doctor approves."

"I do, and thank you."

Annabel gave his hand a squeeze and went to pull away, but he held tight.

"You know, I do believe I owe you a dinner out." Thomas leaned closer. "Are you free tomorrow night?"

Oh, those bursts exploded into a dizzying array of bright colors. It was like last month's Fourth of July was repeating itself all over again. "Yes, I'm free."

"How about we try out the Gallatin Room at the Thunder Canyon Resort?"

"Oh, Thomas, that place is so fancy."

"So, let's get fancy. What do you say?"

Chapter 7

"Dinner reservation for North."

The Gallatin Room maître d' looked up from his station, then smiled. "Ah, Dr. North. It's good to see you again."

"It's good to see you, too, Robert."

"Your table is ready, if you and your companion will follow me."

Thomas placed a hand at the small of Annabel's back, gently guiding her ahead of him as they walked deeper into the restaurant, enjoying the heat of her skin almost as much as the way she jumped at his touch.

The first time it happened she included a breathless gasp that matched his own when he'd gotten his first look at the wide expanse of skin shown by the open back of her clingy black dress. The lacy shawl she'd casually thrown over her bare shoulders and sexy black heels completed the picture.

Thomas had wanted to stop right there in her family's crowded driveway and kiss her until they were both out of breath.

The hell with the fact her parents and two sisters were probably spying on them from inside the house.

Thomas hadn't picked up a date at her parents' home since his senior prom. And according to Annabel, there were still two more sisters, their husbands and a lone brother that he hadn't met yet!

Well, that wasn't exactly true, but for the moment, for this evening, it was just him and Annabel.

As they walked past tables covered in fine white linen, candlelight and crystal centerpieces of red roses, Thomas acknowledged a few friends of his parents and fellow staff from the hospital, with a quick nod.

He didn't know if the slight kick to his gut was from being seen in the company of a beautiful woman or the fact he'd actually asked Annabel out for another date.

And that she so readily accepted.

Somewhere between the gossip and witnessing the positive effect she was having at the hospital in just a few days, Thomas found himself wanting to spend time with her and damn the consequences. A feeling he hadn't experienced in a long time.

His sudden invite had surprised him as much as it did Annabel. Impulsive decisions had never been his strong suit. Thanks to his scientific mind, he tended to think long and hard about everything, but the moment the words had left his mouth yesterday he knew he wanted tonight to happen.

"Here we are, sir." The maître d' stood to one side

at the opening to a private area just off the main room, separated by a slight stairway. "The wine you requested has been laid out for you. Your server will be with you shortly."

"Thank you, Robert."

The man's slight nod told Thomas all of his plans were in place, which didn't surprise him. The Gallatin Room was a five-star eatery and one of the finest dining establishments in the entire state of Montana.

He entered the space behind Annabel in time to hear her gasp again as she stood before the floor-to-ceiling windows that looked out over the entire mountain.

"Oh, Thomas! This is glorious!"

He smiled and walked past the perfectly set table for two and joined her at the curved wall of windows. "Have you never been here before?"

She turned to face him, her hair gliding slowly across her shoulders. "Once or twice for a special occasion, but never in this spot and never with this view." Her gaze moved to the table. "Never this fancy."

"Didn't we agree *fancy* is the chosen word for tonight?" Thomas teased, pulling out the closest chair and waiting until she sat before he moved to the other side of the table.

"I think you and I have different definitions of the word." Annabel accepted the glass of wine he poured for her.

"Maybe so," Thomas said, raising his glass in a toast to her. "So I'll go with another word, *beautiful.* You look very beautiful tonight, Annabel."

Pleasure flashed in her eyes, but before she could respond their server appeared with the first course of their meal. Thomas enjoyed Annabel's confusion as a colorful salad plate was placed before her.

Once they were alone again, he reached for his own fork and dug in, but paused when he noticed Annabel hadn't moved. "What is it? Is something wrong?"

"Ah, no." She opened her cloth napkin and laid it across her lap. "Is that a Caesar salad you're having?"

"Yes, it is."

She looked at her plate again. "Mine's a garden salad without the shredded cheese, croutons or onions."

Thomas fought to keep his features passive. "I can see that."

"And the ranch dressing is served in a separate dish on the side," Annabel persisted, "because there's nothing worse than soggy lettuce."

"That's an interesting reason."

"Thomas, this is exactly the way I like my salads." She leaned forward, her voice a low whisper. "What's going on?"

"Just eat," he replied, matching her tone.

"Thomas—"

He waved his salad-laden fork at her. "I heard your visit with Mr. Owens went well today."

"Yes, it did." Annabel reached for her fork. "He told me the most amazing stories about serving in the navy during the Second World War and how he met his wife in San Francisco after the war ended. Did you know she was a nurse?"

Thomas nodded around a mouthful of food, waiting until he swallowed to speak. "Yes, he mentioned you pointed out how she would expect him to be a better patient."

Annabel laughed. "I did no such thing. He's the one

who made that admission. When he told me they'd shared over fifty years of marriage together I agreed that she must've known him better than anyone else in the world."

"Well, I would think so."

"Did you know they fell in love and married within a month of meeting each other?" Annabel paused to take another sip of wine, then sighed. "He told me he knew she was the one for him after their first date. Do you think it's really possible to be so sure that you want to spend your life with someone that quickly?"

"I don't know. My grandparents were married for fifty-five years, after they dated for four years first. Of course, that was because my grandfather was a freshman in college when they met and my grandmother wasn't even out of high school yet."

"My folks have been together for over thirty years. Let's hope long marriages run in the family, huh?"

Thomas's mouthful of salad lodged in his throat.

He coughed and reached for his wine, thankful that Annabel didn't notice his distress due to the amazing sunset outside that grabbed her attention.

"Are you okay?"

Okay, so she did notice. "Yeah—ah, yes, I'm fine."

They finished eating just as the server returned. The empty plates were whisked away and moments later, the main course was served with a flourish.

Annabel's eyes widened as she stared at the offering in front of her. "Surf and Turf?"

"North Atlantic lobster tail with porcini-rubbed filet mignon and apricot-glazed green beans." Thomas provided the specifics as the server silently disappeared again. "Hope it tastes as good as it looks."

"I've only had lobster and steak together a few times, but I've always considered this combination my favorite meal in the world."

"Yes, I know." Thomas smiled and reached for the wine. "Can I refresh your glass for you?"

Annabel only nodded, holding out her glass toward him, her gaze still on the food before her.

When the idea to create a meal made of her favorite foods first came to him, Thomas wasn't sure it was a good one, but seeing Annabel's reaction was just what he'd hoped for.

"But how?" She finally looked at him after setting her glass down. "How did you know?"

"After you left the hospital yesterday I stopped by ROOTS, introduced myself to your sister Abby, and asked what your favorite foods are." He decided the direct approach was best. "Then I made arrangements to have them served tonight for us."

Annabel's gaze dropped back to the table. The candlelight danced over her shocked features and when she captured her bottom lip with her teeth, Thomas wanted nothing more than to lean across the table and release the fullness from its imprisonment.

And cover her mouth with his.

"Does this mean we're having strawberry chocolate devil's food cake for dessert?" she asked, cutting into the steak.

Thomas laughed, loving the playfulness in her eyes. "You'll just have to wait and see."

The meal was terrific and they talked while they ate, sharing stories that covered everything from childhood experiences to college escapades. When dessert arrived, Annabel claimed she was too stuffed to eat, but the cake was perfectly sized for two and they managed to make a pretty good dent in it. "Mmm, that is just too delicious for words," Annabel purred after sliding her fork from between her lips. "This has got to be the best meal I've ever had."

"I'm in complete agreement with you." Thomas signaled for the server, who came into the room. "Do you think we could meet the chef? We'd like to thank him for this amazing meal."

"I'll see if he's available."

A few minutes later a tall man with black hair arrived at their table. "I'm Shane Roarke, the executive chef here at the Gallatin Room."

Thomas introduced himself and Annabel, offering his compliments before his date took over the conversation as only Annabel could, with charm and grace.

"I can't believe Thunder Canyon was able to lure you away from the big city, Mr. Roarke," Annabel said after the man admitted to working in Los Angeles, San Francisco and Seattle before taking his current position at the resort.

Thomas noticed the quick tightening of the chef's jaw for a moment, but then the man blinked and it was gone. "Well, I've only been here since June, but I'm finding I like the slower pace of Thunder Canyon," Shane said. "I'm glad you enjoyed your meal."

The man left and Thomas saw Annabel's gaze follow him as he walked away. A flare of heat raced through him that could only be jealousy, but Thomas quickly squashed the emotion.

"I need to tell my cousin DJ about him," Annabel said, turning her attention back to the dessert. "I think they would get along great."

"Why's that?" Thomas asked.

"DJ owns the Rib Shack, another restaurant here in the resort. Not that he could get Mr. Roarke to work for him, but he'll probably try." She took another mouthful of cake and then laid the fork on the plate. "Oh, this really is so good, but I can't possibly eat another bite. I've probably gained five pounds from one meal."

"How about we work some of that off by dancing?"

Annabel's shocked gaze locked with his. "Dancing?"

The idea surprised Thomas just as much the moment the words left his mouth, but right now he wanted nothing more than to hold this woman in his arms.

"Why not? There's wonderful music coming from the main area and we've got plenty of room." Thomas stood and held out his hand.

"Oh, I'm not the best dancer." Annabel sat back in her chair, the candlelight highlighting the pretty blush on her cheeks. "The whole two left feet thing."

"Maybe you just haven't met the right partner yet." He waited, knowing it wouldn't take her long to match up his words with her earlier declaration about him not having met the right dog. "Dance with me, Annabel. Please."

She placed her hand in his and Thomas gently pulled her to her feet and into his arms. He easily maneuvered her until they were in front of the windows again, the star-filled night sky a beautiful backdrop to the dimly lit room.

Her left hand rested at his shoulder and he tucked her other hand in his and brought both of them to rest over his heart. The softness of her hair brushed against his jaw and he inhaled, pulling her sexy vanilla scent deep into his chest. His hand flattened across her back, seeming to startle her, but he just pressed her tighter to him, her curves wreaking havoc with his attempts at controlling his libido.

Despite all the time they'd spent together over the past two weeks, and the few times they touched, they'd never been this close.

Thomas now knew why he'd worked so hard to keep distance between them. Holding Annabel in his arms wasn't like anything he'd ever felt before.

And that scared the hell out of him.

"You are a liar, Miss Cates."

"Am I?" Her words caressed his neck with warm breaths.

"You're a wonderful dancer." Thomas lowered his head a few inches until his cheek rested against hers. "I think you like keeping me off balance where you're concerned."

"Now why would I do that?"

He leaned back, hating how their bodies separated, but wanting to see her eyes. "I don't know. I'm normally not a man who likes surprises."

"Well then, what I'm about to say next shouldn't be a surprise," she said, looking up at him, "but I'm going to tell you anyway."

He stilled, having absolutely no idea what she was going to say.

"This has been the most magical night of my life, Thomas." Annabel gazed at him, her eyes wide. "Thank you...from the bottom of my heart."

Annabel had no idea what time it was when Thomas pulled his sleek sports car to a stop in her family's driveway.

The last time she'd looked at the glowing digits of the car's clock it had been almost eleven-thirty. That had been when they left the resort, and as hard as she tried, Annabel just couldn't keep her eyes open during the drive home.

They'd stayed at the restaurant for another hour after her heartfelt thank-you that she'd been so sure would end in a kiss.

Only she hadn't been brave enough to rise up on her tiptoes and press her mouth to his.

Instead Thomas had replied with a simple "you're welcome" and they continued to dance until coffee arrived, which they enjoyed while finishing off the last of that decadent cake.

He shut off the engine and the car stilled. She heard him turn toward her, but again, her eyelids were too heavy even though she'd love to see the expression on his face.

"Annabel?"

He spoke her name in a soft whisper that sent shivers up and down her spine. Something she'd been experiencing from the moment he walked onto her front porch dressed in a charcoal-gray suit that fit him to perfection. Heck, even her sisters had sighed as they peeked at him through the dining-room window.

"Are you asleep?" he asked, his voice back to its normal level, which was still sexy.

"No, but if I lived another mile or so away I probably would be." This time she succeeded in opening her eyes and smiled. "Did I thank you for an amazing evening?"

"Many times."

"Good." She closed her eyes and stretched, pointing

her naked toes in a perfect arch. The heels had slipped off the moment she got into his car. The pair were her favorite, but she didn't wear them too often.

Or this dress, because while she loved what the bandage-style dress did for her curves, it tended to ride up whenever she sat.

Or stretched.

The sound of the driver's side door opening and the inside light coming on had Annabel bolting upright in her seat. She grabbed the hem and yanked it back into place before looking at Thomas, but he was already out of the car.

The interior went dark again when he closed the door, but she'd found her purse, shawl and shoes by the time he walked around the car.

Sliding out of the passenger seat, she gently closed the door behind her. Except for the porch light at the kitchen door, the house was dark and the last thing she wanted was an audience when she and Thomas said good-night.

"I was going to get the door— Hey, you're shorter."

Annabel smiled and held up her shoes dangling from her fingers. "Sore tootsies."

"You okay to walk in bare feet?"

"Of course. I'm outside all the time— Thomas!" Annabel felt the ground disappear beneath her feet as Thomas lifted her into his arms and headed for the side porch.

"We can't—" he paused and cleared his throat, his grip tightening on her bare thighs "—can't take any chances."

She looped her arm around his shoulders, grateful when she didn't knock him in the head with her purse.

Moments later, they stood in the soft glow of the light and he gently set her feet to the ground, his arm staying around her waist.

Her hand slid to his upper arm, but she tightened her hold, keeping their bodies close, hating that her other hand was filled with her shawl and shoes.

"There you go. Home safe and sound."

She tried to read the emotion in his gaze, but he dipped his head, the shadows making it impossible for her to see.

Did it matter?

Was he finally going to kiss her?

"Thanks for tonight," he finally said, releasing her and stepping away. "I haven't had... It was a great night."

The lump of disappointment in her throat when he made no move to give her a good-night kiss made it impossible for Annabel to speak. She could only nod as she reached for the screen door.

He stepped off the porch and she spun around, opening the inside door and slipping into the kitchen before he even made it back to the driveway.

Not knowing why she did, Annabel stood at the door and watched through the window as he climbed back into his car and started the engine.

What had gone wrong?

Tonight had been pure magic from the moment he'd picked her up. He'd been gracious with her family, attentive to the point of distraction from the first moment he touched her and that meal—who goes to the effort of making sure they had a private table, finding out a date's favorite foods...

He should've kissed her.

She should've kissed him.

She dumped her stuff on the counter beside her, her hand hovering over the light switch, and still his car stayed.

Was he waiting for her to—

She dragged her fingers downward, flipping the lever and the porch went dark. Then she twisted the lock on the door, the click echoing in the quiet.

Suddenly the car's engine cut off, and Thomas emerged, sprinting back across the drive. She undid the lock, yanked open the door and pushed at screen. Seconds later, he had her wrapped in his arms as he pushed her up against the wall, his mouth covering hers in a searing kiss.

Her hands plunged into his hair, pulling him closer and loving how his kiss was thorough, possessive and exploded with an intensity that had started the moment they met. His hands moved lower until they cupped her backside, pulling her tight to him. He leaned into her, lifted her until their bodies aligned perfectly, allowing her to feel the evidence of his arousal.

She moaned low in her throat, their tongues stroking against each other, eager to share the heat and hunger. He echoed that moan back to her with his own, and regret pulsated through her because she knew they had to stop.

Finally, he lifted his head, his hands sliding back to her waist. He pressed his forehead to hers, his rapid breathing matching her own as her hands moved to lie against the restless rise and fall of his chest.

"Wow." Annabel stole another kiss, thrilling at the groan the quick swipe of her lips over his brought forth.

"Please, tell me we are going to do this again. And soon."

Thomas's laugh was husky and warm. "What's that? Go out for dinner?"

"Yeah, that, too." Especially if this man were on the menu as appetizer, main course and dessert because she was already craving another taste of heaven.

Chapter 8

"I think you're doing what mothers do best, sticking your nose where it doesn't belong."

Annabel stilled as her father's voice carried from the kitchen to the stairway.

Wednesdays were her late days at the library so she'd taken a run without Smiley this morning—his habit of stopping at every tree made it a bit hard to maintain a good pace. When she'd returned she'd grabbed a mug of freshly brewed java and her mail from the basket in the hall before heading up the stairs to her bedroom.

Until her father's pronouncement stopped her in her tracks.

"Annabel doesn't have a lot of experience when it comes to men," came a more feminine voice—her mother. "I'm worried she's going to get hurt."

Unable to resist, Annabel sat on a step and waited, sure her sisters had shown up as well and, like the rest of the family, they'd have no problem stating their own opinions about her love life.

Or anything else, for that matter.

"Then why don't you talk to her?" Zeke Cates said. "No one else is home, including me, because I'm on my way out. You can say your piece without it becoming a major discussion."

Bless her dad. He understood how hard it was at times to be part of a big family. Annabel loved her parents and siblings, and living in the house where she grew up made financial sense, but there were times when having space to yourself and a sense of privacy were sorely lacking.

"But she'll think I'm interfering."

"You are, dear, but that's your right as her mother."

Annabel smiled at her father's parting words, knowing the following silence was her parents sharing a goodbye kiss.

Yep, there was the slam of the kitchen door.

Now, should she go back to the kitchen and find out exactly what was bothering her mother or scoot upstairs and see what Smiley was up to since he hadn't made an appearance yet? She still needed to grab a shower—

"Oh, there you are."

Busted.

Annabel took another sip of coffee, enjoying the surprise on her mother's face. "Here I am. Good morning."

"Good morning, dear." Her mother held on to her own coffee mug with a grip so tight Annabel feared the handle would crack. "How was your run?"

"It was good." Annabel eyed the clock hanging on the wall. She had plenty of time before she had to leave for work. Might as well get this over with. "So, tell me why you're so worried about me."

"Oh, Annabel… I'm sorry you overheard that." Her mother sighed. "I'm just concerned that you're falling too fast for your doctor friend."

Her doctor friend. Well, that was one way of looking at what was happening between her and Thomas. After the way he went out of his way to create such a special dinner—and the way he'd kissed her goodnight last Saturday—she'd like to think he was at least a step above being a friend.

A big step.

"Thomas and I are…getting to know one another. So I would hold off on ordering the wedding invitations just yet."

Her mother walked up the stairs and sat beside her. "You like him."

"Of course I like him. The man is smart, funny, caring and gorgeous. What's not to like?"

"I will admit he was very nice when we met him the other night, even if he did seem a bit serious. Have you seen him since your date?"

Annabel wondered where her mother was heading with that question. "Yes, of course I have."

"At the hospital."

"Yes, at the hospital. I stopped in on Monday to talk about the Tuesday and Thursday sessions I'll be having with Smiley, and I saw him again yesterday after the session."

"Are you planning to go over there today?"

As a matter of fact she was, during her dinner break.

Annabel wanted to check on Mr. Owens, whose visit with Smiley yesterday was cut short because the elderly man hadn't been feeling well.

"Yes, I am, but to visit a friend, Mom. Not to see Thomas."

"Don't you think it's strange that outside of your two dates, you've only seen him at the hospital?"

"It's where he works. Not to mention where the therapy sessions take place. Doesn't it make sense that's where we would run into each other?"

"It seems to me you are the one doing all the running into, not him."

Okay, that hit home. Annabel took another sip from her mug, silently acknowledging her mother had a point.

She hadn't heard from Thomas at all on Sunday, even though he'd left with a whispered "I'll call you" after that mind-blowing, body-numbing kiss that really did make her wish she had her own place.

Stopping by his office on Monday to see Marge made sense as the secretary was coordinating Smiley's sessions. Of course, Thomas was there and he did seem happy to see her. They'd even gone down to the hospital café for a light dinner.

At her suggestion.

And he'd walked the two of them all the way to her car yesterday after she'd run into him when leaving Mr. Owens's room.

He'd teased her about parking in the farthest corner of the lot. She'd flirted back that maybe she'd been trying to lure him away from the crowds.

His smile had disappeared when he took a step closer, crowding her against her car. Annabel had been so sure he was going to kiss her again. Until Smiley had broken the spell by noticing a nearby squirrel and uncharacteristically taking off in pursuit.

Okay, so she'd only seen Thomas at the hospital the past few days, but that didn't stop the man from invading her dreams at night.

She wanted to kiss him again. She wanted more than that. The idea of stripping off that starched dress shirt and perfectly matched tie to find out just what those shoulders of his looked like—

"Annabel?"

Wow, she'd gotten lost there for a moment. "Sorry about that, Mom. Did you say something?"

"It's just that your social life has been a bit slow lately and you don't want to rush—"

"Slow?" Annabel cut off her mother's words with a sharp laugh. "Mom, I haven't dated anyone steady in over three years."

"Which is why I'm concerned that you're doing what you always do. You jump in with both feet when you believe in something, without much thought as to how difficult things might become in the future. Whether it's upgrading the children's area of the library or the therapy training with Smiley."

Yes, those projects had entailed a lot of hard work and effort on her part, coupled with more steps backward than forward at times thanks to the said "both feet" habit, but she'd accomplished both goals, quite successfully she might add. "Hey, both of those other ventures turned out fine. Better than fine."

"Well then, what about when you decided to enter the Frontier Days marathon after only running a few weeks? You ended up in the E.R. with a stress fracture. Or that spur-of-the-moment road trip you and Jazzy took last summer that found you in the middle of nowhere with a busted engine?"

Annabel let loose a deep sigh. Boy, what were mothers for if not to remind you of your shortcomings? "So let's add getting a little starry-eyed over a doctor to the list."

"I'm just worried you're setting yourself up for heartache," her mother persisted, laying a hand on her arm. "Doctors are notorious for not having happy, stable marriages. I want you to be happy, just like I want all my children to be."

Surprised at her mother's claim, Annabel could only stare at her. "That's absurd. Where did you hear that about doctors' marriages?"

"I was chatting with Mrs. Banning the other day—"

"You talked about me with the neighbors?"

"Of course not. We were just visiting and she mentioned her daughter's marriage was ending, and in a very messy way. Her husband is a surgeon. He works terrible hours and wasn't there for her or the children. Now he's decided that the woman who supported him all through medical school is too boring to spend the rest of his life with."

"I'm sorry for what Mrs. Banning's daughter is going through, but it sounds as though there are more issues with that marriage than her husband's working hours."

"Mrs. Callahan was with us, too, and she mentioned a friend whose daughter also married a doctor right here in Thunder Canyon, who was crushed when her husband recently announced he was leaving her so he could marry one of the nurses on his staff. A much younger nurse."

"Who needs reality television when the Thunder Canyon gossip mill is alive and well?" Annabel rolled her eyes. "What about Cade and Abby? Cade has his own business and he works all kind of crazy hours."

"Cade works for his family, he can set his own hours. Besides, your sister was in love with Cade for years before she, or he, ever admitted their feelings."

"And Laila?" Annabel pushed harder, bringing up her other recently married sister. "Jackson is an executive at Traub Oil Industries and from what I've heard he travels a lot. Are you telling me Laila should be worried because they only knew each other a month before getting engaged?"

"By the time your sister met Jackson she'd had more experience when it came to men than all of my girls combined, although Jazzy is giving her a good run for her money. When Jackson came to town and swept Laila off her feet, they were both ready for married life."

Annabel stood. She was *ready* for this conversation to be over. Yes, everything her mother said about her sisters was true, but that didn't mean she was heading for heartache.

"Well, you don't have to worry because Thomas and I are… I don't know what we are, but we aren't thinking about anything close to marriage. I appreciate your concern, Mom, but I'm an adult and it's my life and my decision."

"Oh, honey, I just want you to be careful with your heart."

Evelyn Cates pushed to her feet as well, and Annabel saw nothing but love and concern in her mother's gaze.

"I am being careful," she said, leaning over to give her mom a quick kiss on the cheek. "Trust me, I'm not in over my head. And neither is my heart."

Thomas was so far over his head he didn't have a clue what he was going to do.

About Annabel.

Intentionally skipping the "Smiley Session" this afternoon had been the right decision. He was a busy man with a lot of work to do, which was why he was still sitting at his desk an hour after his official workday was over. An hour after Annabel and Smiley had left the hospital, thanks to Marge's report, who was working late herself.

Because of him.

The woman never left the office until he did. He'd told her often enough that it wasn't necessary for her to stay so late. But with her husband gone and her kids moved away, Marge always said the only things waiting for her at home were three cats and they'd survive just fine without her.

Him? She wasn't so sure of.

So most nights he went home with a briefcase full of work or he'd circle back after grabbing a quick dinner off the hospital campus.

He sighed, leaned back in his chair and scrubbed at his tired eyes. He should get the heck out of here. Reading the same paragraph over and over again in his patient's file wasn't helping the information stick in his head.

Maybe because that space was already filled with

images of a perky, bubbly blonde who'd taken his breath away the moment he'd pulled her into his arms and finally kissed her.

He'd thought about little else after they'd danced at the Gallatin Room. No, that wasn't true. He'd been thinking about kissing Annabel from the moment he'd met her, but last Saturday, the need and want had been building all night. Until he couldn't take it anymore.

There'd been so many chances.

Like when they'd walked to his car after leaving the resort or when he'd pulled into her family's driveway and discovered she wasn't asleep like he'd thought. Not to mention, when he'd set her back on her feet beneath the porch light after he'd carried her to the front door, her body brushing the length of his.

He'd taken none of those openings, having decided during the few minutes it took to reach her front porch it was best to keep things simple. Say good-night and leave. He managed to do both, but only made it as far as turning on the engine, before the porch light went out after Annabel got inside.

He'd missed his chance.

Seconds later, he'd been racing across the yard. The way the door opened immediately said she'd been watching him—waiting. It fanned the flames of his desire for her even higher.

The sureness of how it felt to hold her had taken its time to settle in, thanks to the passion of that kiss, but when it had, Thomas knew he had to get out of there. So he'd given a simple promise to call and then left.

Only he'd never called.

He'd seen Annabel on Monday here at the hospital and they'd grabbed a quick bite together down in the café—not the most private venue—and of course he heard about it the next day from a few colleagues. And while he'd purposely dropped by Mr. Owens's room on Tuesday to see how the visit went with Smiley, he hadn't planned on walking her and her dog out to the parking lot.

It'd just been so easy to talk to her. Thomas rose from behind his desk and walked to the window, drawn to the vivid reds and oranges of the setting sun.

No matter what the subject, Annabel made him feel relaxed and comfortable. Not to mention the crackle of sexual energy that seemed to surround her, a deep pulsing pull that called to him every time he saw her.

But late Tuesday night, after he found himself lying alone in his bed, wishing she was with him and, in turn, had berated himself for feeling that way again, he'd realized the simple truth.

Being with Annabel scared him silly.

Not that he was *with* her.

Two dinners and spending time together at the hospital didn't exactly make them a couple. Of course, Marge or some of the staff didn't need much more than to see them together in the hospital café to come to that conclusion.

Getting involved in a relationship again was the last thing he wanted, or needed, at the moment. He still felt he had to prove himself, to right the wrongs of his past, but he was having a hell of time keeping Annabel out of his head.

"So, what'll it be tonight?"

Marge's voice from the open doorway cut into his thoughts. He turned and found her flipping through the notebook she kept of take-out menus from the local restaurants.

"Chinese or Mexican?" she continued, not looking up at him. "Or are you not planning to stick around much longer?"

He didn't get a chance to choose.

"Mmm, go with the Chinese. The kung pao chicken at Mr. Lee's is to die for."

The lilting voice from his dreams drew his attention past his secretary. "Annabel. What are you doing here?"

Silence filled the air for a moment until Marge cleared her throat. "I think I'll just go down to the lounge and get myself a cup of hot tea. Annabel, would you like anything?"

"No, thanks, Marge, but I appreciate the offer."

Marge smiled at Annabel, shot him a quick wink over her shoulder that caused his stomach to drop to his feet and left the office area.

Oh, hell, maybe it was the sight of Annabel walking toward him in a simple cotton skirt, tank top and wedged heels that did that.

Or the fire-engine red polish on her toes.

He bit back a groan and forced his gaze back above her neckline. "So, what brings you this way so late?"

Annabel waved what looked like the remains of a tattered teddy bear in the air. "I had to come back for Smiley's baby."

Her words threw him. "Excuse me?"

"I know it doesn't look like much now, but this stuffed bear came with Smiley from the shelter." As she glanced down at the toy, her long golden curls tumbled over one shoulder. "He carried it around for weeks after I first brought him home. Then he seemed to only need the thing when he went to sleep."

She offered a quick shrug, and continued, "I don't know why he brought it with him to today's session, but once we got home I realized he'd left it behind. I had to run a few errands anyway. When I pulled into the parking lot, I saw your light was on, so I thought I'd stop by and see if you wanted to grab some dinner…"

Her voice trailed off when she looked at him again. Thomas swallowed hard at the mixture of desire and awareness he read in her blue eyes as their gazes locked. And just like that his world tilted off balance as uncontrolled need and want washed over him again.

Shoving his hands deep in his pockets, Thomas broke free and looked away. "Annabel, I'm not sure that is such a good idea."

"What's not a good idea? Chinese? Hey, if you want Mexican, that's fine with me. I'm easy."

Damn it, the last thing she was doing was making this easy.

Control.

He needed to get this situation back under control, back to what he was used to, a place of organization—of having power over one's actions and emotions.

A place that was familiar to him, ever since his mother pulled him aside after his grandfather's accident and told him tears were not allowed. At the tender age of seven, she'd expected him to handle what happened to his grandfather with the same dignity and grace that the Norths handled everything else.

Which probably explained why he'd thrown himself into his studies, determined that when he became a doctor, no one else would suffer the way his grandfather had. Of course, he'd learned the hard way that doctors weren't miracle workers, but he had a pretty damn good track record so far, at least here at TC General.

If his affair with Victoria had taught him anything, it was that he had the tendency of letting a woman's beauty blind him to everything else around. Considering his lack of judgment and having to learn to live with the regret, the last thing he wanted was to make the same mistake.

He faced her again. "I've got a lot of work ahead of me and now that your dog therapy sessions are in place, I don't think— It's just that my free time is going to be very limited."

Barely a heartbeat passed before Annabel offered him a bright smile. "Oh. Well, you've obviously given this a lot of thought." Her cheery tone and calm acceptance were the last things he expected. "I don't want to make things…difficult for you. I'll just go and let you get back to work."

Thomas wanted to speak, even though he had no idea what else to say. Not that it mattered. His throat was so constricted he could barely breathe.

A nod was all he managed.

She quickly backed up until she reached the door. "So, I guess I'll see you when I see you."

Then she was gone.

Thomas stood rooted to the spot, his blood pounding in his temples at he stared at the empty space. Had he really just told a beautiful and fascinating woman he wasn't interested?

He waited for the cool detachment that told him he'd done the right thing to bring relief that it was over. It was nowhere to be found. In its place instead was an overwhelming rush of regret and panic that filled every ounce of his being.

"Dr. North?"

The sharp tone in Marge's voice caused his head to snap up.

How long had she been standing there? How long had he been standing here staring at the doorway like a fool?

He started to ask, but had to pause and clear his throat first. "Ah, I don't know how much of that you overheard, but for some reason I think I should—"

"Go."

With one word the despair shifted to hope. "She has no reason to let me—"

"What she has is a good head start." Marge folded her hands primly over her stomach. "And you're without a car today, if memory serves. Go."

Thomas automatically reached across his desk for his phone and house keys. "I need to shut down—"

"Turning off a computer, the lights and locking your door is within my scope of abilities." She made a show of glancing at her watch. "If you're not back in fifteen minutes, I'm going home."

Sprinting past his secretary, Thomas headed for the stairs. He raced outside and into the parking lot, praying Annabel was a creature of habit and had parked in the same location as before.

He hoped he hadn't ruined his chance with her. If he had, he'd have a lot of making up to do.

Chapter 9

Annabel couldn't believe how much Thomas's words hurt.

She'd thought things were going so well between them. They hadn't run into each other when she popped in to check on Mr. Owens yesterday, and while she'd hoped to see him today at Smiley's session, it never occurred to her that he'd been avoiding her.

Obviously it hadn't come to mind or she'd have never made the effort to seek him out tonight.

Coming back for Smiley's toy hadn't been an urgent issue. The dog hadn't even noticed it was gone, but Annabel foolishly took it as a sign.

So she'd changed her clothes, spritzed her wrists and cleavage with her favorite perfume and hopped back in her car, daydreaming about more alone time with Thomas and hoping she'd have the good fortune of finding him still at the hospital.

Oh, she'd found him all right.

Shoving the ratty teddy bear in her bag, Annabel marched across the parking lot, proud that she'd at least stayed cool during his little speech and walked away with her head held high.

Okay, so she walked fast once she left his office, but still she managed to keep it together in the elevator, thankful she hadn't run into anyone. She still didn't understand what drove him to say what he did, but the bottom line was the coming days would be empty without him.

The tears began to well in her eyes.

"Hey, wait!"

A voice calling from behind her, followed by hands closing over her shoulders, sent a rush of panic through her. A quick, sharp jab with her elbow was on the mark, punctuated by a male grunt and she was free. Spinning around, keys laced between her fingers, Annabel took a defensive stance ready to scream—

"Thomas!" She dropped her hands, but not before quickly swiping the remaining moisture from her eyes. "Are you crazy? I could have stabbed you with my keys!"

"I'm sorry…didn't mean to scare you." He puffed out the words while rubbing his hand across his midsection. "That was a stupid…stupid thing to do."

At least the man was right about something tonight.

Annabel folded her arms under her breasts, tried to slow her runaway breathing while telling herself he deserved the hard poke to the gut. "Yes, it was."

"No, I don't mean grabbing you— Well, yes, that

was dumb, too." He dropped his hand, but then propped both on his hips. "I'm talking about what happened in my office. I don't know what I was saying. I mean, I know what I said. I heard the words coming out of my mouth. It's just that I've been doing a lot of thinking the past couple of weeks, hell, the past couple of years. Probably too much thinking, but I've been that way since I was a kid."

Annabel blinked hard and tried to keep up with Thomas's ramblings. He didn't mean to scare her, but he did follow her out here. Pretty quickly, too, as she'd only walked out of his office less than ten minutes ago.

She ignored the sharp thrill that zinged through her.

"The thing is, I think I was too hasty. It's just that I've been trying to work through some things from the past and what's been going on between us. You know, weighing the good, the bad, lessons learned, and all that stuff. The next thing I knew you were standing there—"

"Thomas, stop!"

Annabel took a leap of faith that she finally understood what this man was trying to say.

He did as she asked, but the silence only made his words a bigger jumbled mess in her head. She didn't want to sort through them right now. Not with him standing right there in front of her.

Grabbing his already loosened tie, and throwing her concerns—and her mother's admonitions—to the wind, she wrapped it once around her palm and yanked him up against her. "Are you going to kiss me or what?"

He blinked owlishly, then relief filled his eyes, his hooded gaze dropping to her lips. "God, yes."

She didn't wait, but instead rose to her toes and covered his mouth with hers before pulling back just enough to gently suck his lower lip between hers.

His large, capable hands circled her waist, holding her in place as a deep groan rumbled in his chest. He quickly took over, ravishing her mouth with hot, deep skims of his tongue against hers. She boldly matched his every move, surrendering to the craziness of the moment.

And it was crazy.

He pressed her up against her car door, his hips brushing in a slow back and forth motion that brought forth a husky moan of her own. A delicious ache for more, much more, filled her, spreading like wildfire until every corner of her body vibrated with need.

His mouth slipped from hers, his lips trailing across her cheek to her ear. "I know how insane this sounds, but I want you, Annabel."

A victorious thrill raced through her and she couldn't hold back the nervous giggle that escaped. "Well, I would say your place or mine, but I'm afraid my father would be blocking your path, his shotgun firmly in hand."

Thomas leaned back, an unreadable emotion in his eyes. Then he blinked and it was replaced with an amused gleam. "Then I guess we'd better go to my place. Problem is my car is in the shop."

Annabel jiggled her keys in front of him. "You know, I'm not even going to ask how you planned to get home tonight. You want to drive or play navigator?"

He gave her a crooked grin as he slipped the keys from her hand. "We can decide that later, but for now, it'll be faster if I drive."

Less than fifteen minutes later they pulled into his condo's garage, located in an upscale complex Annabel had never been to before. When he went to shut off the engine, she slipped her fingers from his, smiling at how they'd became entangled in the first place. Seemed a little teasing finger action back and forth across his powerful thigh was too much of a distraction for the sexy doctor.

But she couldn't help herself.

The man drove her quirky little bug as if it was a luxury car, with purpose and speed. What could she say? It was a turn-on.

"Nice place," she said, popping out of the passenger side as the garage door slid silently closed behind them.

"It's just the garage," Thomas shot back, taking her hand again as he headed for the stairs. "Wait until you see the master bedroom."

At the top of the stairs, he opened a door and wrapping his arm around her waist, pulled her close and kissed her again. She clung to him as he walked her backward into what she guessed was the front foyer.

He broke free of their kiss and flipped on the lights. She blinked as everything came into focus. Then she gazed around in curiosity.

Soft lighting highlighted fine leather furniture and the shiny chrome and glass tables that sat atop an oversize plush Oriental rug her toes itched to dig into. The best "boy toys" money could buy filled the room, as well. An enormous flat-screen TV hung over an empty fireplace while nearby floor-to-ceiling bookshelves held numerous black boxes that must be a high-end stereo system.

Gleaming hardwood floors stretched the length

of the room, including a dining area with a table big enough to seat six. Off to the left, she saw a kitchen.

His home was beautiful, but her first thought was "professional decorator." She wondered how much of Thomas was even reflected here.

"Please don't tell me you want a tour." He nuzzled her from behind, his lips warm against her neck, and Annabel was glad she'd secured her hair to one side with a large clip. "If so, let's start with the second floor."

She couldn't agree more, with one minor change.

Facing him again, she dropped her purse to the floor and quickly stripped off his tie, tossing it to one side. "Oh, I think we'll start—and finish—right here."

It seemed to take a moment for Thomas to get her meaning, but once he did, he lifted her in his arms and headed straight for the sofa.

Anticipation flooded her insides as she kicked off her shoes along the way, waiting until he sat, her straddling his lap before she leaned in and captured his mouth again.

Just like she'd hoped to do in his office.

While their mouths tasted and nipped, devoured and shared, her fingers went to work on the buttons of his dress shirt, releasing them all the way to his waist. Yanking the material open as far as it would go, she reveled in the feel and heat of his naked chest, at the way he jumped at her touch.

Time to get serious.

When she lightly dragged her fingernails over his nipples, his hands gripped her hips, cradling her heated center over the thick ridge of his arousal. The loose swing of her skirt made sure that the only barrier between her nakedness and the silkiness of his slacks were the simple thong panties she wore. Unable to resist, she rotated her hips in a slow circle.

"Damn, that feels good," he rasped, breaking free of their kiss. "You feel good."

Their eyes met and held as he gently pulled her tank top free from the skirt's waistband, his hands slowly sliding underneath and up over her belly. He kept going, taking the material with him until she had no choice but to raise her arms as he tugged the top over her head.

While her hands were raised, she'd reached back and freed her hair, loving the heat in his eyes as her breasts pressed against the bra's lacy cups. Shaking her head sent loose waves flying over her shoulders, but it was the way his fingertips traced the delicate straps of her bra that sent shivers dancing over her skin.

"You cold?" His words came out in rough whisper. "The air-conditioning is pretty strong."

"I think it's more about what you're doing to me than artificial cooling." He proved her point when he caught the lobe of her ear gently between his teeth and another shudder rolled through her. "Oh, see what I mean?"

"Here, let's get you warm." In one swift move, he had her flat on her back against the cool, soft leather of his sofa as he stretched out over her.

Soft except for the object pressing into her lower back.

"What the—" Annabel reached beneath her and pulled out a large rectangular object covered in buttons of all shapes, sizes and colors.

He took the device from her and tossed it to the side. "It's just my remote."

She gave a half laugh, lowering her voice to a purr. "A remote for what?"

Thomas deftly pulled down the zipper of her skirt while his lips left behind a trail of wet kisses over her collar bone. He then returned his focus to the lace edging of her bra, his tongue dipping inside the delicate border to wet the skin beneath. "Everything."

As sinfully wonderful as his focus was, Annabel persisted. "Everything?"

He groaned and lifted his head, bracing himself on one elbow. "Don't tell me you really want to know?"

Annabel shifted, his erection now in perfect alignment between her thighs. "Mmm, impress me."

"I thought I was."

She laughed, and he joined her, his deep chuckle vibrating the length of her body and at that moment, as sure as if her heart had flipped over and displayed the words *I Belong to Thomas North* etched in a pretty scrolled font, she knew.

She was in love with this crazy, wonderful man.

It wasn't a sentiment she had a lot of experience with, but the pure joy and elation pouring from her heart was something she planned to embrace with both hands and never let go of.

He surprised her when he reached over, picked the remote up and placed it back in her hand. "Press the numbers 3-1-7-3 on the bottom keypad."

Annabel did as instructed, focusing on the device. The last thing she wanted was Thomas to see the new-found emotion going off like skyrockets inside her before she had a chance to examine the feeling.

In private.

As soon as she pressed the last number, a fire blazed

to life in the fireplace, blanketing the room with dancing shards of light and a warm glow.

"Oh!"

His lips nibbled up the side of her neck. "Now enter 6-8-7-4-2."

Her fingers shook as she pushed the correct buttons and seconds later a faint beep filled the air, before it was replaced with the smooth strains of classic jazz flowing from the stereo.

"Okay, I'm officially impressed." Annabel blinked hard, refusing to allow her head, or her heart, to even imagine Thomas showing these tricks to someone else. Mentally shaking off that thought, she playfully pointed the remote at him. "Now, what's the magic combination that works on you?"

A smile tipped one corner of his sensual mouth as he took the device from her hand and tossed it farther away this time in the direction of the closest chair. "I think you already know what buttons to press."

He pushed up to his knees and peeled off his shirt. Annabel found herself thankful for the fire's glow that showed off his wide shoulders and washboard abs to perfection. Next was his belt and darn if he didn't take his time letting the strip of leather slide from his belt loops.

Loosening the button at his waist, he reached for the zipper, but she brushed his hand away and slowly lowered the zipper.

She only caught a glimpse of dark boxer briefs and the length of him pressing against the material before he reached for her, tugging gently at her skirt. Raising her hips, he eased the material down over her legs, leaving her in nothing but her bra and matching panties.

"You are perfection, Annabel."

The naked desire in his gaze called to her. She crooked her finger in a come-hither motion and he quickly complied, molding his hard planes with her curves.

He took her mouth again as his fingers nimbly opened the front clash of her bra, his warm hand cupping her breast. His thumb rasped over the hardened bud, drawing it even tighter until he ended the kiss and drew the peak into the moist heat of his mouth.

A blast of shameless need flared deep inside her. Annabel arched, offering him more, and he took, moving his mouth from one breast to the other, leaving behind a shimmering wetness that tingled in the cool night air.

She reached low, her fingers brushing across his stomach as the need to touch him overpowered her. He shuddered when she slipped beneath the cotton waistband and curled around him. She stroked him once, twice, before he pulled her hand away.

"Don't," he rasped. "It's been...a while since I've done this."

His words made her heart soar. He released her wrist and she clutched at his shoulders as his fingers easily moved aside the damp material covering the most imitate part of her before slipping into her wet heat.

"Oh, for me, too. Thomas, please..."

Moments later, the rest of their clothes disappeared and Thomas paused only to sheathe himself with a condom he grabbed from his wallet. Then he was back between her legs, cupping her bottom and tilting her hips. He entered her with a long, slow thrust, capturing her gasp with his mouth.

Their bodies moved together in a natural, instinctive rhythm. A burning caught fire deep inside her, growing stronger and stronger, taking her higher with each demanding stroke.

Those same fireworks she'd felt deep inside from the moment they met threatened to explode, shattering her heart and soul in a million colorful pieces.

His lips moved to her neck, whispering words against her skin, pushing her even higher as she dragged her nails over his back, demanding the sweet release only he could give.

Then the fuse of her passion ignited, sending her spiraling into the heavens. She clung to him, crying out his name, loving the moment when he gave up his last remnant of control, buried himself deep inside her, joining her.

They lay there together afterward, trying to catch their breaths and failing when he pressed his lips to the pulsing in her neck and she tightened around him.

Annabel had never known a moment like this before in her life. Was it because her heart had already laid claim to this charming, honest and dedicated man?

Her wonder was interrupted by their stomachs suddenly rumbling in sync. She laughed aloud, the sweetness of the moment almost too much to bear. "Boy, I guess you do want dinner."

"I'm starved." Thomas lifted himself off her while flashing a grin of total male satisfaction as he helped her sit up. "Even more so now."

"Chinese from Mr. Lee's still sounds good to me."

"Me, too." Thomas reached for his pants, pulled

out his cell phone and hit the speed dial number. "Any special requests?"

"I'm happy with anything."

He rattled off a list of appetizers, his arched brows silently asking for her approval with each item. Annabel nodded in agreement as she scooped up her clothes, suddenly wishing for a light blanket to throw over her naked body.

Not that she was ashamed of being like this with him, but Thomas had been right. The air-conditioning was going at full blast and the air was chilly despite the fire.

Or was it reality setting in?

Goodness knows, she had no idea where things were headed between them now, other than dinner and hopefully more moments like what they just shared.

But what did this mean to Thomas?

She still wasn't sure exactly what he'd been trying to tell her back in his office, or the parking lot. Did he want more? Did he want her? Could he possibly love her in return?

"Okay, we're all set."

Thomas's words pulled her from her thoughts. He stood, the cool air obviously not affecting him, and then before she realized what he was doing, he easily lifted her into his arms.

"Hey!"

"You think I'm going to let some high school delivery boy get an eyeful by staying downstairs? No way." He gave her a quick squeeze. "Besides, we've got twenty minutes until the food gets here."

Annabel laughed again. "You've got to stop carrying me around."

"You feel…good in my arms."

She cupped his face with both hands and placed a chaste kiss, one that carried all the love in her heart, on his mouth. He carried her up the stairs to his bedroom and laid her on the silky comforter. Never breaking eye contact, Thomas lowered his mouth to hers, returning her kiss with one that was just as soft and sweet, even more so because of the slight tremble when his lips met hers.

Sunlight tried to make its way through the room-darkening shades with little success. Exactly how Thomas preferred it on those few mornings when he tried to sleep in.

Like today. Lying on his stomach, he cracked open one eye to focus on his bedside clock: 8:00 a.m.

Blinking hard, he looked again. That had to be wrong. For him, sleeping in usually meant staying in bed until six, six-thirty at the latest.

Nope, the numbers were an eight, a zero and now a one.

He bolted upright, coming to a fast realization of two things. The first, he was alone in his king-size bed, even though that's not the way he'd gone to sleep last night. The second was the aroma of frying bacon hovering in the air.

Annabel.

He quickly grabbed his cell phone from the bedside table, and checked his calendar. He breathed a sigh of relief. Yes, his first appointment of the day wasn't scheduled until noon.

Pulling on a pair of briefs and sweats, he stopped to use the bathroom and brush his teeth. After tossing his toothbrush back into the holder, he paused and stared into the mirror, his reflected image blurring as he thought back to the madness and passion that had consumed him last night.

They hadn't even made it past his living-room sofa that first time. Not that he was complaining. Being with Annabel had been amazing, and afterward, they'd spent the rest of the night in his bed, sharing Chinese takeout, a bottle of wine and each other.

Not the evening he'd thought he'd have after the way he'd fumbled through explaining his "I'm too busy" speech. A decision that hadn't lasted all of five minutes before he chased after her. Did she understand any of what he'd tried to say? Both in his office and in the parking lot?

Hell, he wasn't sure *he* understood the logic and reasoning that still swirled inside his head when it came to her, them.

But she'd dismissed his ramblings with a hard kiss, and he'd thrown caution, and control, out the window.

Yet again. Letting down his guard like that was something he hadn't done since—

Refusing to confuse things even more with thoughts of the past, Thomas stalked out of the bathroom and followed his nose downstairs. He started across the living room when he noticed a blanket draped over one of the chairs—a patchwork quilt, done up in rectangular-shaped blocks in shades of brown, dark red, black and beige that reminded him of the glass-tile pattern in his kitchen. Tucked into the folds of material was a dog-eared copy of a romance novel featuring a half-naked cowboy on the cover.

"Good morning, sleepyhead." Annabel strolled in

from the kitchen, looking impossibly sexy wearing only his wrinkled dress shirt from last night and her long hair pulled back in a messy ponytail. "You saved me a trip back upstairs to get you. Hope you're hungry."

She set two plates piled with scrambled eggs, bacon and buttered toast on his dining-room table, drawing his eye to the vase brimming with daisies perched in the middle.

Daisies?

He hadn't realized he had that much food in his kitchen, but he was quite certain the flowers hadn't been there at all.

"Ah, yeah, I'm starved." Thomas ignored the quick twist in his gut and held up the quilt. "Where'd this come from?"

"I made it." Her voice carried over her shoulder as she disappeared back into the kitchen, and then returned with glasses of orange juice and silverware. "Pretty, isn't it?"

"Yes, but what's it doing here?"

"I couldn't figure out how to lower your air-conditioning when I got up this morning." She sat at the table and motioned for him to join her. "So I grabbed it from my car to wrap around myself. Come on, let's eat before all of this gets cold."

"The food and the flowers came out of your car, as well?"

A piece of bacon stilled halfway to her mouth. "Is that a problem?"

"No, just curious." Proud of his causal tone, Thomas sat opposite her.

"When I went to get the quilt I remembered I stopped at the store last night before coming to the hospital. The flowers needed water and I thought the groceries could camp out in your fridge until I left." She took a bite. "Then I saw the inside of your fridge and figured a healthy breakfast was needed. You do know those things are made to hold food, right?"

He smiled and the knot in his stomach eased.

Everything Annabel said made perfect sense. It just threw him at how easily those things seemed at home here.

How easily she fit into his home.

And how much he liked it.

Chapter 10

Three days later, Thomas stepped out of his car, having parked at the far end of the already-crowded driveway at the Cates family ranch.

Tightening his grip on the bottle of wine and the bouquet of flowers he'd brought, he silently counted the number of cars and pickup trucks scattered around.

Six in total, which meant at least two more would be coming. Sunday dinner with Annabel's family.

Her entire family.

Fighting the urge to turn and bolt, he forced himself to keep walking forward, remembering how Annabel had offered the invite just last night.

They'd been lying together on his couch watching their second choice in a classic black-and-white movie night. The screwball romantic comedy featuring Lucille Ball had been Annabel's choice after viewing one of his favorite Jimmy Stewart dramas.

Her words had been casual, not even glancing away from the movie as she spoke, but Thomas could tell by the way her arm had tightened over his stomach how much she wanted him to say yes.

And the sparkle in her eyes when he had accepted.

A thank-you kiss followed, and they never saw the closing credits of the movie. She'd finally left in the wee hours of the morning.

They spent the past three evenings together at his place, but thanks to Smiley, who was like a child to Annabel, she hadn't slept over again since that first night. Not that her family minded taking care of the dog, she assured him. She'd shared the text message she'd sent on Thursday to her sister Jazzy, asking her to make sure Smiley was fed and let outside in the morning, but Smiley was her dog, her responsibility.

Knowing she couldn't stay hadn't cooled their love-making; if anything the time they spent in his bed had been hotter and sexier because they didn't have all night to be together.

Still, Thomas found himself tempted to tell Annabel to bring Smiley with her the next time she came over if it meant he could hold her in his arms all night.

And didn't that rock the already wobbly ground beneath his feet?

Walking up to the same kitchen door where he'd kissed her like crazy a week ago, Thomas remembered Annabel's light quip the first night they'd made love about how her father would've been waiting with a shotgun. He hadn't been quite sure if she'd been joking or serious, but now he pushed those thoughts from his head. Thinking about sex and Annabel at this moment probably wasn't a good idea.

Looking down at the wine and flowers in his hands, he wondered again if they were a good idea. Raised by parents who always insisted a gift for the hostess was a requirement, he'd felt strange leaving his house empty-handed.

So he'd turned around and gone back, grabbed a bottle from his private collection and stopped along the way to pick up the flowers, just in case her parents didn't drink wine.

A deep breath, pulled in through his nose and slowly released, helped a little, but not as much as he'd hoped.

Damn, he shouldn't be this nervous.

Having already met half of her family, how bad could it be to spend an afternoon with all of them?

"Psst! Hey, doc. Over here."

Thomas turned and saw Annabel standing at the far end of the porch. She sent him a saucy grin and signaled for him to join her. He did and she took his face in her hands and pulled him close, their lips meeting in a long, slow kiss that Annabel tried to deepen, but he held back.

"Spoilsport," she teased.

"With the size of your family? And your father's shotgun? I think not."

She laughed. "You just keep on impressing me, Dr. North."

Thomas again refused to let his mind wander back to how he'd impressed her on the couch, in his bed and beneath the dual-headed shower over the weekend.

She stepped back and he admired the simple sundress she wore, bright colors splashed in a wavy, tie-dyed pattern that seemed perfect for the hot August afternoon. He was already sweating beneath his collared shirt, despite the short sleeves, but he doubted that had anything to do with the temperature.

"You know, when I invited you here today I forgot to ask you one thing."

The seriousness of her tone got his attention. "What's that?"

"Who's your favorite baseball team?"

That's what she needed to know? "Ah, the Dodgers, I guess."

"Hmm, Dad and Brody are Rockies fans. Well, it should be okay. We're still a few weeks out from the start of football."

"The preseason is already under way."

She waved off his words. "Preseason games don't count. Not around here."

Thomas didn't realize she was such a fan of professional sports. "Tell that to the guys on the field."

"Who's your favorite team?"

He guessed they were still talking about football. "The Broncos, of course."

Annabel graced him with a bright smile and grabbed his arm. "Perfect! Let's go join the others."

Instead of going inside the house, Annabel led him around the backyard and to a large stone patio. Numerous chairs sat scattered around a raised fire pit, piled with fresh cut wood. Two steps led up to the main area where tables, one covered in an array of dishes, and more chairs filled the space.

Another gut check and a deep reach for confidence. How could one family have so many members?

"Dr. North." Zeke Cates, Annabel's father, rose from

one of the chairs and greeted them first. "Glad you could make it. It's good to see you again."

Thomas quickly maneuvered the flowers and wine into one hand so he could take the older man's out-stretched one. "It's good to see you, too. Thank you for including me, Mr. Cates. And please call me Thomas."

The man's sharp gaze moved between Thomas and Annabel. He tightened his grip and held it for a long moment before releasing him. "You know anything about barbecuing, Thomas?"

Not sure if he remembered Zeke's greeting being quite so strong the first time they met, Thomas resisted the urge to flex his fingers. "Ah, no, sir. Not much."

"That's too bad. Dad can use all the help he can get." A younger version of Annabel's father walked past, a plate piled high with uncooked steaks, burgers and hot dogs in his hands. "Hey, we can use his surgical precision when it comes to slicing the meat."

"That's Brody, one of my many annoying siblings," Annabel said with a grin.

Thomas nodded and acknowledged the younger man he guessed to be in his early twenties with a wave. The flowers started to slip from his grip but then he realized Annabel had reached for them. He released his hold on the bouquet, but held tight to the bottle of wine.

"Oh, aren't these pretty!" She buried her nose in the fragrant stems. "Yellow roses, white mums and my favorites, daisies."

A whisper of unease tagged Thomas as he glanced at the flowers. He hadn't noticed the specific types in the cluster when he grabbed them at the local florist in town.

Daisies again?

"So, you've already figured out my daughter's favorite flowers? How sweet." Evelyn Cates joined them and, thanks to his training, Thomas immediately picked up on the hint of anxiety in her tone. The older woman placed a hand on her daughter's arm. "Annabel, let's go find a vase for those."

"Actually, the flowers are for you, ma'am." Thomas slipped the tissue-wrapped bunch from Annabel's grip and presented them, along with the wine, to her mother. "And this is from a winery that's been in my family, on my mother's side, for years. I hope you enjoy it."

"Thank you." The strain around the woman's mouth eased for a moment, but when she looked at Annabel, the lines deepened and her smile appeared forced. "This was very kind of you."

Still confused, Thomas looked at Annabel hoping she wasn't upset over the flowers, but she offered him a full-blown smile that he felt all the way to his toes as she leaned into him, giving his arm a squeeze.

"Annabel?" Her mother headed toward the double glass doors. "You coming?"

"Don't worry, we won't scare off the good doctor while you're gone." Jazzy, one of the two sisters Thomas had already met, stepped outside through the same doors. "Annabel, I'm letting Smiley out. He started freaking out as soon as he spotted— Oops, watch out!"

The warning came too late as seconds later Thomas let out a rush of air when two large paws landed right on his stomach.

"Smiley!" Annabel cried out and reached for the dog's collar. "Get down!"

"It's all right." Brushing her hand away, Thomas

gently lifted the dog's paws, forcing the animal to rest back on his haunches. "Sit," he added, trying for a stern tone, just in case a verbal command was needed.

The dog obeyed, but stayed in the middle of all of them, tail wagging wildly, his attention solely on Thomas, with a few side glances at his owner.

Returning the dog's grin, Thomas reached down and scratched behind his ears. "Hey there, Smiley. Good to see you, boy."

"Well, you seem to have a fan," her father said.

"Oh, Smiley just loves Thomas." Annabel bent and gave Smiley a quick kiss on the snout. "Don't you, baby?"

Annabel's mother whirled around and hurried to the house.

Annabel sighed softly and looked at him. "I better see if she needs any help."

He gave her a quick nod and she left.

"So, what's your poison, doc?" Jordyn Leigh, the other sister who still lived at home and was here last Saturday, too, stood at a nearby table holding a bottle of beer in one hand, a pitcher of iced tea in the other.

The beer would've been great, bathing his dry throat with its tangy coldness but Thomas decided to play it safe. Moments later, he found himself sitting with Jazzy and Jordyn Leigh, a glass of iced tea in his hand and Smiley at his side.

Annabel's dad had joined his son at the oversize grill, keeping watch over their dinner as they argued about last night's Colorado Rockies game and the proper way to cook the steaks.

"Will you two knock it off?" a feminine voice called

out from behind Thomas. "Jackson, go over there and play referee."

Thomas stood when four more people joined them, assuming the tall blonde and pretty brunette were the last two Cates siblings.

"Hi, Jackson Traub, glad to meet you." A tall man wearing a Stetson held out his hand, his voice laced with a Texas twang. "I'm Laila's husband and it seems the designated arbitrator for this afternoon's festivities."

"Thomas North." He returned the handshake, liking Jackson's easygoing manner. "And is that really necessary?"

"In this family, you bet. I'm Laila," his wife said, taking Thomas's hand next after handing off a foil-covered bowl to one of her sisters. "It's nice to finally meet the man who's been making my little sister even more bubbly than usual."

"We're all your little sisters," the woman standing beside her said. "Even if Annabel has the market cornered on bubbly. Hi there, Thomas," Abby said. "This is my husband, Cade Pritchett."

Thomas shook her hand first and then her husband's. "Nice to meet you, Cade."

"You're looking a little shell-shocked, North." Jackson Traub grabbed a beer from a nearby ice bucket as his wife and Abby moved away to fuss over the food table. "I remember the feeling well."

Thomas was surprised by the frank assessment. "Is it that obvious?"

"Only to someone who was in your shoes this time last year." The man headed for the barbecue, but then turned back. "Hey, thanks for all you've done for my cousin. The entire family appreciates the surgery you did on Forrest."

"I haven't heard from him in a while. Hope things are going well."

"Me, too," Jackson replied, his voice a bit cryptic as he joined the men grill-side.

Soon the three were debating loudly the finer points of cooking over an open fire, with both an oversize spatula and tongs being used for emphasis.

"Come on, doc," Cade said, grabbing a beer for himself. "We should probably join them. Just in case medical attention is needed."

Thomas took his iced tea with him just so he'd have something to do with his hands, and walked across the patio with Cade.

Minutes later, the noise level grew as the conversation switched from cooking to the current standings of their favorites baseball teams. Jackson was the lone holdout with his assurance of the Texas Rangers being play-off bound, but his opinion was voted down so boisterously that Thomas decided just to keep his mouth shut where his Dodgers were concerned.

The men shot statistics and scores back and forth until finally Jackson bet a prized saddle against one of Zeke's horses on the outcome of the World Series.

"I won't hesitate to take that beauty off your hands," Zeke said. "Doesn't matter if you're married to my daughter or not."

"And I'm looking forward to adding that stallion to my growing collection," Jackson shot back. "In fact, I might take him out for a run after dinner. Thomas, do you ride?"

Surprised at the question, Thomas glanced quickly

at the feet of all four men. All wore cowboy boots that looked well loved and lived in. Not quite the same as his Italian leather loafers.

"Ah, I haven't in a while," he finally said, realizing he still hadn't answered the question. "Not since my days at boarding school."

Silence filled the air for a moment before Evelyn called out, asking for the status on the meat as everything else was ready. Thomas stepped back as the men all turned to the grill and in fluid movements that showed they'd worked together before, quickly gathered the food that was fully cooked.

Soon everyone was seated around the largest table; a radio perched nearby was tuned to the local country-music station. After shooing Smiley out of the way, Annabel patted a chair next to her for Thomas to take, handing him a plastic plate and a matching set of silverware. Platters of meat and bowls of salads were passed around and he was encouraged to take whatever he wanted as arms reached back and forth across the table.

Someone spilled a drink, good-natured insults followed and a couple of flying pretzels joined in the mix. The banter flowed from sports to the economy to politics. Everyone talked at once, speaking over each other with no one afraid to voice their opinion no matter what the topic.

Thomas didn't know what to make of it all.

His childhood family dinners had been made up of classical music playing softly in the background, artfully arranged food served on the finest china and dinner conversation with one person speaking at a time. Even now when he dined with his parents and grandmother the evenings were exactly the same.

This…this was chaos.

"Hey, we're going to pull together a game of flag football after dinner," Brody said, elbowing Thomas from where he sat on the other side of him. "You want to join us?"

"Somehow I don't think rolling around in the grass chasing a leather-covered ball is something Thomas would be interested in," Jazzy said, with a wink.

"Do you like football, Thomas?" Jordyn Leigh asked. "I warn you, it's pretty much a prerequisite to joining the family."

"No, it's not," Annabel protested. "Besides, his favorite team is the Broncos."

"Is that right?" Zeke asked, his eyes bright.

Thomas nodded, feeling as if he'd finally scored points with the man. "Yes, sir."

"Hey, do you feel that?" Cade lifted his beer in a mock salute. "I think the balance of power has shifted ever so slightly."

"What are you talking about?" Laila and Abby asked in unison.

"There's always been six women sitting around the Cates family table, but now we're up to five men." Cade leaned over and clinked his bottle against his father-in-law's. "All we need now is to get your last two daughters married off and the majority power will be all male."

"Amen to that," Zeke offered with a wide smile.

Laughter, jeers and catcalls filled the air but all Thomas felt was the rising panic at how everyone at the table already had him walking down the aisle while Annabel said nothing to ebb their train of thought.

Suddenly, he couldn't breathe, his chest and throat

tight. The need to escape was so overwhelming Thomas almost missed the ringing of his cell phone. He reached for it, trying to ignore the hard lump in his gut, and peered at the display.

"I need to answer this," he gasped in Annabel's ear. "Is there somewhere I can go that's a bit quieter?"

"Of course." She wiped her hands and rose to her feet.

Thomas did the same and addressed the table. "Please excuse me. I need to make a call to the hospital."

The lively talking paused for a moment, then started back up as they walked away, diminishing slightly as they entered the cool interior of the house.

Annabel waved him into the kitchen, but stayed by the door as he walked farther away and hit the button that would connect him directly to TC General. As he listened to the call, the lump in his gut grew.

Damn, not the news he was hoping for.

After a few minutes he ended the call and walked back to her. "I'm sorry. I have to leave."

"What's wrong?"

He paused, weighing exactly what he should say. "It's Maurice Owens."

"Oh!" Her eyes filled with concern. "That poor, sweet man. Is it bad?"

Thomas knew Annabel had come to care for his patient over the past week, often stopping in to see the old man even without Smiley, but he couldn't go into the details with her. "Serious enough that I need to say my goodbyes and get to the hospital right away."

They went back outside. Thomas explained he'd had an emergency come up and offered his apologies for having to leave early. He returned her father's handshake, thanking the man for having him in his home and again read concern in her mother's eyes when Annabel grabbed his hand and insisted on walking him to his car.

"Will you call me later?" she asked and hurried to keep up with his quick strides. "I'd like to know how Maurice is doing."

Thomas glanced at his watch as he opened the driver's side door. It was after six already. "I don't have any idea how late that might be."

"I'll be up." She leaned in and gave him a quick kiss. "I can come over, too, you know, later on. If you need me."

He didn't know if it was her offer or the heat of her lips on his that caused that hard lump in his gut to rise up to his throat.

Unable to spare the time to figure out which the correct answer was, he shoved the thought from his head and slid behind the wheel. His focus right now had to be solely on his patient. "I can't make any promises."

"I know that, I was just…" Her voice trailed off as she stepped away from the car. "Please drive safe."

Eight hours later, Thomas finally dragged his tired self inside his home. Alone. It was after two in the morning and he was dead on his feet.

Maurice Owens had suffered a series of seizures and they were still trying to find the cause. The last one had been so strong they had no choice but to place the man in a medically induced coma to prevent brain damage.

The elderly gentleman had been doing so well ever since Smiley had started to visit, his recovery progressing much faster than estimated that Thomas had almost been willing to admit—

No. He shut down that thought, refusing to go there. Not now. Not tonight.

Thomas had sat in his office for the past two hours going over the man's medical records and test results, certain that he'd missed something. A leg with multiple fractures wasn't good for anyone, least of all a man who was close to celebrating his one hundredth birthday. And the chances of someone Maurice's age not suffering any additional side effects from the seizures or the coma were slim at best.

Eyes glazed over and a headache on the edge of erupting, Thomas had finally noticed the time. Realizing he'd never called Annabel, he decided to head home. His place was so quiet after the craziness at Annabel's and the constant noise of the hospital. The silence seeped into his bones and he realized just how tired he was.

Heading upstairs, he toed off his shoes and socks and stripped off his shirt. He undid his belt and yanked down the zipper on his pants, pausing when his gaze landed on the multicolored quilt folded neatly over the back of a chair in the corner of his bedroom.

It was the same quilt he'd found in his living room the morning after they'd made love the first time. Annabel had brought it back with her last night, insisting he keep it as the blanket's muted shades fit perfectly in his home's color scheme.

Besides, she'd said, she was always cold, despite the warm summer night, and they'd cuddled beneath the quilt until soon the soft material was the only thing protecting their bare skin from the cool air-conditioning.

Thomas grabbed the blanket off the chair, brought it to his face, and breathed deeply. Annabel's scent filled his head, but soon memories of this afternoon and tonight did, as well.

Her family's comments linking him and Annabel, the sight of Maurice's body flailing uncontrollably, the soft blue eyes offering to come to him when he called, the aged, unseeing gaze, clouded with confusion, pain and then no expression at all....

Thomas still didn't know what he missed when it came to his patient's health, but he knew one thing.

If he hadn't been spending so much time over the past three days with Annabel, thinking about her when they weren't together, and anticipating when he was going to see her again, he would have seen this coming. He should have known his patient was heading down the wrong path, a path that could take the man's life.

Tossing the blanket down, Thomas turned and headed for his bed, ignoring the urge to call Annabel even at this late hour.

He was not going to pick up that phone.

No matter how much he wanted to.

Chapter 11

"Please, I need to see him." Annabel leaned over the counter, doing her best to persuade the nurse on duty, who happened to be an old high school friend, to bend the rules just a little bit. "I need to know if he's okay."

After waiting for hours with no phone call from Thomas on Maurice's condition, she'd finally fallen asleep around two this morning. When she'd woken up and still didn't have an update, she'd taken a quick shower and headed for the hospital, determined to find out what was going on.

"I'm sorry, but only family can visit patients in intensive care," Jody replied, her voice a low whisper. "You know that, Annabel."

"Maurice Owens doesn't have any family." A sense of hopelessness weighed heavily on her shoulders. She glanced at her watch, noting she needed to be at the library in forty-five minutes for a mandatory budget meeting. "He's over ninety years old and he's all alone in this world. Smiley and I have been by to visit him a few times last week and I've come by myself even more often. He was doing so much better. I don't understand—"

She broke off when the tears threatened, but pulled in a deep breath instead of letting them overpower her and forced herself to continue. "Jody, please. Can you at least tell me how he'd doing? Why he was moved here from his regular room?"

Jody's fingers flew over the keyboard in front of her for a moment, then her expression changed from stern to surprised. "If you'll follow me, I'll take you to his room."

"You will?" Shock radiated through Annabel. "But how? You just said I couldn't go in."

Her friend smiled as she rose and walked around the desk. "Your name just appeared on the approved visitors list. Believe me, it wasn't there a few minutes ago when you first asked. The attending physician must have made the change. Doctor's orders."

Doctor's orders.

Thomas's orders.

He had to be the one who granted permission for her to follow the petite nurse through the security doors into the hush of the intensive-care area.

Did he somehow know she was here this morning? Was he here?

The urge to look around and see if he was nearby flowed through her, but she kept her gaze firmly on her friend as they walked down the long corridor.

"Okay, here we are." Jody stopped outside a glass

door, her voice a hushed whisper. "All I can tell you is Mr. Owens suffered a series of seizures last night. As far as I know the doctors don't know why yet, but he is currently in a coma in order to keep him stable."

The tears threatened again, but Annabel held them off as she nodded her understanding.

"You only have fifteen minutes until the morning's visiting hours are over," Jody continued. "But you can come back later."

Annabel leaned in and gave her friend a hug. "Thank you, Jody, so much."

Entering the room, Annabel's eyes were drawn right away to the elderly man lying so still in the bed. She walked to a chair next to him and sat down, instinctively reaching out to grasp Maurice's hand. His skin was almost gray in color, wrinkled, and covered with age spots, but until now his grip had been strong whenever she'd held his hand.

"Hey there, Maurice." Annabel's heart ached for her new friend, but she kept her voice light. "Boy, when you said you were ready to get out of that room upstairs I don't think this is what you meant."

She swallowed hard and kept talking. "You know, they'll never allow Smiley to come into the ICU. You're going to have to get better so you two can spend some time together again. You promised to play catch with him, and Smiley just loves to chase a ball...."

Pressing a hand to her mouth as her voice faded, Annabel closed her eyes and offered a quick prayer for this very special man. A man who'd fought valiantly for his country during both the Second World War and the Korean Conflict. A man who often spoke of his wife, who he'd fallen in love with long after he thought his chance at happiness had passed him by, and how much he missed their simple home while being stuck in the hospital.

"You rest and get better, Maurice," she whispered. "I'll be back to see you very soon."

Rising, Annabel released his hand and leaned over to place a light kiss on the elderly man's forehead. After leaving his room, she walked out to the main corridor, her mind once again filled with thoughts of Thomas.

She still didn't know why he hadn't called her last night to give her an update on Maurice's condition. Not even a message on her cell phone. He had to know how worried she'd be…how much she'd wanted to make sure that Maurice was okay.

That he, too, had been okay.

As thankful as she was that he'd added her to Maurice's visitors list this morning, she still had no idea what was going on with Thomas. Deciding there was no time like the present to find out, Annabel quickly took the stairs up to the second floor, her high heels echoing on the polished linoleum as she made her way toward his office.

She had no idea what she would say to him once she got there, but she wasn't worried. The words would come. They always did. Except for yesterday when her family had so easily lumped her and Thomas together.

Heck, the way they'd carried on during the barbecue, they practically had them married!

While she had pleaded with them beforehand to make Thomas feel comfortable and at home, she'd never expected her brothers-in-law to go as far as they did.

As much as she liked the tingling that filled her

bones at the idea of someday being Mrs. Thomas North, she'd known she needed to say something to downplay their teasing. Something along the lines of how she and Thomas had only been on a few dates, while leaving out the part about the great sex over the past three days for her parents' sake.

She'd been about to do just that when Thomas had gotten the call that forced him to leave early.

And yes, he did seem intently focused on Maurice when he'd left, but she was smart enough to pick up that a small part of him was relieved to be out of the line of fire where her family was concern.

Not that she blamed him, because despite how easily the subject matter had changed from the two of them to something else once he'd left, she had to put up with the "I told you so" look and a few underhanded remarks from her mother about what life would be like married to a doctor.

Not that any of that excused him from not calling and letting her know about Maurice.

Confusion swamped her as she entered his office area, surprised to find both Marge's desk and Thomas's inner office empty. From the half-empty mug of coffee and paperwork scattered across his desk, she could tell he'd arrived already, he just wasn't here.

She checked her watch again and then grabbed a small pad of paper, determined to leave him a quick note. Three tries, three crumpled balls of paper later and she still didn't know what to say.

Why didn't you call?

I miss you.

When will we see each other again?

Oh, all of those openings seemed so…so…desperate? And Annabel didn't want him to think of her that way.

Yes, she was in love.

Yes, he was the one for her.

Two amazing and wonderful facts she'd carried in her heart since the first time they'd made love. But she wanted Thomas to come to those same conclusions on his own, in his own way and time.

Deciding it was best to just call his office later and speak to him in person, she tossed the pad back onto Thomas's desk and headed for the doorway when voices from the outer office stopped her.

"And who would've thought the guy had enough time on his hands to steal my wife."

What?

Annabel's hand stilled on the door knob. Instead of moving to the other side of the door, she stood there, frozen.

"I mean, we've only been married a year," the man continued. "Aren't we supposed to still be in some damn honeymoon phase?"

"That's rough. Sorry you're going through all that."

Okay, that voice she recognized as Thomas's. The other man must be a friend of his.

"You know, people warned me about getting married during my residency, but we'd been together since college. I loved her. I thought she loved me," the friend went on. "Then I find out she's been spending time with some hot-shot lawyer while I'm busting my ass working long shifts here." The man sighed. "Sorry I'm unloading my problems on you."

Annabel's heart ached for the poor guy's obvious pain over his wife's infidelity. She should make her presence known, but the last thing she wanted was to embarrass the man, or Thomas. Better to step back and give them as much privacy as—

"I understand it's tough, but you can't let your personal life get in the way of your work here. That minor slip you had earlier with your patient could have become a major issue, if you hadn't caught it in time." Thomas's voice was low, but strong and filled with certainty. "Love and medicine don't mix. I found that out the hard way."

His last statements stunned her and Annabel found it impossible to move.

"Look, I'm the last person who should give out advice on something like this," Thomas continued.

"No, please," his friend pushed. "I want your opinion."

Silence filled the air for a long moment and Annabel found herself holding her breath waiting to see how Thomas would respond.

"I've learned that being one hundred percent committed to your career is a prerequisite for our profession. Anything less and people's lives are at stake," he finally said. "Some can find a balance between a personal life and a professional one, some can't. You need to find out which group you belong to."

"Have *you* figured that out yet?"

She pressed a hand to her mouth to stop herself from blurting out how wrong he was, how finding a balance was a part of being in love no matter what someone's line of work. Annabel closed her eyes, her heart pounding in her chest as she waited for Thomas to answer.

"All I know is you have to weigh the facts against

the evidence. In my experience, trusting in love is crazy and I— Ah, hello, Marge."

Thomas cut off his words as his secretary arrived, ending the men's discussion. Turning away, Annabel walked to the windows, brushing away the tears before they could fall. She wrapped her arms tightly around herself, suddenly very cold despite the suit jacket she wore.

Wishing a hole in the floor would open up and swallow her would do no good. All she could do was wait and—what?

Hope that Thomas and Marge left again so she could sneak out unseen? Where would that leave her?

Still waiting for Thomas to come to her?

No, what she needed was to make a few things clear to him. At least one thing in particular. She knew what was in her heart and now seemed like the perfect time to share—

"Annabel?"

She whirled around.

"What are you—" Thomas stood in his doorway, shock on his face. He quickly glanced back out at the outer office before closing the door behind him. "How long have you been in here?"

"Long enough. I'm sorry. I didn't mean to eavesdrop." She waved one hand toward his desk. "I stopped by to see you, but you were gone. I was going to leave a note. Then I heard… I didn't want to interrupt a private conversation."

"So you just listened instead?"

"It was pretty hard not to. Oh, Thomas, I can't believe you really feel that way about love."

He moved to the other side of his desk, his attention

on the paperwork in his hand. "Now is not the time to talk about this."

"I think this is the perfect time." Annabel reached deep inside for that certainty she'd been so sure of just a moment ago. "Thomas, I—"

"I'm guessing you came here to check on Maurice," he interrupted her. "I didn't call you last night because it was late when I finally got home. Actually it was very early this morning." Thomas dropped the folder to his desk. "I can't go into any detail about my patient's care—"

"I know he's in intensive care and I know I have you to thank for allowing me to see him." Annabel waved off his explanation, determined not to let him pull away from what they really needed to talk about. "Thank you for that. I'm sure you and the rest of the staff are doing all you can for him."

His gaze remained focused on his desk. "Yes, we are."

Annabel remained silent, but when he didn't say anything more, she purposely walked to him, invading his personal space as she slid between him and his desk.

He tried to step back, pushing his chair to one side, but the credenza behind him stopped him.

"Do you really believe it's crazy to trust in love?"

Thomas purposely kept his gaze away from her. "Annabel…"

"I don't, and do you want to know why?" She placed her fingertips at his jaw and gently forced him to look at her. "Because I love you, Thomas."

He closed his eyes and pressed his mouth into a hard line before he spoke. "No, you don't."

Yes, she did. Saying the words aloud for the first time made her even more certain of her feelings for this man.

"Yes, I do."

He opened his eyes again, the glacial chill in their blue depths surprising her. "You can't know that."

"Of course I can and I wanted you to know." Undeterred, she dropped her hand to his chest, the steady beat of his heart beneath her fingers reminding her of those nights when he'd held her close. "This may seem a bit sudden considering—"

"Sudden?" Thomas turned away from her, moving out from behind his desk. "Yes, I would say so. We've only known each other a couple of weeks."

"I'm sure of my feelings, Thomas, but knowing that I love you doesn't mean I have the future all planned out." Pushing aside the panic that the distance he was putting between them was more than physical, Annabel followed him. "Goodness knows, I'm very much a live-in-the-moment kind of person, but what I'm certain of is that I want you in every one of those moments."

"After such a short period of time?" The disbelief was evident in his voice as he crossed his office; this time he was the one staring out the windows. "How is that possible?"

"I don't know how." She wanted to reach out, to make him turn and look at her, but the stiffness of his posture held her back. "I just know that what we have is special and worth all the craziness that might come our way as we muddle through this."

"Worth it to whom? My patients? I can't allow my personal life to get in the way. To distract me from…"

Thomas's voice trailed off as he pinched the bridge of his nose hard and sighed.

"Is that what you think?" Annabel quickly connected the dots. "That because you and I have been spending time together over the past few days you missed something in Maurice's treatment—"

"It doesn't matter what I think." Thomas spun around. "What I rely on are facts, while you place all of your trust in your feelings."

"Yes, I guess I do. And from what I overheard, you've been hurt in the past, but please don't let that affect what's happening now between us. You must know what we have is wonderful…"

"What I know is that I have a lot of work to do." Thomas's gaze traveled the length of her. "And you look like you're on your way to an important meeting."

Annabel glanced down at her business suit. "Yes," she finally admitted. "I need to get to the library."

"Well, please don't let me keep you."

The distance on his face spoke volumes at how far apart they were despite standing right in front of each other. For the first time, the words wouldn't come and Annabel had no idea how to reach him.

"I'm free tonight." She pushed the invitation past her lips, already knowing deep inside the reception her words would receive. "If you want to get together?"

"I'll probably be working late again." Thomas grabbed a white medical coat off a nearby hook. Sliding it over his shoulders, he pulled it on like a suit of body armor, leaving Annabel standing there alone and defenseless.

"Thomas, I—"

"Annabel, please." He started to reach for her, but

curled his fingers into a tight fist and jammed it into his pocket. "I can't talk about this right now, and I really need to get back to work."

Pressing her palm hard against her chest as if she could actually stop her heart from breaking, Annabel could only nod before she turned and walked away, certain that this time he wouldn't be coming after her.

Chapter 12

It amazed Thomas how much life could change in a mere seventy-two hours.

On Monday morning he had no clue as to the reason for Maurice Owens's seizures. Today the man was scheduled to be released from intensive care. They'd finally determined a blood infection was the source of the problems. After a heavy dose of IV antibiotics, the man now fully awake, alert and, according to his nurses, asking when that rag mop of a dog and his pretty owner were coming back to see him.

Annabel and Smiley.

Thomas's fist tightened on the bag he carried as he crossed the parking lot and headed inside the hospital.

Yeah, life had certainly changed since that Monday morning when he'd done the one thing he'd wanted to avoid from the moment he'd met Annabel.

Hurt her.

After he'd made it clear he didn't believe her declaration, the pain and disappointment in her eyes before she'd turned and walked out of his office had filled him with such remorse he'd actually started after her. Then common sense took over. Even so, stopping himself from chasing after her had taken every ounce of strength he had.

Let her go. Let her go. Let her go.

The words had echoed in his head, a resounding anthem that told him he'd done the right thing.

He hadn't seen her since.

His daily rounds and Maurice's unstable condition had kept him occupied for the next twenty-four hours until his boss ordered him to go home and not return until he'd gotten some much-needed rest. He'd obeyed and fell into a dreamless sleep for over fifteen hours, woke long enough to choke down some food, check in with Marge and then slept again.

But this time he'd dreamed of Annabel.

Her looking at him smiling and happy, her beautiful blue eyes filled with joy as she chatted about her work at the library, the therapy dog program, her family.

But then the joy faded, replaced with the same bewilderment and hurt that *he'd* put there as she faded farther and farther from his outstretched hands until she disappeared in swirling mist….

He'd shot awake, drenched in sweat and tangled in the sheets of his empty bed, his heart pounding in his chest. The urge to call her, to hear her voice, had been so powerful he'd grabbed his phone and held it in a grip so tight his knuckles ached.

But he couldn't do it. He couldn't put her through that again.

She'd laid her heart in his hands, and he'd all but thrown it back at her. He hadn't believed her when she poured out her feelings about how she felt about him, about *them.*

He couldn't do it because he hadn't changed his mind.

No matter how hollow and empty he might feel at the moment, making the choice of his patients over a personal life had been the right one.

He meant what he'd said to the young resident on his staff. Some in their profession managed to balance both a career and a life outside of the hospital, but others, the majority, tried and failed.

The consequences could be much worse than a broken heart.

He couldn't take that chance.

After his shower this morning, he'd dressed and started to leave his bedroom when the quilt Annabel had given him caught his attention.

He'd reached for it, ignoring how his fingers shook as he grabbed the soft material. Marching downstairs and into the kitchen, he quickly stuffed the blanket into a paper sack.

Returning the gift was a necessity for the both of them.

Annabel had her Thursday session with Smiley this afternoon at the hospital. He was certain she would be there, just like she'd been every day this week visiting with Maurice, her name scrawled on the visitors' log in her loopy handwriting, which made his chest hurt every time he saw it.

He didn't have any idea what he was going to say when he came face-to-face with her, but he would think of something over the next six hours.

Even if it was only goodbye.

Exiting the elevator, he walked down the hall to his office and had to swallow the hard lump in his throat before he greeted Marge, who sat at her desk, the phone receiver in her hand.

"Morning, Marge."

"Oh, Dr. North." She looked up at him, surprise in her eyes. "I'm glad you're here. I was just about to page you."

He disregarded the natural quickening of his pulse. "What is it?"

"Mr. Owens is being a bit cantankerous this morning." She placed the receiver back in its cradle. "The head nurse in ICU just called to say he's insisting on seeing you *before* they move him."

Thomas dropped his briefcase and the bag into the closest chair. "I'll go right now. Can you please put these in my office?"

"That's quite a big lunch you're brown bagging today."

Turning to grab some much-needed coffee, he snapped a lid on the disposable cup and kept his gaze from returning to the bag. "That's not food."

"Is it something I can take care of for you?"

For a split second Thomas almost agreed to Marge's request. He could easily ask her to take it down to the session or even mail it to Annabel at her home, but he quickly squashed the idea. "No."

He softened his tone when the woman offered him

a raised eyebrow. "Thank you, but that's something...
it's something I need to handle on my own."

Three hours later Thomas returned to his office.

He'd gone ahead and completed his morning rounds
after making sure Maurice was settled in his new room,
which wasn't the same one he'd been in before. A fact
the elderly man found very unsettling until Thomas
had promised him the staff would make sure the new
room number was available for anyone who asked for it.

Anyone meaning Annabel.

He hated to admit it, but he'd been disappointed to
find out she hadn't made it in yet to see Maurice this
morning unlike the past two days when she'd come by
during the early visiting hours.

Another reason Maurice had been upset.

Thomas met up with Marge in the hallway just as
she was leaving. "On your way out for lunch?"

"Yes, I need to pick up my cats from the vet." She
pulled her keys from her purse. "They went in this
morning for their checkups and the poor things hate
it there. I want to get them home as soon as possible."

He peeked at her desk, noting the bag and his briefcase were gone, but he asked anyway, gesturing toward
the still-closed door to his inner office. "Did you put
my things inside?"

"I started to, but she insisted on taking that beautiful quilt into your office herself."

He stilled, his feet suddenly rooted to the floor.
"She?"

"The bag tipped over when she bumped the chair
and we couldn't help but see what was inside," Marge
called out over her shoulder as she kept walking. "I
tried to put it back, but she insisted and I knew it was

useless to argue. Oh, and she was also adamant about waiting for you, too. Be back soon."

Before Thomas could say another word, Marge disappeared with a quick wave.

He remained standing there, staring at the door, trying to grasp the fact that Annabel was waiting for him on the other side.

Her coming back here to his office was the last thing he'd planned on, the last thing he expected. It was too early for Smiley's session. She must have come to see Maurice.

And him.

He pulled in a deep breath and moved forward, regretting that he didn't have the afternoon to figure out exactly what he was going to say to her. That he'd brought the quilt to the hospital was probably explanation enough, but still she'd persisted on waiting for him.

Determined to keep his focus completely on the facts and not the wild beating of his heart, he straightened his tie, turned the latch and stepped inside. His gaze was immediately drawn to the woman sitting at one end of his couch, the quilt spread over her lap, her fingertips tracing the mutely shaded blocks and the intricate stitching.

"Grandmother?"

Ernestine's hand stilled as she raised her head. "Good morning, Thomas. Or should I say good afternoon. You know, this quilt is a beautiful piece of work."

He walked farther into the room, bombarded with regret when he realized it wasn't Annabel who was waiting for him.

He tried to control the emotional roller coaster he

was riding, knowing the fact he was on this ride in the first place was of his own doing. "Ah, yes, it is."

"The time and attention to detail it took to create such a lovely work of art." She returned her attention to the quilt, her hands again moving lightly over the fabric. "Someone must have been working on this for a very long time."

"Almost two years."

The words left his mouth before he'd even realized he spoke, remembering Annabel telling him about how she'd started the quilt as a way to keep busy during a crazy winter storm that dumped almost two feet of snow on Thunder Canyon.

He'd spent that same long weekend holed up in his empty condo with nothing but a home designer's catalog to flip through. It still amazed him how the colors she'd chosen had perfectly matched the furniture, carpeting and drapes he'd picked for his place that first weekend he'd been back in town.

Deciding he'd better sit before his shaky legs gave out on him, Thomas moved to the chair behind his desk.

"And it fits so perfectly with both your office and your home. Wherever did you have it made?"

"I didn't. I mean, it wasn't created specifically for me. For my place. The fact it matches is...just a fluke."

"Oh?" His grandmother slightly tilted her head, a familiar motion that spoke volumes despite her abbreviated question.

"It was a gift, actually." He paused and cleared his suddenly tight throat. "An unplanned gift. From a friend."

That caused his grandmother's gaze to sharpen with curiosity. "A lady friend?"

Thomas remained silent.

"A very special lady friend." Her words were spoken as a statement of fact as she answered her own question. "Well, that's even better."

"No, it's not."

She laced her fingers together and rested them primly on her quilt-covered lap. "I'm intrigued. Please go on."

"There is nothing to be intrigued about, Grandmother." He leaned back in his chair, forcing himself to appear relaxed as he returned her direct stare. "There is no special lady friend."

"But there was."

A heartbeat passed. "Yes, but it's over."

This time her head tilted ever so slightly in the opposite direction. "And does Miss Cates share in that assessment of your relationship?"

Thomas couldn't contain his shock. "How did— How did you know it was Annabel Cates?"

"Oh, my darling, you'd be surprised at the things I know." Ernestine gently folded the quilt into a neat package and laid it next to her on the couch. "With age comes wisdom, as the saying goes."

"What exactly does that mean?"

"It means I was hoping you would find more here in Thunder Canyon than just a brilliant career that you've worked so hard for and deservedly so."

Then it hit Thomas that his grandmother knew everything that happened back in California. "How did you find out?"

"Haven't you learned by now that there's little that

goes on in this hospital that I don't know about? Including the professional backgrounds of our staff?" She held up a hand when he started to speak. "And when one of those staff members is related to me you can be certain my fellow administrators made sure I was aware of what exactly led to you looking for work away from Santa Monica."

Thomas leaned forward, bracing his elbows on his knees. "I'm sorry. I should've told you about all of that myself—"

"No apologies necessary, Thomas." She cut him off. "The way your personal and professional lives collided, and the fallout it created, was not something you could control."

"It was my fault."

"You were lied to. Your feelings were manipulated. How can you take responsibility for that?"

"I have to." Thomas rose and walked to the window, unable to take the sympathy he saw in his grandmother's eyes. "I have to make sure that 'collision,' as you called it, never happens again."

"By closing off your heart?"

"By choosing to focus all of my attention on my patients." Despite the rudeness of the gesture, he kept his back to her. "I missed something last weekend that could've cost a man his life."

"But it didn't."

"No, but to take that chance again..." He turned and looked at his grandmother. Pride welling inside him at all she'd accomplished here at the hospital, at what his family has achieved in this town. "To do anything that would result in a repeat of what happened in the past, to bring shame to this hospital, our family…to you. I won't take that risk."

"Thomas—"

"Besides, love and marriage and medicine aren't a good mix. Look at all the people here at TC General going through breakups and divorces."

His grandmother smiled as she stood, using her cane for balance as she walked toward him. "Thomas, you could say the same thing about any profession. Love and marriage take a lot of hard work, commitment and attention to keep it strong and healthy, just like any career does."

"Mother and Father haven't had to work that hard."

"Yes, they have," she countered. "Children don't always see all that goes into their parents' relationship, especially you because you were away so often at school and such. Believe me, with the two of them being hardheaded lawyers, like your grandpa Joe, they made some of their arguments more entertaining than most federal court cases."

His grandmother's assessment of his parents' stable and rather sedate marriage surprised him. Even more so was the hint that her own marriage had suffered its share of ups and downs. "You and Grandpa Joe?"

"We had our troubles as well, darling." She reached out and laid a hand on his arm. "Both long before and after that horrible accident. When we first met, your grandfather told me on our third date that we were going to spend the rest of our lives together. To an eighteen-year-old girl that sounded crazy, but he was so sure we were meant to be together."

Thomas did the math quickly in his head. "But you were married just before your nineteenth birthday."

"Yes, we were. With a lot of promises of forever from him and a big leap of faith on my part." Her eyes filled with long-ago memories. "Your grandfather told me he loved me enough for the both of us and that would carry us through until I was sure. And he was right. When he lost his legs all those years later, it was my turn to be the one to convince him our love was strong enough, that I could be strong enough, for the both of us."

"But you'd been married over three decades when that happened." Thomas remembered his own devastation at what his grandfather had suffered through when Thomas was a child. To picture those events again from his grandmother's point of view put a totally new spin on things. "Looking back now, as an adult and a doctor, I can see all he had to deal with, both physically and mentally, but I honestly never thought your marriage—"

"Our marriage lasted another twenty years because we found a way to make our love strong again, a feat achieved many times over." Her attention was back fully on him. "The ups and downs, the good times and bad, the strengths and weaknesses…when you find the right person, when you're that lucky, you need to grab ahold of that love and never let go. Fifty-five years or fifty-five days… I would've been happy with either because I was with the man I loved."

Thomas turned back to stare out the window again, folding his arms over his chest after his grandmother released her hold on him. His head swirled with everything she'd said, making sorting it into logical steps and facts difficult.

Falling back on his training, he started compartmentalizing, pushing away his emotions even as the desire to find Annabel, to go to her, surged inside of him.

The gentle cuff to the back of his head caught him completely by surprise.

He turned to stare at his grandmother, his mouth rising into a grin that matched hers. It'd been years since she'd swatted him one.

"What was that for?"

"I know you're going to think and reason and debate all we've talked about, because that's who you are and that's what you do, but don't take too long." She turned and headed for the door. "Your young lady doesn't seem to be as naive as I once was. I think it might take a lot more than fancy words and heartfelt promises to show her how wrong you were."

"I didn't say I was wrong."

"Not yet, you haven't." She glanced back and gave him a quick wink. "You're a smart boy. You'll get there eventually."

Thomas turned back to the window after his grandmother departed, closing the door behind her.

He didn't know how long he stood there, reflecting on the past few days, weeks and years. Thinking about all he'd gone through in California thanks to both his own choices and the things that had been out of his control.

Yes, he'd fallen hard and fast for Victoria and he'd overlooked—or just didn't want to see—the obvious signs that something was wrong with their relationship from the start. All the hiding and secrecy over the months they'd spent together should've been red flags that everything wasn't as it seemed.

She wasn't all she seemed.

While his day-to-day work at the hospital hadn't been affected, his career had suffered because of his own actions, even more so, by all that Victoria had done. Not just to him but to the poor schmuck still married to her.

Annabel wasn't Victoria though.

Yes, they'd only known each other a few weeks, but the way he felt when he was with her was so much more than he'd ever experienced with Victoria. With anyone, for that matter.

And the only one trying to keep their crazy and wonderful courtship a secret had been him, because of the past.

When he'd finally admitted to himself—and to her—how much he wanted her, wanted to be with her, everything fell in place so easily. It was almost scary at how perfect they fit.

Another reason why he'd tried to run.

Not that everything would always fit so flawlessly. They came from two different worlds. Her loud and adoring family, so different from his small and demure one, would require some getting used to. His demanding career, her devotion to her dog and their equally strong commitment to both would also require a lot of give and take.

The bottom line?

Finding a way to bring his world and hers together would be challenging and fun and well worth the effort.

Thomas moved back to his desk and sat, thinking about everything his grandmother had said about the hard work and commitment that came with making a relationship last.

He kept coming to the same conclusion.

Why was he running away from the best thing that ever happened to him? Fighting his feelings, hiding from them was useless because they weren't going to change.

Not now. Not ever.

But what to do to show that he'd finally understood? That he was finally sure?

The idea came to him quickly and while it might be a small first step, it was an important one.

He quickly booted up his computer, typed a simple request in the search engine and waited. As soon as the website appeared he scanned the images, one after the other, until he found the perfect one. Blonde, bubbly and a face that showed all the love in the world to give.

With one click he checked his calendar, relieved to find it empty for the afternoon. Rising, he rounded his desk and headed for the door.

"I'm out of here for the day, Marge," he said to his secretary, glad to see she'd returned. "I'll have my cell phone on if any emergencies arise."

"Has your grandmother left?" she asked.

"Yes, she did." He didn't even slow down as he hurried past her desk.

"Where are you going?" she called after him.

"To see a woman about a dog."

Chapter 13

Forcing a smile had never been something Annabel needed to do, but today, despite stopping in and finding Maurice sleeping comfortably in his new room, it took all the energy she had to remain positive during this afternoon's Smiley session.

She'd left behind a note and an arrangement of brightly colored daisies for Maurice to find when he awoke, ushering Smiley away from the bed after he'd nudged at the sleeping man's hand.

Once they arrived at the therapy area, they'd found a roomful of patients already waiting, with more coming and going as the two hours passed. Annabel had already contacted a few members of her therapy group with the idea of adding more dogs to this weekly open session. Having two or three additional animals would allow each person to have more one-on-one time as many were often reluctant to allow Smiley to move on.

Of course, she still needed to get approval from—Thomas.

Still on bended knee, Smiley at her side after they'd said goodbye to the last child, Annabel bowed her head, blinking hard against the endless supply of tears.

Would they ever stop?

After the past three days one would think she'd exhausted her supply. But after Annabel had responded to her mother's innocently asked "how was your day" on Monday night by bursting into wrenching sobs, her mother had lovingly pointed out to her that the tears would end when the healing began.

Annabel wasn't sure that would ever happen.

Something deep inside told her that while the crippling ache in her heart might one day ease, the empty space left behind would always belong to the one man she'd been so sure was the love of her life.

A man who couldn't—wouldn't—accept her love.

Smiley's snout nuzzled her shoulder, his nose cool against her neck. Annabel sighed and her pet moved even closer, instinctively knowing how much his owner needed his faithful and unconditional love.

"Thank you, sweetie." Annabel wrapped her arms around the dog's shoulders and gave him a gentle hug. Smiley had rarely left her side since greeting her at the door on Monday. "I don't know how I'd get through all of this without you."

"I was just thinking the same thing."

The low masculine voice caused Annabel to look up. Shock filled her at the sight of Forrest Traub standing in front of her. Rising, she brushed the tears off her cheeks. "What are *you* doing here?"

The tall man leaned heavily on his cane as he held out one hand for her dog to inspect. "I'm here to see you. And Smiley."

Seconds later, Smiley offered a quick lick to the man's fingers and was rewarded with a firm scratch behind his ears.

Forrest leaned over and spoke gently to her pet. Annabel silently thanked him, sure he'd seen her crying, and used those few moments to pull in and then release a deep shuddering breath.

She had no idea why Forrest Traub was back in town or why he'd come looking for her. "No, what I meant was what are you doing back in Thunder Canyon? I was told you'd returned to your family's ranch."

"I did, for a while." Forrest straightened. "But my brother Clay and I have decided to move to Thunder Canyon on a permanent basis."

Her gaze flickered for a moment to his leg and the brace still visible beneath his faded jeans. "For your treatment?"

His grip again tightened on the curved handle of his cane. "Among other reasons."

"Ah. Would you like to sit?" Annabel waved at a pair of nearby chairs, already inching toward the one farthest away. "Smiley's session ended a few minutes ago, but I don't think they'll kick us out just yet."

Forrest sank into the chair, his injured leg stretched out in front of him. Smiley moved in, placing his chin immediately on the man's good knee, just like he'd done that first day.

"I've been standing in the corner for the last few

minutes, watching you work," Forrest said, his lips rising into a small grin when Smiley lifted his head and looked up at him. "Watching both of you work. I'd heard from my cousin about how popular your sessions have become. I guess you were able to convince Dr. North to give your idea a go."

Annabel ignored the kick to her gut at the memory of how she and Thomas first met, just a few short weeks ago. "Yes, I did."

"Do you have any interest in expanding them?"

Pushing aside her heartache, Annabel was happy for the distraction and equally surprised at how Forrest's question echoed her own thoughts from a moment ago. "I have been thinking of bringing in more dogs to spread the attention around."

"My idea is different."

"What's that?"

"I'd like to start a support group just for veterans."

Annabel thought back to the two servicemen, both recently returned from Afghanistan, who'd come to the first private session she held on Tuesdays. Despite the small size of the group, neither had been back since even though both were still patients here in the hospital.

They'd admitted to being strangers to one another during introductions, but had instinctively sat next to each other that first time. The chairs had formed a large circle, but the two men had remained emotionally, if not physically, separated from the other patients, both choosing not to speak, even during their turn with Smiley.

"That's an interesting idea," she said, watching as Forrest finally reached out and began scratching Smiley's ears again. "What made you think of it?"

Silence filled the room. Annabel waited, hoping he would share his inspiration when he was ready.

"I often thought about Smiley over the last few weeks. Just that short amount of time I spent with him really had an impact on me." Forrest kept his focus on her pet as he talked. "Being back on the ranch was harder than I'd thought it'd be. I honestly don't think I would've gone down to the barn to see the horses I still can't ride if I hadn't felt—if Smiley hadn't made me realize how much I missed…"

Annabel remained silent, watching the array of emotions that crossed the man's handsome features. It was almost as if she could see his attempts at gathering his thoughts after his voice had faded with his last words.

"Animals offer an unrestricted love, don't they?" he finally said, his attention still focused on the repeated motion of his hand moving easily over Smiley's fur. "No questions, no divided loyalties, no demands or restrictions."

Everything Forrest said resounded deeply inside Annabel and made all her hard work with Smiley worthwhile. "You've obviously thought a lot about this."

"I haven't had much to do with my time lately but think."

"And heal," Annabel added.

Forrest lifted one shoulder in a shrug. "Physically, maybe, although that's taking longer than everyone, including myself, ever thought it would. But it's what's going on inside, the learning to let go of…certain behaviors, certain memories, that I think Smiley could help with. Not just for me, but others who have served their country, as well."

She could easily understand how letting go or at

least learning to live with the memories of serving in a war might be difficult. From the straightforward hurting of being away from their loved ones to the unimaginable horror of living day to day, moment to moment, in a place where each decision could mean life or death, these men and women had been to hell and back.

"What do you mean by certain behaviors?" she questioned. "If you don't mind me asking."

"Soldiers tend to keep their problems to themselves. It isn't easy for them to rely on other people." Forrest's voice was low, his gaze now focused straight ahead at the large expanse of windows across the room. "Even the men and women we serve with, people who know better than anyone else what you've gone through— even talking with them isn't easy. Throw in family members who are often eager to help, but they sometimes don't realize how difficult answering even the simplest question can be.

"We're trained to lock away our emotions, to focus on the task at hand, to get the job done. Use your head and keep your heart out of it." Forrest punctured his last words with imaginary quotation marks drawn in the air. "Simple to do during the extreme moments when everything you've been taught comes as naturally as breathing, but when the job is done and things get quiet, when you're alone with your thoughts…it's a lot harder to keep your feelings under control. For some people denying any sentiment is the only way they can survive."

Annabel couldn't stop comparing Forrest's words to what Thomas had said to her as they stood in his office just a few days ago.

He'd been so adamant that there was no room in his

life for anything but his work. Somewhere along the way, he'd come to believe he couldn't have both love and his career.

In my experience, trusting in love is crazy.

Had someone taught him that? Was that why he refused to believe her when she told him how sure she was of her love for him?

"So learning to allow your feelings to be a part of your life again, that it's okay to even acknowledge the everyday emotions most people take for granted—is that what you mean?"

Forrest nodded. "I think it's a good place to start."

"So do I." For the first time in days, Annabel allowed her own emotions to flow freely, the pure joy of what she felt for Thomas to once again fill her heart.

"I'm sorry, I didn't mean to turn our talk into a personal session just for me." Forrest offered her that same slight grin as before. "See how easy it is to start jawing when this mutt of yours is around?"

"That is exactly why Smiley and I are here." Annabel reached for Forrest's hand and gave it a quick squeeze. "And I think your idea is wonderful."

"So you'll work with me on this?"

"I'd love to. We'll need to talk to people here at the hospital in order to pull it together, but I don't think that'll be a problem."

Forrest pushed himself to his feet. "You didn't let it stop you before."

"Nope." Annabel stood as well, her smile reflecting her renewed sense of confidence. Hadn't she told Thomas the first time they'd met that she could be persuasive when she wanted something? "And nothing is going to stop me this time, either."

* * *

The gravel drive crunched beneath the tires of her car as Annabel slowly pulled to a stop outside the over-size, tree-shaded building. There were only a few other vehicles in the Thunder Canyon Animal Shelter parking lot, but none that she recognized.

Was she too late?

Smiley pawed at the back of her seat when she turned off the engine. The sounds of their surroundings filtered in through the open windows.

"Yes, I know." She twisted around to look in the backseat. "You remember this place well, don't you?"

Smiley offered a low woof in response.

Removing her seat belt, Annabel got out of the car and freed Smiley, as well. She held tight to his leash as he eagerly headed for the front entrance. The office area was empty, but Annabel walked on through until they emerged back out in the bright sunshine as a familiar face met them.

"Hey there! It's good to see you two again." Betsy greeted them with a bright smile. "What brings you here this afternoon?"

"Hi, Betsy. I was hoping to find a friend of mine, but I didn't see his car out front."

"We only have one visitor here at the moment so I'm guessing that's who you're talking about. He parked around the other side in the employees' section." The woman smiled and gestured over her shoulder. "You'll find him right around the corner. Seems to be having a hard time making up his mind. Not everyone is as sure as you were that day."

Suddenly unable to speak, Annabel could only nod her thanks as she allowed Smiley to lead her to the familiar path. Rounding the corner, she stopped short at the sight in front of her.

Thomas, still dressed for work in dark slacks, a buttoned shirt now wrinkled with the sleeves folded back to his elbows, and his tie yanked halfway down his chest, sat on the grass inside a gated area, his lap overflowing with at least a dozen wiggling, happy puppies.

Three years ago, she'd come here to the Thunder Canyon Animal Shelter, drawn by a flyer advertising how a special pet could change a person's whole world. Finding Smiley within a few minutes of her arrival had been the most wonderful moment of her life...until the day the two of them walked into a certain doctor's office.

Her heart soared as she watched the ease of his smile and listened to his husky laughter as the playful pups vied for his attention. She had no idea exactly why he was here, but it was a sight she could've enjoyed for hours.

Except her pup had other ideas.

Smiley let loose with two happy yips of his own, causing Thomas and the dogs to jerk their heads their way.

"Annabel."

She offered a small wave, enchanted by the bright flush of embarrassment that crossed his features. "I'd ask if you're enjoying yourself, but that would be a silly question."

Thomas hurried to his feet, brushing at his clothes with one hand because the other cradled one petite pup in the crook of his arm. "Ah, yes. Well, you know... puppies."

"Yes, I know." She signaled for Smiley to sit. He

obeyed, but that didn't stop his back end from wiggling back and forth in time with his swishing tail. "You seem to have found a new friend."

He took a few steps forward until only the wired fencing separated them, his gaze dropping for a moment to the surprisingly docile pup, whose tiny head rested contently against his chest. "I guess so."

"I didn't know you were interested in getting a dog."

His gaze returned to look at her, the icy blue coloring of his eyes reflecting a contentment she hadn't seen there before. "I guess it was a spur-of-the-moment decision."

Was that a good thing or not? Was he ready to make more spontaneous choices in other areas of his life? And could she possibly be included in any way?

The questions filled her head, but engaging her mouth seemed impossible at the moment.

"How did you know I was here?"

Before she could answer Betsy came around the corner with a young family, complete with two boys, who seemed as excited as the puppies were to have someone new to play with.

"Hold that thought. I'd like to continue this conversation face-to-face." He waited until the shelter's director entered the gated area that allowed visitors to interact with the available pets before he slipped out and started toward her, the pup still in his arms.

To Annabel's trained eye the animal seemed to have at least some golden retriever in him, or her. She guessed the pup to be only a few months old, but the familiar coloring of its coat reminded her of Smiley when she'd first brought him home.

But it was the mixture of tenderness and purpose

in Thomas's eyes that drew her gaze back to his face. Gone was the aloof detachment he'd so easily displayed in his office a few days ago.

He stopped right in front of her, leaning down to give Smiley a quick pat hello. "Hey there, Smiley." His attention returned to her. "Okay, now. How did you know where I was?"

"We were on our way to your office when we ran into Marge at the elevator. She mentioned you'd left the shelter's website up on your computer when you left for the day." The words tumbled from her mouth, her eyes drawn to the ease with which Thomas stroked the pup's soft fur. "She, for whatever reason, thought I might like to know that."

"Of course she did."

Annabel couldn't stand it. She once again decided to jump in with both feet and trust in the love she felt in her heart and the warmth in Thomas's gaze.

"You know, I don't want to ruin a good thing. Correction, this great, amazing and wonderful thing that's happening right at this very moment, but to say I'm a bit confused is putting it mildly."

Thomas motioned toward a nearby bench. "Do you think we could sit for a moment?"

Annabel nodded, a thrill racing through her when Thomas laid his free hand at the small of her back as they made their way across the yard. Smiley sat again when she and Thomas did, his gaze moving between her, him and the pup that settled easily in Thomas's lap.

"Everything's okay, sweetie." She reassured her pet with a gentle pat, hoping the simple phrase would calm her, as well. "You can say hello."

Smiley quickly sniffed at the now-snoozing puppy

then offered a low sigh before stretching out at her feet, his head resting on his paws.

"Wow, two quiet dogs. That's a bit unusual, isn't it?"

Thomas's words had Annabel returning her gaze to his. "Yes, it is, especially for a puppy. Do you have any idea what you're in for? Puppies demand a lot of time and attention. They need to be cared for, fed, bathed, trained, but most of all they need your love."

"I know all that." His smile was genuine. "I guess I've finally found the right one for me."

The whirlwind of emotions battling inside her was suddenly too much to contain. Annabel squeezed her eyes closed, but a single tear managed to escape anyway. "Thomas, you're driving me crazy here."

His touch was gentle as he cupped her jaw, his thumb brushing over her cheek to wipe the tear away. "Then the feeling is mutual. You've been nothing short of a beautiful, passionate and maddening presence in my carefully controlled world from the moment we met."

She opened her eyes. "What exactly does that mean?"

"It means my life changed in a way I never expected a few short weeks ago and as hard as I tried not to allow it to happen, you found a way past my defenses. And no matter how hard I pushed, you never gave up on me."

"I'd say that's pretty evident considering I followed you here," Annabel whispered, following her heart and all the love she carried inside for this amazing man. "I meant what I said to you three days ago. My feelings haven't changed. I love you."

This time it was Thomas who closed his eyes, his head dropping forward, pressing his forehead gently to hers. "I was so afraid I'd waited too long. That I was too late."

"Late for what?"

"To ask for another chance?" He pressed his kiss to her temple for a long moment, and then leaned back again. "Will you take a chance on me?"

Annabel's heart beat wildly in her chest. This was exactly what she wanted, what she'd hoped for when she'd decided less than a hour ago not to give up on him, but to believe in the sincerity of his words? "Thomas, you have to be sure of what you want, what you need in your life."

"I want you. I need you." He pulled her closer, his arm moving to wrap low around her waist. "I think I've known that all along. That's what was so scary, how easily you came into my life, as if you were meant to be here, with me. I love you, Annabel, and I'm going to for the rest of my life."

She laid a hand over his where it held the tiny bundle in his lap. "This…all of this is going to take a lot of hard work and commitment."

He smiled, his fingers lacing through hers. "And time, attention and love. Yeah, I got it. So, do you think you and Smiley have enough of all those things to share? For both of us? I think me and this little guy come as a package deal."

Annabel leaned forward and met Thomas's kiss while Smiley offered a resounding bark of approval. They broke apart with a shared laugh. "Two for one? How could we resist?"

* * * * *